Praise for bestselling, award-winning author

JOAN JOHNSTON

and her New York Times *bestseller*

THE PRICE

1011 1 0090 0910 0909 0610 0508

JOAN JOHNSTON

THE RIVALS

POCKET BOOKS
New York   London   Toronto   Sydney

This book is a work of fiction. Names, characters, places and incidents are products of the author's imagination or are used fictitiously. Any resemblance to actual events or locales or persons, living or dead, is entirely coincidental.

An *Original* Publication of POCKET BOOKS

POCKET BOOKS, a division of Simon & Schuster, Inc.
1230 Avenue of the Americas, New York, NY 10020

ISBN: 0-7434-5440-5

First Pocket Books printing September 2004

10 9 8 7 6 5 4 3 2 1

POCKET and colophon are registered trademarks of Simon & Schuster, Inc.

Cover illustration by Alan Ayers
Cover design by Lisa Litwack

Manufactured in the United States of America

For information regarding special discounts for bulk purchases, please contact Simon & Schuster Special Sales at 1-800-456-6798 or business@simonandschuster.com

ACKNOWLEDGMENTS

I had the joy of doing on-site research in Jackson Hole, Wyoming—the most beautiful place in the world, really!—in the course of writing this book. I'm deeply indebted to a number of people for sharing their time and expertise.

My thanks and appreciation go to Detective Cindy Leeper, who generously and patiently answered all my questions, and to Sergeant Lindsey Moss (retired), both with the Teton County Sheriff's Office. To my friend, Judie Schmidlapp, for helping me to locate Bear Island and for helping me to decide where I could hide my yurt. And to Captain Gaylen Merrell for giving me a tour of the Teton County Jail and explaining how a murderer gets arrested.

Much thanks to Teton County Circuit Court Judge Timothy C. Day for taking time to explain the intricacies of a bail hearing and to Teton County Clerk of the Court Jeannine Hawkins and District Court Clerk Carol Hammond for their kind assistance. My thanks also to Rod Newcomb with the American Avalanche Institute for the quick class on avalanche blasting.

Finally, thanks to Jeffrey Schmidlapp at the Jackson

Hole Historical Society for helping me figure out where my modern-day Forgotten Valley should lie.

Any mistakes are mine.

My move to Colorado has brought many joys, not the least of which has been the new friends I've made, including Libby Howard, who runs a tow service with her husband in Coal Creek Canyon; Claire Collins, who's always willing to see a movie with me; and my hiking partner Barb McCleary.

I also want to thank my writing friends Roberta Stalberg, Gloria Dale Skinner, Sally Schoeneweiss and Margie Lawson for their continuing support.

*This book is dedicated to
all the booksellers
over the years
who've put my books into a
new reader's hands
and said,
"I think you'll enjoy this one."*

THE RIVALS

PROLOGUE

&

"My dad is going to flip when he finds out I've skipped out of school in the middle of term," the young woman said to the attractive man sitting on the barstool to her left.

"Where is your dad?" he asked.

She took a sip of her cosmopolitan and stared out the window of the ski lodge at the snowboarders racing down the steep, powdery slopes. "He lives back East," she said at last. "We have a . . . strange . . . relationship."

The handsome man smiled indulgently. "Strange?"

She met his gaze and said, "Sometimes I think he wishes I'd never been born."

"You don't get along?"

"I didn't say that," she said. "We just . . . I hardly ever see him. When I do, he just . . ." She turned to stare wistfully at the happy families making the most of the new snowfall on the majestic Tetons, trying to remember the last time she and her father had gone skiing together. A long time ago. Ages ago.

"Why is that?" he asked.

"What?" she said, distracted from her memories by the warmth in his voice.

"Why don't you get along with your father?"

"I don't know." She shrugged. "It doesn't matter now. I'm a grown-up. If I want to take off and bum around the ski slopes, that's my business, not his."

"I see," the handsome man said. "I have to admit I wondered if you were old enough to order that drink."

She grinned conspiratorially, leaned close and said, "I have a false ID. I'm really eighteen. Well, seventeen-and-three-quarters."

She felt woozy and almost fell off the barstool. She wrapped her ankles around its unique ax-handle base, struggling to sit upright. She yawned, squinted at the setting sun through the wall of windows framed by enormous logs, and said, "I didn't realize it was so late. I'd better get going."

"Let me walk you to your car," the man offered.

"No thanks. I can manage." But as she stood, shrugging her backpack onto her shoulder, her knees buckled. "No sleep last night," she muttered. "One drink and—"

Strong hands were there to rescue her.

She smiled up into the handsome face. "Thanks. I guess I will take that hand. I don't have a car. Would you mind calling a cab for me?"

"It'll be my pleasure," he said in a husky baritone. He took her backpack and slid it over his shoulder, then wrapped a strong arm around her slender waist as they headed for the door.

She felt nauseated as the heat from the moose-calf-high stone fireplace assaulted her, and she turned her face into his shoulder. He smelled good, some piney aftershave.

The frigid February air did nothing to revive her, and when she stumbled down the steps, he picked her up.

"I'm sorry," she muttered, her tongue thick. "All of a sudden, I can hardly keep my eyes open."

It had been a long flight from Virginia, and she'd felt relieved to finally be home, as the American flight circled its way down amid the Tetons and landed like a nesting bird in Jackson Hole. She'd called her mother from Chicago when she'd changed planes, but no one had been home, nor had her mom answered her cell, so she'd left messages both places.

Once on the ground, she'd called her mom again—and gotten no answer. She'd called her uncle North, who owned the ranch where she and her mother lived—and gotten no answer. She'd even called her father in Washington, D.C., and been told by his secretary that he wasn't taking calls—from anyone.

By now the Ethel Walker School in Charlottesville would have called her mother to report her missing. She'd felt too antsy to go home and sit in an empty house and wait, so she'd hitched a ride to Teton Village, the resort community at the base of Wyoming's Grand Tetons. She'd rented a snowboard and taken the tram all the way to the top of Rendezvous Mountain— 10,450 feet up—and raced down the treacherous double diamond slopes with defiant, life-threatening speed.

No wonder she was so exhausted.

She felt herself being laid down and opened her eyes long enough to realize that she was in the backseat of an extended-cab pickup. She tried to rise, but her body felt as though a couple of boulders had tumbled onto her chest. She stared up in confusion at the handsome face looming over her. "This isn't a cab," she whispered.

He smiled at her and said, "No, my dear, it isn't."

1

Because of the shadows at dusk, Libby saw the patch of ice on the curve too late to downshift. Hitting the brakes on her Subaru Outback would have sent her into a skid. With mountains to her left and the icy Hoback River on her right, the winding two-lane road didn't allow for mistakes.

She'd been speeding twenty miles over the limit ever since she'd left Cheyenne, racing for the past five hours, west through Rock Springs, then north through Pinedale, despite the ice and the terrifying fog, trying to stay ahead of a threatening snowstorm.

She had to get home. What could have caused her daughter to leave her boarding school so precipitously and fly home? The tremulous message Kate had left on Libby's answering machine had said only, "I have to talk to you. It's important." Not a word of what disaster had befallen her daughter.

Libby's immediate thought had been, *She's pregnant.* She'd felt her heart sink. She knew what it was like to be an unwed teenage mother. She'd been one herself. She wouldn't have wished that fate on her only child.

Why, oh why, hadn't she checked her messages sooner? Libby loved her work as a back-country guide because it kept her out-of-doors. But being in the mountains—or the middle of nowhere—often meant her cell phone was out of service.

Her three hunting dogs, one bluetick and two red-bone coonhounds, whined anxiously in their cages in the rear of the car.

"You can tell I'm upset, can't you?" she said, knowing the dogs would understand her comforting tone, if not the content of her speech. "It's just that Kate is my whole world. When something goes wrong in her life, I want to rush in and rescue her. Only, you know Kate. She insists on doing everything for herself. Self-sufficiency personified, that's my Kate."

She'd left several messages on Kate's cell phone once she'd gotten back to civilization, but her daughter hadn't returned her calls.

Where could Kate be? Libby had called her brother North, hoping Kate had contacted him, but he refused to take a cell phone with him when he worked his cattle, and she'd been forced to leave a message for him to call her as soon as he got her message.

The worst part was knowing Kate wouldn't hesitate to hitch a ride home from the airport with some stranger. Her daughter was foolishly fearless.

Libby's knuckles whitened as she steered into the opposite lane of traffic to avoid a treacherous patch of ice, uneasy because there was always a chance someone would be coming from the other direction on the deserted highway.

Ohmigod. Someone was.

Libby hissed in a breath and jerked the steering wheel, but her tires didn't hold when she hit a patch of ice, and she skidded directly into the path of the oncoming vehicle. She tried to stay calm, turning the steering wheel into the skid and keeping her foot off the brake.

When the oncoming pickup swerved to avoid her, it also hit a patch of ice and began to spin out of control. A head-on crash seemed inevitable.

Libby could see the driver's grim face for a single instant in her headlights as his speeding pickup raced across the ice on a deadly T-bone collision course with her car.

Libby watched, amazed, as the pickup suddenly accelerated with a loud roar and shot sideways across the nose of her car, barely missing her right front fender before taking a flying leap into the Hoback River. She could hear the rumble of crumpling metal behind her as the pickup landed, and then a horn blaring.

A second later, Libby was past the patch of ice and hit the brakes. The dogs tumbled in their cages as she screeched to a halt on the narrow berm. Her head fell forward onto her hands, and she took a shuddering breath as she slowly sat up and shoved her blond curls out of her face.

"Ohmigod," she whispered. "That was close."

She opened the window on the river side and listened for any sounds from the other vehicle. The truck's blaring horn had stopped, but her dogs were barking excitedly, making it hard to hear anything else.

She kept her voice low and calm as she said, "Quiet Magnum." The older dog stopped barking immediately. "You, too, Snoopy. Doc, quiet."

It took a moment longer for Snoopy, the youngest of the three hounds, to obey her command, but suddenly the car was silent. All she could hear was the frigid river rushing on its way.

She bent and peered out the passenger window, but the truck was too far below and behind her to be seen from where she was. There was no human sound to be heard.

Her legs were trembling so badly she was afraid they wouldn't hold her as she stumbled out of her car. A quick word reassured the dogs before she hurried back to the steep incline where the pickup had left the road. The river wasn't deep, but if the pickup had overturned, the driver might very well drown.

There was no guardrail. She could make out the tracks on the edge of the road where the pickup had taken off and looked to see where the dark-colored truck had landed. The headlights were on, and the pickup appeared to be upright.

But no one emerged from the vehicle.

The winter sun had disappeared behind the mountains, and Libby realized she was going to need a flashlight to make her way down to the partially submerged truck. "I'm coming!" she shouted, hoping the occupant of the pickup could hear her over the burbling water. "I'm going to get a flashlight. I'll be right back."

Her legs still felt wobbly, and she could hear her heart pounding in her ears. "Stay calm," she told herself. "You can do this."

Libby shivered, then remembered that the digital sign she'd passed on the Pinedale First National Bank building had said it was five below zero. She'd taken her parka off while she was driving, and she opened the passenger door and grabbed it. The dogs barked excitedly, and she said, "That's enough, Magnum. Quiet, Doc. Settle down, Snoopy. Everything's fine."

Her fiber-filled coat was still warm from the heater, and she reached into the pockets for her gloves and put them on before reaching under the passenger's seat for the flashlight she kept there.

She turned it on, grateful the batteries were working. She'd checked them in the fall, but it was February. She breathed a prayer of relief as she turned back toward the river.

As she skidded down the hill of shale toward the riverbank, she realized she wasn't going to be able to call 911 on her cell phone. She'd driven this road often enough to know the mountains prevented her from getting a signal.

Which made her even more anxious. What if the driver was hurt? They were at least thirty minutes from the hospital in Jackson. Luckily her car was still on the road and running.

In her mind's eye, Libby had a fleeting glimpse of Kate's worried face as she wondered where her mother was, and why she hadn't returned her calls. She was going to be even later getting home, with the delay caused by this accident.

"Hello? Can you hear me?" she yelled as she stumbled down the slope to the river. It wasn't more than fifteen or twenty feet down, and there was enough brush on the hillside to give her feet purchase, but she wondered how well the other driver had survived the sudden drop. "Are you all right? Can you answer me?"

To her surprise and relief, the window rolled down and the man inside said in a calm baritone voice, "I can hear you fine."

Libby stopped at the edge of the frigid river, uncertain how strong the current was, reluctant to step into its rocky depths in the dark. One slip, and she'd be sopping wet. With the temperature below zero, it wouldn't take long for hypothermia to set in. If both of them were incapacitated, the situation could quickly become life-threatening.

She aimed her flashlight at the pickup's occupant, who put up a hand to deflect the beam from his eyes. She could see blood streaming from his forehead. "Can you make it out of there on your own?" she called. "Do you need me to come and get you?"

As he lowered his hand to peer at her, she suddenly recognized him.

"Drew?" she said incredulously. "Drew DeWitt? Is that you? What are you doing here? I thought you were practicing law with your family's firm in Texas."

"Who are you?" he said. "I can't see you."

"It's Libby Grayhawk," she said. "How badly are you hurt?"

"I'm more angry than hurt, Libby," he said in that same tranquil voice. "What the hell were you doing in the wrong lane?"

"I was—" Libby realized there was no excuse for the

risk she'd taken. "I'm sorry. I can see blood on your head, Drew. Are you sure you're not hurt?"

He touched a hand to his head and seemed surprised when it came away red. "I bumped my head when I landed."

"You might have a concussion," she said. "You must be freezing. How much water is there under your feet?"

"None. It's dry as a bone in here."

Libby aimed the flashlight at the front wheel well and realized the water came up that far, but no farther. She'd never thought she would be grateful for the drought that had kept the rivers so low, but the dearth of water in the Snake River had kept a bad situation from becoming a disaster.

"I think I should come and get you out of there," she said. "You need to be checked out in a hospital."

"Look, Libby," he said. "I'm safe and dry in here. Why not drive on in to Jackson and send someone back to tow me out?"

"I don't want to leave you here." She knew how she would have felt sitting in the dark in the middle of a river in freezing weather. She would a hundred times rather have slogged her way through the icy water to safety.

"I'm in more danger trying to make my way across the river on foot than I will be if I stay right here and wait for a tow truck to pull me out," Drew said. "Go for help, Libby."

"I'd call for help, but—"

"I've already tried 911 on my cell," he said. "Without any luck. The sooner you take off, the sooner someone will be back here to get me."

"If you're sure—"

"Go," he said. "Get."

Libby headed back up the hill, which turned out to be a lot more difficult than the trip down. She stumbled once and her knee came down hard on a piece of shale. She could feel her oldest, most comfortable jeans rip and then felt a warm trickle of blood. Considering everything, she felt lucky to get off so easy.

On the rest of the drive into Jackson, she kept her speed a little slower than the limit, still trembling with the realization of how narrowly she and Drew had both escaped disaster. She kept trying her cell phone, wanting it to work, hoping there would be some blip in the atmosphere that would allow the satellite to hone in on her signal.

She wondered what had brought Drew DeWitt here at this time of year. He owned half of a ranch called Forgotten Valley outside Jackson, but it was run by a manager. Drew sometimes came to hunt in the fall, but deer and elk season was long past. Maybe he'd come to ski.

She wondered if Clay Blackthorne was with him. The two men were cousins. Their mothers, Ellen DeWitt and Eve Blackthorne, had inherited Forgotten Valley from their mother and decided to give it to two of their sons. Libby had no idea why Clay and Drew had been chosen, when both of them had siblings. Maybe their mothers had drawn straws.

Libby wondered if Clay had ever told Drew the awful truth about what had happened all those years ago. How sixteen-year-old Elsbeth Grayhawk had misled and seduced twenty-seven-year-old Clay Black-thorne.

Libby felt her face flush as she remembered how foolish she'd been. It had all been a childish game to her, one which she'd deeply regretted when she'd realized just how much pain she'd caused. What she'd done was unforgivably cruel. No wonder Clay had been unable to forgive her.

Libby tried to remember what was going through her head at the time. Excitement at attracting the attention and admiration of a man so much older than she was. Brand-new—and very powerful—feelings of arousal and desire. And a cockeyed notion that she could finally avenge the wrong done to her father.

It was asinine, immature sixteen-year-old thinking.

But not surprising, considering how often during her youth she'd heard her father damn Clay's father, Jackson Blackthorne, to hell for stealing the woman he loved, Evelyn DeWitt, right out from under his nose.

King Grayhawk had married and divorced three times and had indulged in an equal number of affairs seeking a replacement for Eve DeWitt. But no woman had been able to measure up to his lost love.

Libby had learned to hate and blame Blackthornes for every ill wind that blew in her life. But most especially for the women who came and went in her father's life, none of them willing to mother some other woman's brat.

She and her two older brothers, North and Matt, had been the offspring of her father's first wife. The two stepmothers passing through her life had given her two half brothers and two half sisters that she was left to care for.

When the chance had come for revenge against the Blackthornes, she'd wrapped her arms around the son of her father's enemy, whispered lies in his ear, and kissed him until she didn't know which way was up. It had seemed a sweet irony to have Clay Blackthorne fall in love with her—and then walk away.

They'd spent the whole glorious month of June making love every day. Morning picnics. Afternoon assignations. Secret evenings under the starry night skies. She'd planned to spend the Fourth of July with him and, after the fireworks, simply disappear without a word or a clue as to who she really was or where she'd gone.

She hadn't counted on falling in love with him. Hadn't counted on getting pregnant. Hadn't counted on her father's damaging interference when Clay Blackthorne had wanted to do the right thing and marry her.

"What he did was statutory rape," her father had said in a steely voice. "You go after him and I'll have him arrested. You let him near my grandchild and I'll have him arrested. I want him out of your life. Is that clear?"

It had been years before she stopped to wonder why her father hadn't had Clay arrested anyway. Years before she'd realized that Clay's father had had enough money and power and influence to keep his son out of jail despite her father's threats.

Because she'd loved Clay, she'd sent him away, telling him enough lies to make sure he never came back.

She'd left home with her two-year-old daughter on the day she turned eighteen. North had given her a refuge at his ranch in Jackson Hole, in an old cabin that was a legacy from their departed mother, a place that must have been used by settlers in bygone days. That was where Clay Blackthorne had found her when he'd finally come looking.

He hadn't come right away. In fact, not long after the fateful day she'd sent him away, he'd gotten engaged. Libby had died inside, wishing she could be the one that he was marrying. She'd felt torn when she'd learned that Clay hadn't gotten married after all, because his fiancée had been murdered a week before the wedding.

Libby hadn't been able to keep from indulging in the fantasy that Clay would come looking for her someday. That they would marry and raise their daughter together.

It had never happened.

In the end, Clay had come, all right—to seek out his four-year-old daughter. That first visit had been awkward. Amazing how cordial two people could be for the sake of a child. Amazing how well she'd been able to hide her aching heart.

Clay had never publicly acknowledged Kate. A bastard daughter sired on a sixteen-year-old mother wouldn't have been good for a politician's career. And Clay's family had great plans for him.

No, that wasn't fair. Clay hadn't wanted Kate to be forced into the spotlight. But with a grandfather like King Grayhawk, the spotlight had been unavoidable. And devastating for a vulnerable child.

The Grayhawks might be Jackson Hole royalty, but King had made a lot of enemies over the years. There were plenty who snickered when his eldest daughter had become an unwed mother. They were quick to brand King's granddaughter with the label of bastard—behind her back. No one would have dared to say such a thing to her face, fearing King's swift and certain retribution.

Nevertheless, Kate had been aware of the slights, the sniggers, the whispers behind her back.

Which was why Libby had spent every penny she'd earned, and money loaned to her by North, to send her daughter to a boarding school in Virginia, where Kate could make friends who didn't know about her birth or her family.

King had offered Libby money for Kate's support, but Libby had known better than to take it. With such webs were sticky familial traps laid. And Libby had told Clay, when he offered, that if he wanted to give Kate money, he should put it in trust for her until her twenty-first birthday.

Libby had been proud of managing on her own, and Kate had never wanted for anything. Except a full-time father.

Over the years, Clay had spent his holidays vacationing in Jackson, as did many other politicians, and found time to spend with Kate. But Libby had borne her daughter's tears each time Clay left. And it had broken her heart.

After Clay married Giselle Montrose, the daughter of the American ambassador to France, he'd spent even less time in Jackson. But he and his wife had never had children, and Giselle had died a year ago of cancer.

Clay was on his own again.

So was she. Libby had tried marriage, and when it hadn't worked out, had gone so far as to get engaged to another man. She'd backed out three weeks before the wedding, realizing that she didn't love her fiancé enough to marry him. She was no more able than her father to find someone to measure up to her first love.

Libby had resigned herself to being alone. That was better than repeating her father's mistake and kept her from putting any more men through what her stepmothers had endured. It wasn't fair to them or to her or to her daughter.

Libby forced herself not to yearn for what she could never have. Clay had loved her once upon a time, and she'd betrayed that love. She wasn't going to get a second chance to make things right. Blackthornes weren't any more forgiving than they were merciful.

Kate had remained the center of Libby's life until she'd headed off to boarding school in the ninth grade. Since then, Libby had focused on her work.

She loved taking city folk into the mountains and showing them the savage beauty of the wilderness. She never embarrassed them by exposing their ignorance, just did her best to ensure they enjoyed the pristine wilderness that still existed in so much of Wyoming. She'd established a reputation as someone who was friendly and competent, and her guide services were much in demand.

It wasn't a perfect life. But it was satisfying.

Libby felt her heart clutch. *Please God,* she prayed, *don't let Kate be pregnant. Anything but that.*

Libby wondered if she ought to call the sheriff's office to report the accident with Drew but realized if she did they were liable to tie her up filling out forms and answering questions. Instead, she called the local garage that had towed her car in the past.

"Hello, Theresa? I need help. A friend of mine went into the Hoback south of Jackson. He's sitting in his pickup in the middle of the river. He needs a tow."

Libby gave Theresa the mile marker where Drew's truck had gone into the river. "Please hurry," she said. "Oh, one more thing. I haven't reported the accident yet."

Theresa said her husband Mike would be there as soon as possible. And if the police needed to be called, Mike could call them.

"Thank you. Thank you so much," Libby said. She clicked off her cell phone and hurried through town toward home. Kate's plane had long since landed. Libby only hoped her daughter had come home and stayed there. She called her home number but got the answering machine. Then she called North. She felt her heart race when he picked up and said, "Hello."

"North, is Kate there with you? Did you pick her up from the airport?"

"She's not here, but I found a message on my machine when I got home that she's in town. Is something wrong?"

"She probably hitched a ride home with someone, but she's not answering her cell phone. Will you go by my place and see if she's there? I'm coming home now. Give me a call to let me know either way."

"Will do," North said.

North's ranch was north of Jackson, and Libby broke the speed limit again getting there. She hit the brakes hard in front of her cabin. The lights were on inside, and she shoved her way through the door, expecting to see Kate.

"Oh. I thought Kate was here," she said, when North rose from a leather armchair. Her eldest brother was tall, broad-shouldered and lean-hipped. His blue eyes cut at her like two chips of ice, and his mouth was thin, almost cruel.

"There's a message from her on your answering machine," North said, "saying she's in town and that she needs to talk to you. Nothing else."

"Oh, God," Libby said.

"What's she doing here, Libby?" North asked. "What's wrong?"

Libby clenched her teeth to keep her chin from quivering. "I don't know. But when she finally shows up, I'm going to give her a good piece of my mind!"

"I'll start some coffee," North said.

An hour later, Libby said, "I can't sit here doing nothing. I'm going looking for her."

"I'll go with you," North said.

"No. Please. Stay here. Something terrible must have happened for her to come home like this. She'll need someone to be here when she shows up."

Libby bit her lip to keep from blurting out her fear that Kate might be pregnant. She was terrified, but if she'd learned one thing growing up, it was to hide her fears. She met North's piercing gaze and realized he wasn't fooled.

She wished they were the sort of family that hugged one another, but they never had been, and she didn't expect North to start now. She needed someone to tell her everything would be all right, that Kate would turn up in a minute safe and sound. North wasn't that person.

Sometimes Libby wondered if her eldest brother had any feelings at all. He never lost his temper. He rarely smiled. He made every decision with cold-blooded reason. And he never made a mistake—or at least, never admitted to one.

"Anywhere in particular you plan to start looking?" he asked.

"I've called all her friends," Libby said. "None of them have seen her."

"You might try the bars."

Libby frowned. "Kate's too young to drink."

"Your choice," North said.

He never imposed his will. Just made it impossible to ignore his reasoning. And he was always right. "All right," she said. "Maybe she went to a bar with a friend to wait until she could reach me by phone. I'll check them out."

Libby looked in every bar she could think of in Jackson. No one had seen Kate. She returned to the house at seven o'clock, her heart in her throat, her stomach a knot of pain.

"No sign of her?" North said, as she stepped inside.

"Nothing. It's as though she's disappeared into thin air."

"I called the hospital. They haven't checked in anyone matching her description. It's time to call the police, Libby."

Libby felt the blood drain from her face. "You don't think—"

"She would have called," North said. "She wouldn't have made you worry like this. So yes, I think something has happened to her."

Libby's knees buckled and she sank into the nearest chair. This was every mother's nightmare. Even worse was the knowledge that two other young women had disappeared from Jackson Hole over the past fifteen months. Someone bad was out there. And he might have taken her daughter.

"Wait," she said, rising abruptly. "Before you call the police, let me make a call."

"Have you thought of someone who might know where she is?" North asked.

"Yes," Libby said. "I don't know why I didn't think to call him sooner."

North raised a brow. "Who did you have in mind?"

"Kate's father."

2

Sarah was making oatmeal raisin cookies after dinner when she got the call from her sister-in-law that Sarah's brother Mike was drunk again and had run the tow truck off the road on his way to a job. Theresa couldn't leave the kids alone and wanted Sarah to please rescue Mike and then go tow some idiot out of the Hoback River.

"The call came in more than an hour ago," Theresa said. "The guy must be going crazy waiting for his tow."

"No problem, Theresa," Sarah said. "I'm leaving now."

Sarah yelled for her stepson. "Nate, can you come and keep an eye on the cookies in the oven? I've got to go do a tow for Uncle Mike."

"I'm playing Metroid," Nate shouted back. "I'm about to defeat Mother Brain. Can't Brooke do it?"

"Brooke is getting Ryan ready for bed."

"Is Uncle Mike drunk again?"

Sarah headed into the living room, wiping her hands on a dish towel, and got there in time to meet Nate's eyes as he finished speaking.

"Yes, he is," she said. "Which should be a lesson to you about the dangers of drinking."

Nate flushed. He'd been caught the previous Friday night drinking at the Valentine's Day dance at school and had been suspended for three days. He set down the controller and rose from his seat on the floor facing the TV, heading for the kitchen. "You've made your point, Mom," Nate said. "Endlessly," he muttered under his breath.

Once upon a time, Sarah would have ruffled her stepson's hair as he passed by her. But Nate was already six feet tall and still growing. He had her husband Tom's wiry build and Tom's warm brown eyes, sandy hair and freckles. She brushed a hand down the sleeve of Nate's black-and-gold Jackson Broncs sweatshirt instead, wanting the contact, wanting to reassure him that they were going to be all right, despite the hardships of the past fifteen months.

"Thanks, Nate. I appreciate the help. Don't eat all of them before I get back," she said with a grin. "Save one for me."

"Sure, Mom," he said, shrugging free of her touch.

As she was putting on her coat, her eight-year-old son Ryan came running toward her, his pajama top still unbuttoned. Brooke came stalking in behind him, her hands on her hips—her jeans a few inches below that—and her fifteen-year-old eyes so caked with mascara that it was hard to tell they were hazel behind the black fringe.

"Where you going, Mom?" Ryan asked as he launched himself at her.

Ryan was too big to be picked up, really, but Sarah picked him up anyway. If Tom were still around, he could easily have hefted Ryan's weight. But Tom was gone.

Sarah knew there was debate in town about whether Tom Barndollar had finally gotten tired of his wife wearing the pants in the family and taken off. In fact, she and Tom had argued the morning he'd disappeared about the long hours Sarah was spending as a Teton County Deputy Sheriff hunting for some missing teenage girl, instead of staying home and taking care of her own family.

Sarah might have believed Tom was mad enough that morning to walk out on her, but she couldn't believe he would have left without a word to Nate and Brooke, his children by his first wife, and Ryan, who was Sarah and Tom's son.

Sure they'd argued, but in the past, they'd always worked things out. Only, that long-ago morning Tom had given her an ultimatum. He'd threatened to leave her if she didn't put her family first.

He'd only *threatened* to leave. Which meant he was giving her a chance to change her priorities. But when she'd come home that evening, both Tom and his truck had been missing.

That had been fifteen months ago. She hadn't heard a word from him since.

Sarah knew her husband was dead. Because if Tom Barndollar had been alive, he would have contacted her. Whatever the town of Jackson thought, Tom had loved her. And he would never have walked out on Nate and Brooke and Ryan.

Nate had been seven and Brooke six when Sarah

married Tom. She'd been twenty-two and looking for an escape. She'd found it in Tom's arms. It hadn't been easy winning her stepchildren's love. She'd persisted, despite the setback when Ryan had been born, and Nate and Brooke had feared she wouldn't love them anymore, now that she had a child of her own.

Sarah's relationship with all three kids had been tenuous lately. A second girl had disappeared from Jackson three months ago, and Sarah was suddenly spending more time at work than ever before. She'd called on Nate to take care of the housework and on Brooke to keep an eye on Ryan.

Neither of them were happy about the additional responsibility. Both of them had heard that final argument between Sarah and Tom. Both of them had recently accused Sarah of reverting to the behavior they believed had caused their father to leave home.

To make matters even worse, Sarah's husband and her brother Mike had run the tow service together, but since Tom's disappearance, Mike had had trouble managing on his own. The added pressure had caused him to start drinking again.

Sarah didn't see that she had any choice but to help out when Theresa asked. Her sister-in-law needed the money too much to send the business elsewhere. And Sarah would rather do the tow herself than let her brother drive drunk. In any event, some reckless cowboy needed his pickup hauled out of the Hoback River.

"I shouldn't be gone more than a couple of hours," Sarah said. "Ryan, you can have some cookies and milk before you go to bed."

Brooke had already dropped into the spot on the floor in front of the couch her brother had occupied and picked up the controller to finish his game of Metroid.

"Is your homework done?" she said to Brooke.

"Why should you care?" Brooke shot back.

Sarah felt her stomach clench at the defiant—and hurtful—response. "I'm still your mother, young lady. I asked you a question."

When Brooke ignored her, Sarah's hands balled into frustrated fists. She was at the end of her rope with her stepdaughter, who grew more rebellious by the day. "Well?" she demanded.

"It's Friday," Brooke muttered. "I don't have any."

"Fine. Help yourself to some cookies when they're done."

"I don't want any of your damned—darned—cookies," Brooke quickly corrected, eyeing Sarah sideways from beneath straggly brown bangs.

Sarah surveyed Brooke's thin frame, wondering if the girl was eating enough. A few months after Tom had disappeared, Brooke had stopped eating entirely for a twenty-four-hour period—something no healthy, happy teenager would do.

Sarah had caught Brooke, who was swaying, ready to faint, when they were cleaning out the garage one Saturday morning and confronted her about whether she was ill. Brooke had denied being sick. When Sarah asked when she'd eaten last, Brooke admitted she'd had "a potato chip" at a party the previous evening, but that was all she'd eaten since Thursday supper.

That same afternoon, Sarah had handed her step-daughter all the books she could find in the Teton County Library on anorexia. Nowadays, she made sure Brooke at least ate dinner—when she was home to make sure Brooke ate.

Lately, that was less and less often.

Sarah released her balled fists and said, "I'd appreciate it if you'd help Ryan read the next chapter in *Harry Potter and the Order of the Phoenix* before he goes to bed."

Brooke rolled her eyes. "Fine."

Sarah knew her stepdaughter loved Ryan, and that she'd likely help him for his own sake, rather than Sarah's.

"Thanks, Brooke," she said. "Good night, Ryan," she called. "Thanks for the help, Nate."

Then she was out the door.

She drove her Teton County Sheriff's vehicle, a white Chevy Tahoe, to pick up her brother and returned him to his home above the Teton Valley Garage. She picked up a pair of waders, since she was going to find herself in cold water before the night was out.

As she headed south out of Jackson in the tow truck, she could see how the cowboy's pickup might have ended up in the river. The roads were icy and fog hindered visibility. She slowed when she neared the mile marker she'd been given and looked for signs of a vehicle off the road. A pair of headlights flashed on in the river, and she pulled to the side of the road, angling the tow truck so its headlights lit the vehicle, and hit her overhead flashing yellow lights.

As she stepped out, the driver rolled down his window. She shouted to him over the rush of water, "Are you all right?"

"I'm fine," he said. "I'm waiting for a tow."

"I'm your tow," she called back, as she began unwinding the cable she would need to pull the pickup out of the river. She stumbled down the hill, sliding in the shale, a flashlight in one hand and the frame hooks attached to the winch cable in the other.

As she headed into the river, the driver's door opened and the passenger started to get out.

"Stay in your truck until I get you to the edge of the river," she said.

"You're going to need help," he said.

"Stay in your truck," she said more firmly, flashing the light in his eyes. "You'll only be in my way."

Sarah picked her way carefully across the shallow river to the front of the pickup and bent to locate the openings in the frame and attach the mini-J-hooks. She swore when icy water splashed her leather gloves. She finished the job as quickly as she could, then pulled her leather gloves off and substituted a pair of fleece ones she'd brought along.

When she flashed her light at the driver a second time, she realized his head was bleeding. "You're hurt! Why didn't you call the paramedics? An accident with injuries needs to be reported to the police."

He dabbed at his head with a bloody kerchief and said, "It's just a bump. I'm fine."

She eyed him dubiously, then said, "I think I can get your truck out of here in one piece. Be sure the brake is off and the transmission is in neutral. You can help by steering till I get you closer to the riverbank. Then you're going to have to get out. There's always a chance this rig will tip and roll when it comes out of the water and heads up that incline."

Sarah climbed up the hill and began winching the pickup toward the edge of the river. The tires bumped over the stones in the river bottom, then came up against some sort of obstacle that held the truck fast. She eased the slack on the cable and headed back down the slope.

"I should have known this wasn't going to be easy," she muttered.

When she got to the truck, the driver already had the window down.

"It's stuck," he said.

She nodded curtly, then did a quick search with her flashlight to see if she could find the problem. When she checked the right rear tire, she found it hooked on a submerged log. She kicked at the log a couple of times with her booted foot, but it wouldn't budge.

She came around to the driver's window and said, "It's stuck on a log. Try starting it up. Maybe you can back it off."

"The engine won't turn over," the man said. "I've already tried it." He looked down at the water. "Damn. Guess I'm going to get my feet wet after all."

"I can attach the winch to—"

Before Sarah could explain how she planned to re-arrange the mini-J-hooks, run the cable around a nearby pine and winch the truck backward, the man had stepped down into the frigid river.

He almost fell face-first into the water. Sarah caught him with an arm around his waist and felt him sag against her.

"You *are* hurt," she said.

"I'm fine," he said, straightening. "I was a little dizzy there for a moment. Water's freezing."

Sarah lifted his arm around her shoulder, slid her arm more snugly around his waist and said, "Next time the roads are icy and it's foggy, maybe you'll take your time around the curves."

"It wasn't my fault."

Sarah sighed. "It never is."

She couldn't help noticing how tall he was. She was five feet ten in her bare feet, and he was several inches taller, lean and lithe and muscular, like most cowboys she knew, who spent their days doing physical labor from the back of a horse.

"I'm fine. Really," he said, straightening and freeing himself from her supporting grasp. "Let's take a look at that log."

"I can winch it from—"

He was already slogging through the frigid water toward the rear of the pickup. "Mmm. I see," he said as Sarah focused her flashlight on a branch of the log that stuck out above the waterline.

He gave the submerged log a couple of hard kicks with the heel of his boot, and it broke in half. He reached down and yanked the log from under the wheel. "That should do it," he said.

Sarah caught him as he swayed and almost fell. He tried shrugging her away, but she slid her arm firmly around his waist and said, "All right. You've proved you have the muscle. Now let's see if you have brains enough to let me help you."

The flashlight was in the hand she was using to support him, with the light aimed up at his face, and she saw a grin flash as he sagged against her.

"Yes, ma'am," he said. "Whatever you say, ma'am."

Sarah helped him up the hill and into the cab of the tow truck, where the heater was running full blast. In the light that came on when she opened the door, she saw his face was pale, and his teeth were clenched to keep them from chattering.

"Those boots need to come off," she said, suiting word to deed. It wasn't easy getting wet cowboy boots off his feet, but she knew he'd warm up faster that way. She peeled his socks off, revealing feet that were long and narrow and ice cold. She rubbed each of them briskly and realized his Wranglers, wet from the knees down, were dripping ice water onto her hands.

She tugged at his soggy jeans and said, "Those better come off, too."

He lifted a brow suggestively, then reached under his anorak for his belt buckle and undid it, before unsnapping and unzipping his jeans. He lifted his hips and she pulled on the hems of both legs until they came off. He was wearing some kind of snug black underwear that hit him midthigh.

She handed him a gray wool blanket and said, "Wrap yourself in this. I'll be back in no time."

Once back down the hill, she checked to make sure his pickup was still in neutral, that the brake was off, and that the mini-J-hooks were attached properly. Then she headed back to the tow truck to take up the slack.

She took her time getting the truck up the hill, moving back and forth between the pickup and the winch, making sure the wheels were headed in the right direction, so the truck came up clean and easy. Once the pickup was secure for the tow back into town, she removed her waders and stowed them.

Within fifteen minutes she was back in the cab expecting to find the cowboy warmed up. She was troubled to see that his eyes were closed. "Hey, are you all right?"

His eyes blinked open and he scooted upright.

"Sorry to fall asleep like that. I had a late night last night."

"You shouldn't be driving when you're tired. That's what causes accidents."

"It wasn't my—"

"I know," she interrupted. "It wasn't your fault. At least you were wearing your seat belt. You might have been killed, taking a flying leap off the road like that." She reached over to peer into his eyes, her flashlight angled slightly away to keep from blinding him. His eyes were blue. An astonishing blue. The sort of blue that made you want to keep on looking.

He looked right back at her. And grinned. "Last time a woman looked that intently into my eyes, she—"

Sarah flushed and backed away, shutting off the flashlight, buckling herself in and putting the tow truck in gear. "Spare me the details. Where do you want me to drop you and your pickup off?"

"You can leave the pickup at the Jackson Hole Garage. I could use a ride to my ranch, if you don't mind."

Sarah didn't usually provide cab service, but it was late and he was wet, half-naked and hurt. He might very well collapse or get frostbite before a cab finally showed up at the garage to take him home.

"Where's your ranch?" she said, eyeing him curiously. She knew most of the ranchers around town, and she didn't know this man. The way he'd been dressed, in a plaid wool shirt, worn jeans, and boots, she'd figured him more for a cowhand than an owner. "Is there someone who can take care of you overnight? You shouldn't be alone. You might have a concussion."

He cocked another brow at her. "There's nobody at the main house right now except me."

"Where is that?" Sarah asked.

"Forgotten Valley."

Sarah turned to stare at him. "Forgotten Valley is owned by a couple of guys from Texas."

"Drew DeWitt, at your service, ma'am."

Sarah frowned. "I didn't think the owners lived there."

"I moved back in December."

"Moved back?" Sarah said skeptically. "I didn't realize you'd ever—"

"Moved in," Drew corrected. "Quit my job in Houston and moved here to . . ." He paused and said, "That's another story."

"I've got time. It's a long ride back to Jackson."

Drew shrugged. "I needed a change of scenery."

"You could afford to quit your job?"

He shrugged again. "It was only a job."

"Your work wasn't important? What did you do?"

"I was a litigator with DeWitt & Blackthorne."

"A lawyer? I can see why you wanted to get away," Sarah said. As a policeman who caught the bad guys, she was leery of the lawyers who got them off. "What is it you plan to do now that you're here in Jackson?"

"I haven't decided."

"I suppose if I'd quit my profession and moved a couple thousand miles away, I'd need more than six weeks to figure out what to do with the rest of my life, too. Just don't do your thinking on the highway," she said. "That way you're more likely to stay among the living long enough to come up with another life plan."

"I was forced off the road," he said.

Sarah frowned. "Where's the other vehicle? Didn't the driver stop? Do I need to be looking for another reckless driver out there somewhere?"

"It was a friend of mine—and no, I'm not going to tell you who it was," Drew said. "It was an accident. No one was hurt—"

"That bump on your head should be looked at by a doctor," Sarah interrupted.

"I'm not going to a doctor," Drew said firmly.

"Have you got someone to stay with you overnight, just in case?" Sarah asked. "A girlfriend? A wife? A friend? You shouldn't be alone."

"I'm not married. And I don't have a girlfriend . . . anymore," he said bitterly.

"Ah," Sarah said, eyeing him speculatively. "So you came here to nurse a broken heart."

He didn't say anything, which Sarah took as a confirmation of her guess. She figured he must really have loved the woman to have quit his job and moved away when the relationship ended. "She dumped you?" Sarah asked.

"I don't want to talk about it."

"She dumped you," Sarah concluded. "What did you do to her?"

"I didn't do anything. She— Look," he said, "this is none of your business."

"It became my business when you let yourself get distracted and drove off the road."

"I told you—"

"I know. It wasn't your fault. A mystery woman drove you off the road. That woman wouldn't have been the one you broke up with in Houston, would it? You let yourself get distracted by thoughts of her and—"

"I wasn't thinking of Grayson Choate. She never crosses my mind. I'm over her," Drew insisted. "Your job is to drive, not to interrogate me."

"Well, actually . . ." Sarah hesitated, then said, "I'm a detective with the sheriff's office. I only showed up to hook this wreck because . . . I'm helping someone out."

From the corner of her eye, she saw Drew slowly run his eyes down her body. She shivered, as though he'd touched her with his hands.

"Well, well, well," he said. "So you're the law in Teton County."

"One of many deputy sheriffs."

He turned to face her and said, "Are you going to write me a ticket?"

"For what? Being in the wrong place at the wrong time?"

His gaze stayed on her as he said, "Or maybe being in the right place at the right time. I met you, didn't I?"

Sarah frowned. She hadn't been flirted with in so long, she wasn't quite sure Drew DeWitt was actually showing that sort of interest in her. If he was, she had to nip it in the bud. The DeWitts and Blackthornes were rich folks. All he could possibly want from her was a quick roll in the hay.

Sarah sucked in a silent breath at the thought that crossed her mind. *Why not? He's not going to be in town long. The rich folks never stay. And it's been so long. . . .*

Sarah felt guilty for what she was thinking. But it wasn't possible to have a casual affair with someone local, because the gossip would be devastating. And until she knew for certain that Tom was dead, she wasn't willing to get emotionally involved with anyone. She missed being kissed and touched and held in a man's strong arms.

She returned Drew's gaze as long as she dared, then turned her eyes back onto the road.

The tension in the truck was palpable, like static electricity ready to spark the instant Sarah dared to touch. Drew said nothing, just kept looking at her, caressing her with his eyes.

Sarah was remembering his long, muscular legs and long, narrow feet, and the bulge in his fitted briefs when she'd stripped off his jeans.

She felt a growing tautness in her breasts and belly, as though he were already touching her. She took a hitching breath and let it out, then loosened her iron grip on the steering wheel.

Part of her wanted to take him up on his unspoken offer. She wanted to go to bed with him and have incredible, mindless sex. She needed a man. And he seemed willing.

Sarah pulled up at the Jackson Hole Garage, lowered the pickup and unhitched it. Drew could call the garageman tomorrow with instructions. When she stepped back into the truck, she noticed Drew had pulled on his jeans, which were still soggy below the knee, and his wet socks and boots.

"You look uncomfortable," she said.

"My place isn't far from here. They'll be off soon enough."

There was enough sexual innuendo in his voice to cut with a knife, but Sarah neither acknowledged nor deflected it. "I think I know the way, but why don't you go ahead and give me directions."

Sarah followed Drew's instructions, heading down Spring Gulch Road, which quickly turned to dirt as she left the main highway. The ranch was located in a valley thirty miles wide and eighty miles long that lay between the east and west Gros Ventre buttes. Forgotten Valley Ranch was bordered beyond the butte on the west by tributaries of the Snake River,

which was marked by the growth of aspens and cottonwoods.

It was an idyllic spot, with a one-story, split-pine
ranch house that had been added onto for the better
part of a century, surrounded by cottonwoods that had
been planted by pioneers. It was a working ranch that,
even in this modern day, ran black baldies and Here-
fords and the occasional longhorn steer. Cowhands
grew hay in the summer that was baled in rolls to feed
stock from a sleigh in the winter.

Sarah pulled up in front of the main house, which
was dark. The foreman's house, which was set across an
open yard, was also dark. She looked at her watch. It
was shortly after eight o'clock, but the foreman was apparently already in bed. That wasn't unusual, since his
day probably started around 4:30 A.M.

"I appreciate you coming to the rescue," Drew said.

Which reminded Sarah she hadn't charged him yet
for the tow. "I'll be sending you a bill."

"I'd better get inside and get warmed up," Drew said.

He opened the door and Sarah squinted her eyes
against the excruciatingly bright dome light. He hesitated, then pulled the door closed again, leaned over,
and touched his mouth to hers in the darkness.

Sarah was too shocked to resist.

His lips were soft. His touch gentle.

Sarah's throat ached with longing. Her lips pushed
back against his and opened to his probing tongue. She
gasped at the warm wetness. And drew back with a
shudder, staring into his glittering eyes.

"Come inside with me," he said.

Sarah opened her mouth to explain why that was impossible. She was a married woman. She had to get home to her three kids. She was a Teton County Deputy Sheriff, for heaven's sake, with a reputation to protect. There was no way she could indulge in sex with a stranger.

What came out was, "Okay."

3

Sarah shivered as she stepped down from the tow truck. The wind had picked up and made the freezing temperature feel glacial. She followed Drew to the kitchen door and stood hunched in her coat as he unlocked the back door, stepped inside and flipped on a light switch. Then he turned and reached out a hand to her.

She was running out of time to turn back.

Sarah laid her hand in his and allowed him to tug her inside.

"It's cold in here," he said. "Would you like me to make some coffee?"

She wondered if Drew was getting figurative cold feet. She was pretty sure his real feet must be freezing. Sarah pulled her hand free and crossed her arms over her chest. "Maybe I should—"

That was all she got out before his arms folded around her and his mouth found hers. His hands slid down to her hips to pull her snug against the hardness in his jeans, then up under her jacket, one on her back, the other resting just under her right breast.

She felt herself tense, waiting for him to touch.

But he didn't reach for her breast. His hand slid back

down across the front of her belly and stayed there, making her want, making her anticipate where he would send it next.

Sarah was suddenly too warm in her fleece coat and reached for the zipper.

"Let me," Drew said in a husky voice. He kept his hips pressed against hers as he slowly zipped it down, his eyes riveted on her as though he were exposing her naked body, rather than a soft black wool turtleneck.

He slid the coat off her arms and let it fall onto the worn linoleum floor behind her. Then he tugged his anorak off over his head and let it drop, leaving him in a plaid wool shirt and long john undershirt.

His hands, warm and callused and, she realized, more experienced than she'd imagined, sought her flesh beneath the sweater. He teased her, almost touching where she wanted him, then moving elsewhere.

Sarah realized she wanted to touch his muscular chest, and she tugged at his shirt buttons, pulling his shirt down his arms, forcing him to release her long enough to get it off. As he reached down to pull his long john shirt off, she reached for her sweater and pulled it off over her head. Her plain brown hair was secured in a French braid, but strands of it came loose and fell around her face.

Her eyes met Drew's as her hands found their way across his chest and up around his neck. He lowered his face as she raised hers, and their lips met. His hands circled her hips and he pulled her tight against him, so her breasts were crushed against the dark blond curls on his chest. Their tongues dueled as she arched her hips into his, feeling the hardness of him, wanting him inside her.

She thrust her tongue into his mouth and heard a guttural groan as his hands tightened on her buttocks. One of her hands gripped a handful of his silky, golden blond hair as the other slid down his back, her nails raking his naked flesh and making his body arch into hers.

Suddenly, he was picking her up, cradling her in his arms. Sarah was stunned because Tom had always said she was too big—too tall—for that sort of romantic gesture. Drew made it seem like she weighed nothing as he headed through the darkened house.

"Don't you need a light?" she asked.

"I know where I'm going," he answered with a teasing grin.

Moonlight streamed through the bedroom window, hitting the old-fashioned sleigh bed. It looked small, when she was used to the king-sized bed she and Tom had shared. He let her feet drop to the floor, then reached over to pull down the covers.

He sat on the bed, tugging her down beside him, and pulled off his wet socks and boots, then stood and unbuckled his belt and unsnapped his jeans. Sarah froze when she heard the zipper coming down. She exhaled audibly as he pulled his jeans off—along with his thigh-length briefs, leaving him unbelievably, delightfully naked.

She could see the gleam of Drew's white smile in the moonlight as he said, "You want to take those jeans off yourself, or do you want help?"

"To be honest," she began, "I'm . . ."

The word that sprang to mind was *terrified*. Of course she was also exhilarated. Mostly, she couldn't believe what she was doing. It was so unlike her. She was a responsible, law-abiding member of the community, a devoted mother . . . and wife.

But Tom was gone. Dead, she believed. Because the alternative, that he'd abandoned her, was impossible — too unbearably painful — to believe.

Sarah stood and unsnapped her jeans, unzipped them quickly and shoved them down, then sat and pulled off her Sorel boots and socks before tugging her jeans down her bare legs. She left on her plain white bra and white cotton underwear. Then, she stood again, facing Drew.

"My God," he said.

"What's wrong?" she asked.

He caught her wrists to keep her from covering herself. "You're goddamned beautiful."

Sarah relaxed in Drew's grip. "Thank you."

He let go of her wrists and reached out and unsnapped the front clasp of her bra, letting it fall away before covering her breasts with his large, warm hands. She felt his mouth on her nipple, felt him suck and then tease with his teeth.

Her hands threaded through his soft hair and her mouth latched onto his shoulder to bite and suck. She felt him shoving her panties down her legs and used a foot to push them out of her way so she could spread her legs for his searching hand.

His head came up and they stared into one another's heavy-lidded eyes.

"Are you sure you're okay with this?" he asked, placing his fingertips tantalizingly low on her belly.

Sarah couldn't believe he'd stopped to ask. She hadn't exactly been fighting him off. She wondered what he would think if he knew she hoped never to see him again after tonight. That she felt guilty and grateful for what was about to happen all at the same time.

She swallowed hard over the painful lump that had formed in her throat, making speech impossible anytime soon. She nodded soberly.

He tipped her chin up with his forefinger and lowered his mouth to touch her lips with his. "I just wanted to be sure," he murmured. He turned away, opened the bedside table and retrieved a condom.

She breathed a silent sigh of relief that she wouldn't have to ask, then gulped when he handed the foil package to her and said, "When the time comes, we'll need this."

He picked her up again and laid her on the bed, then covered her with his body. They were intimately joined from breast to thigh, with his legs caught between hers. His callused hands caressed as his mouth promised rapture.

Sarah was determined to give as good as she got. She reached out to touch warm flesh, and had the satisfaction of hearing Drew grunt in surprise and pleasure.

They were both breathing hard, both slick with sweat, both moaning with pleasure, when Sarah's pager went off.

It didn't pierce her consciousness immediately. She was too wrapped up in the salty taste of Drew's skin, too enamored of the lithe muscle and sinew along his flank, the soft dusting of hair on his muscular forearms, the hard budding of his nipples.

She felt his arms grasp hers, heard him gasp, "What the hell is that?"

Sarah sat up abruptly. "Oh, God."

Only two parties had the number to her pager. Her children. And the Teton County Sheriff's Office.

Which was when she realized she'd never called Nate and Brooke to tell them she'd be later than she expected. They were probably worried. Ever since Tom had disappeared, they'd kept close track of her whereabouts whenever she was out of the house. It made her sick to her stomach to imagine that they thought she might have run away—or become the victim of some dire act—too.

She slid off the bed and went searching for her jeans in the dark, looking for the pager she kept clipped to her belt. She found it and hit the button that lit the caller's number. She was relieved to see it was the sheriff's office calling and not her children.

"I left my cell in the truck. May I use your phone?" she said.

"Can't that wait?" Drew said, leaning across the bed and pushing the tail of her French braid aside to kiss her nape.

Sarah lowered her head to give him better access and let him kiss her for another moment before she groaned and pulled away. "I'd better call."

"Sure." Drew turned on the brass lamp beside the bed, revealing the portable phone on the nightstand and the digital clock, which read 8:52.

Sarah pulled the sheet free and wrapped it around herself. When she turned back to Drew, she felt ashamed, because the bump on his head showed purple in the lamplight. She hadn't given a thought to his injury. "Your poor head," she said. "Does it hurt?"

"It was fine until your pager went off," Drew said with a wry smile.

Sarah smiled back as she reached for the phone beside the bed. She took it across the room, keeping a good grip on the sheet with her arms, as she dialed the sheriff's office.

"It's Sarah," she said to the dispatcher. "What's up? Oh, no. Not another one. Really? Maybe we'll have a chance to find her this time. I'll be there in twenty minutes."

Sarah clicked off the phone and said, "I have to go."

"What's the rush?"

"A teenage girl has gone missing, the third over the past fifteen months. This is the first one we've known about in the first twenty-four hours. In fact, she's only been gone six or seven hours."

"Isn't it a little early to presume something bad has happened to her?" Drew asked as he retrieved his shorts from the floor and began dressing.

Sarah realized she was either going to have to dress under the sheet—a ridiculous proposition, considering the fact that Drew had already seen her naked—or drop the sheet and put her clothes on. She opted for the latter.

Sarah couldn't help feeling pleased at Drew's gasp as the sheet fell to her feet. She stepped over it, found her panties and bra and put them on, then put on socks, jeans and boots.

As she dressed, she explained, "If it weren't for the two other local girls who've gone missing, I don't think we'd be so quick to jump on this."

"Why do you have to go?" Drew asked, his arm slipping around her waist from behind, his coaxing mouth on her throat almost making her swoon. "Can't someone else do it?"

"I was the detective originally assigned to investigate the disappearance of the other two missing girls."

"That sounds like a lot of responsibility."

Sarah's lips twisted sardonically. "I'm only in charge because when the first girl disappeared everyone figured it was a simple missing persons case—some girl who'd run away from home. It happens."

"What makes you think the missing girls didn't just run away?"

Sarah buckled her belt before she met Drew's eyes. "Because we found the body of another young woman last spring—not one of the two reported missing— buried in a shallow grave in the mountains. She'd been shot once in the back of the head."

"How did you find her?" Drew said.

"I wish I could claim it was good detective work," Sarah said. "It was pure accident. An out-of-bounds skier found her. She turned out to be a runaway from Nevada."

"You have no clue who's taking these girls, or why?"

Sarah shook her head. "Nothing. We're not even sure the cases are connected, or we'd get the FBI involved. The girl who went missing three months ago is from a family living in Driggs, Idaho, about ten miles north over the Teton Pass, who came from Mexico illegally to work in Jackson," Sarah said.

"The girl reported missing fifteen months ago has no family. She came here from California to bum around on the slopes and worked in one of the motels. She hooked up with a local ski instructor, who reported her missing, or we might not have known anything had happened to her. Folks come and go on the drop of a dime around here."

Sarah frowned and added, "Which is what makes the third girl's disappearance different. This girl has family here in town."

"So she decided to kick up her heels for the evening, and she'll show up at home in the morning," Drew said.

"I hope so," Sarah said. "A lot of parents have panicked since that girl was found dead in the mountains. A mother calls and says, "Susie's late getting home." Then Susie shows up and she's been making out in the backseat of Johnny's car for the past three hours. This might be one of those calls."

"Or it might not," Drew said.

"Right," Sarah said. "If this disappearance is connected, and we can find the girl, it might lead us to the other two missing girls." Sarah pulled free of Drew's embrace and turned to face him. "This was . . . tonight was . . . nice."

"Come back when you're finished and we can—"

Sarah's grimace cut him off. She'd been saved by the pager, given a reprieve. But there was no sense tempting fate. She'd liked everything Drew had done way too much. But there was simply no future in it. It was sex merely for the sake of the pleasure it could bring. Better to cut all ties now.

"I don't think we should—"

"I'll be here in Jackson a while," Drew said. "We've got time to give it another try. By the way," he said, "what's your name?"

Sarah stared at him, stricken. She'd almost had sex with a man who didn't even know her name! What had she been thinking? "You don't need to know my name," she said. "Since we won't be seeing each other again."

She turned to leave, but he caught her arm.

"I'm sorry," he said. "I should have asked sooner. It didn't seem to matter."

She stared at his hand until he let her go. Then she headed through the darkened house toward the kitchen door, Drew flipping switches behind her to light her way.

Sarah snatched up her sweater and coat from the black-and-white checkerboard linoleum floor in the kitchen and realized she couldn't race out the door in this frigid weather without stopping to put them back on.

"I can ask at the garage who you are," Drew pointed out. "Or at the sheriff's office."

Sarah shuddered at the thought of Drew making inquiries about her in town. "My name's Sarah Barndollar," she said, glaring at him. "Don't ask about me. Don't try to contact me. I don't want to see you again."

By then, she had her coat on but couldn't get the zipper to work.

Drew stepped in front of her and moved her trembling hands away, then slowly and surely inserted the two sides of the zipper together and pulled it up to her chin. He tucked the stray hairs behind her ears, then leaned forward and gently brushed her lips with his.

"It was nice meeting you, Sarah Barndollar."

Sarah waited for him to say that he planned to pursue her, that he wasn't going to let her get away. He didn't say anything of the sort. He was letting her walk out of his life, exactly the way you'd expect a man to be glad to see the backside of a one-night stand.

"Good-bye," she said. She barely managed to keep herself from thanking him. For the pleasure. For making her feel beautiful. For making her feel like a desirable woman again.

Sarah turned on her heel, yanked open the door and let herself out into the cold.

Libby paced the confines of her chinked log cabin wearing cowboy boots that echoed on the hardwood floor. She glanced at her watch, appalled to see it was 9:03, and still no word from Kate. She'd finally called the police around eight-thirty, feeling more and more frantic as she listened to the dispatcher's calm demeanor as she wrote down answers to a seemingly endless list of questions she asked.

Libby crossed back and forth past North, who sat on the saddle-brown leather couch, one booted foot crossed over the other, sipping a mug of coffee.

"Sit down and take a load off, Libby," North said.

Libby scowled at her brother. "If I want to worry, I'll worry!"

Libby stopped and listened. The Teton County Sheriff's Office was dispatching someone to get a picture of Kate to send out over the Internet to nearby law enforcement offices and to ask more questions about her daughter's disappearance. "Is that someone at the door?" she asked.

"The dogs would have heard if it was," North replied.

Libby realized he was right. Her two sleek redbone coonhounds lay on the braided rug in front of the roaring fire she'd built in the rock fireplace, following her with watchful eyes, their tails thumping each time she passed. Her twelve-year-old bluetick hound stayed on her heels as she paced.

Libby turned to North and demanded, "Why would she do it? Kate knows better. Leaving school without permission, flying halfway across the country on a whim, not waiting for me to pick her up at the airport. She knows how dangerous it is to hitchhike!"

The younger of the redbone hounds rose to its feet, stretched, and whined. Libby crossed to the dog, rubbed its smooth red shoulder, ran a hand over floppy ears that fell below the dog's jaw, and said, "It's all right, Snoopy. Lie down."

The dog hesitated, then settled back on its haunches. But his large brown eyes remained riveted on her.

Libby's gaze blurred with tears as she stared at the hound. Snoopy was a silly name for a hunting dog, but

Kate had taken one look at the puppy, with its long ears and sorrowful eyes, and despite its all-over red color, said, "He reminds me of Charlie Brown's Snoopy." Snoopy he'd become. The last time Libby had gone hunting in the mountains, Snoopy had treed a snarling, full-grown mountain lion.

Libby dropped onto her knees beside the bluetick hound, whose graying muzzle settled into her lap. She stroked the dog's coarse, speckled black-and-white coat and said, "We'll go looking for her, Magnum, I promise you, if she doesn't show up soon."

A moment later, Libby was on her feet pacing again, railing against her absent daughter. "What was she doing in a bar in the first place? She's not old enough to drink!"

Libby had gone into town with Kate's picture, showing it in every bar in Jackson, including the tourist-laden cowboy bars. She'd been to the Silver Dollar Bar at the historic Wort Hotel, with its two thousand silver dollars laminated into the bar, the Shady Lady at the Snow King Resort, the Million Dollar Cowboy Bar with its saddles for bar stools, the Cadillac Grill, and the Stagecoach Bar in Wilson, on the chance that Kate might have stopped in one of them.

When she got no results, she headed to Teton Village, the ski resort outside of town. Where she got a hit.

When she stuck Kate's picture under the nose of the bartender at the Mangy Moose, he said, "Sure. Stunner like that, long black hair and those silvery gray eyes, you notice her. She was in here when I started my shift, around four. Left with some man."

"What man?" Libby demanded.

"Haven't seen him in here before," the bartender said. "Doesn't mean he isn't a regular. I just started working here a couple weeks ago."

Jackson Hole was a resort town, and the hired help came and went as quickly as the tourists. The perennially young bartenders and waitresses worked long enough to earn the money for a season ski pass, then disappeared to the black diamond slopes. The transient town had an infinitesimally small local population—less than ten thousand—but ten times that many passed through during the summer on their way to Yellowstone National Park, a mere hour's drive away.

"What did the man who left with this girl look like?" Libby asked, holding the picture of Kate in front of his face.

The bartender shrugged. "Six feet maybe. Brown hair, maybe brown eyes, I don't know. Wearing ski clothes like everybody else."

Libby realized the bartender's description probably fit half the men in town. "Was there anything different about the man with my daughter, anything that would help us find him?"

The bartender frowned in concentration. "He was good looking. Clean shaven." He shook his head. "Sorry. He was just a normal guy."

Normal. Except that he might have been a kidnapper, Libby thought, as her stomach clenched with fear. Though she'd persisted, the bartender hadn't been able to remember anything else.

As she paced her living room, Libby didn't let herself think the worst. It was too frightening.

There wasn't much breaking news in a small town like Jackson, and the *Jackson Hole News and Guide* had reminded everyone—when the most recent young woman had gone missing three months ago—of the girl who'd disappeared fifteen months ago, and the girl who'd been found shot to death in the mountains.

"Why didn't Kate just come home and wait here for me?" Libby wailed. "Why would she go to a bar, of all places?" Libby couldn't help thinking of the phone message Kate had left for her. Now she saw all sorts of sinister possibilities. What kind of trouble was Kate in? Was her disappearance related to her desperate message?

"Why did I have to be gone at just this time?" she said to her brother. "Why couldn't I have driven faster?"

Which reminded Libby of her nearly catastrophic accident on the road south of Jackson. No, she couldn't have driven any faster than she had. But that didn't make her feel any better. She glanced at her watch. "It's nearly nine-fifteen. She would have called by now if she could."

North set his coffee cup on the table beside his chair. "Kate's a Grayhawk. She knows how to handle herself when the chips are down."

"I'll bet the mothers of those other two girls thought the same thing." Libby had a bad feeling, deep in her gut, that wouldn't go away.

North pounded a fist into the palm of his other hand and said, "When she shows up— and I think she will—

that sonofabitch who was with her at the Mangy Moose is going to answer to me."

Snoopy was up and headed for the door a half second before the knock sounded. Doc and Magnum joined him, nearly tripping Libby as she crossed in front of them to get to the door.

Libby reached for the doorknob with her heart in her throat, hoping against hope that it was Kate, or if not her, that the police would have some word of her whereabouts. At the same time she was terrified that it might be someone coming to tell her Kate had been hurt in an accident—or that they'd found her body dumped beside the road.

Libby put a hand over her pounding heart and opened the door. And gasped when she saw who stood there.

"May I come in?"

Libby didn't move. Couldn't move.

A second later, North was standing by her side, his body wired tight as a bowstring. "You can say whatever you have to say from right there, Blackthorne."

Libby stared at Clay Blackthorne, whose gaze had never left hers. His gray eyes were as ruthless and remote as they'd been since the day she betrayed him, his cheekbones chiseled, his jaw square and determined. He had crow's-feet at the corners of his eyes and his black hair showed gray at the temples, but his powerful shoulders were still broad, and at six feet four, he towered almost a foot above her.

He looked imposing in a long black cashmere coat. He unbuttoned it to reveal a tailored Armani tuxedo jacket and a crisp white tux shirt with the tie gone, open at the throat to reveal a thatch of dark hair. Black tuxedo trousers with a satin stripe along the side emphasized his long legs. His patent leather shoes looked out of place in her log home. Clay had come from a world of power brokers and politics. He didn't belong here.

"You must have been at a party," Libby blurted.

"At the British Embassy," Clay confirmed. "With Dad and Ren and Jocelyn."

Libby looked behind him, as though expecting to see Clay's father Blackjack, his second wife Ren, and Clay's late wife's sister Jocelyn Montrose on her doorstep. "Where are they?" she asked.

"I came alone."

"What are you doing here?" Libby said.

"Has Kate shown up?"

Libby shook her head. "No. What are you doing here?" she repeated. "Why did you come? How did you get here so fast?"

"You called me a little over four hours ago and said our daughter was missing," Clay said. "I'm here to make sure she's found."

"We don't need your help," North said.

"She's my daughter," Clay said.

"I told you not to come," North said.

Libby turned to North. "You talked to Clay?"

"He called here while they were doing the preflight check on his jet. You were out showing Kate's picture around." North turned to Clay and said, "Now get the hell off—"

Libby turned on North and said, "This is my house. I'll decide who's welcome here."

North grabbed his Stetson and sheepskin coat from the antler rack behind her and said, "Call me when he's gone." He shoved past Clay, who held his ground, resulting in the inevitable collision of two hard-muscled male shoulders.

Libby's jaw clenched. North had taken up the gauntlet against the Blackthornes and carried it every bit as fervently as their father. Ordinarily, Libby would have sided with her brother. She wished she could hate Clay. But what had happened between them had been entirely her fault.

She stepped back and said, "Come in."

Clay gave each of the three hounds a pat and a word of greeting as he entered. He took off his coat and hung it on the antler coatrack, then discarded his tux jacket before turning to her. "What's being done to find Kate?"

Libby bristled. "The presumption being that I'm incapable of handling the situation."

"I didn't say that," Clay replied with irritating equanimity. "I just want to know what's going on."

Libby was itching for a fight, but she knew better than to provoke Clay. He didn't fight fair, and he fought to win.

"I'm waiting for someone to show up from the Teton County Sheriff's Office," Libby said. "Kate was seen leaving the Mangy Moose with a man who hasn't been identified."

Clay slipped the gold cuff links from his starched

cuffs and dropped them into his pants pocket, then rolled up his sleeves, revealing strong, veined forearms. He looked like a man who spent his days manhandling barbed wire, but as attorney general of the United States, Clay only exerted his muscle figuratively.

His current job was only a stepping stone, Libby knew. Clay had been groomed all his life for higher office. He would likely go from Washington to the governor's mansion in Texas, where his father owned an empire called the Bitter Creek Cattle Company, with a ranch the size of a small northeastern state. From the governor's mansion, it was a short step to the White House

The fact that Clay had gotten a sixteen-year-old pregnant when he was twenty-seven might very well put those aspirations in jeopardy. Which was why Kate's relationship to him had remained a secret.

Libby wondered why Clay would risk coming here at a time like this. There was liable to be news coverage of Kate's disappearance, since she was King Grayhawk's granddaughter. If Clay was here, someone might ask what his connection was to the Grayhawk family, who were known adversaries, politically and otherwise, of the Blackthornes.

Clay's visits with his unacknowledged daughter at his ranch in Jackson had been done in a way that kept their true relationship a secret from the outside world. To maintain the deception, Kate had never addressed her father as Dad or Daddy or Father or Pop. He was simply Mr. Blackthorne. Or when they were alone, Clay.

"What was Kate doing in a bar?" Clay asked. "She's not old enough to drink."

"When did that ever stop a determined teenager?" Libby retorted. "There's no reason for you to be here. I'm handling the situation."

"Then why did you call me?"

"I thought Kate might have called you when she couldn't reach me about whatever was troubling her. And I thought you should know your daughter was missing."

"If I'm not mistaken, she'd only been out of touch a couple of hours when you called. Why did you think something had happened to her?"

Libby wondered now why she'd made that giant leap on such insubstantial evidence. Maybe it was a mother's intuition, but she'd had a premonition since she'd first listened to Kate's voicemail that her daughter was in trouble. She turned the question back on Clay and said, "Why did you come?"

Clay's gray eyes locked with her blue ones as he said, "I don't know. I can't explain it. I had a feeling something was wrong. It's strange enough that Kate would leave school in the middle of the term like that. Since she called you, I presume she wanted to talk to you about something. So why didn't she come straight here and wait for you?"

"I know what you mean," Libby said, her hands clutched together to keep Clay from seeing that they were shaking. "I can't stop thinking about those other two girls who disappeared. And the third one, who was found dead." She met Clay's gaze and said, "I'm scared."

In the eighteen years since they'd been lovers, they'd never once touched. But the child they'd made together was missing, perhaps in mortal danger. When Clay opened his arms, Libby walked right into them. His body was warm and he smelled faintly of some masculine cologne. His arms were strong and she felt safe within them.

Memories swamped her, of long lazy afternoons in the sunlight. Of his callused hands on her flesh. Of his long, tanned flanks in the leaf-dappled sunlight. It had been a heady time, she'd been so much in love. So had he.

Until she'd sent him away.

Libby felt Clay's body tense as she turned her face up to his, saw his eyes narrow as she reached up to curve her hand around his nape and draw his head down to hers.

But he didn't release her. And he didn't turn away.

"Clay," she whispered.

His shoulders were rock hard under her hands, and she caught her breath as she stared up into gray eyes that had turned dark and stormy. His lips were surprisingly soft as they met hers, and Libby felt a sudden surge of desire as his tongue traced the seam of her mouth, urging her to open to him.

His arms tightened around her as she let him in. The kiss was searing, and Libby felt overwhelmed by sensations. The silkiness of his hair under her hands, the warm wetness of his tongue, the crush of her breasts against his muscular chest. She couldn't catch her breath, couldn't catch up to the powerful rush of emotions that made her throat ache with love and regret and need.

He backed her up against the wall, capturing her there with his hardened body, grasping her breast and kneading it, thrusting his tongue into her mouth as his hips sought the welcoming cradle of her thighs. He reached for the button of her jeans, growling when it wouldn't come free, ripping the cloth as he shoved his hand inside to reach skin.

Libby moaned and pressed her hand against the front of his trousers, feeling the hot, hard length of him.

Suddenly, he separated them with a guttural sound of torment. They were both panting, and she stared with stunned surprise into gray eyes that looked equally shocked at the violence of their mutual desire.

"Libby, I—"

Someone knocked hard on the door.

Libby refused to look away, willing Clay to finish his thought. *"Libby, I need you."*

A muscle worked in his jaw, and his gray eyes became inscrutable. He might want her, Libby realized. But he was never going to forgive her. She swallowed hard over the sudden lump of sadness in her throat.

She reached up with a trembling hand to caress his cheek. When he flinched, she gave a cry of woe, then pulled free and ran for the door.

4

When the petite, worried-looking blond woman opened the door, Sarah held up her badge, a five-point gold star in a leather folder, and said, "I'm Detective Sarah Barndollar, with the Teton County Sheriff's Office. I'm looking for Libby Grayhawk."

"You've found her."

"May I come in, Ms. Grayhawk?" Sarah asked.

"Please, call me Libby," the woman said as she stepped back and opened the door wider. "I wasn't expecting a woman. I don't know why I thought—"

"No problem," Sarah interrupted. "I'm here about your daughter's disappearance."

"Of course," Libby said. "The dispatcher said you'd want a picture of Kate. Let me get it for you."

When Libby Grayhawk turned, she ran into the tall, black-haired, gray-eyed man who'd come up behind her. Sarah managed not to hiss in a breath when she recognized him. U.S. Attorney General Clay Blackthorne was one of Jackson's many celebrity residents. She hadn't recognized Drew as a part owner of Forgotten Valley, but she'd seen Clay Blackthorne more than once on television, standing beside the president of the United States.

Sarah saw the tightening of Clay Blackthorne's jaw as he took the woman's shoulders in his hands and moved her away. Evaluating people was an important part of Sarah's job, and she was aware of the tension between them.

Libby was clearly flustered when she turned back to Sarah and said, "This is Clay Blackthorne." Libby hesitated, and Sarah waited with bated breath to hear how the petite woman would explain the U.S. attorney general's presence this late at night—in his shirtsleeves. "A friend," Libby said at last.

Clay reached past Libby and shook Sarah's hand. "Thanks for coming, Detective Barndollar. How soon will the Amber Alert go into effect?"

Sarah turned to Libby before she could escape and said, "How old is your daughter?"

"Seventeen."

"Almost eighteen," Clay said.

"We've never done an Amber Alert in Wyoming," Sarah said. "Kids around here that go missing are mostly taken by divorced parents. We're too small a town to have a local TV station, and the only flashing sign we have to announce an Amber Alert is on the Snake River at Hoback Canyon, and it's used to warn folks there's road work ahead."

"Christ." Clay shoved both hands through his hair in agitation.

"I'll have the dispatcher alert everyone to be on the lookout for your daughter, and we can e-mail your daughter's picture to statewide law enforcement. We usually wait twenty-four hours to post information on missing persons with NCIC."

"What's NCIC?" Libby asked.

Sarah had made the explanation so many times, she had it memorized. "The National Crime Information Center," she said. "It's a centralized computer system with statistics and information about crimes and missing persons that allows different jurisdictions to make comparisons of data."

"Does it work?" Libby asked.

"It's how we identified the girl who was found last spring buried in the mountains. NCIC came up with a match on a missing persons report out of Las Vegas."

Sarah realized the mistake she'd made when Libby's face paled and she began to tremble. Before Sarah could reach out to the other woman, Clay Blackthorne had stepped up behind Libby and steadied her by wrapping an arm around her waist. Libby immediately turned and buried her face against his shoulder.

Blackthorne's cold-eyed gaze dared Sarah to say anything. She kept her mouth shut, but that kind of body contact between a man and a woman suggested a relationship beyond that of mere friends. Was the U.S. attorney general having a clandestine affair with Libby Grayhawk? Then she remembered reading that Clay Blackthorne's wife had died a while back of cancer. Not clandestine, then. Just private.

"In a special case, you could put the information on

NCIC without waiting the full twenty-four hours, couldn't you?" Blackthorne asked.

"In a special case," Sarah agreed.

"I want Kate Grayhawk's info put on now," Blackthorne said.

"I don't think—"

"I don't like pulling rank, but I will," Blackthorne said, his arms tight around Libby Grayhawk. "I want that information posted on NCIC immediately."

"I'll see to it."

"I'll go get that picture," Libby said, pulling free of Blackthorne's embrace and heading toward the back of the house.

Sarah pulled her purse strap higher on her shoulder and said, "I didn't realize you were visiting in Jackson, Mr. Blackthorne. Usually the Secret Service asks that someone from our office be assigned to help protect dignitaries when they're in town."

"I'm not here on official business," he said.

"Where are you staying?" Sarah asked.

Blackthorne's gray eyes turned to ice. "That's none of your business."

Sarah flushed. She glanced at Libby, who'd returned with the picture of Kate, then turned back to Blackthorne and said, "I just dropped off Drew DeWitt at the ranch house at Forgotten Valley. He mentioned the two of you own it together."

"We do," Blackthorne said.

"I asked where you were staying because I towed his truck out of the river tonight—that's another story—but he was hurt in the accident and it might be a good idea if someone stayed with him tonight to make sure he doesn't have a concussion," Sarah said. "So I wondered if—"

"I see," Blackthorne said. "I am staying at the ranch. I promise to keep an eye on him, Detective."

"Here's the picture of Kate," Libby said, handing over a 5x7 color photo of an extraordinarily beautiful black-haired, gray-eyed young woman. "I gave a lot of information to someone over the phone. Is there anything else you need from me?"

"Is there anyone in town your daughter might have gone to see? A girlfriend? A boyfriend?" Sarah asked.

Libby shook her head. "I already gave a description of the stranger Kate left the Mangy Moose with to someone at the sheriff's office. I can't imagine who the man was. No one I know, for sure. I called all of Kate's friends here in Jackson when I got home around four-thirty, but none of them had heard from her recently. Kate has been attending a private school back East for the past four years, so her friends live all over the country."

"There's no one—"

"I said there's no one here in Jackson," Libby said sharply. "Just my brother North and me."

Libby was caught up in her thoughts when the detective asked, "What about Kate's father? Any chance he might—"

"Kate's father doesn't live around here," Libby said quickly.

Too quickly, Sarah thought. She watched Clay Blackthorne stiffen beside the petite woman.

"Have you been in contact with him?" Sarah said, her eyes on Blackthorne. "Maybe your daughter—"

"He's been informed," Libby said. "He doesn't know where she is, either."

Sarah looked from Clay Blackthorne to Libby and back again and waited, letting the silence do its work. She wondered what Blackthorne had to do with this situation. She'd learned better than to make guesses, but her gut told her there was more going on than she was being told.

When it became clear that Blackthorne wasn't going to offer any further explanation for his presence, she handed her card to Libby and said, "If you think of anything you believe might be useful, give me a call."

"I will," Libby said as she followed Sarah to the door. "Thank you, Detective."

"You're welcome, Libby. And please, call me Sarah. I'll go back to the Mangy Moose and see if anyone noticed your daughter leaving or saw the vehicle she left in. If I find out anything more, I'll be in touch." She didn't offer platitudes. They weren't going to help find Libby Grayhawk's missing daughter.

Sarah didn't look back as she headed for her Tahoe. She had a bad feeling about this one. Clay Blackthorne's presence lent more weight to the girl's disappearance. Why had he come here? What, exactly, was his relationship to Libby Grayhawk? And why did he seem to care so much about Libby Grayhawk's daughter?

* * *

"I should have told her Kate is my daughter," Clay said.

"Why?" Libby asked. "What difference can it possibly make?"

"They'll do more to find her if they think she's the daughter of someone important."

"She's a Grayhawk," Libby said. "In Jackson, that's enough. I'd rather you say nothing."

Clay lifted a brow in question and Libby explained, "Whoever has her may kill her if he realizes that both the Grayhawks and the Blackthornes will come down on him for taking her," Libby said. "I don't want her connection to you made public yet. Besides, aren't you afraid of the political repercussions if it gets out that you have a grown daughter you've never told anyone about?"

"I think my career can survive it."

"And if you thought it couldn't, would you still make the ultimate sacrifice for your daughter?" Libby said bitterly.

"You know I would." Clay put his hands on Libby's shoulders, looked into her eyes, and said, "I love Kate. She's all I have left in the world."

Clay saw Libby wince before she pulled free and turned away. He'd known the words would hurt, but he hadn't been able to curb his tongue. At forty-six, it was getting harder not to say exactly what was on his mind. To hell with diplomacy. He'd spent his whole life being careful not to offend the right people. If ever there was a time for plain speaking, this was it.

"What's going on, Libby? What is it you haven't told me? Why did Kate leave school and fly back here?"

Libby turned to face him, her arms crossed protectively over her chest. "That's the worst part. I don't know. She called to say she was coming home, that she had something important to talk to me about. She never said what it was."

"She's pregnant," Clay said flatly.

He watched as Libby sucked in a breath. "I thought the same thing," she said.

"So maybe Kate met the father here, and that's who she was with at the Mangy Moose," Clay speculated.

Libby shook her head. "I don't think so. The bartender seemed to think they didn't know each other. He overheard a little of what they said," she explained when Clay lifted a skeptical brow.

"How could this have happened?" Clay demanded.

Libby's eyes looked bleak.

Suddenly Clay was remembering how he and Libby had met. How easily he'd succumbed to Libby's flirtatious smile and her young, supple body. She was still slim, still beautiful. But the smile was gone. He rarely let himself think about the good times they'd shared. Staying focused on her betrayal was the only way he'd been able to keep his distance from her. She was a dangerous flame, and this moth already had singed wings.

"I'd better go," he said, crossing to the door.

"Clay . . ."

He unrolled his sleeves before putting on his tux jacket, then turned to her as he slipped into his cashmere overcoat. "Any ideas where I should start looking in the morning?"

"I've already looked everywhere I thought she might be," Libby said.

"I'll go by the sheriff's office—"

"You can't do that," Libby protested.

"Why not? I'll go as a friend of the family."

"You're being naive if you don't think someone will call the newspapers to tell them you were there," Libby said.

"Thanks to you, there's nothing to connect me to Kate," Clay said bitterly. "My name doesn't appear anywhere. I've never contributed a dime to her support."

"You've never complained," Libby retorted.

"Would it have done any good?" Clay pulled on his black leather gloves. "You've had everything your way for nineteen years," he said. "That ends now. I'm going to do whatever I think needs to be done to find my daughter."

"*Your* daughter?" Libby said, her chin up, her eyes sparkling with anger.

"*Our* daughter," Clay corrected.

"Even if it means the past will come out?"

"It was never my choice to keep the fact I have a daughter a secret," Clay said angrily. "I did it because you convinced me it was the best thing for Kate. The only thing I'm concerned about now is getting Kate back home safe and sound, and then helping her through whatever crisis got her into this mess in the first place."

Clay was nearly out the door when Libby said, "I want to go with you."

He turned to stare at her. "Now?"

She flushed. "No. When you go hunting for her to-morrow."

"What purpose will that serve?"

"I won't be here worrying all alone."

"What if she calls and there's no one here to take the call?" Clay asked.

"I can have the calls forwarded to North's house. He can call me on my cell if there's any word."

Clay didn't want to spend the day with Libby. He still found her far too attractive. Holding her in his arms tonight, kissing her, touching her, had brought back memories he would rather forget.

But from a practical standpoint, it would be easier to get information from the sheriff's office if he was with Libby. And she might know places to look in Jackson that he didn't know.

"All right," he said. "I'll pick you up after breakfast."

"I could make breakfast for you here," Libby said.

Clay pictured Libby with her shoulder-length blond curls in tangles, her eyes sleepily seductive, her rosy nipples barely hidden beneath a thin cotton shift, then said curtly, "I'll meet you at Bubba's at seven."

Libby nodded.

Clay figured breakfast at the popular restaurant in town was a safe compromise. He wouldn't be tempted because they wouldn't be alone, and they could start their search that much earlier.

He let himself out, closing the door firmly behind him. It was snowing, the flakes big and fluffy and coming straight down, rather than being blown sideways, for a change.

Clay wondered if his daughter had been in an accident. Maybe she was lying injured on the side of the road, and the snow was covering up her body. Or maybe she was tucked up under a blanket in front of a fire with the love of her life, so caught up in passion that she wasn't aware of the worry—and terror—she was stirring in her parents' hearts.

Clay raised his face to the sky and let snowflakes land on his eyelashes, opening his mouth to feel the coldness on his tongue. The snow would make a wonderland of the landscape. But right now, it was more menace than miracle. If it kept up, it was going to make the search for Kate much more difficult.

He got into the SUV he'd rented at the airport and tried not to speed during the twenty-minute drive to Forgotten Valley. He wondered if Drew would still be awake. He needed someone to talk to, someone to make him feel less afraid for his daughter. Someone to tell him he was a fool for having the carnal thoughts he was having about Elsbeth Grayhawk.

Hell, if Drew was asleep, he'd wake him up. Someone with a concussion wasn't supposed to sleep anyway.

Clay had his own key, but the kitchen door wasn't locked. He flipped on the light switch and was surprised to see a man's shirt in the middle of the floor. He left his overcoat on the stand by the door and followed the trail of clothes down the hall to Drew's bedroom, realizing that someone of the female persuasion had obviously come to make sure Drew wasn't suffering alone.

Clay made a face. There was no way he was going to drag his cousin out of bed to talk to him when he was with some woman. What he had to say would have to wait until morning.

But as he passed Drew's door, it opened, and he found himself facing the barrel of a shotgun.

"Whoa, there," Clay said, instinctively putting his hands up in the classic Western pose.

Drew's blond hair was standing up in spikes, his forehead was bruised and he was stark naked. He squinted at Clay and said, "What the hell are you doing here?"

Clay reached out and moved the barrel of the shotgun away. "You look like something somebody rode hard and put away wet."

Drew let the barrel of the shotgun fall, opened the door wider and said, "Sexual frustration will do that to you."

Clay could see through the open door that the bedcovers were mussed, but the bed was otherwise empty. "From the trail of clothes leading in here, I figured some woman was in there easing your pain."

Drew hung the shotgun back up over the fireplace in his bedroom, then headed straight for the bed and crawled into it. "She had to leave. Duty called."

"Duty? What kind of female are you bedding these days?"

Drew grinned. "This one's a deputy sheriff."

Clay put two and two together and said, "Her name wouldn't be Sarah Barndollar by any chance?"

Drew's grin disappeared. He started to frown, then winced and put a hand to his bruised forehead. "How did you know?"

Clay took a breath and said, "Kate's missing. The detective came by to ask some questions and pick up Kate's picture."

"Missing?" Drew sat up abruptly, then gingerly touched his head.

"How's your head?" Clay said. "You seeing double or anything?"

"It's just a bump," Drew said irritably. "Tell me about Kate."

Clay crossed to sit in a cowhide and burled-wood chair near the crackling fire. "Don't know much. She called Libby to say she was coming home, then left the Mangy Moose this afternoon with some stranger, and we haven't heard from her since."

"Let me get my hands on the sonofabitch, and he'll be sorry he touched a hair on her head," Drew said.

Clay had been forced to tell Drew that Kate was his daughter because they both vacationed at Forgotten Valley, and he wanted Kate to be able to visit him there. Kate had taken an instant liking to Drew—most females did—and the two of them had become fast friends.

"Why aren't you out looking for her?" Drew said, sliding to the edge of the bed and reaching for his shorts.

"You're not going anywhere until I'm sure you don't have a concussion," Clay said.

"To hell with that. She could be lying hurt by the side of the road."

Clay's hands tightened on the arms of the chair. "There's nothing we can do until it gets light. I'm meeting Libby for breakfast at Bubba's. You're welcome to join us."

"You're damn straight I'm going to join you!" Drew staggered, then sat down. "As soon as this damned headache is gone."

"Have you taken anything for it?"

"I'm not supposed to take anything," Drew mumbled as he got back into bed and pulled the covers up over himself.

"Get some sleep," Clay said.

"I'm not supposed to sleep," Drew muttered.

Clay slid his tuxedo jacket off, then slumped down into the chair. He didn't think he could sleep himself. But he needed to get some rest if he was going to spend tomorrow hunting for his daughter.

He was almost asleep when he remembered he hadn't called Jocelyn to tell her what he'd found out about Kate's abrupt departure from boarding school. His wife's sister had been a great comfort over the past year since Giselle had died. He and Jocelyn had been dancing at a British Embassy ball when Clay had gotten the call on his cell phone from Libby that Kate was missing. He'd taken Jocelyn's hand and sought out his father to tell him he had to leave.

"There you are, Clay," his father had said when he saw him. "I've been looking all over for you."

"It looks to me like you and your partner have been enjoying the music," Clay said, glancing at the attractive woman dancing with his father.

Clay still had trouble making himself say his stepmother's name. He'd hated her for too many years when she was the wife of his father's mortal enemy, Jesse Creed, to feel comfortable being cordial to her. She shamed him by smiling up at him with genuine affection.

"I'm having a wonderful time, Clay," Ren replied.

Though she was well into her sixties, Lauren Creed—for the past twelve years Lauren Blackthorne—was still a beautiful woman. His father had loved Ren his whole life, even while he'd been married to Clay's mother Eve. The doomed love triangle had finally destroyed Clay's mother, who'd committed suicide rather than lose her husband in a divorce to *that woman*.

Clay had to admit his father was happier living with Ren than he'd ever been during the years he'd been married to Clay's mother. But his father's remarriage hadn't dampened his political ambitions for Clay one iota.

President of the United States.

Clay had lived all his life with the knowledge that his family expected him to reach the highest office in the land. He'd been groomed for it since he was a boy and had always been conscious of needing to lead a blameless life.

With one—notable—exception, he had.

Clay swore under his breath. Just thinking about Libby Grayhawk, her seductive body and her betrayal, made his heart pound. He told himself it was anger that sent the adrenaline rushing through his bloodstream every time she came to mind. Anger was part of it. But there was a great deal more.

"There are some folks here tonight from Texas that I want you to meet," his father said.

"Can't that wait, Jackson?" Ren said, laying her hand on her husband's heart. "You can see Clay and Jocelyn want to dance."

"You just want me to finish this dance with you," his father grumbled.

Ren smiled up at him, and Clay watched his father, a man who crushed his enemies with a mighty hand and without a second thought, melt like butter in the hot Texas sun.

"All right, Ren," his father replied, his eyes soft as they looked down at his wife. "We'll finish this dance." He turned flinty gray eyes on Clay and said, "No lolly-gagging, son. When this dance is done, I expect you to join me."

Clay answered evenly, "I have to leave, Dad."

"You can stay long enough to meet a few of the gentlemen here from Texas," his father replied.

"No, I can't."

His father had looked at him with sharp gray eyes and said, "Business?"

Clay's reasons were his own, and he didn't choose to share them. "I have to leave," he repeated. "Can you take Jocelyn home for me?"

"Of course," Ren said. "We'll be glad to."

He'd walked Jocelyn a few steps away to say his good-byes to her. Jocelyn was a politician's daughter, used to interruptions at social engagements due to more important business, but he apologized anyway. "I'm sorry," he'd said. "This is important. I want to be there if Kate needs me."

"No need to apologize, *mon cher.*"

Despite the fact her father's family were Connecticut blue bloods, Jocelyn had spent enough time in Paris while her father was ambassador to France that her voice had a charming French lilt and her speech was unselfconsciously peppered with French expressions.

"I was looking forward to holding you in my arms tonight while we danced," he said with a regretful smile.

Her cheeks pinkened, and he was reminded how young she was, only twenty-four. She looked up at him from beneath lowered lashes and he could see the desire in her lavender eyes. Clay's eyes locked on her slightly parted lips, imagining what it might be like to kiss her, wondering what she would taste like. He'd actually lowered his head toward hers when he was shoved from behind by a dancing couple.

Whatever spell she'd cast was broken.

Clay realized suddenly where he was. And how many photographers there were in the room. The future president of the United States couldn't afford to have his picture splashed across the tabloids kissing his late wife's sister. At least, not before she was his wife.

"I have to go," he said in a voice guttural with sudden desire. It was surprisingly hard to walk away from her.

Clay was nearly to the door when someone stepped in front of him. "Damn it all to hell," he muttered.

"Your jet is being fueled at Dulles," Clay's chief of staff said. Dressed in a tux, Morgan DeWitt looked as influential as he was in real life. As Clay's right-hand man, he vetted anyone who wanted to see Clay in his office, and made sure Clay only had to deal with those issues that deserved his personal attention. "Are you sure you don't want me to go with you?" Morgan asked.

"This is a trip I have to make on my own," Clay replied. "I trust you to take care of things for me while I'm gone."

"Where are you going to be?" Morgan asked.

"Wherever the hunt for my daughter takes me."

Within minutes he'd been in the air on his way to Jackson. He'd expected Kate to be home, but he'd wanted to be there to help solve whatever problem had sent her running from school. But she hadn't been home. And it seemed the situation was far more dire than he'd imagined.

Clay sighed and shoved a hand through his hair. He ought to call Jocelyn. She would be anxious to know what he'd found out. He knew she was in love with him, though neither of them had ever discussed it. But he wasn't sure yet what he wanted to do about it. He'd never even kissed her, except on the cheek.

He'd told himself he wasn't ready yet to make another commitment to any woman. And since it would be a couple of years before he made his bid for governor of Texas, let alone the presidency, he could afford to stay single a while longer.

He saw Jocelyn's perfect, heart-shaped face in his mind's eye, her stunning violet eyes teary, her lower lip bitten raw with worry. He glanced at his watch. Hell. It was two hours later on the East Coast, too late to call and apologize for not phoning sooner. Likely she was sound asleep. He'd have to remember to call her in the morning.

5

~~

Kate reached for a blanket to cover herself because she was cold—and realized the thermal covering wouldn't pull up any higher over her shoulder. Oh. It was a sleeping bag. Where was she?

She saw what looked like a domed tent above her. White canvas walls framed by some sort of wooden lattice surrounded her, and she was lying on a wooden floor. She'd never seen a structure like this. It was a sort of tent, but not like any tent she'd ever been in.

Her mouth felt full of cotton and she was painfully thirsty. "Dear Lord," she groaned. "How much did I have to drink last night?"

She sat up slowly and reached for her head to keep the room from spinning. She stared in shock at her hands, which had both come up together. She was handcuffed!

"Are you okay?" a voice asked in Spanish.

Kate started and stared at the girl sitting on the foot of the sleeping bag she was wrapped in. She'd taken Spanish all through school, so she understood the question. But she had no idea why someone who spoke

Spanish was here with her. Or why she was here, for that matter.

And speaking of *here*, where the hell was she?

She squinted up into long-lashed, wide-spaced dark eyes, in a very young, very beautiful face and asked the girl in Spanish, "Where are we?"

"I don't know," came the response.

Kate winced at the streams of sunlight coming in through the slatted boards that covered the single window. Was it morning or evening? The last thing she could remember was being laid in the backseat of that stranger's pickup.

She'd been kidnapped. And brought to this . . . place.

Kate looked around. The circular white canvas tent was maybe twelve feet in diameter. The bottom four feet of the walls were framed by a wooden, diamond-shaped lattice, while the domed ceiling was held up by what looked like teepee poles attached at the top of the lattice. A hole in the ceiling vented smoke from an old-fashioned woodstove. There was one plastic-covered window, but it was boarded up with wooden slats.

It was only a tent. But it was a prison, all the same.

She curled her legs closer and wrapped her arms around them when she noticed the raised wooden floor had spaces between the lumber and missing knotholes where crawly things could come inside. She shuddered at the sight of the spiderwebs in the lattice.

Kate considered herself a dauntless, courageous person, but she hated bugs. Wouldn't squash one for all the money in the World Bank. Screamed like a banshee and jumped like a frog whenever she felt something crawling on her. She knew it was silly to be scared of something she could kill with a swat of her hand. But she'd been bitten by a black widow when she was nine and gotten deathly ill. And been terrified of bugs ever since.

She wanted out of here. Now.

Kate staggered upright to look between the slats of wood covering the window, then dropped back down and scooted back under the thermal covering. It kept her surprisingly warm, even though the air was cold enough for her to see her breath.

"It must have snowed," she murmured. The olive-colored pines—which seemed to lose their forest green color in the winter, Kate thought—were shot with a layer of snow. Snow didn't stay on the trees long before the wind blew it off or the sun melted it. "How long have I been here?" she asked the girl in Spanish.

"Since last night," the girl answered.

"How long have you been here?" Kate asked.

The girl held up three fingers and said something that Kate couldn't quite believe.

"Three days?" Kate asked.

"Three months," the girl repeated.

"Three months!" Kate exclaimed. She looked around the empty structure. No table or chairs, no bed, no bathroom that she could see, just a metal pail in the corner. Nothing but these canvas-covered wooden lattice walls and the old-fashioned woodstove in the center of the room, which wasn't burning at the moment.

No wonder it was so damned cold.

Which was when Kate realized her coat was missing. And her snow boots. She was dressed only in a sweatshirt and jeans and white socks. A look at the other girl showed she was dressed no more warmly, with black corduroy trousers and a red pullover sweater with a sequined Christmas design and black socks.

Both of them were handcuffed.

Kate shivered as she left the warm sleeping bag, but made her way to the wooden door and tried to open it. She wasn't really surprised when it wouldn't budge. "Probably barred from the outside."

"*Que?*" the other girl asked.

Kate repeated what she'd said in Spanish.

The girl nodded and said, "A man comes once a week to bring food and water and wood for the fire. He left food and water when he brought you." She pointed to an old trunk near the woodstove. "But he forgot to bring more wood."

"You mean we're going to be here for a week without heat?" Kate said. "We'll freeze to death!"

The girl shook her head. "He said he will be back tonight for me—and bring some wood for the stove."

"Where is he taking you? Why are you here? How did you get here?" Kate asked without waiting for the girl to answer. "Why is he taking you somewhere and not me?"

The girl put up her hands to slow Kate down. "I was kidnapped from the hotel where I work," she said. "I don't know why. The man who comes here wouldn't tell me. And he hasn't told me where he's taking me."

The girl looked at Kate and said, "I'm scared. I don't

think my mother and father went to the police when I disappeared. It is likely no one even knows I'm gone."

"Why not?" Kate asked.

"I'm . . ." The girl searched for a word and finally said, "Illegal. No green card. My father came here from Mexico in the spring to work in the kitchen of a grand hotel. In the fall he sent for my mother and me and my three younger brothers to work in the hotel cleaning rooms. He had found a small place for us in Driggs, just over the Teton Pass in Idaho. We were happy to be together again."

"I see," Kate said. If they were all illegal aliens, the girl's parents wouldn't want to say anything to the police for fear of discovery and deportation. "Well, that certainly isn't the case with me. My mother will roust every cop from one coast to the other to look for me. She'll probably even call my father."

Kate wondered for a moment if her father would come. And whether he would risk his relationship to her becoming public. Probably not. But he could still pull a lot of strings from the background.

"We're going to be found," Kate said. "Don't you worry about that." Kate realized she still didn't know the girl's name. "I'm Kate Grayhawk," she said. "What's your name?"

"Lourdes Ramirez," the girl replied.

"Pleased to meet you, Lourdes," Kate said, reaching out her cuffed hands to the other girl. "Like I said, my mother will have the cops searching high and low for me by now." But as she stared out through the slits in the window at the thick pine forest that surrounded the white tent, which sat atop the even whiter snow, she realized a helicopter might not be able to see them from the air. And if Lourdes had been here three months and no one had found her, this place was far from ski or snowshoe or snowmobile trails.

"Considering how long you've been here without being found," Kate said, "and the fact someone's coming back later to take you away somewhere, I think we'd better figure out a way to get ourselves out of here."

It was a long day for Kate.

It rapidly became apparent that the lattice framework inside the tent and the wooden floor were there to stay. They had nothing to dig out with, even if the ground under the wooden floor hadn't been frozen solid.

Wyoming was still a savage land, with predators that included gray wolves, mountain lions and the odd irritable moose. Even if they managed to avoid getting eaten, they would very likely freeze to death without shoes and coats long before they found any signs of civilization.

Kate greedily drank the water Lourdes offered her, until the girl stopped her, telling her she would need to conserve, that the water had to last them a week. Kate looked at the packaged food and realized there was barely enough to keep them from starving. Moreover, there was only one large sleeping bag for the two girls to share.

Which they did. Huddling together under the thermal covering, Kate found out everything there was to know about Lourdes and her family—and about the behavior of the handsome man who'd apparently kidnapped them both in essentially the same way. Which was when she realized that both she and Lourdes had seen his face. Kate didn't allow herself to consider what that might mean.

"So he's never touched you . . . physically?" Kate asked.

Lourdes shook her head. "He has always been very polite."

It was almost more frightening that whoever had kidnapped them hadn't made any sexual overtures. He'd kept Lourdes fed, kept her warm, kept her healthy. What did he want with her? Where was he taking her tonight?

Kate had the awful feeling that something bad was going to happen to Lourdes. That she was here as a replacement for the other girl. And that, eventually, whatever bad thing that was going to happen to Lourdes would happen to her, too.

"Was there anyone here when you got here?" Kate asked.

Lourdes shook her head. "But there were girls here before me."

"How do you know?" Kate asked.

Lourdes rose from her perch at the foot of the sleeping bag, reached for Kate's hand, and led her across the width of the circular space. She pushed aside the trunk that held wood for the stove and pointed at the wooden floor. "See here? Two names have been carved here, where they wouldn't be seen."

Kate saw the names etched in the wood beneath the

trunk and felt a chill run down her spine. "Oh, no. No. No. No."

"What is it?" Lourdes asked, looking as frightened as Kate felt.

"One of those girls was found dead," Kate said. "And another one is missing."

"*Dios mio,*" Lourdes whispered.

Kate's mother had given her a subscription to the *Jackson Hole News and Guide* to keep her in touch with what was happening at home. Kate had seen the coverage of the two missing girls.

She felt a chill as she realized that one of the girls who'd carved her name on the wooden floor beneath the trunk had been found shot in the head and buried in a shallow grave. Now it seemed the other missing girl had been brought here. As had Lourdes. And herself.

Kate simply hadn't connected the disappearance of the other girls to her own situation. Until now.

"We have to get away from here," Kate said. "We have a better chance of surviving barefoot and—"

Lourdes started to cry. Kate slid her cuffed hands over Lourdes's head, so her arms surrounded the other girl, and pulled her close, fighting the knot in her own throat. "Crying isn't going to get us out of here," she said, staring at the beams of redeeming sunlight streaming through the slatted window. "We have to think!"

6

Clay searched the Saturday morning crowd at Bubba's, looking past wagon wheels and other Old West memorabilia for Libby, and found her at a table toward the back of the restaurant. "There she is," he said to Drew.

They were halfway to Libby's table when Clay nodded toward a woman dressed in a tan shirt and dark brown pants, the uniform worn by Teton County Sheriff's Office patrolmen, and said, "Isn't that Sarah Barndollar?"

"Looks like her," Drew said.

"Are those her kids with her?"

"I have no idea," Drew said. "Let's find out."

Before Clay could stop him, Drew headed straight for Sarah's booth. He stopped there and said, without even a good morning, "I didn't know you had kids."

Clay saw the blush rise on Sarah's cheeks. An admission of the omission.

"This is Nathan," Sarah said, indicating the older boy, "and Brooke and Ryan," she said, introducing the girl and the younger boy. "This is Mr. DeWitt."

Ryan waved and smiled, his mouth too full of pancakes to speak, while Brooke blurted, "You have really blue eyes."

Nate said in a snide voice, "Where did you meet him?"

"That's no way to speak to your mother," Drew said. "Especially when your mom was obviously working overtime when she towed me out of the Snake River last night."

Nate's look turned sullen, and Clay watched Sarah Barndollar's claws unsheathe like a mountain lion who sees her cubs threatened.

Clay was surprised Drew hadn't used humor to deflect the boy's comment, since his cousin was normally the picture of charm. As he watched Drew's glance slip from Sarah to her three kids and back again, Clay realized why his cousin was acting so out of character. He'd heard Drew swear—more than once—that he'd never bring kids into this world, because he wanted nothing to do with being a parent. Clay knew enough about Drew's miserable childhood to understand the rationale behind his cousin's choice.

Obviously, it had been an unwelcome shock for Drew to discover this morning that the sexy woman he'd entertained last night was also the mother of three very-much-a-part-of-her-life children.

"My son's behavior is a matter between him and me," Sarah said to Drew.

"I can speak for myself," Nate snapped belligerently. He turned to Drew and said, "Stay away from my mom."

"Nate!" Sarah said in a shocked voice.

Drew's wintry glance stayed focused on the older boy. "I think your mom can decide whom she wants to see without your help."

Sarah rose from her seat, setting her napkin carefully beside a half-eaten plate of scrambled eggs and bacon. Clay imagined her police training at work. Staying calm to handle a subject who was likely to be bigger and stronger than she was. Her voice, when she spoke, was quiet, but there was an edge to it. "Back off, Drew. Now. And Nathan, behave yourself!"

Clay was aware of powerful undercurrents between the two adults as they squared off and realized that Drew must be way more attracted to the woman than he'd let on last night. If his cousin had only been interested in a quick lay, the fact that Sarah Barndollar had three kids wouldn't have mattered.

Clay tensed as sexual sparks arced between Drew and Sarah. It was plain that Drew wanted Sarah, and from Sarah's flushed face, it was clear she wanted him, too. Clay didn't think it would take much provocation for Drew to act on his desire, children or no children.

In an effort to avoid getting caught in the middle of a lover's quarrel that was bound, with the dearth of exciting news in Jackson, to end up on the front page of the local newspaper, Clay pitched his voice low and firm and said, "Come on, Drew. We came here to have breakfast. And to see what we can do to help find Kate."

It was the mention of Kate that finally turned Drew away from Sarah. He acknowledged what Clay had said with a sharp nod, then turned back to Sarah and said, "We'll finish this later."

Without giving her a chance to reply, he turned his back on her and headed toward the table where Libby was sitting.

Ever the politician, Clay stayed a moment longer. He diverted Sarah's attention from Drew's retreating back by asking, "Have you gotten any response overnight from posting Kate's information with the NCIC?"

Sarah quickly recovered and said, "There's been nothing. I'm sorry."

"What happens now?" Clay asked. "Is there anything else we can do?"

"I'd suggest that Libby contact her daughter's friends at the school she was attending back East," Sarah said. "Maybe one of them will know something about Kate's whereabouts. I'm picking up a shift for a friend, so I can follow up on whatever leads there are here in town."

"Thanks," Clay said. "We'll be in touch if we find out anything."

Sarah lifted an eyebrow. "You're going to stay in town and help Libby with the search for her daughter?"

"Mom, I want more pancakes," Ryan interrupted.

"In a minute, Ryan," Sarah said. She turned back to Clay and asked, "What's your relationship to Libby?"

"We're just old friends," Clay said with a casual smile. It was time he got out of here, before the detective started asking questions that required lies.

"I'd better get going," Clay said.

As he walked toward Libby, Clay admitted he was

still physically attracted to her. Even knowing how she'd betrayed him, he wanted her.

There had been only two women in his life since he'd fallen in love with Elsbeth Grayhawk at twenty-seven—three, if he counted his late wife's sister, who'd been his escort whenever he'd needed one over the past year.

Clay had regretted getting engaged so quickly after the debacle with Libby. His terrible grief over Cindy Ridgeway's untimely death a week before their wedding had been more a result of guilt and remorse than anything else. He'd felt relieved that he wouldn't have to go through with the wedding, about which he'd been having second thoughts. He'd discovered too late that he didn't love the woman he'd asked to be his wife.

He'd been determined not to make that mistake again. But it seemed no woman could match up to the image of Libby that was imprinted on his heart and soul. Clay might never have married, except a politician needed a wife.

And then he'd met Giselle Montrose.

Clay had never met a person with a kinder soul or a more cheerful outlook on life. He didn't know what he'd done to earn Giselle's love, but there was no doubt she was devoted to him. It was hard not to love her back. Except for the fact his wife had been unable to conceive and they'd had no children, he'd been content.

But in the dark, when he should have been sated and replete, he lay there remembering. Angry and resentful that memories of a woman who'd shoved him

out of her life—and taken his only child with her—
should still hold him in such thrall.

But he was unattached now. And Libby was free.
And they were going to be spending time together until
they found Kate. She seemed to want him. He definitely wanted her.

The question was whether he could enjoy Libby
physically without allowing himself to fall back into the
emotional trap that had left him wounded so many
years ago. It might be worth the risk to try. Maybe he
would find that the reality no longer lived up to his
memories, and he could free himself from the chains
that had bound him to the past.

As he approached the table, where Drew had already seated himself across from Libby, Clay said, "Detective Barndollar says there's no new word on Kate."

"I spoke with Sarah earlier myself," Libby admitted.
"I've been sitting here making a mental list of who else
Kate might know here in town."

Clay seated himself at the end of the table next to
Libby and said, "Sarah suggested we also talk to
whomever Kate might have confided in at school."

"Kate only had two close friends that I know about,"
Libby said. "I called them last night. They promised to
ask around and get back to me."

"I can have a private investigator follow up with
them and take a look in her dorm room for anything
that might give us a hint about what's happened to her,"
Clay said.

Their gazes met, and Clay watched as Libby con-
quered the terror that momentarily appeared in her

eyes. She obviously wanted to believe that Kate would reappear healthy and happy and sorry to have troubled her parents for disappearing without a word. She was also apparently very much aware of the other two girls who'd gone missing over the past fifteen months and never been found, and the teenage girl who'd run away from her home in Nevada and been found with a bullet hole in the back of her skull.

The ring of Libby's cell phone startled all of them. Libby grappled for the phone in her purse and answered with a breathless, "Kate?"

Clay watched as Libby pressed her lips flat, then shook her head to let him know it wasn't Kate and said, "Thank you for calling, Patricia. What did you find out?"

Libby frowned. "An e-mail? Who sent it? That's odd. Would you forward it to me?"

Clay listened as Libby gave her e-mail address.

"Thank you so much, Patricia. Please call if you hear anything or if anyone thinks of anywhere else we might look for her," Libby said.

She clicked off her cell phone and said, "I asked Libby's roommate to check Kate's e-mail, if she could. She says Kate received an e-mail late Thursday night, telling her to fly to Jackson on Friday. That she was to tell no one she was leaving school, but to call her mother en route and ask her to meet her when she arrived in Jackson."

"We need to take a close look at that e-mail," Clay said.

Drew shoved his chair back noisily and said, "I'll go

tell Sarah what you've found out. I presume you'll forward that e-mail to the sheriff's office as soon as you receive it?"

"Of course," Libby said, as Drew turned and headed back across the restaurant toward Sarah Barndollar's table.

Clay clasped Libby's hand when she reached out to him, her eyes stark, her chin quivering.

"It sounds like someone planned to take her all along," she said in a strained voice. "But why not kidnap her from school? Why make her come all the way home first?"

"I don't know," Clay said. "Did Kate's roommate tell you who sent that e-mail to her?"

"Patricia didn't recognize the return address. It seems to have arrived out of the e-mail ether."

"We'll see about that." Clay pulled his cell phone from his belt and dialed a Washington, D.C., number. "Hello, Morgan. No, she's still missing. I need a favor." Clay explained what he wanted and nodded his approval as Morgan DeWitt said he'd get right on it.

"Drew's stepbrother is as good with a computer as it's possible to get," Clay reassured Libby. "If that e-mail can be traced, he'll be able to do it—or know someone else who can."

During the sixteen years they'd worked together as a team, forty-year-old Morgan DeWitt had become closer to Clay than Clay's twin brother Owen, who was a Texas Ranger. Morgan knew all—or almost all—of Clay's secrets.

Clay had told Morgan about Kate, but he'd never

confided the depth of his love for Kate's mother. Clay had more than once turned to Morgan and gotten good advice. He intended to take his friend with him all the way to the White House.

"Do you want to stay and eat?" Clay asked.

Libby shook her head. "I can make us something at my house. Let's go."

Clay was about to rise, when he felt a strong hand grip his shoulder and hold him in place. He turned to shake hands with the man who owned most of the oil in West Texas. "Hello, Niles. What are you doing here in town?"

"I think the better question is what are you doing here, Clay? And who is this lovely lady?"

Clay avoided the oilman's first question and said, "Libby, this is Niles Taylor. He's an oilman from Midland, Texas. Niles, this is Elsbeth Grayhawk."

"Grayhawk?" Niles repeated. "You wouldn't, by any chance, be related to King Grayhawk, would you?"

"He's my father," Libby replied.

"Hell's bells! I had dinner with your father last Sunday at that ranch of his outside of town, Kingdom Come. Near talked my ear off about all his oil wells in Wyoming and Texas. Never said a word about having such a beautiful daughter."

Clay felt a jolt of possessiveness when he saw the assessing look Niles gave Libby. Niles was dressed in an expensive Western-cut suit and cowboy boots. He was tall and barrel-chested, with a head of wavy, salt-and-pepper hair and an engaging smile that stretched from ear to ear. The oilman was married, but his wife stayed home in Midland, and Clay had often seen Niles at parties with a pretty young woman on his arm.

"This little filly yours?" Niles said with a nudge and a wink at Clay.

"I don't belong to anyone," Libby said in a cold voice.

"No offense meant," Niles said with a grin. He turned to Clay and said, "I'm having a party tonight at a friend's house on Bear Island. As long as you're in town, why don't you come? In fact, why don't both of you come?"

"I have other plans," Libby said.

"I'm afraid—" Clay began.

Before he could finish his refusal, Niles said, "Don't say no. There are at least three congressmen from Texas and a passel of contributors to the party who can be a real help to you when you make your bid for governor."

Clay didn't pretend he had no aspirations in that direction. But he wasn't in the mood to shake hands and smile and get patted on the back by political sycophants. Not while his daughter was missing under mysterious—and threatening— circumstances.

"I don't think—"

"Don't think," Niles interrupted. "Just come. You won't be sorry you did. In fact, if you come, I promise to make a substantial contribution to your campaign myself."

"I'll think about it," Clay said to Niles. "I can't promise anything."

"I'll be looking for you." Niles tipped his hat to Libby and said, "You too, little lady, if your plans change."

* * *

Sarah felt totally rattled by Drew's appearance at Bubba's this morning. She'd known he was a rich playboy. She should have expected the shock and displeasure she'd seen on his face when he realized she was the mother of three kids. But she couldn't help feeling a little sad and disappointed.

In light of his attitude, she'd been stunned and appalled by the heat that had nevertheless leaped between them. She was actually sweating beneath her bulletproof vest!

Sarah hadn't mistaken Drew's last words as anything less than what they were—a warning that he would be back to claim her, at a time and place where her children would not be there to act as a buffer.

She forced herself to take a bite of pancake and chew.

"That guy's a total jerk," Nate said under his breath, his narrowed eyes focused on Drew across the room.

"I think he's cute," Brooke said. "I don't think I've ever seen eyes that blue."

Sarah wanted to correct her children, but they were both right. Drew had overstepped his bounds. And his blue eyes amazed her every time she saw them.

She turned to her stepson and said, "I want you to keep an eye on Ryan today while you're on the slopes."

"Aw, Mom," Nate said. "If I have to stay with Ryan, I can't snowboard the black diamond runs. Why can't Brooke—"

"You heard me, Nate. Brooke watched him last Saturday." She turned to Brooke and said, "I don't want you driving the car."

From the color that appeared on Brooke's face, her daughter had already been negotiating with Nate, who'd had his driver's license for nine months, to make use of her driver's permit. "Not with Ryan in the car," she amended.

"Can we go now, Mom?" Brooke asked.

"If you're all done eating," she said.

Nate and Brooke jumped up and pulled on their ski jackets, then each took one of Ryan's arms and shoved him into his jacket.

"Have fun!" Sarah said as the two older children hustled the younger one out the door. "And be careful," she said under her breath.

She knew Brooke would spend most of the day with her girlfriends, sitting on the deck outside one of the ski lodges drinking Coke and talking about boys. Nate wouldn't come off the slopes until darkness—or Ryan's nagging that he wanted to go home—forced him off.

She was lucky the sheriff's office provided her a vehicle, so the kids could make use of her pickup. So far, Nate had proved to be a responsible driver, but she worried about Brooke driving, since she never seemed to focus her attention on anything for very long.

The children hadn't been gone more than a minute before Sarah caught sight of Drew heading back in her direction. She wasn't about to let him catch her in Bubba's, where any scene he created would become fodder for gossip. She grabbed her jacket from the back of the chair and headed for the door.

She made it outside before Drew caught up to her, but he caught her arm before she could make it to her Tahoe.

"Wait up, Sarah."

Sarah stopped abruptly and turned and stared at Drew's grip on her arm, then focused her gaze on his. "Get your hands off me."

Drew let her go, but he stood between her and her SUV, an immovable object. "You look different in uniform," he said.

"It's the Glock," Sarah replied.

Drew shook his head. "Nope. It's the sharp creases and the badge and all that gear on your belt. You look like a real cop."

Sarah bristled. "I *am* a real cop."

Drew grinned. "And just as feisty in uniform as out."

Sarah glared at him. "If you're finished gawking, I've got work to do."

"We need to talk," he said.

"It'll have to wait. I'm on duty."

"I've got news about Kate."

"Why didn't you say so?" Sarah said, not hiding her irritation. "What is it?"

"Let's go somewhere we can talk in private."

Sarah shook her head. "If you have information about Kate, let's hear it. Otherwise, we have nothing to discuss."

"You're wrong about that."

Sarah's fisted hands landed on her hips. "What is it you want from me, Drew?"

"I want to finish what we started last night."

Sarah felt a flush rise on her throat. "Last night was a mistake. You caught me at a . . . vulnerable moment. I'm a married woman."

"Whose husband hasn't been seen for more than a year."

"That doesn't make me any less married," Sarah said stubbornly. She wondered where he'd found out about Tom's disappearance. "Who have you been talking to?"

"If your husband was coming back, he would have returned by now," Drew said, avoiding her question.

The truth was hard to hear. Sarah gritted her teeth and said, "What is it you have to tell me about Kate Grayhawk?"

Drew opened the door to the Tahoe for Sarah and said, "It's cold out here. Get inside and I'll tell you."

Sarah hesitated, then stepped inside the SUV. She was tempted to drive away and leave Drew standing there, but she still hadn't learned what information he had about the missing girl. When Drew got inside, she said, "I'm listening."

"I could use a ride home."

"I'm not a taxi service. Say what you have to say and get out."

Drew shrugged. "Fine. Kate's roommate at school found an e-mail instructing Kate to come here."

Sarah frowned. "Who sent it?"

"We don't know. Libby's going to forward it to you as soon as she gets it."

"That e-mail makes Kate's disappearance sound a lot more sinister. Could her father have sent it?" Sarah asked, thinking of all the custody battles that had been resolved by one parent stealing the children and running.

"It didn't come from her father," Drew said.

"How do you know that?" Her eyes narrowed as she asked, "Do you know who Kate's father is?"

Drew looked wary. "No, I don't."

"You're lying."

"I can't tell you," he amended.

"Whoever it is needs to be warned about what's going on here," Sarah said.

"He knows."

"It's Clay Blackthorne," Sarah guessed.

"If you think so, why don't you ask him?"

Sarah wasn't ready to face the consequences of asking a prestigious political figure like Clay Blackthorne whether he had a secret child. With the instructions about leaving school and coming home to Jackson Hole that Kate Grayhawk had received, it might be important to know whether Clay Blackthorne was Kate's father. And whether he had any enemies who might be using his daughter to get to him.

"What are you going to do now?" Drew asked.

"I'm going back to the Mangy Moose to ask more questions," Sarah replied. "And I want to make sure that someone who knows a lot more about computers than I do takes a look at that e-mail Kate received telling her to head home."

Drew turned in his seat to face her and said, "I want to see you again."

"No."

"That sounds pretty unequivocal," Drew said with a wry smile.

"I made a mistake last night," Sarah said. "I used bad judgment and put us both in a situation that—"

Drew reached for her hand and Sarah felt a jolt of electricity all the way up her arm. She jerked free and stared at him, shocked by her response.

"You're not alone," Drew said. "I felt it, too. I don't pretend to understand why we make the kind of sparks we do, but it's extraordinary enough in my experience for me to want to pursue this."

"This?" Sarah said. "What is *this* but plain old ordinary *sex*?"

"I don't think sex between us would be the least bit ordinary," Drew countered. "I think it would be spectacular."

"It would still just be sex," Sarah said. "You've made it plain it could never be more than that."

"I have?"

"I saw your face this morning when you realized I have three children," Sarah said. "And they aren't going anywhere."

Drew rubbed the back of his neck. "Yeah. The kids are a problem."

Sarah was stung by his brutal honesty. "If they're a problem, what are you still doing here?"

He looked at her, his blue eyes fierce, and said, "I want you."

"Well, you can't have me," Sarah shot back. "Not without the baggage that comes along with me."

"Those kids are—"

"Don't you dare say anything bad about my kids," Sarah warned.

He smiled suddenly, a self-deprecating curve of his mouth that Sarah knew was intended to be charming. She fought against being charmed as he said, "I admit they're a complication."

"I wouldn't want to complicate your life," Sarah retorted. "Better to end *this* before it gets started."

"I don't want to do that," Drew persisted, his blue eyes intent on hers, making her stomach do little flips.

"You don't have any choice," Sarah said, determined to fight the attraction she felt. "Now get out of my car. Stay away from me. Otherwise, I'll—"

"Don't make threats you can't enforce," Drew said. The words were threatening, but his smile cajoled her to let him into her life.

Distressed by her urge to throw caution to the winds, Sarah glared at him. "You've forgotten whom you're talking to."

"No, I haven't," Drew said.

Before Sarah realized what he intended, Drew's hand caught her by the nape and his mouth covered hers, his tongue thrusting between her startled lips. The surge of passion she felt was powerful—and undeniable. Rational thought was impossible. All she could do was feel.

And she felt too terrifyingly much.

She put her gloved hands on Drew's shoulders to shove him away, but they ended up in his hair, where she grasped hold and hung on tight, as he took her deeper, to places she'd never been.

A moment later he was back on his side of the car, his eyes heavy-lidded.

She put a trembling hand to her lips and shook her head in denial.

"Don't try to say you didn't feel anything. I won't believe you," Drew said in a voice harsh with unrequited desire. "Sooner or later we're going to finish what we started last night. I'm not going away, Sarah. Make up your mind to that."

A moment later he was gone, and Sarah was left alone with her quivering, sexually unsated body and her tumbling, jumbled thoughts.

7

After making sure that the threatening e-mail that had sent Kate running home was forwarded to Morgan De-Witt in Washington and to the Teton County Sheriff's Office, Libby spent a long and frustrating day contacting everyone Kate had known since the first grade, asking questions.

What became painfully obvious after a few visits, was that Kate only had one or two close friends, the ones she'd brought home to meet Libby and had kept in touch with sporadically since she'd gone to boarding school in Virginia. Kate was a loner. Or, to be more honest, an outcast.

Everyone Libby had spoken to agreed that Kate was smart—she got straight As. And that she was a superb athlete—she'd been a cross-country runner in junior high and also competed in shorter, faster dashes with amazing success. And that she was pretty—a lot of boys said they'd wanted to ask her out.

But more than one person who might have be-friended Kate said that they were intimidated by the signals she sent out that said, *Come closer at your peril.*

Libby had believed her daughter when she'd said

she wanted to go to high school back East so she'd be able to visit her father more often in Washington, D.C. But once Clay's wife got sick, which was almost as soon as Kate began attending boarding school, visits with him had been difficult to manage. Nevertheless, Kate had stayed in school far from Jackson.

Now Libby wondered whether Kate hadn't wanted to be away from Jackson Hole to escape the small-town gossip that she'd so obviously silenced with her unapproachable demeanor. What troubled Libby most was the thought that she hadn't detected her daughter's deception. The last overt signs of trouble she'd seen had been the bruises and bloody scrapes Kate had brought home when she was six years old.

Libby's heart bled for her daughter.

Clay had gone with Libby when she questioned Kate's junior high classmates, and Libby had watched his eyes become increasingly unfriendly as the day wore on and he realized the isolation in which Kate had spent her life.

"Why didn't you tell me how alone she was?" he demanded, when they pulled up at Libby's cabin after the last of the visits.

"I didn't realize the truth," Libby said. "She was always busy with after-school activities. And she participated in school events on the weekends. Her life seemed a lot like mine when I was growing up. I never had many friends over, either, because I was busy taking care of my younger brothers and sisters. It never occurred to me that Kate was—"

"Ostracized," Clay said angrily.

"She never complained," Libby said. "She never said a word."

"She wouldn't," Clay said. "She never cried when she skinned her knee, not even when she was little. The one time I saw her get bucked off a horse, she got right back on. That girl doesn't know the meaning of quit. She's got guts."

"And why not?" Libby said. "She comes from stubborn, mule-headed stock on both sides."

Clay's lips curved in a rueful smile. "Too true."

Libby cut the engine and turned to Clay, her throat suddenly choked with fear. "Are courage and persistence going to be enough to get Kate out of whatever predicament she's in?"

She caught the worried look in Clay's eyes before he focused his gaze on the snowcapped Tetons in the distance. "What I don't understand is why Kate was targeted. If she was kidnapped for ransom, why haven't you gotten a note asking for money? No one knows I'm her father, so she can't have been taken to get to me."

Libby shivered. If Kate hadn't been kidnapped for ransom, she didn't want to think what her daughter's kidnapper might have wanted with her. "It's cold. I'm going inside. Do you want to come in and wait with me."

"That's not a good idea," he said.

"Why not?"

"Because we're liable to turn to one another for comfort. And end up doing something both of us will regret."

"Contrary to what you might believe," Libby said, "I haven't been living without sex."

Clay snorted. "I have."

Libby laughed in surprise, then sobered as she realized why Clay might have been celibate for the past couple of years. "I'm sorry about Giselle," she said. "She seemed like a lovely woman."

"She was."

"Please come inside," Libby said. "I promise to resist you," she added with a smile. "And I could use the company."

"All right," he said. "For a little while."

The first thing Libby did was check with the Teton County Sheriff's Office to see if anyone had reported any news about Kate or if they'd had any luck tracing Kate's e-mail. She met Clay's somber gaze and shook her head, then hung up the phone. She hurried into her office to check her e-mail, but there was nothing new.

She pulled up the e-mail that had sent Kate home, hoping she'd find something she hadn't seen before. When it appeared on the screen, Clay leaned over her shoulder to read it along with her.

Kate,

Your family is at risk unless you obey what you read here.

Take the first flight you can get and go home. Call your mother and tell her you're coming and need to talk with her about something important, but don't mention this e-mail to her or anyone else.

Everything will be explained when you arrive.

This is not a joke or a hoax. The consequences for ignoring this e-mail will be serious and immediate.

"She must have been terrified when she read this," Libby said. "No wonder she sounded so desperate to talk to me. And I wasn't even available when she called."

"Neither was I," Clay said. "Only Morgan and my personal secretary, Helen Witlock, know that Kate is my daughter. Helen took Friday off for a visit to the dentist. I told the temp who replaced her that I didn't want to be disturbed. I never thought to make an exception for Kate Grayhawk."

Clay's comforting hand suddenly tightened on Libby's shoulder. "Who would know we'd both likely be inaccessible by phone on Friday?"

Libby looked up into his frowning face. "You think someone who knows us—both you and me—sent that e-mail?"

"I don't have a temp that often. Any other day, Kate's call would have been put through to me."

"Kate called you? Even though she was told not to?"

"You know Kate. I'd bet money she tried to reach me. There was no message that she called, but she might have figured it wasn't safe to leave a written record that she'd contacted me—just in case."

Libby knew very well how little Kate liked following directions. "But if she was willing to call you, why not go all the way and call the police."

Clay met her gaze and said, "She couldn't be sure whoever sent that e-mail wouldn't have harmed us."

"Us?"

Clay reached across her shoulder and pointed to the screen. "This e-mail specifically says *family*. Why use that term if they only meant you?"

"Who else knows you're Kate's father?"

"Only people I'd trust with my life," Clay said.

"And with Kate's life?"

"Someone else must have found out," Clay said grimly.

Libby felt a shiver run down her spine. The Grayhawks had many enemies. The Blackthornes had even more.

"I can't believe this is happening," Libby said, blinking back tears. "It could be anyone. Where is she, Clay? What's happened to our baby?"

They were questions without an answer that either one wanted to voice aloud. When Clay slid a comforting hand under the hair at her nape, Libby turned and lurched into his embrace. He held her close and rocked her in his arms, his body a bulwark against all the terrifying thoughts that kept running through her mind. Libby clutched at him, pressing her face against his oxford cloth shirt, stifling the moan of despair that sought voice.

His voice rumbled against her ear as he admitted, "I keep thinking of all the times Kate phoned me over the past three years, wanting to see me, and I told her I couldn't get away. Giselle was sick and she needed me, but her sister could have stayed with her for a couple of hours.

"After Giselle died . . . I'm not sure why I didn't make more time for Kate."

"You were grieving," Libby said.

She felt Clay's hands on either side of her head, turning her face up to his. She looked at him through tear-glazed eyes, seeing her own anguish reflected back at her.

"I was—"

The ringing phone interrupted him.

Libby pulled free and grabbed for the phone. "Yes? What?" After a pause she said, "We'll be right there!"

Libby hung up the phone and ran into her bedroom, calling over her shoulder to Clay, "An out-of-bounds skier found Kate's backpack and called the authorities."

Clay was right behind her as he asked, "What are you doing?"

"I'm getting dressed to go skiing."

Clay caught her arm. "Hold on. You're going skiing?"

Libby kept her gaze riveted on the cross-country ski gear in her closet as she said, "The place where they found Kate's backpack isn't far from where they found that missing girl earlier this year."

Libby didn't say "that *dead* missing girl." She was sure Clay would remember how the girl had been found. And saying it was too frightening.

"Have you considered using a snowmobile to get where you want to go?" Clay asked.

Libby freed herself and reached for her ski pants. "Too risky. The avalanche control guys don't always get to all of the back-country ski areas to explode shells and start mini-avalanches and—"

"Where are we talking about, exactly?" Clay asked.

"Teton Park—25 Short."

Clay swore under his breath. "You know I don't ski there anymore. And you know why."

Libby grabbed her wool cap and scarf from the top of the closet and turned to face Clay. "I know," she said. "I'm not asking you to come with me."

"Dammit, Libby! You shouldn't be skiing there, either. That mountain is always an avalanche waiting to happen, and with all the snow we've had lately—"

"I said you don't have to come with me."

Clay glowered at her. "Have you checked the avalanche report? Do you have the equipment you need to dig out—an avalanche shovel, probe poles, a transceiver?"

"I have everything in my backpack in the garage. I'll call for the avalanche report on the way, but it's obviously safe, if someone else has already been up there skiing today."

"Don't assume anything," Clay said. "That's how Drew ended up in a ravine on 25 Short, buried under five feet of snow. I was damned lucky to dig him out before he suffocated."

"I'm going," Libby said stubbornly. "I need to see for myself where Kate's backpack was found."

"Sonofabitch," Clay muttered. "Libby, you shouldn't be taking risks—"

"Nothing you say is going to stop me, Clay. You don't have to—"

"I'm not about to lose you, too!"

Clay seemed as surprised by what he'd said as Libby

was. There was an awkward pause, while Libby waited for Clay to explain himself. Instead, he said, "Let's go. I'll drive."

They made a stop at the ranch house in Forgotten Valley so Clay could change into ski clothes and pick up his cross-country ski gear, then headed north from Jackson, turning left twelve miles out of town at Moose onto the Teton Park Road.

"The wind's picking up," Clay said. "You know what that means."

Libby knew that strong winds after a heavy snow increased the chance of an avalanche. She could see Clay's jaw was clenched. She didn't remind him again that he didn't have to come along.

Libby had an annual pass on her windshield that got them into Glacier National Park without stopping to pay a fee. She drove a few miles farther to the Bradley-Taggert Lakes parking area, which was as far as the road was plowed in winter. Three cars were parked in the lot, including the park ranger's and Teton County Sheriff's vehicles.

"Do you know which deputy is up there?" Clay asked.

"The dispatcher said she sent Sarah up there to meet the park ranger who answered the original call and retrieve Kate's backpack," Libby said.

"You ready?" Clay asked, as he stepped into his skis.

"Yeah," Libby said.

They skied west across the flats in the direction of the mountains until they reached a hillside, an old glacial moraine, then angled south into the Beaver Creek drainage. The sun was hot on Libby's shoulders, the air brisk enough to make her breath fog, as they followed the hillside above the creek until it gradually turned back toward the west. After a mile and a half they crossed Beaver Creek and headed into an open meadow.

As they crossed the meadow, which led up the mountain, Libby glanced at Clay, whose face looked grim. She wondered what he was thinking. She didn't ask, because she didn't want to hear her own fears confirmed. When they reached the beginning of the thick timber, he stopped abruptly.

"Why are we stopping?" Libby asked.

"You realize the detective is probably already on her way back down the mountain with Kate's backpack," he said. "It's crazy for us to be skiing 25 Short in these conditions."

Libby looked around her. The sky was clear, as blue as she'd ever seen it. A breeze played at her hair, but it was rare when the wind didn't blow in Wyoming. Clay was right, of course. Disaster could be a short step away. The snow beneath the bends on the mountain could fracture and take them down the mountain with it. But it could just as easily remain right where it was.

"You can go back if you want." She squared her shoulders and focused her gaze on the mountain above them. "My baby might be up there somewhere. If she is, I intend to find her."

Clay was having trouble catching his breath, he was so scared. The danger of avalanche on 25 Short—which had gotten its name because the ridgeline above the slopes was 25 feet short of 10,000 feet—was real. But he knew his fear was way out of proportion to where they were on the mountain. The real danger occurred farther up, in the ravines south and north of a series of benches in the open slopes between the thick timber.

Before the avalanche that had tumbled both him and Drew down one of the ravines on 25 Short nearly a hundred feet, and then buried Drew alive, he'd loved out-of-bounds skiing and been as much a daredevil as anyone on the slopes. After the incident, he'd gotten right back on skis and done some of the riskier runs down the Tetons at the Jackson Hole Mountain Resort.

But something had happened to him when he left the groomed ski trails for the first time after Drew had been buried alive and headed into the back country by himself. He'd never told anyone, not even Drew, that he'd gotten so scared that his body had become paralyzed. He'd stood frozen on the trail, unable to go forward or backward, certain that the snow around him was moving, sliding, and that any moment he would be buried and suffocate as Drew almost had.

He'd stood there trembling, his knees threatening to buckle. He'd struggled to draw breath, and gasped because there didn't seem to be any air. He could remember the world spinning and then everything going black.

When he'd awakened and realized where he was, he'd been grateful there wasn't anyone around to witness his humiliation. Then he'd looked up at the glistening white mountain above him and distinctly heard the sound of snow fracturing and felt the earth trembling beneath him. His heart had started to pound. And he'd gasped for air that, once again, wasn't there.

When he'd woken up the second time—and the snow was still right there on the mountain where it had been the first time—he'd realized that, once again, he'd fantasized the danger. He'd given himself a stern lecture about how ridiculous his fears were. He wasn't even in a high-risk avalanche zone. But it had taken him a long time to convince himself that moving an inch in any direction was not going to start an avalanche of snow that would bury him.

He'd managed, somehow, to get back onto his feet. He'd turned himself around and skied, very slowly and carefully, back down the mountain.

Clay hadn't told anyone about the incident, not even Drew, who had more reason than he did to be frightened of skiing out-of-bounds. Nor had he repeated the experience. He'd simply found reasons why he couldn't go skiing whenever Drew or Kate headed out-of-bounds.

Right now, his legs were still responding when he demanded they move forward another step. But his breathing had become labored, and his heart felt like it might burst, it was beating so hard with terror.

Above them lay thick timber, fir and pine and aspen, and beyond that the series of benches and open slopes through which they would have to climb, where the danger of avalanche was real. He wasn't sure how long he could keep his feeling of panic under control. In another moment, he was going to have to tell Libby the truth.

"Someone's coming," Libby said.

Clay looked up and saw Sarah Barndollar skiing toward them. "It's the detective."

Clay caught Libby's arm to keep her from skiing off to meet Sarah halfway. "No sense skiing up to meet her when you're just going to have to turn around and ski back down."

A few minutes later, Detective Barndollar reached them.

"You didn't have to come out here," she said.

"Yes, I did," Libby replied. "Do you have Kate's backpack?"

Sarah nodded. "I had no choice but to retrieve it. I marked the spot where it was found, but a small avalanche uncovered it, and I was afraid another avalanche was going to bury it before I could get anyone else up there. The park ranger's taking one last look around."

Clay exchanged a glance with Libby, then asked, "Could you tell if Kate was actually up there?"

Sarah shook her head. "No other gear was uncovered. I had the dispatcher contact Teton County Search and Rescue to canvass the area, but conditions at the top of the mountain are hairy."

"But if she's up there—" Libby began.

Sarah fixed her gaze on Libby and said, "It's too dangerous to let civilians up there right now. I'm sorry."

"Sorry won't cut it," Clay said. "If there's any chance my daughter—"

The words were out of Clay's mouth before he could stop them. He glanced at the detective and noticed she didn't seem particularly surprised by his revelation.

"You guessed," he said.

"I considered it a possibility," she admitted.

"I'd appreciate it if you'd keep that information to yourself," Clay said.

"I will as long as I can." Sarah looked from Clay to Libby and back again as she said, "I don't know if your daughter was up there skiing and got caught in an avalanche, or whether someone buried her backpack up there to hide it and an avalanche uncovered it. The last time your daughter was seen, it was late in the day. It seems unlikely she would have come here to snowboard after that. But it's not impossible she was here—"

"And got caught in an avalanche," Clay finished for her.

The detective nodded. "I've already contacted Teton County Search and Rescue, but based on the conditions when I was up there, I can tell you they aren't going to be able to look for her until that crest of snow breaks loose."

Clay realized the problem. "And that might bury her even deeper."

Sarah nodded.

Clay realized Detective Barndollar hadn't pointed out the obvious. If Kate had been buried for the entire time she'd been missing, it was unlikely she was still alive. Most avalanche victims suffocated within a few minutes. He grasped Libby's hand like a lifeline, staring up at the mountain that had almost taken Drew's life, wondering if it had claimed his daughter.

"I'm going up there," Libby said, yanking her hand free.

Clay grabbed for her arm and missed, but Detective Barndollar was there to block Libby's way.

"I can't let you do that," Sarah said.

"You can't stop me!" Libby said.

"I can and I will," she replied in a calm voice.

"Libby, you can't—" Clay began.

Libby whirled on him and said, "You don't have to come!"

"You heard what the detective said," he shot back. "The whole mountain's about to come down. What good will it do Kate if you end up suffocating under a ton of snow?"

"Mr. Blackthorne is right," Sarah said.

Clay watched Libby's shoulders slump and realized she'd given in to reason. He turned to the detective and said, "Is there anything in Kate's backpack that indicates where she might have gone or where she might be now?"

"I haven't had a chance to look inside yet," she said. "I suppose it's safe enough here if you want to check it out." She slipped the backpack off her back and handed it to Clay.

Clay had seen too many cop shows not to wonder why she wasn't "preserving the evidence"—the assumption being that there might be some sort of hair or fiber adhering to the backpack, or fingerprints on some item inside the backpack, that could be used to prosecute whoever might have abducted Kate.

But it was obvious why Sarah had picked up the backpack and run with it, and even more obvious why it made sense to look as soon as possible to see if there was some clue inside the backpack that might lead them to Kate's whereabouts.

Clay unzipped the backpack and held it open wide enough for the three of them to look inside. The first thing he saw was Kate's gloves and hat. Which was when he realized she hadn't been snowboarding or skiing or anything else on that mountain. Otherwise, she would have been wearing them.

"Oh, no," Libby whispered.

Clay carefully pulled the tasseled wool cap and fleece gloves from the pack and handed them to Libby to hold. She pressed them against her face, and he heard her inhale. He wondered if she could smell Kate on the clothing, realized she probably could, and envied her that closeness to their daughter.

He tipped the backpack, saw a spiral notebook, a pen and a mechanical pencil and a folded up piece of paper. He reached in for the paper and pulled it out. He handed the backpack to the detective to hold as he opened the paper and read it.

"It's a printout of the e-mail instructing Kate to come home," he said. "She's written her flight information on the bottom of it."

"We're checking with the server to see who has this e-mail account," the detective said. "But if whoever sent this wanted to remain anonymous and hid his tracks, it'll take time to hunt him down."

"And every minute counts now," Clay said, refolding the paper.

Sarah Barndollar nodded. "The first twenty-four hours a child is missing are crucial."

And they were almost gone, Clay realized. He pulled the spiral notebook from the backpack and opened it, expecting to find notes from one of Kate's classes.

"It's a journal," he blurted.

"Let me see!" Libby said, leaning over his shoulder.

He flipped through it, hoping that something would leap out at him.

"You're going too fast," Libby protested.

Each entry was marked with the date and time. He turned to the end of the book to see what Kate's last entry had been. He could hear Libby reading it aloud as he read it more quickly in his head.

I wish Dad would have taken my call.
I don't know why I thought he would.
He hasn't been there for me in the past.
Why should I expect him to be there when
I need him now?

Clay felt his stomach clench as he imagined Kate trying to reach him—and failing.

"Anything jump out at you?" the detective said.

"No," Clay said.

"We can examine everything more closely once we get off this mountain," she said. "Maybe there's something in your daughter's journal that will give us a clue to what's going on here."

"What do you think is going on?" Clay asked, meeting the detective's eyes.

"I don't know," Sarah said. "But I'm every bit as determined as you are to find out."

They heard a deep rumble and felt the ground shaking beneath them.

"Avalanche!" Clay said, staring at the mountain in the distance. He could see the powdery snow rise above the tree line in the distance. His heart was pounding and he felt his lungs constrict. He waited to take a breath of air, afraid there wouldn't be any. At last he gasped, and his lungs filled.

Both Libby and the detective were focused in the direction of the slide, and he managed to get himself under control before they turned around.

"Please, God," Libby murmured. "Don't let her be on that mountain. Don't let her be buried under all that snow."

Clay put a supporting arm around Libby's shoulder and said, "She isn't there, Libby."

Libby pulled away and said, "How do you know that? You can't know that!"

"Use logic," he said. "We know she wasn't snowboarding or skiing there. Otherwise, she'd have been wearing her hat and gloves. Agreed?"

Libby nodded reluctantly.

"I think the backpack was put there to lead us away from where she really is," Clay said, as he pushed off and began skiing back toward the parking lot.

"Why do you say that?" Sarah asked, following behind him.

"Because this mountain is where the other girl was found," Clay said. "The person who took Kate—"

"We don't know she was taken by someone," Libby interrupted.

"If Kate weren't being forcibly detained, she'd be home," Clay said implacably.

"Unless she ran away," Detective Barndollar said.

"Runaways don't usually run *toward* home," Clay pointed out. "That note Kate received at school makes me believe someone wanted her here so she could be abducted. Whoever took Kate wants us to believe her disappearance is related to what happened to that other girl, so they planted that backpack near where the other girl was found. What if there's some other force at work here?"

"Why would you think something like that?" Libby asked.

Clay feared that someone had found out Kate was his daughter and intended to use that fact to blackmail him, knowing his eventual aspirations for the presidency. But if that was so, he didn't understand why no one had contacted him to make a ransom demand.

Then he remembered the appearance of Niles Taylor at Bubba's, and the invitation to the private party that seemed to have come out of nowhere. Was he going to be approached in person? Was he going to be asked for something other than money in exchange for his daughter's life? His office was investigating an oil consortium Niles had set up. Was there a connection between his investigation and Kate's disappearance?

Clay recalled that Taylor had mentioned visiting King Grayhawk. Did Libby's father—who hated Clay—have something to do with his granddaughter's disappearance? That might have sounded too diabolical to be true, if Clay didn't have his own experience with the man to convince him how nefarious Kate's grandfather could be.

"Clay?" Libby said.

Clay realized he'd been caught up in his thoughts and had never explained why he believed Kate hadn't been kidnapped at random by some serial murderer. He didn't want to voice his suspicions about Niles Taylor or King Grayhawk without thinking them through first, so he said, "It's just a gut feeling."

But he made up his mind to attend the political party on Bear Island. Maybe someone would approach him to deal for Kate's life in exchange for some political favor. He was in a position to launch an investigation that could cost Niles's oil consortium billions of dollars—or exempt them from scrutiny. Lives had been sacrificed for less. He didn't intend to let Kate become a victim of corporate greed.

8

Sarah followed Clay and Libby back to the parking lot, then back to Jackson and the county government building on South King Street, where they took a more thorough look through Kate Grayhawk's backpack.

The second search, conducted in Sarah's small office, revealed a condom in the small zippered pouch—which caused both parents to take a long look at each other—half a Snickers candy bar, a hundred dollars in twenties, fifty-seven cents in change and a VISA credit card.

Sarah saw Clay and Libby exchange another anxious look when they realized what the presence of the cash and the credit card in their daughter's backpack might mean. The bag hadn't been stolen, or the money would have been gone. And it was unlikely Kate would have taken off on her own without her cash and credit card.

Their daughter was either buried under the snow on 25 Short, in which case she might not be found until spring, or she'd been abducted by the stranger she'd been seen with at the Mangy Moose and the backpack discarded, or some other option that was equally frightening.

"What happens now?" Clay asked.

"Teton County Search and Rescue will head out to 25 Short to see if they can find your daughter—or any more evidence that she was there," Sarah said.

"What else are you doing to find Kate?" Clay said.

"What else did you have in mind?" Sarah asked.

"What about a nationwide Amber Alert?" Clay asked.

"We sent a BOL—be on the lookout—around the state last night. We can see about getting Kate's picture on the TV stations in Colorado and Utah that air in this region. And I have the local police in Charlottesville questioning Kate's roommate and friends. I promise you we're doing everything we can to find your daughter, Mr. Blackthorne."

"I have a private investigator asking questions in Charlottesville as well," Clay said. "It's not enough."

"I'm open to any suggestions you might have," Sarah said. She knew the despair Clay and Libby must feel, because she'd felt it herself when her husband disappeared, especially since Tom's disappearance had been a nightmare from her childhood repeating itself.

When Sarah was fourteen, her sixteen-year-old sister Paige had disappeared from a party and never been seen again.

Paige had gone to the party with Sarah, and she'd been determined not to go home without her. Sarah was having too good a time dancing and had refused to leave with her sister. She remembered telling Paige, "You never want to have any fun. Go, if you want. I'm staying."

Paige had left alone. And disappeared. And never been found. Sarah had never stopped feeling responsible.

Many, many nights since then Sarah had woken up in a cold sweat, fleeing nightmares of what had happened to her elder sister, feeling regret and guilt and wishing she could relive that night and make a different choice. Sarah was certain that if she'd gone home with her sister, Paige would be alive today.

Sarah had tried to explain to her husband why it was so important to her to find the girls who'd gone missing in Jackson. That it was a way of seeking absolution for her part in Paige's disappearance, a way of sparing the families of those girls the hell she'd lived with for the past fifteen years.

Tom had insisted the past was done and over, and that he was here now and needed her. She'd ignored him. And he'd disappeared. And she'd felt she was to blame. Again.

Sarah desperately wanted to find the three missing girls. Alive. It was almost an obsession. It was the only way she could make up for the past, the only way she could escape her guilt, if not her pain.

When Clay wasn't able to offer another suggestion for how to find his daughter, Sarah said, "You might want to question Kate's friends at school again. Maybe they'll remember something."

"All right," Clay said.

"You can call me anytime," she said. "Here's my home number." When she saw their looks of surprise, she repeated, "Anytime."

"Thank you," Libby said. "We'll call if we find out anything."

After they left, Sarah sighed and dropped into the chair behind her plain wooden desk. Her small office was at the end of a labyrinthine hallway, but at least she had a door she could shut, which she did now.

It was much worse, she knew, not to know what had happened to a loved one, than to face the knowledge of their death from foul play. At least when you knew what had happened, you could bury the dead and go on with your life. Sarah had never been able to put Paige to rest. She would always wonder what had happened to her sister.

Which was why she'd spent so much time, to the detriment of her marriage, searching for the missing teenage girls. Once a trail went cold, it was only a matter of waiting for a body—or in this case, bodies—to show up.

Sarah fought against accepting that eventuality. Which was why she was going to spend some of her time today looking around Jackson to see if she could find any more clues that would lead her to Kate Grayhawk.

Sarah straightened when she heard a knock on the door and said, "Come in."

"Well, now. Here you are, Deputy Barndollar."

"Detective Barndollar," Sarah said, bristling at the smile on Drew DeWitt's face because she was so glad to see it. "What can I do for you, Mr. DeWitt?" she asked in her most official voice.

Drew made a *tsking* sound. "It was Drew and Sarah last night."

"Last time I looked the sun was up. What do you want?"

"That's no way to treat a citizen of the county, Detective Barndollar. Especially one who's come here on an official visit."

Sarah ground her teeth. Trust Drew to put her on the defensive. And on the spot. She rose and put her hands on her hips above her utility belt, because she was feeling intimidated by his towering male presence on the other side of her desk. "I'm listening. Talk."

"I had an idea where we might look for Kate."

"I'm surprised you didn't suggest it to Mr. Blackthorne, since I believe he's your friend."

"It's because Clay's my friend that I don't want to go looking for Kate with him," Drew said.

Sarah met his gaze and realized what he was implying. "You think she's dead."

Drew nodded. "Clay called and told me you found Kate's backpack on 25 Short, and that her money and credit card were still inside."

"Where is it you think we should be looking for Kate?" Sarah asked.

"There's a hunting cabin in the woods near 25 Short. I think whoever took Kate might have hidden her there."

Sarah frowned. "I've been in those woods. I've never seen a cabin."

"It's not much of a cabin, just a place some mountain man put together as a shelter a hundred and fifty years ago. It's completely hidden by brush and trees."

"How did you find it?"

"Clay and I used to ski 25 Short. We got separated one day and I found it."

"You never told your friend about it?"

Drew shook his head. "A lot happened that day. It kind of slipped my mind."

"Until now."

"Until now," Drew said. "Do you want to take a look with me or not?"

"Sure," Sarah said. "My shift is over. I need to change out of uniform and check in with my kids first."

Drew's mouth twisted, and Sarah said, "You don't have to like the fact that I have kids, but I could do without the aggrieved faces whenever I mention them."

"I don't have anything against your kids personally," Drew said. "And I admire people who think they can raise good kids. I just don't happen to believe I could manage it myself."

Sarah grabbed her coat and headed for the door as she asked, "Why not?"

She felt Drew's hand on the small of her back urging her through the door as he said, "Too much uncertainty."

"About what?" Sarah asked, edging away from his hand as they made the trip through the maze of corridors to the back of the building where her Chevy Tahoe was parked.

"About whether you'll fail," Drew said.

"I've got skis on the roof," Sarah said. "Did you bring yours?"

Drew pointed to a shiny black Porsche with a ski rack mounted on the roof holding a pair of cross-country skis.

"Nice wheels," Sarah said.

Drew grinned. "It pays to be rich."

"And modest."

Drew shrugged. "No sense pretending. Might as well enjoy the fruits of my forebears' labor." He transferred his skis to the Tahoe's roof as he muttered, "Couldn't spend it all if I tried."

"Have you been trying?" Sarah asked, standing on the opposite side of the Tahoe.

"I've earned every penny I've spent," Drew said as he finished lashing on his skis and let himself inside the SUV.

Sarah frowned, then got in behind the wheel. "You just said—"

"I can't help the fact that my grandfather's money came to me," Drew said, fastening his seat belt. "But I can choose whether or not to spend it."

Sarah fastened her seat belt and started the vehicle. "It sounds like you didn't care much for your grandparents."

"My stepgrandmother was a Bitch—with a capital B. She's the reason my brother—"

Sarah eyed Drew sideways as she pulled out of the lot, wondering whether she should prompt him to finish his sentence. She wasn't sure how well she wanted to get to know him. From the hint of anguish she'd heard in his voice, whatever had happened to his brother hadn't been good.

Once home, Sarah quickly changed her clothes in her bedroom, leaving Drew to wander around her living room. She took advantage of the moment of privacy to check in with her kids on the phone.

"How are you doing?" she asked when Brooke answered the cell phone the kids shared.

"I haven't seen Nate since he took the tram up to the top of Rendezvous Mountain this morning," Brooke complained. "I've been stuck with Ryan all day."

"I'll talk to Nate when he gets home," Sarah promised. "Let me speak with Ryan."

"He's skiing," Brooke replied.

"By himself?" Sarah asked.

"He's a good skier, Mom. Anyway, I told him to stay on the bunny slopes."

Sarah knew that was no guarantee that he had. "Please go find him, Brooke."

Silence met her on the other end of the line. Finally, Brooke said, "All right."

"I mean it, Brooke," Sarah said, hearing not only reluctance, but defiance in Brooke's response. She felt helpless, torn in two. She needed to go be a mother. Yet she felt compelled, in a way she couldn't deny, to search for the missing girl.

"You worry too much, Mom," Brooke said. And then, before Sarah could interrupt, continued, "I'll find him. I promise."

"Thank you, Brooke."

Brooke clicked off the phone in response.

Sarah took a deep breath to calm her agitation, then headed back to the living room.

When she reappeared, Drew pointed to a picture on the piano and said, "Is that your husband?"

"That's Tom." Sarah was surprised by the sudden lump in her throat. She missed her husband, missed their normal, up-and-down married life. She wished . . .

"You miss him," Drew said flatly.

She met his gaze. "I loved him. Of course I miss him."

"Even though he walked out on you?"

"I don't think that's what happened," Sarah said. "He did a repair job on Bear Island that morning. There was nothing to indicate anything out of the ordinary. He just . . . didn't come home that night."

"He didn't pack anything? Nothing was missing?"

"Nothing. No pictures, no money from the bank. Only Tom's truck. And Tom."

"Did you search Bear Island?" Drew asked.

"We did. And found nothing," Sarah replied.

"Did you drag the river for his truck?"

Sarah frowned. "There was no reason to do that."

"Why not?" Drew asked. "Maybe he had an accident, went into the river and—"

"There's no road leading to the river that he could have driven off of," Sarah said. "There's only a walking land bridge from the houses to the actual island."

Drew shrugged. "Just a thought."

Sarah didn't want to think about Tom. It hurt too much. "Let's go," she said.

They drove in silence through Jackson, past the quaint town square. A lot of towns had preserved a plot of grass in the middle of the business district, but in Jackson, each of its four corners was adorned with an impressive, freestanding archway of sun-and-wind-bleached elk antlers.

Like most of the tourists who passed through Jackson on their way to Yellowstone National Park, an hour's drive away, Sarah had taken her share of pictures in front of the unique arches. The antlers also provided a temptation for tourists and local teens—to take just one—that was hard to resist.

Sarah waited for Drew to comment about the elk preserve on their right as they headed out of town, but he acted as if the enormous herd of elk that wintered every year on Jackson's outskirts was nothing out of the ordinary.

She would have used any comment he made as an opening to find out more about him, but at last she decided simply to ask the question on her mind. "Does whatever happened to your brother have anything to do with your attitude toward children?"

Drew slanted a glance in her direction but didn't answer. She'd learned long ago that the best way to get a perp to talk was to stay silent herself. They traveled for ten more minutes before he spoke.

"I've never understood what would make someone decide that the best solution to his problems is to kill himself," Drew said.

"Ah," Sarah said. Now she knew what had happened to Drew's brother. All she lacked was the details. "I don't suppose it's a person's first choice," she said. "Maybe when all else fails—"

"Death is never a better choice than life."

"Was your brother ill?" Sarah asked, wondering if he might have chosen death over the disintegration of his body during a terminal illness.

"He was only twenty-three and healthy as a young bull. He'd just finished law school and been recruited by a high caliber New York firm. He had his whole life ahead of him."

"Oh," Sarah said.

Silence reigned in the Tahoe for another five minutes.

"I blame my grandfather's second wife. The proverbial wicked stepgrandmother," Drew said. "She made sure Dusty felt unwanted and unimportant and . . . useless."

"How did you escape her clutches?" Sarah asked.

"It's a long story."

"I've got time.

Drew stared out the window as he spoke. "My grandfather had two daughters, my mother Ellen and Clay's mother Eve. He fell in love with a woman named Shelby and divorced my grandmother, who fell apart and turned to alcohol and drugs. She finally slashed her wrists three years later."

"That's terrible!" Sarah said.

"I wasn't born yet when all that happened," Drew said sardonically. "The good part comes later."

Sarah made a face. "How can you make fun—"

"My life was anything but funny," Drew said bitterly. He turned and looked out the window again, regaining his composure, then began talking as though he hadn't stopped.

"Shelby had a daughter Elizabeth, my aunt Liz, who became the favored daughter."

"That sounds way too much like the fairy tale about the wicked stepmother and the ugly stepsisters," Sarah said.

Drew glanced at her and said, "Only the wicked stepmother part applies in this case. Aunt Liz was always nice and very pretty. Shelby was hell on wheels. She thought she ought to run all three of her daughters' lives."

"Uh oh," Sarah said.

"She couldn't stop my mother Ellen from marrying the man she loved, but Shelby didn't like Dusty's and my father, so she hounded him until he divorced my mother. Mom married a second husband, my stepbrother Morgan's father. He lasted a couple of years before Shelby ran him off.

"If Shelby didn't like you—and for some reason, she took a dislike to Dusty—she knew what to say to make you feel like a bad person," Drew said.

"She sounds like an awful woman."

"She was," Drew said. "She's the reason Aunt Eve married Jackson Blackthorne instead of King Grayhawk."

Sarah turned to him in surprise. "Really?"

Drew nodded. "Aunt Eve was being courted by King, but Shelby didn't want her stepdaughter going so far from home, so far from her grasp and control. So she told a few lies to convince Aunt Eve that Blackjack was the better choice. My aunt became a Blackthorne, and the rest is history."

"Whatever happened to the wicked stepgrandmother?"

"She's still alive and kicking in the hill country of Texas, madder than a peeled rattler because my grandfather left his ranch in Texas to his daughters—and her daughter. My grandfather's will stipulated that each of the three sisters had to name the other two as their heir to the DeWitt property, so the ranch would stay in one piece. My aunt Liz, the only sister living, owns the entire DeWitt ranching operation."

"I'm confused," Sarah said.

"About what?"

"If you know your grandmother was a terrible person—and the exception, rather than the rule, as grandmothers go—why do you think you wouldn't be a good parent?"

"Kids need too much."

"You've just told me you have more money than you can spend in your lifetime," Sarah pointed out.

"They need attention," Drew qualified.

"You could hire a registered nurse or a nanny."

"Love," he said curtly. "They need too much love."

"I can't disagree with that," Sarah said. "Everyone needs to be loved. Surely you—"

"I'm done loving," Drew said, cutting her off.

"Right," Sarah said. "I forgot about the girlfriend who dumped you."

"She's none of your business."

"I suppose she was the straw that broke the camel's back."

Drew made a disgruntled sound in his throat. "Let it go."

"I have to admit true love wasn't any part of what I had in mind last night," Sarah said. "Just some satisfying sex."

Drew eyed her with interest. "That can still be arranged."

Sarah laughed. "It wouldn't work now."

"Why not?"

"I should have said that what I wanted was *anonymous* sex. Now I know too much about you."

"Lady, you know nothing about me," Drew retorted.

"Very little, I'll admit," Sarah said. "What I do know makes any involvement between us impossible."

"You should know better than to throw down a gauntlet like that."

"I wasn't offering a challenge, just stating a fact."

Drew snorted. "You're lucky my head still hurts."

Sarah eyed his bruised forehead. "Did you have that checked out by a doctor?"

"I'm fine."

"Except your head still hurts."

"It's nothing," he insisted.

Sarah suspected Drew, like many of the men she worked with, would have to be prostrate before he'd seek out a doctor. Which made her wonder whether she should head up into the mountains with him on skis. "Maybe you should tell me where this cabin is and let me go on my own."

"I would have done that, if I'd thought you could find it without me," Drew admitted. "It's tucked into the trees so well I didn't see it myself until I nearly tripped over it."

"Why are you so sure you can find it again?" Sarah asked.

"I know exactly where I was, because thirty seconds later I was on my way down that mountain in the middle of an avalanche."

Sarah stared at Drew. "And you're willing to go back up there?"

"For Kate I will," Drew said soberly.

For the first time Sarah noticed the beads of perspiration on his upper lip. "What's your relationship to Kate Grayhawk?"

He turned to stare at her and said, "Let's just say I care about her and leave it at that."

Sarah believed Drew knew full well that Clay was Kate's father, but in case he didn't, she couldn't admit she knew the truth. "How did Kate Grayhawk get under your 'no kids' radar?" she asked instead.

"She never acted like a kid," Drew said. "Didn't cry, mope, moan or wail. Game to try anything. Brave, loyal, trustworthy—a real Boy Scout."

"Shouldn't that be Girl Scout?" Sarah said with a smile.

"Real tomboy," Drew explained. "Never saw her in anything but jeans and a T-shirt and cowboy boots."

"I'm surprised she didn't call you when she couldn't reach her mother."

"Kate wouldn't have known I was here," Drew said. "I've been living like a hermit. Haven't wanted to be bothered."

"Home nursing your broken heart?"

Drew shot her a sideways look. "I don't have a heart."

Sarah wasn't so sure, but she wasn't going to argue. They'd reached the parking lot at the foot of 25 Short, and she pulled in and parked the Tahoe. "How long is it going to take us to get to this cabin?"

"Maybe thirty minutes," Drew replied.

Sarah stood with her face to the wind, gauging its speed, then looked up at a gray sky heavy with snow clouds. Finally, she looked at the unpredictable, avalanche-prone snow cresting 25 Short, which she knew, having just been up there, was a risky place to be skiing.

"How high up do we have to go?" she asked.

"Not far. Just across the base and up a ways," Drew replied.

"Let's get on and get off," Sarah said, eyeing the mountain above them.

They'd been skiing fifteen minutes when Sarah felt a thirty-mile-an-hour gust of wind. "That isn't good," she said, staring up. "Wind like that's going to shift the snow on the crest."

"What do you want to do?" Drew asked.

"Go back," Sarah said. "Wait till the wind dies down." She felt a shiver roll down her spine as she heard the sharp crack of snow breaking free.

"Is that what I think it is?" Drew asked, raising his gaze to the top of 25 Short.

"We need to get off this mountain."

Drew turned to her, his blue eyes fierce and said,

"What if that cabin gets buried by snow before we get back?"

Sarah was used to making hard choices, but she didn't like the one Drew had presented to her. If they moved forward, they could very well end up buried under an avalanche started by the gusting wind thousands of feet above them.

But if Drew could find the cabin, and if Kate Grayhawk was inside, they might be able to rescue her and escape, since snow from an avalanche might not get this far down the mountain.

What if they turned around, and later discovered that Kate Grayhawk had been in the cabin and been buried alive? Sarah would never forgive herself.

"Sarah?" Drew prodded.

Sarah made a frustrated sound in her throat. There was no more time for what-ifs. It was time to act.

"How far to the cabin?" she asked.

"Maybe five minutes."

"Let's go."

Sarah's breath created trails of fog as she sucked oxygen open-mouthed. She was fast on skis, but Drew could have won prizes racing. She struggled not to lose sight of him as he pressed forward through the spruces and pines.

"Wait for me," she called out. "We don't know what—or who—we'll find at that cabin."

"If Kate's abductor is there," Drew replied, "he must be as aware of the avalanche danger as we are. He might already be high-tailing it out of there."

"Maybe, maybe not," Sarah said. "Don't go in there without me." *And my gun*, she added silently.

Drew glanced over his shoulder, and Sarah realized that he wasn't going to wait for her. She increased her stride, using every bit of strength and skill she had to close the distance between them.

Sarah felt the ground shudder, or maybe she only imagined the earth shaking beneath her feet, and acknowledged the fact that they'd run out of time—and luck. She was aware of her heart beating like the drum in a marching band and the taste of copper in her throat.

Under the circumstances, a healthy dose of fear was a good thing. She could use all the adrenaline her body cared to shoot into her veins. Tons of snow were on their way down the mountain. She was racing for her life.

The sad thing was, they'd risked their lives for nothing. They'd never found Drew's mysterious cabin.

"There!" Drew said, pointing in the distance. "See it? There!"

Suddenly, Sarah saw the tiny cabin through the trees, every bit as ramshackle as Drew had said it was, half a football field away.

She could also hear the snow thundering its way down the mountain, could see the mist rising along its path, like a powerful steam engine billowing white smoke.

"Our Father, Who art in Heaven," she began praying.

"Move your butt!" Drew shouted.

Sarah realized he'd stopped and was waiting for her. She spurred muscles that were already screaming to even greater effort, and together they made it to the cabin door. She stepped out of her skis and pitched both skis and poles inside. The snow appeared like a giant tidal wave at the edge of her vision.

"Inside!" he snapped, throwing his skis and poles in after hers and pushing her inside ahead of him.

There was no time for caution, no time to see whether the cabin was occupied by friend or foe, before Drew closed the door behind them.

It took Sarah a tenth of a second to realize that the cabin was empty. In a glance she took in a broken table. Spiderwebs. Dust. A single boarded-up window.

She turned and met Drew's gaze. It was all going to be over in another tenth of a second.

Sarah launched herself into Drew's open arms, her face buried against his shoulder as the thundering snow cracked trees like matchsticks on its way down the mountain. She held tight and waited for the moment when the ancient logs that protected them would crack, and they would be crushed under tons of snow.

Sarah's chest hurt, and she realized she was holding her breath. She gasped a life-saving breath of air as the thundering sound moved beyond the cabin, and she realized the walls hadn't come down, and they hadn't been buried alive.

Or maybe they had.

Sarah's fear was that the cabin was buried under so much snow that they wouldn't be able to dig themselves out, that eventually they'd suffocate. She had to try the door. She had to know for sure whether snow had trapped them in a cold white tomb.

She pulled free of Drew's grip, but her legs were trembling so badly they wouldn't hold her upright. She grabbed at him as she started to fall, and his arms once more tightened around her.

"Whoa, there," he murmured in her ear. "Take it easy."

"We're alive," she said. And then felt stupid for announcing the obvious.

"Yeah," he said.

She realized he was trembling, too. She lifted her head and looked into his eyes. "Are you all right?"

"Getting there."

Then she remembered what Clay Blackthorne had said about Drew being buried in an avalanche on 25 Short. She slid her arms around his waist and held him tight, giving back the support he'd offered her. "That was close," she said.

"Yeah."

She heard him swallow and looked up to see he had his eyes closed and his jaw clamped tight.

She raised a hand and cupped the back of his head, drawing it down to her own, so she could lay her icy cheek against his. "We're safe," she murmured.

Maybe saying it would make it true.

She heard him swallow hard again, and realized her own throat was tight with emotion. She was no more willing to admit her own fear than to force him to admit his.

They stayed clutched together until the rumbling snow had passed beyond their hearing.

Sarah was so caught up in comforting Drew that it took her a moment to realize what she was seeing. "Thank you, God," she murmured.

"What?" Drew said.

Sarah smiled up at him and said, "You'll be pleased to hear we haven't been buried alive."

"Damn pleased," Drew said, returning her smile with a lopsided grin. "How did you come to that conclusion?"

Sarah pointed at a crack in the chinking near the front door of the cabin. "Sunlight."

Drew left her and crossed to the door, which faced the downslope, and opened it. A foot of snow blocked the threshold, but that was all. He turned to her and smiled. "I'm feeling damn lucky right now. How about you?"

Sarah felt something lurch inside her at the sight of Drew's brilliant smile. She'd found him attractive from the start, but the heightened emotions of the past half hour had made her even more susceptible to whatever it was about this man that made him stand out from all others. Lucky? She'd be damn lucky to get out of here with her heart intact.

She forced her gaze away from him, back to the interior of the cabin. "Too bad there was no one here for us to find," she said, as she surveyed the dilapidated one-room cabin.

"Yeah," he said. "I guess I was hoping . . ." He met Sarah's gaze and said, "I wanted her to be here."

What he meant, and hadn't said, was that he wanted Kate Grayhawk to be alive. Sarah wanted the same thing. More than he knew.

"We'd better go," she said. "I need to check on my kids."

She watched Drew curb the reflexive twist of his mouth at the mention of her kids. He looked at her and smiled ruefully.

Her heart was thumping heavily, and her body felt languid. She resisted the urge to move in his direction. So what if he'd allowed her to comfort him? So what if he'd comforted—and protected—her? So what if he had a thousand-watt smile?

He was a rich playboy. He couldn't stand kids. Well, most kids. All he wanted from her, if he wanted anything at all, was sex.

Sarah looked into Drew's striking blue eyes and felt her insides take the kind of uncoordinated flying leap a bullrider takes off a ball-breaking Brahman.

She realized she was trembling again, and wondered if it was a leftover response from the avalanche or anxiety about what might happen next. She stumbled over her own feet when she tried to walk. She must have looked like she needed someone to hold her up, because Drew crossed the room in two seconds flat and tucked his arms around her.

"You okay?" he asked, staring down into her eyes.

She stared back up at him, feeling her insides clench in a way she recognized all too well. "No," she rasped. "I'm not okay."

"What's wrong?"

She closed her eyes to shut out the concern she saw in this near-stranger's eyes.

"Hey," he said, holding her close and rocking her. "We're okay. It's all over. We're fine."

He kissed her on the forehead. Purely in comfort, she was sure. Then on the cheek. And then his mouth slid down to hers.

And she felt the world turn upside down.

9

Adrenaline was still running hot through Sarah's veins. That was the only explanation she had for the voracious need she felt to be kissed, to be touched, to somehow climb inside the skin of the man whose need seemed as ravenous as her own.

"Sarah," he said in a guttural voice.

Just her name. She answered his call with the wanton desire that had gone from tight bud to full bloom in the seconds since his mouth had claimed hers.

His eyes glittered avidly in the shafts of sunlight that streamed through the cabin walls, as the snow settled on the countryside around them.

Their mouths meshed, their hands searched urgently for flesh, discarding mittens and shoving coats and sweaters aside. Sarah gasped as Drew's warm hand surrounded her breast and heard his gasp in return as she slid her hand inside his long johns.

Her mouth sought his in a frenzy, her tongue dueling with his, hot and wet and urgent. He lifted her and she clasped her legs around his waist as he impaled her. She heard a ragged murmur of satisfaction in his throat and answered with a moan of her own. Everything was feeling—hot, liquid, pulsating need.

He took the few steps necessary to brace her against the wall and give him the leverage he needed to thrust. Her body tightened around his and she groaned as she convulsed in a sweet agony of joy and pain. He uttered a savage, guttural sound as she felt the heat of his seed inside her.

Her breath hissed from her in smoky clouds, as it did from him. The air felt painfully cold as she sucked deep breaths to feed desperate lungs.

The sudden knowledge that they hadn't used anything to prevent conception woke her abruptly from the fantasy she'd created with him. "Oh, God," she croaked. "Let me down."

She kept her face pressed against Drew's chest and her arms on his shoulders as he released her cramped legs.

She resisted the touch of his fingertip under her chin until he said, "Sarah, look at me."

She wasn't brave enough to deny him. She lifted her chin defiantly, ready to confront him.

When their eyes met, she saw a glint of humor, and then the amused twitch of his mouth.

"I have to admit I wasn't expecting that," he said. "From near death to spectacular sex in the space of a heartbeat."

"It's the 'near death' part I could have done without," Sarah admitted. "The 'spectacular sex' was . . ." She ran a fingertip over his still-damp lips and felt her insides quiver. "Spectacular."

"Except now I'm about to freeze my ass off," Drew said with a smile that threatened Sarah's heart rate. Her nipples peaked as he straightened her sports bra back over her breasts. She held her breath as he lowered her long john shirt, trailing his hand enticingly across her pubis. She fought the urge to arch her hips against him.

She grabbed his hand and said, "Don't."

He looked surprised but didn't push the matter. "I think your sweater's over there on the floor."

By the time she'd retrieved her sweater, he was dressed again and holding her coat, scarf, hat and mittens in his hand. She allowed him to help her into the coat, then took everything else from him and finished dressing.

They'd abandoned their cross-country skis and poles on the floor inside the door. Sarah picked hers up and stepped outside into the powdery foot of snow with Drew on her heels.

"Are we going to talk about this?" Drew said.

"No." She stepped into her skis, grabbed her poles and shoved off in the direction of the parking lot.

Sarah felt surprisingly self-conscious when she and Drew ran into a Teton County Search and Rescue team heading up the trail as she and Drew were going down. She knew her eyes must be bright, and her lips felt bee-stung from Drew's kisses. But no one seemed to notice anything different about her.

"Hey, Sarah," the team leader greeted her. "Should have known you'd be up here ahead of us. Who's that with you?"

Sarah had no choice but to introduce Drew. "This is Drew DeWitt. A . . . friend."

Too late Sarah realized she shouldn't have tried to put a label on Drew, because once she did, eyebrows went up all around. Detective Sarah Barndollar was a notorious loner. Ever since Tom had disappeared, she'd claimed she had no time for anything except work and family obligations. Yet, here she was skiing with a stranger none of them had ever met—in a town where local folks knew each other—and calling him a friend.

"Any suggestions where we ought to go looking for the Grayhawk girl?" the team leader asked her, his curious eyes on Drew.

To Sarah's surprise, Drew answered, "Above the avalanche, because if she was anywhere below it she's dead and buried now."

He shoved off without giving anyone a chance to reply. Sarah stayed only long enough to say, "Head up to where we marked her backpack was found and work your way downhill. Good luck."

Drew reached the Tahoe ahead of her and was leaning against the front fender, his skis already strapped to the roof, waiting for her. "They aren't going to find her," Drew said flatly.

"Probably not," Sarah agreed as she lashed her skis to the SUV. "But they have to look." She paused and added, "Just as we did."

Drew turned his back on her and looked up at the mountain. "Where the hell has she gone?"

"We may never know," Sarah said. It was a brutal truth she'd been forced to live with before.

He turned angry blue eyes on her and said, "That's not good enough, Detective Barndollar."

"I've done all I can do today," Sarah replied. "There are a lot of dedicated officers searching for Kate. I'll start again tomorrow, and I won't ever stop searching until I find her. But right now, I have to go home to my kids." She got into the Tahoe and waited for him to join her.

They made the trip back to town in a silence all the more provocative because of what had passed between them on the mountain. When they reached the parking lot where Drew had left his Porsche, Sarah killed the engine and reached for the door, hoping to escape without talking to him.

He caught her arm and said, "This isn't over."

She forced herself to meet his gaze and said, "It was sex. Precipitated by—"

He caught her nape and kissed her hard on the mouth. Her blood thrummed through her veins, and she felt completely alive as she hadn't since long before Tom had walked out the door. She didn't try to escape. She simply stopped returning his kiss.

When he let her go, she put up a wall behind her eyes to keep him from searching out the chaos his kiss had created inside her. "Good-bye, Drew," she said.

His lips curved in an ironic smile. "I'll be seeing you, Detective Barndollar."

Sarah didn't contradict him. She was just glad to get him out of the car and out of her life, before she got involved with him anymore than she already was. She stayed where she was until he'd removed his skis from the Tahoe and strapped them onto his Porsche. He gunned the engine, so she could hear the horsepower under the hood, but since it was a police parking lot, he eased the Porsche onto the street like he was taking his dog for a pleasant walk.

Sarah leaned back against the headrest and closed her eyes and let the remorse flood over her. What had she been thinking?

Well, the answer to that was simple. She hadn't been thinking. She'd been feeling. Oh, God, had she been feeling. So much. So wonderfully much.

A knock on the window jerked her back to reality, and she stepped out of her Tahoe. "Hi, Jim," she said, greeting the investigative sergeant who'd taught her everything about police work that she hadn't learned during the FBI course she'd taken at Quantico. Sergeants didn't work on weekends, and yet Jim was here, on his way out as she was coming in. "What's up?" she asked her boss.

"Anything new on the Grayhawk girl?" he asked.

"Unfortunately, no."

"We're getting a lot of pressure to find her," Jim said.

"From Blackthorne?"

"Yeah, from him. And from King Grayhawk. He wants his granddaughter found. Now. The sheriff has every available deputy working double shifts."

"I've already done my extra shift," Sarah said. "I've got some paperwork to do and then I need to go home."

"I need you to—"

"Not today," Sarah said firmly. "My kids need me at home. I'll be back at work first thing in the morning."

"All right. I'll cover for you."

"Thanks, Jim," Sarah said. She'd only planned to spend an hour at the office, but several calls came in regarding Kate. By the time Sarah had taken them, it was dark outside. She felt guilty for having worked so late as she hurried out to her Tahoe and headed home.

Sarah's house was on the hill above Snow King Mountain. Most locals could no longer afford to live in Jackson because the dearth of real estate—97 percent of Teton County was forest service land—made it incredibly valuable, and the influx of politicians and Hollywood types had pushed property values sky-high. When folks couldn't keep up with the property taxes that escalated along with the property values, they sold out.

So far, Sarah had held on to the house, a simple wood-frame home with a brick fireplace. It had three bedrooms but only one bath, and a water heater too small for five people to get hot showers one after another.

Tom's disappearance had reduced that problem by one, but had created a financial, as well as an emotional, nightmare for Sarah. Instead of two incomes, she and the kids had been managing for the past fifteen months on one and a half—the half being all the extra shifts Sarah worked for any patrolman who was on vacation or had a family emergency. It was still tough to make ends meet.

If Tom had died, his life insurance would have kept them afloat. But until Tom's body was found, he wasn't "officially" dead. So Sarah worked long hours and endured the accusing faces turned on her by her children when she arrived home at odd hours.

Nate and Brooke were old enough to understand her financial dilemma, but she'd worked too much overtime before this emergency for them to accept the need for it now.

Sarah pulled the Tahoe into the driveway and cut the engine, then let her head fall forward onto the steering wheel. She'd willingly take ice-cold showers the rest of her life if Tom would just show up and explain why he'd left in the first place.

Sarah needed to go inside and be a mother to her kids, but her feelings were still raw. She couldn't believe what she'd done with Drew. For the first time since she'd promised to love, honor and cherish Tom Barndollar, till death should part them, she'd betrayed her marriage vows. She was surprised at how guilty she felt.

And how angry she felt.

"Where are you, Tom?" she raged. "Where the hell did you go?"

It was time, Sarah realized, to file for divorce. Time to move on. Time to admit, at last, that Tom was never coming back.

"Oh, God." She gasped with the pain the mere thought of taking such a step caused her. She hadn't grieved her loss, because she hadn't admitted to it. What had happened with Drew had been a shock. She'd felt alive again. She'd wanted to live again.

Recognizing her loss meant grieving. And grieving meant the wrenching pain of letting go, knowing that she would never really let go until Tom—or his body—was found.

Sarah shivered and realized she must have been sitting in the Tahoe long enough for the last of the heat to dissipate. She shoved open the door and headed inside to see her children.

Which was when she realized her pickup wasn't in the driveway or parked on the street. There were lights on inside the house, which meant the kids had been home after dark. But where were they now?

Sarah hurried inside, suddenly worried. She depended on Nate and Brooke to take care of Ryan, and they'd always acted as responsible baby-sitters. She stepped into the living room and found Ryan lying on his belly, Brooke beside him, both already dressed in pj's, playing a desperate game of Metroid on the TV.

She wanted to grab both of them up in her arms and hug them, she felt so grateful to find them safe and sound. She got a quick, "Hi, Mom!" from Ryan, who remained focused on the game, and no greeting at all from Brooke.

"Where's Nate?" she asked.

"Out with some friends," Brooke replied, not looking up from the game.

"He was supposed to be home before dark," Sarah said.

"Yeah, so were you," Brooke said.

Sarah felt mortified.

"I win!" Ryan shouted gleefully.

Brooke looked at the screen, groaned and said, "No fair. Mom broke my concentration."

"Have you had supper?" Sarah asked.

"Ryan was hungry," Brooke said, staring her in the eye. "So I fed him."

"Thank you, Brooke," Sarah said, swallowing her pride. "Did Nate say when he'd be coming home?"

"Before curfew," Brooke replied.

Nate's curfew was midnight, which meant that despite how tired she felt, Sarah would be up late waiting to make sure he got home safely. "Did you have a nice day with your friends?" Sarah asked Brooke.

"Yeah. When Ryan wasn't bugging me to death."

"You like me," Ryan said, grinning at Brooke as he dropped the controller and sat up. "You know you do."

Brooke ruffled Ryan's hair and grudgingly said, "Yeah, bug, I do."

Ryan jumped up and crossed to Sarah and hugged her around the waist. "I'm glad you're home, Mom. Brooke and me were getting scared."

Sarah met Brooke's gaze and saw the fear behind the sullen mask on her stepdaughter's face. "I'm sorry I didn't call to let you know I was running late. I'll try to do better."

Brooke turned away without acknowledging the olive branch she'd extended. Ryan grabbed her hand and said, "I'm nearly finished with Harry Potter. Will you help me read an extra chapter tonight?"

"Sure," Sarah said as she slid her arm around Ryan's narrow shoulders and walked with him down the hall.

By the time Ryan had finished reading two chapters of Harry Potter and Sarah returned to the living room, Brooke had disappeared into her bedroom. She could hear her stepdaughter talking on the phone. Sarah realized she was famished and headed into the kitchen, wondering if Brooke had made something for dinner that had resulted in leftovers.

She opened the fridge and found it nearly empty. She was supposed to have shopped for groceries this afternoon. She wondered what the kids had eaten for supper. The kitchen counters, she noted, were wiped clean. The sink was empty of dishes. She had Brooke to thank. And hadn't thanked her.

Sarah sighed. She wasn't doing a very good job as a mother. She felt frustrated that her work as a deputy sheriff hadn't produced the results she would have liked, which is to say, that she hadn't found any of the missing girls . . . alive.

"Mom?"

Sarah turned to find Brooke standing in the kitchen doorway, her eyes wide and frightened. "What is it?" she asked.

Brooke held out the cordless phone and said, "It's the Jackson police. They want to talk to you. About Nate."

Sarah's heart leaped to her throat. A call from the police when your teenage son was out driving around at night was every mother's nightmare. She didn't dare let her terror show. Brooke already looked scared to death.

Sarah took the phone from her daughter and said in as calm a voice as she could manage, "This is Sarah Barndollar. To whom am I speaking?" She kept her face blank as she said, "I see. Thank you, Harry. I appreciate the professional courtesy."

She hung up the phone and met Brooke's gaze.

"Is Nate all right?" Brooke asked, her eyes bright with unshed tears.

"He's fine," Sarah said, crossing to Brooke and hugging her tight.

"Where is he? What happened?"

Sarah sighed. "He's been arrested."

"Arrested?" Brooke jerked free and stared up at Sarah, shocked. "What for?"

"Vandalism. He and a couple of other boys apparently tried stealing antlers from the town square. The other boys got away. Nate got caught. A friend of mine is holding him for me in an interrogation room."

Brooke's eyes were huge. "Will Nate have to go to jail?"

"No. The officer who caught Nate is going to give him a warning and release him into my custody."

"Nate must be scared shitless."

Sarah realized Brooke was so scared that she hadn't even been aware of the language she'd used—which was strictly forbidden. "I'm sure he is," she said. "I'd better go get him."

Before she could take a step toward the door, the phone rang again.

"That's probably for me," Brooke said.

Sarah handed her the phone and headed for the door, but before she reached it, an anxious-looking Brooke said, "It's for you, Mom. Sounds like somebody else is in trouble."

Sarah took the phone and listened, then shook her head and smiled. "Congratulations, Buck. No problem.

I promised I'd cover for you when Bobbie Sue went into labor, and I will. Don't worry. Tell Bobbie Sue to breathe deep and relax."

When Sarah hung up the phone, she saw a mutinous look on Brooke's face. "I don't have a choice, Brooke. I have to go."

"You just got home. You were barely here an hour. What about Nate? Are you going to leave him in jail?"

"I'll pick up Nate and bring him home before I go back on duty," Sarah said as she headed back to her bedroom to change once more into her patrolman's uniform. "I'm sorry it worked out this way."

"It always works out this way," Brooke accused. "You're never home. I can see why Daddy left!"

Sarah paled as Brooke shoved past her and ran down the hall and into her room, slamming the door behind her.

"What's going on?" she heard Ryan call out. "Is everything all right?"

Sarah hurried down the hall and into Ryan's bedroom. "Everything's fine," she said. "I have to go out again tonight to work. Brooke will stay with you and Nate will be home a little later. I'll see you in the morning."

Ryan yawned. "Will you make blueberry pancakes for breakfast?"

"Sure," Sarah said. And realized she was going to have to stop by the grocery on her way home and get milk and eggs and blueberries and pancake mix.

She knocked on Brooke's closed door, then opened it and said, "I'm leaving now. Nate should be back soon. Thank you for cleaning up in the kitchen."

Brooke said nothing, just curled into a tighter ball in her bed.

Sarah had a sudden thought. Maybe the kitchen was so clean because Brooke hadn't eaten anything. But Ryan would have insisted on being fed, so something had been cooked. She wanted to confront her step-daughter about whether she'd eaten, but right now didn't seem like the time. Nate was being held at the police station and was probably scared and worried. And she had to go back to work, to cover for Buck, whose pregnant wife had finally gone into labor.

"Good night, Brooke," she said.

There was no answer as she closed her stepdaugh-ter's bedroom door.

The phone rang again. Sarah was afraid to answer it, afraid of more bad news. She picked up the cordless phone and said, "Sarah Barndollar."

"Are you taking Buck's shift?" the dispatcher at the sheriff's office said.

"Yes."

"There's been an accident with injuries south of town." The dispatcher gave her a mile marker to locate the scene.

"Got it," Sarah said. And then she remembered Nate. She wondered if she dared take the time to pick him up on the way, and then realized that the scene of an accident with injuries was no place to take her teenage son.

Sarah grabbed her coat and headed out the door. Nate would have to wait.

10

Clay had thought the day couldn't get much worse, but the moment he stepped inside Libby's cabin, he realized he'd been wrong.

"Hello, King," he said when he spied Libby's father.

King Grayhawk sat in a studded leather armchair near the fire, like a head of state on his throne, Libby's three hounds at his feet. Magnum rose and stretched. King had one hand on each redbone hound's head, and it wasn't until he released them that Doc and Snoopy bounded over to greet Libby, sad eyes adoring, tails wagging and tongues lolling.

"Clay." The older man should have risen to greet Clay, but King used the fact that his left knee was stiff from an old bronc-busting injury, and stretched out on an ottoman in front of him, as an excuse to stay where he was. An impressive, gnarled oak cane with a golden hawk, wings outspread for a handle, remained in place, leaning upright against the chair.

Clay wanted to turn around and walk right back out the door, but Libby was behind him, and it would have looked too much like the retreat it was if he'd tried to get past her. And really, what was the point? This confrontation was bound to come sooner or later. It might as well be now.

"Who told you?" Clay asked as he took off his coat and hung it on an antler hook by the door. He stopped to help Libby take off her coat, then hung it beside his own.

"Hello, Daddy," Libby said as she crossed into the living room.

Clay noticed she made no move to touch her father, not to hug him or kiss him or greet him in any familiar way. She headed directly to the crackling fireplace and stood there, her hands held out before her, as though its heat could warm the cold inside her.

Clay knew better.

There was no love lost between King Grayhawk and his eldest daughter. Clay didn't know all the details of what had transpired between them when Libby had finally told her father she was pregnant, but he knew King had struck her, because he'd seen the bruise on her cheek.

Someday, he'd vowed, he would repay King for that injury.

"North called me," King said, his eyes focused on Libby in condemnation. "I expect to be told when something as monumental as the disappearance of my only granddaughter occurs."

"There isn't anything you can do that we aren't already doing," Libby said.

"You're wrong," King said. "As usual."

Clay saw the flush rise on Libby's cheekbones, saw the firm set of her lips as she bit back whatever retort had sprung to them. He opened his mouth to defend her but was never given the chance.

"I've hired private detectives to backtrack Katherine's steps," King said. "They've already discovered—"

"They've found her?" Libby exclaimed, taking a step toward her father in her anxiety to hear good news about Kate.

"No," King conceded.

Libby stopped in her tracks.

King continued, "But they've got an artist's rendering of the man who apparently kidnapped her, which they're circulating among—"

"The police have already done that, Daddy," Libby said scornfully. "We've talked to everyone, we've—"

"You didn't issue an Amber Alert," the old man contradicted.

Clay watched Libby's eyes brim with tears that she fought not to shed.

"You know how few roads there are in and out of here," she said. "They were all blocked by police within hours of Kate's disappearance."

"That doesn't mean someone couldn't have taken Katherine across state lines," the old man said stubbornly. "I've got a nationwide Amber Alert in place."

Clay was grateful for any effort that might help locate Kate, but he'd be damned if he'd thank the old man. "What has your investigator found out?" he asked.

The old man snorted. "Not much! But I have every confidence that—"

"Why did you come here?" Libby interrupted.

It was plain to Clay that, far from finding comfort in her father's presence, Libby seemed irritated by it.

King Grayhawk seemed impervious to his daughter's rebuff. "I'm here to find my granddaughter."

"I don't need you here," Libby retorted. "I don't want you here."

"I have no intention of going anywhere until—"

"This is my home. You're not welcome in it."

"I'll be at the Big House," the old man said. "I thought you might want to know—"

"I don't care why you left that Big House of yours at Kingdom Come and showed up here. I don't care what you think you can accomplish. I want you out. Get out!"

Clay could see she was on the verge of hysteria. King apparently realized the same thing, because he reached for his cane, eased his left leg off the ottoman, and shoved his way upright. Clay had forgotten how tall he was, how imposing he looked. King Grayhawk was wearing what any cowboy might wear, jeans and a flannel plaid Western shirt and boots. But he looked far from ordinary.

The face above the clothes bore snakelike, unblinking eyes, a hawk nose, and sharp cheekbones etched into stone by wind and weather. The shirt did little to conceal broad, powerful shoulders, and the jeans revealed a wiry leanness that came from years in the saddle. The tooled leather belt, with its broad silver buckle, cinched a narrow waist, and the boots were scuffed and crusted with dirt that made it clear this man stood his ground.

King Grayhawk was not a man Clay admired, but he recognized a powerful adversary when he saw one. Clay had grown up with a father very much—almost exactly—like the man he faced now. They were two giants cut from the same rugged cloth, both shaped by the vast, unforgiving frontier.

Both men were descendants of English noblemen—the Duke of Blackthorne and the Earl of Grayhawk.

Despite the objections of her nearly grown son, a widow named Cricket Creed had married the first American Blackthorne, which had begun the feud between Blackthornes and Creeds that had lasted to modern times.

The Earl of Grayhawk, the family black sheep, had been banished from England by his father and made his living in the American fur trade. He'd used his profits to buy land in eastern Wyoming that happened to have a fortune in oil underneath it.

Several descendants of that original Grayhawk black sheep, King and North among them, seemed to have inherited a bit of his dark soul. Clay knew how ruthless such a man could be. How totally untouched he could be by the feelings of those whose lives he manipulated and controlled.

When he was a younger man, Clay had been caught between the desires of King Grayhawk and Jackson Blackthorne—and barely managed to escape without being crushed.

He could see Libby was still fighting a battle he'd

opted out of years before. He didn't want to play knight in shining armor to her fair maiden and ride to the rescue. But he couldn't stand by any longer without doing something.

"We don't need your help," he said.

"*We?*" King shot back sarcastically. "I must have missed more than I thought. When did you and my daughter become a *we?*"

Clay was surprised when Libby took the steps necessary to stand beside him.

"We're Kate's parents," she said. "She's our responsibility. You don't belong here."

"I'm her grandfather," King said. "Which makes this my business."

"No," Libby said, shaking her head. "You never wanted Kate to be born. You wanted that foul Blackthorne seed torn from my womb," she said, her voice vibrating with feeling. "It's only because I defied you that she exists. It's too late now to say you care about her."

"The girl's last name is Grayhawk," King said implacably. "Not Blackthorne."

"Because you—"

King cut Libby off with a wave of his hand. "I take care of what's mine." His cane made a thumping sound on the hardwood floor as he limped his way to the door.

Clay hadn't realized he'd slid his arm around Libby, but she'd backed up against him so they presented a solid front to her father as he turned to look at them one last time.

"I should have shot you," King said to him. "No one around here would have convicted me if I had.

Don't use what's happened as an excuse to go sniffing around my daughter. I won't make the same mistake twice."

The deadly threat might have seemed melodramatic if it weren't King Grayhawk speaking. King controlled the judges and politicians in Wyoming the way Clay's father Blackjack controlled the judges and politicians in Texas. But Clay was no longer a young man in love, vulnerable and confused. He was a man who wielded a great deal of power himself.

"There's nothing you can do to me, King—short of shooting me dead—that will keep me from pursuing whomever I damn please."

"You've been warned," King said. "That's the most I feel obliged to do."

It was strange to hear King suggest that he adhered to the Code of the West, rules of behavior established by cowboys over time, not unlike the code of chivalry observed by the knights of old England, which held that you could never shoot an unarmed man—or an unwarned man.

It dawned on Clay that from now on, he'd better watch his back.

When the door closed behind King, Libby pulled free of Clay's embrace and headed once more for the fireplace, crossing her arms and rubbing them with her hands as though she were freezing.

"Are you all right?" he asked.

"You shouldn't provoke him," she said. "It's exactly what he wants."

"I meant every word I said."

She glanced at him over her shoulder. "He'll ruin you. He can do it. All it would take—"

"Let me handle King," he said. "What else can I do to help you?"

She turned to face him, her arms clutched tight around her middle, as though she would fly apart if she let go. "Hold me, Clay. Please."

He couldn't have refused her. Didn't want to refuse her. In all these years, he'd never gotten over her. Libby Grayhawk was unfinished business. Maybe it was the way they'd been dragged apart by their respective fathers. The woman he'd loved in his youth, and been forced to leave, was a dangling string he couldn't help pulling, even though he knew that pulling that string might very well unravel the political life he'd been building.

When his arms closed around her, it felt like he'd come home. He pressed his nose into her hair and inhaled, wondering if he would recognize whatever scent it was she used now. But there was no hint of perfume, only the clean, fresh smell of soap and woman.

Her breasts were soft against his chest. He felt himself becoming aroused and kept their lower bodies separated so she wouldn't realize the effect she was having on him. He was supposed to be offering comfort.

He tried to imagine how any relationship between them could possibly thrive. He needed a wife who could be a political hostess, someone who could face liars and thieves with a smile on her face and never bat an eye.

Libby was too honest to put up with that sort of bullshit. And she wouldn't have recognized a pair of pantyhose if they bit her in the ass. It was no coincidence that their daughter thought jeans and boots were appropriate attire for all occasions.

Libby had made a life for herself here in the West, acting as a guide to hunters and fishermen and naturalists who wanted to see the land up close. Could he ask her to walk away from a life spent out-of-doors to join him in the political arena?

He had a brief, traitorous thought about his dead wife. If not for Giselle, he might have returned to ranch life in Texas long ago. His wife had found the endless South Texas prairies, with their abundance of dangerous wildlife, intimidating. She was much more comfortable dealing with the sharks in Washington's political waters.

That would never have been true of Libby. She was even more comfortable in the wilderness—mountain, plain or prairie—than he was.

The problem was their checkered past. It was easy to see how it could rear its ugly head to spoil whatever relationship they tried to carve out in the future. Not to mention the interference of two powerful, angry older men—their fathers—certain to be bitter rivals to the bitter end.

Clay would have dismissed the idea of pursuing Libby out of hand, except it was hard to ignore the way his body hummed—that was the exact word for what happened to him—whenever it came in contact with hers. He could feel it now, a sort of thrumming rush in his blood, a lightness in his head from the mere thought of pressing his mouth against hers.

Action followed impulse. He lowered his head as she raised hers, and their lips met in a kiss of utter tenderness. It was comfort of a sort he hadn't imagined he could feel with this woman, who'd always been the source of so much passion. He felt the moistness of her lips, the pliant softness as she pushed back against his own.

He wanted to tell her how he was feeling but feared he'd break whatever spell had fallen between them. He'd expected passion in her arms. He hadn't expected peace. And need. And, yes, there it was, simmering beneath the surface now and always . . . the ache of desire. The insatiable hunger. The desperate need to put himself inside her.

He slid his tongue into her mouth to taste. Slid his hand up to caress her breast. And heard her breath quicken.

He couldn't believe how good she tasted, how perfect she felt in his arms, how soft her breasts felt in his hands, how naturally her hips sought out his own. He was lost in sensation, his body hard, his need urgent, when the phone hanging on the clip attached to his belt rang. He swore bitterly at the interruption, then realized it might be news of Kate and grabbed for the phone.

"Blackthorne," he snapped.

"Is it Kate?" Libby asked anxiously.

It took Clay a moment to recognize the female voice on the line. He took a step back from Libby and said, "It's nothing to do with Kate." Clay realized he couldn't talk to the woman he'd considered making his next wife with Libby looking up at him, her eyes still dilated by passion.

He turned his back and walked a few steps away to speak quietly into the phone. "I'm sorry I haven't called to update you. No, I don't think I'll be back on Monday for dinner. Please give them my apologies. I can't talk right now. I'll call you later tonight."

He closed the flip phone and turned to face Libby.

Her face had paled, but as he met her gaze, a blush rose on her cheeks. "Who was that?" she asked.

"Jocelyn Montrose."

Libby frowned. "Giselle's sister? Why would she be calling you?"

"We've been . . . She's been acting as my hostess since Giselle died. Lately we've been . . . dating."

"You're dating your late wife's sister?"

Libby's look was incredulous, and Clay could hardly blame her. He hadn't expected Jocelyn to end up helping him out with the political entertaining that was a necessary part of his job. But she'd been living with her father in Washington when Giselle died. He'd leaned hard on his sister-in-law in those first few weeks after Giselle's death, when he'd fallen apart. She'd been a great comfort. After that, it had seemed natural to call Jocelyn when he needed a companion for political dinners.

There was no denying she would make the perfect political wife. When her father had been ambassador to France, she'd often presided at his dinner table. Not only was she beautiful, but Jocelyn knew how to dress so she always looked her best. No matter how harried people around her got, she remained the picture of calm composure.

Beauty, tact, kindness—it was hard to believe one woman could possess so many good qualities. Clay knew she must have flaws, but so far he hadn't discovered any. Except that she was his late wife's sister, and no more likely to be comfortable in the wilds of South Texas than Giselle had been.

That was the only reason—the main reason—he hadn't moved in the direction Jocelyn seemed to be leading him. That is, toward the altar. But he hadn't discounted the possibility of marriage to her, either. He was still riding the fence, waiting for something to push him one way or the other.

If Kate hadn't disappeared, he wouldn't be here now, his insides twisted by feelings for the woman standing before him that he'd stuffed away nearly twenty years ago and kept a tight lid on ever since. And then he realized he might not be the only one who was dating someone else.

"Been seeing anyone lately?" he asked.

"Not recently."

"I'm surprised," he said.

"Why is that?"

He shrugged rather than say what he was thinking. The truth was, he couldn't imagine why any man wouldn't snap her up. She wasn't classically beautiful. Her eyes were too far apart and her mouth was too large. But her eyes, a bright sky blue, were always filled with emotion, her curly blond hair wrapped like silk around his fingers and her mouth could curve into the most enticing smile he'd ever seen.

"I think you'd better go," she said. "I'll call you if I hear anything."

"I'll keep my cell phone handy," he said. But he didn't move. He just stood there staring at her.

Clay wanted to cross the chasm that separated them, to pick up where they'd left off a lifetime ago. But he was afraid. Not of her father, but of what would happen if he gave her his heart and then lost her again.

It had been bad enough watching Giselle's body being eaten away until her skin was thin parchment over bones. But Giselle hadn't been his soul mate. Although a part of him had died with her, he'd been able to keep on living. He'd been able to think about the future. He'd been able to imagine his life in the years ahead.

Losing Libby the first time had nearly killed him. He didn't think he could survive it again.

Sometimes discretion *was* the better part of valor.

"Good night, Libby," he said.

"Good night, Clay."

He didn't go near her as he made his way to the door. She didn't see him out. He was in the car before he admitted that he'd rather have spent the evening talking with her than be anywhere else.

Then he remembered there was somewhere else he could go—needed to go.

He had an invitation from Niles Taylor to a party at a house on Bear Island. He had to stop at Forgotten Val-

ley to change his clothes and he might as well see if
Drew wanted to join him.

"Hey, Drew, you here?" he called as he stepped inside the back door of the ranch house.

"Yo," Drew called back. He trotted down the hall
dressed in sweatpants, a long john shirt and socks. "Any
news?"

Clay shook his head. "Niles Taylor invited me to a
party on Bear Island. Want to come?"

"Anyone I know going to be there?"

"Know any politicians? Oh, yeah, and Niles will
have some pretty girls there."

"You're the only politician I care to know," Drew
said. "And I'm not in the mood for games of seduction.
Think I'll spend the evening here. Besides, someone
might call about Kate."

Clay felt a spurt of guilt. Shouldn't he be sitting here
on his hands waiting for the phone to ring? He knew
he'd go crazy if he didn't have something to distract
him. He was terrified. And terrified to admit how scared
he was of what might have happened to his daughter. "I
know it's a long shot," he said. "But I'm hoping someone will approach me tonight and ask for a political
favor in exchange for releasing Kate."

"You're right," Drew said. "It's a helluva long shot.
But who knows? It could happen."

Clay took the time to change into a suit, knotted a
rep-striped tie and grabbed his black cashmere topcoat.
Even in a place as casual as Jackson, the politicians
wore suits. Western suits, sometimes. But suits.

On his way out, he passed Drew in the kitchen nuking a cup of coffee in the microwave. "I won't be late," he said.

"I'm not your mom. Stay out as late as you like."

"What the hell is your problem?"

"I don't understand why you'd leave Libby sitting home alone to go to some political cocktail party," Drew said angrily.

"I don't understand why you'd leave a perfectly good job in Houston to hide out here," Clay shot back.

"It's none of your business," Drew retorted.

"Back at you," Clay said.

Drew snorted. Then laughed. "God, we're in bad shape. Have a good time. Kiss a pretty girl for me."

"Come along and kiss your own pretty girl."

Drew shook his head. "The only girl I want to kiss is—"

"Back in Houston," Clay finished for him.

"That isn't what I was going to say."

Clay lifted an interested brow. "Really? Must be the detective then."

Drew made a gun with his thumb and forefinger and shot it. "Bingo."

"So, why are you sitting here?"

"Believe it or not, she's on duty. I called her house and her daughter said she was working another shift for some poor schmoe whose wife is having a baby."

Clay didn't think any man whose wife was giving him a child would think of himself as a "poor schmoe." When he'd married Giselle he'd hoped desperately for a child, until they'd discovered that she couldn't have babies. They'd considered adoption, but before they'd gotten around to it, Giselle had gotten sick. Then it had been out of the question.

He only had one child. And she was missing.

He needed a drink. Several drinks. And the company of men who wouldn't know to ask him whether he'd heard any news about his missing daughter. "I'm out of here," he said.

"Stay in touch," Drew said.

Clay patted the cell phone on his hip. "Yeah."

Clay had once considered buying a house on Bear Island. The lots were large—forty acres—and there were enough ponds around that a pair of trumpeter swans had taken up permanent residence. Buck-and-rail fences lined the properties. The cypress trees grew tall and the aspen made it a magnificent, golden place to be in the fall.

In the days before the town had decided to take an environmental stand, the homes had grown as large as twelve thousand square feet. Small by Hollywood standards, maybe, but most of the people who could afford enormous homes in Jackson only lived in them a week or two a year.

The town had put an eight-thousand-square-foot limit on new construction, but Clay was pretty sure, as he gazed at the lighted mansion at the end of a long drive, that this one fell under the old rule. He passed a guesthouse that was four times as large as Libby's cabin.

A beautiful young woman wearing a low-cut aqua cocktail dress and a dazzling smile answered the elaborate chime that served as a doorbell and led him into a room thick with cigar smoke, hearty laughter and glazed eyes.

He found himself facing Niles Taylor. The Texas oilman slapped him on the back and asked, "What'll you have?"

"Scotch. Neat," Clay replied.

Niles called the order to a bartender dressed in a tux without the jacket, who poured Clay's drink. "There are a few folks here I think you know," Niles said.

Clay took the drink Niles handed him and turned to greet the senior senator and three congressmen from Texas.

"Gentlemen, look who's joined us," Niles said. He smiled broadly at Clay and announced, "I give you the next governor of Texas."

"That announcement is premature," Clay said automatically.

"No need for modesty, Clay," Niles said. "You're among friends. We all want to see you make that move to Austin."

Clay spent the next two hours meeting an array of party movers and shakers, Niles always at his side greasing the wheels, making certain Clay never had to speak his ambition aloud. He'd learned over the years not to take more than a sip of any drink and to surreptitiously set the glass down. But at least three an hour were being slipped into his hand, and he was feeling light-headed.

He'd hoped someone would approach him about Kate, but it hadn't happened. And the longer he was in Niles's company, the more ridiculous it seemed to imagine the jovial politician involved in a kidnapping.

It was time to leave while he could still make it on his own two feet. "I've got to take off," he said.

"It's the shank of the evening," Niles replied. "You haven't met everyone yet." The Texas oilman pulled him along to another room to meet a cluster of his cronies, other oilmen from Texas with money to contribute to his campaign.

Clay suddenly realized that several of these men belonged to the oil consortium his office was investigating. He would have to be careful to watch what he said. It was often impossible to avoid fraternizing with the enemy in Washington circles, but it was wise to keep your hand on your wallet while you did.

He waited warily to see whether one of them would broach the subject of his investigation of the consortium. But they were either too cautious—or too shrewd—to mention it.

"That drink of yours needs refreshing," Niles said, and signaled the bartender for another drink.

Clay's glance followed Niles's hand and became riveted on a woman who stood at the bar in a stunning, form-fitting backless red dress. He sucked in his breath when the young woman turned around and he saw how very beautiful she was, dark-eyed and dusky-skinned and voluptuous. Then he realized the bartender had handed her his drink to deliver to him.

She kept her eyes fixed on the crystal glass, carrying it with both hands, as though it were nitro that might explode if jostled.

"Japan always needs more oil," Niles said to one of his cronies, momentarily distracting Clay's gaze from the girl. When she reached his side, Niles slid his arm around her bare shoulder and said, "This is Natalie. She's been wanting to meet you all evening. Natalie, this is Mr. Blackthorne."

Clay thought the girl looked young enough to be his daughter. She also looked nervous, understandable in a crowd of less-than-sober men. "It's nice to meet you, Natalie," he said, reaching out to take his drink from her.

"*Mucho gusto, señor,*" Natalie replied, barely touching his fingers as she made the exchange and then putting both hands behind her back.

Clay shot a questioning look at Niles.

"She doesn't speak a word of English," Niles said. "Not even *no,*" he added with a salacious grin. "If you know what I mean."

Clay felt sick. More than half the cowhands on his father's South Texas ranch had been Mexican, and he'd learned Spanish right along with English when he was growing up. In Spanish, he asked the young woman if she was all right.

She glanced at Niles before she replied that she was fine.

Clay didn't know why he didn't take her at her word. Maybe it was the quick glance she took over her shoulder toward a man in the corner after she answered. Maybe it was the knowledge that his own daughter might be in a compromising situation somewhere and need to rely on the kindness of some stranger.

"Why don't you and I step away where it's not so crowded, so we can talk?" Clay said, as he slid the girl's arm through his own. He wanted to get her somewhere she would feel safe enough to tell him whether she really was all right.

"Now you're talking," Niles said, winking at Clay.

When Clay tried to lead the girl toward the brightly lit kitchen, she resisted.

"I cannot," she said.

"You can't leave?" he asked. "Why not?"

"I cannot," she insisted.

She glanced over her shoulder again, and Clay looked to see whom she might be trying to find. The man he'd seen in the corner was gone, and nobody looked like they had any particular interest in the girl.

"Do you have a boyfriend here?" he asked, wondering if that might be her problem.

"No," she said.

"Would you like to go home?" he asked.

She shot him a look that told him that was exactly what she wanted. And then shot another look around the room.

"Who are you looking for?" he asked.

She bit her lip and stared at the ground. "No one."

"What's wrong?" he said. "I want to help."

"Nothing is wrong," she said hurriedly. "I will do whatever you want."

"I want us to go somewhere a little less noisy where we can talk."

Clay glanced around the crowded room and was surprised to see North Grayhawk with his arm around a very beautiful woman. North met his gaze for a moment, his eyes narrowing, but Clay was distracted from confronting the other man by a female touch on his hand.

"There is a bedroom upstairs," Natalie said in a voice that was barely a whisper.

Clay swore viciously under his breath. He knew girls were hired to be consorts at parties like this. He'd turned a blind eye in the past, but this was coming a little too close to home. What if his daughter were forced into a situation like this?

He took the young woman by the arm and headed for the front door.

"No, señor," she protested. "Please. I cannot leave. I will be—" She looked up at him, clearly terrified.

"Nothing is going to happen to you. I promise you'll be fine."

"Upstairs, señor," she pleaded. "Let us go upstairs."

Clay grimaced. She obviously thought he wanted sexual favors. And was prepared to provide them. She would find out the truth soon enough. "All right," he said. "Upstairs, then."

She looked relieved and smiled at him. "Sí, señor," she said. "Follow me."

She grasped his hand and led him up a spiral staircase and then along a maze of hallways. He thought of how large the house had looked from the outside and tried to imagine where she might be taking him. Finally, she opened a door at the end of a hall and he found himself in a Western-decorated guest bedroom.

A cowhide lay on the hickory floor, and the bed frame consisted of stripped-pine logs. The lamp base had been created with deer antlers, and the shade was oiled skin that cut the light and gave the room a yellow glow.

An elaborate display of the different types of barbed wire that had been used to fence the range hung above the bed. Clay ran his fingertips along the painted board, searching for the double-twist wire that ran along the borders of Forgotten Valley, and finally found a sample. He was more than a little surprised also to find the single-strand barbed wire that had been used in the early nineteenth century in Texas to fence his family's ranch, Bitter Creek.

The collection of barbed wire was a lot more rare than he would have expected. Another look revealed that nothing in the room was a reproduction, and everything was in mint condition. He felt resentful that someone had collected all these relics of past frontier lives, all this heritage, and put it in a place that was only visited by a few wealthy politicians and businessmen, most of whom probably had no idea what they were seeing.

He turned abruptly to face the girl and experienced a spell of dizziness that nearly toppled him. "What the hell?" he said, grabbing the post at the foot of the bed to steady himself. He looked at the drink in his hand. The glass hadn't been full in the first place, and most of the liquor was still in it. Then he thought of all the other glasses that had passed through his hand during the evening and realized he must have drunk more than he'd thought.

"I am here to serve you," the girl said.

"I don't want . . ." Clay realized his voice was slurred,

and that he couldn't keep his eyes in focus. "I want to help you," he said. "Talk to me. Tell me what's wrong."

He took a step toward the girl, and the glass dropped from his hand. He stared at his empty hand in confusion. He couldn't be that drunk. He never got drunk. So why did he feel so dizzy and uncoordinated. What the hell was going on?

He took another step toward the girl and stumbled into her waiting arms.

"Come sit on the bed, señor," she said, helping him take the few steps backward.

"I know a girl your age," he muttered. "Kate Grayhawk. I keep imagining her in your situation, you see. That's why I want to help you."

The girl's eyes went wide. "You know Kate? Kate Grayhawk?" the girl said excitedly.

Clay realized his tongue was too thick for speech and he nodded instead.

"I know her, señor. She is in trouble. We are both in trouble. Bad men held us captive in the mountains."

Clay grasped her wrist tight enough to make her wince and said, "Where?"

"I do not know," the girl said. "I am sorry, señor. I had to put the drug in your drink. I had no choice. He promised me it will all be over soon."

Too late, Clay realized he'd been set up. Kate's disappearance had been about him after all. Whoever had taken Kate had somehow found out she was his daughter. Otherwise, why had she been held with this girl? What was it they hoped to accomplish by drugging him? Maybe they planned to take compromising pictures of him to use as blackmail. He couldn't allow that to happen. He had to get out of here.

But he couldn't move. His legs wouldn't work.

He tried to think, to figure out what he should do next. He grasped at the phone at his belt, but his hands were too clumsy to retrieve it. His eyelids were heavy. His mouth would no longer work. He tried to push himself off the bed but fell back onto it instead.

The last thing he heard was a man's voice, and the girl's tearful voice in reply.

11

Drew was sound asleep when the phone woke him. He grabbed for it and missed, sending it clattering to the floor. He swore with great eloquence as he hunted for the cordless phone in the pile of junk on the floor beside the bed. He glanced at the digital clock, which told him it was 10:38 P.M., and realized he must have dozed off while reading in bed.

"Who is it?" he said in a surly voice, as he clicked the phone on and shoved it against his ear.

At almost the same moment he remembered that Kate was missing and said, "Kate? Is that you?"

"It's me."

Drew tried to place the male voice and said, "Clay? You don't sound like yourself. What's going on?"

Drew's heart was racing. The only reason he could imagine Clay calling was some news about Kate, and he felt sure that if it had been good news, Clay would have given it to him right off the bat. "Have you found Kate? Is she okay?"

"I need a lawyer," Clay said. "And a friend. How quick can you get here?"

"Where are you? What's happened?"

Clay gave him the address of the house on Bear Island where he'd gone for the party earlier in the evening. "As far as I can tell, the party's still going full roar. I need you to come find me. I'm in a bedroom upstairs, at the west end of the house, last room on the right. I'll be waiting for you."

"What's going on, Clay?" Drew asked.

Drew heard silence on the other end of the line, then a sigh, before Clay said, "You wouldn't believe me if I told you. I don't believe it myself."

"Believe what?" Drew said. "What's happened, Clay?"

"There's been a murder. A young girl."

Drew hissed in a breath. "Not Kate."

"No, not Kate," Clay said. "Get here fast, Drew."

"Have you called the police?"

"No! Don't call anyone. Don't talk to anyone. Just come find me. I'll explain everything when you get here."

"Are you all right?" Drew asked.

Clay hung up the phone in reply.

Drew dragged on a pair of jeans, cursing his cousin for being so secretive on the phone. Had Clay witnessed the murder? Had he found the body? Drew wished he knew more details. He'd done some criminal defense work with DeWitt & Blackthorne in Houston, but it had all been white-collar crime. If Clay was involved somehow in a murder, he would need the best criminal defense attorney he could get.

Drew followed the directions Clay had given him and found the house on Bear Island without difficulty.

He tried the front door and it opened, so he let himself in. No one noticed him as he moved through the smoky house. Everyone was busy talking and drinking and making out with nubile women. It reminded him of the few frat parties he'd attended in college, only these revelers were grown men, politicians and businessmen, the leaders of a nation.

Drew tried not to sneer in disgust as he made his way up the spiral staircase and down the west hall to the door on the right at its end. He knocked and said, "Clay, it's me."

The door opened and he saw a haggard figure who looked like he'd aged twenty years in the few hours since Drew had last seen him.

"Come in," Clay said, pulling Drew inside and closing the door behind him.

Drew's impetus carried him toward the bed, where he found a naked woman, her slender throat pierced by a piece of barbed wire that was wrapped tightly around it. He couldn't imagine where someone would have gotten barbed wire, until he saw the display over the bed and noticed that the wood had splintered where a strand had been torn free.

He turned angrily to Clay and said, "What the hell happened here?"

"I was drugged. I woke up in bed with her . . . like that."

"Why didn't you call the police?" Drew asked.

Clay met his eyes and said, "I was naked, too."

"Why didn't you call the police after you got

dressed?" Drew persisted. "Or at least get the hell out of here?"

"Too many people saw me go upstairs with the girl. I've been set up, Drew. Someone wanted me found with her. He glanced at the girl on the bed, then turned back to Drew and said in a steely voice, "Niles Taylor invited me here and introduced me to her. He's the man I want to talk to first."

"I thought Niles supported you politically."

"He does. He did," Clay corrected. "My office is investigating an oil consortium he's organized."

Drew met Clay's eyes and said, "This is going to ruin any political aspirations you might have had. You do realize that."

Clay nodded soberly, his eyes stark.

Drew's mouth twisted. "Of course you do. That's why you called me. You've been trying ever since you woke up naked in bed with a dead woman to figure out a way not to admit you were ever here."

"What I'd really like to avoid is spending the rest of my life in prison for a murder I didn't commit," Clay said dryly.

"If you haven't peed recently you might have enough of whatever drug was used in your system to—"

"Too late for that," Clay said. "Peed and vomited both."

Drew shrugged. "It was a long shot anyway. Some drugs don't leave traces. I hope you didn't call me here thinking I'd help you hide the evidence. I won't. Who do you want me to call?"

"The county sheriff has jurisdiction," Clay said. He hesitated and said, "There's something else, Drew. Something pretty important, I think."

Drew gave Clay his full attention. "I'm listening."

"This girl knew Kate. She said they'd been held captive together somewhere in the mountains."

"Why didn't you say so in the first place? Did she tell you where? Did she give you any idea who might have taken them?"

"I was pretty much out of it by the time she admitted anything. She didn't give me any details. Someone came into the room, someone who frightened her. I saw her eyeing a man earlier in the evening, but I couldn't tell you what he looked like. Whoever put her up to this—she admitted putting the drug in my drink—was here in this room tonight. When I woke up, I looked out the window—"

"To see if there was a way out," Drew interjected.

"To see what time of day it was," Clay said doggedly. "The point is, I saw someone with a flashlight out on the island. There's no reason to be out there in the dark except—"

"Maybe to dig a hole to bury a body," Drew finished for him.

Clay nodded.

"Only they didn't get it dug quick enough," Drew said. "Any chance he's still out there?"

"The light's not there anymore," Clay said. "And no one's been back here to get the body." Clay looked directly at Drew and said, "What if someone plans to use Kate the way they used this girl, as a murder victim?"

He glanced at the girl on the bed and added, "What if they already have?"

Drew looked at the brutal way the young girl's life had been ended. And imagined Kate in her place. "The sooner we get the police involved, the sooner they can question everyone partying downstairs. Someone knows who did this—and why."

Drew used his cell phone to call the Teton County Sheriff's Office. He had the number programmed in because he'd contacted Sarah there. When someone answered he said, "I'd like to report a murder."

Violent crime was practically nonexistent in a remote community like Jackson Hole. There were more suicides from depression and loneliness than assaults against persons. It wasn't the sort of place where you could commit murder and then melt away and hide.

Commercial airlines only flew in and out of the small Jackson Hole Airport a couple of times a day. The Idaho state line was twelve miles north of downtown Jackson, but you had to make it up the narrow, two-lane road that led over the Teton Pass, an icy path through the Grand Tetons with few guardrails to protect you from a precipitous fall. Once you'd made the climb, the closest place to hide was Idaho Falls, ninety miles away.

Pinedale was an hour south, but there was five hours of nothing on a two-lane state road before you hit the next spot of civilization. Yellowstone was an hour east. There was nothing west for the better part of a day, until you hit Salt Lake City.

There was no major crime in Jackson because there was no easy escape from the law.

"When the police get here, keep your mouth shut," Drew said.

"I need to tell them what she said about Kate."

"You've told me. I'll take it from here. You don't say a word. Too bad it's Sunday tomorrow. You're probably going to have to spend the day in jail waiting for a bail hearing on Monday."

Clay's gray eyes turned cold. "I know a few people here in town. Call Morgan in Washington and tell him to get out here. I'll be out on bail in time for breakfast."

"No judge is going to hold court on Sunday morning," Drew said. "Besides, you were naked in bed with a murdered woman, which makes you the likeliest person to have killed her. Who says you're going to get bail?"

"Call Morgan," Clay said curtly. "I can't find out who set me up for murder while I'm sitting in a jail cell. I can manage bail, however much it is."

"Didn't you hear what I said? You're a murder suspect. You may not be allowed to post bail. Judges tend to keep suspected murderers in jail until trial."

"I'm also attorney general of the United States, with close ties to the local community. I'm not likely to flee. The judge will see the wisdom of letting me out on bail."

Drew wondered if Clay could pull it off. They would soon find out. He called the number Clay gave him, then handed the phone to Clay.

"Hello, Morgan," Clay said. "I'm in trouble. I need you to make some calls for me, then get yourself here as fast as you can."

When he hung up, Drew asked, "What about your father? Do you want to call him?"

"No. I can handle this myself."

Drew crossed to the bed to take another look at the dead girl. Which was when he realized he knew who she was. "I recognize this girl. Her picture was on a poster in Sarah's office. She was reported missing three months ago." He met Clay's gaze and said, "Where do you suppose she's been all this time?"

"Wherever she was, that's where Kate is now," Clay said. "She said something about being held in the mountains."

"That's no help," Drew said. "This place is surrounded by mountains."

Drew had been anticipating a commotion, assuming the sheriff's office would arrive with lights flashing and sirens blaring. He was astonished, twenty minutes after his call, to hear a polite knock on the door and Sarah Barndollar's quiet voice saying, "Police. Open up."

Sarah had been skeptical when she got a call from the dispatcher to check out the report of a *murder* at a house on Bear Island. The very exclusive, very private enclave was set along a tributary of the Snake River outside the town limits of Jackson, which meant the county sheriff had jurisdiction.

Sarah's breath caught in her throat when the dispatcher said a young woman had been murdered, so a moment passed before she said, as calmly as she could, "Is this for real?"

"Maybe," said the dispatcher, whose name was Daisy.

"There's no *maybe* about murder," Sarah said.

"What I mean is, I think this might be a hoax."

"Why is that?" Sarah asked.

"The caller's voice was too calm and matter-of-fact," Daisy said. "He said there was a party going on downstairs but he was in an upstairs bedroom with the dead girl. I'm not about to send a bunch of police out to interrupt a party of politicians—who might very well end up being found in compromising situations—on some unidentified caller's say-so."

Daisy gave Sarah directions to the house and then to the upstairs bedroom where the murder had supposedly taken place.

Sarah had gone to the back door, acting like a deputy assigned to dignitary protection, although for some reason, none had been requested for this party. She could see, as she made her way upstairs, why the dispatcher had been so concerned about reputations. She saw famous faces with glazed eyes and arms around young women who were unlikely to be wives.

She released the strap that held her Glock .40 secure in the holster at her waist and knocked quietly on the bedroom door at the end of the hall, announcing, "Police. Open up."

"What are you doing here?" she blurted when Drew DeWitt answered the door. "If this was a ruse to get me here—"

"Come in," he said, opening the door wide. "The victim's over there."

Sarah stepped inside and made a quick visual sweep of the room, noting the naked woman lying still on the bed and Clay Blackthorne sitting in a chair across the room. "So there is a victim," she murmured.

This wasn't the first dead body she'd seen, but her heart was suddenly galloping as she crossed the room to check the girl's pulse. Her flesh was cold.

The apparent cause of death was strangulation. Dried blood made it clear the young woman had been alive when the strand of barbed wire that was still cinched around her throat had punctured her skin. "Poor girl," Sarah whispered.

Sarah noted the splintered wood on the display above the bed. Apparently it had been a crime of passion. She wondered what the murdered girl had done, if anything, to provoke such a vicious attack.

Sarah took out her cell phone and called the dispatcher. "That murder call was no hoax," she said. "Call the sheriff, the captain, the sergeant, and the coroner, along with enough deputies to make sure that no one leaves this place without being questioned first. It's going to be a mess, Daisy."

"Will do," Daisy said.

"You might as well call DCI in Cheyenne, too," Sarah added. There was so little violent crime in Jackson, the town didn't have a CSI of its own. Detectives worked the scene themselves and sent the evidence they collected to the state lab in Cheyenne for processing, or, in high profile crimes—this one certainly qualified—called in the Division of Criminal Investigation from the get-go.

"The politicians downstairs are used to white-glove treatment," Sarah continued. "And they're all drunk as skunks. They aren't going to want their constituents to know they were partying away while a girl was being murdered upstairs."

Once Sarah knew help was on the way, she turned to Drew and asked, "What are you two doing here?"

"Clay called me," Drew said. "I'm here as his attorney."

"Have either of you touched anything?" she asked.

"I closed the girl's eyes," Clay admitted.

"I told you not to say anything," Drew admonished his cousin.

Sarah had avoided the girl's face, but when Clay spoke, she turned to look—and recognized her. "Oh, no," she said. "That's Lourdes."

"She told me her name was Natalie." Clay frowned and said, "Actually, Niles Taylor told me that."

"Clay," Drew said. "That's enough."

Sarah made a mental note to question Niles Taylor, then turned to Clay and said, "What happened here? What was she doing here? What did you do to her? Did you rape her?"

Clay exchanged a look with Drew and said, "I decline to say anything on advice of counsel."

"Did you do this?" Sarah asked furiously. "She was only seventeen! The same age as your own daughter. How could you!"

"I didn't do it!" Clay shot back. "I woke up in bed with her, but I have no idea who killed her or why."

"Goddammit, Clay! I told you to keep your mouth shut," Drew snapped.

Sarah realized she'd blurted the fact that Clay had a

daughter. The fact that Drew hadn't commented on
her revelation confirmed to her that he knew the truth.
She turned to Clay and said, "You're under arrest for
the murder of Lourdes Ramirez." She pulled a pair of
metal cuffs from her utility belt and said, "Put your
hands behind your back."

"Is that really necessary?" Drew asked.

"Shut up and back off or I'll cuff you, too," Sarah
snarled.

"It's all right, Drew," Clay said. "I expected this."

He turned his back and presented his hands to
Sarah, who snapped the cuffs tight around his wrists.
She felt light-headed. She'd found the young woman
she'd been searching for, but far too late to help her.
She dreaded calling the girl's parents, but they would
need to identify the body before the coroner drove it to
Cheyenne to be autopsied.

"You don't belong here," she said to Drew. "You can
see your client once he's been booked."

"I think I'll hang out here," Drew said.

Sarah could have shoved her official weight around,
but Drew had already had time to do whatever damage
he wanted to do to the evidence. When the sheriff and
the captain and the rest of the cavalry arrived, she could
take Clay to jail, and Drew would be their problem.

By the time Sarah left the residence on Bear Island
with her prisoner, the entire house had been surrounded by crime scene tape and the Teton County
sheriff had shown up to supervise and smooth ruffled
feathers.

Clay asked if they could leave by the back door, and

Sarah saw no good reason why not. To her annoyance, Drew followed them. As they headed down the stairs, she heard politicians and businessmen blustering that they shouldn't be detained for questioning since they knew nothing about what had happened. Many of them had their cell phones to their ears waking up lawyers all over the country.

As Sarah locked Clay in the backseat of her Tahoe, she heard Drew tell him, "I'll meet you at the jail."

Sarah drove into the secured sally port at the Teton County Jail and escorted her prisoner inside to be booked and fingerprinted. His possessions were inventoried and he was outfitted in a yellow jumpsuit, which was assigned to prisoners accused of violent crime, and put in a holding cell to await a hearing with a judge.

She kept waiting for Drew to show up, so she could kick him out, but he never did.

"I'm going back out to Bear Island," she told the booking sergeant, "to see if there's anything else I can do."

"Buck is going to be pissed as hell that his wife decided to go into labor tonight," the booking sergeant said with a grin. "We haven't had this much excitement in years."

"This is the kind of excitement I could do without," Sarah said as she threw a wave over her shoulder.

When she backed out of the sally port, she found Drew standing in her way. She rolled down the window and said, "Move it or lose it."

He crossed to the window and said, "We need to talk."

"I've got work to do."

"I want to talk about the girl who was killed. About what she told Clay."

"You want to make a formal statement?" Sarah asked.

"I want to talk to you."

"I'm an officer of the law. Whatever you say—"

"Cut the bullshit, Sarah. This is important. Clay's daughter was being held captive in the same place as the dead girl."

Sarah gasped. "Are you sure? How do you know?"

"Clay told me. He got it from Lourdes before he passed out."

"Is that why Clay killed the girl? Because she wouldn't tell him where Kate is?"

"Clay didn't kill Lourdes. He was set up."

"Somebody did a hell of a job."

"No shit. Are you going to help me find out who set him up, or not?" Drew asked.

"I'm not.

"Why not?"

"I don't think our interests are the same here," Sarah said.

"Of course they are. We both want to find the killer."

"Even if it turns out to be your cousin?"

"There's not a chance in hell Clay murdered that girl."

"How did Lourdes get to Bear Island? Who brought her to the party?" Sarah said.

"I have no idea. But Clay said she was watching a guy in the corner—who disappeared—and Niles Taylor introduced the girl to him."

They were interrupted by a radio call. Sarah picked up the handset and said, "I'll get him now."

"What's that all about?" Drew asked.

"Nothing that concerns you."

"I'm not letting you out of my sight until you agree to help me," Drew said.

"If you want to waste your time following me around, it's no skin off my nose." Sarah closed the window, backed the Tahoe up and pulled into a parking spot. She heard Drew rev the engine of his Porsche before he realized she had parked her SUV and was on foot and headed around the corner.

He caught up to her as she reached the entrance to the Jackson Hole Municipal Building, which housed the Jackson Hole Police Department. It was a two-minute walk around the corner from the Teton County Jail, where she'd dropped off Clay, which was shared by town and county police.

"What's going on?" Drew asked as he leaned up against a counter that separated the public from the police. "What are you doing here?"

Sarah didn't bother replying. She simply headed down a hallway into an area where she knew a civilian wouldn't be allowed to follow.

Sarah had wanted to pick up Nate sooner, but the traffic accident south of town had been a bad one and had taken several hours to clear. Then she'd had a domestic call and a stolen snowboard call and finally the call to the house on Bear Island. This was the first chance she'd had to come for her stepson, who'd been waiting in isolation in an interview room until she could retrieve him.

She wanted to go back to Bear Island and question Niles Taylor herself, but she conceded it would be better to let her boss do it, so she didn't have to spend any more time tonight away from her kids. She would call Jim later tonight and find out what Niles had said.

Thank goodness the Jackson policeman who'd caught Nate vandalizing one of the arches on the town square had been a friend, or her stepson might have found himself caught up in the juvenile justice system.

Harry led her back to a 10x10-foot beige room where Nate sat at a round wooden table, his head in his hands. "Are you ready to go home?" she asked.

He almost leapt off the chair and was across the small room in two gangly strides. "Mom! Where have you been? I thought something had happened to you. I've been going nuts in here. No one would tell me anything."

She didn't apologize for having to work a second shift, or for being late to pick him up, or try to explain where she'd been. She turned to the police officer who'd made the courtesy call to her and said, "Thank you, Harry. I owe you one."

She put a hand on Nate's back and guided him back down the hall past the dying ficus at the front of the building. "Where's my truck?" she asked.

"At the end of our block at Clive's house. He drove to the square," he said. "That cop took the keys from me when I got here, along with my wallet."

Sarah stood with Nate while the policeman who'd arrested him returned the property he'd confiscated. He'd had to hang onto it himself because there was only a receptionist working at the police department, which shared a dispatcher and other facilities with the county.

Sarah intercepted the keys as they were handed to Nate. "You won't be needing these."

Nate shot her an agonized look but apparently realized the wisdom of remaining silent.

Sarah didn't acknowledge Drew as she exited the municipal building with her stepson in tow. She couldn't stand the fact that she was giving him more ammunition for one of his diatribes against the likelihood of raising "good kids." She could just imagine what he would say about her parenting skills after seeing her retrieving Nathan from police custody.

"Hi there, Nate," Drew said, falling into step beside the boy. "What'd they get you for?"

Sarah was surprised to hear her son reply, "Copping an elk antler off the square."

"How'd you get caught?" Drew asked.

"That freakin' Phil started running when he saw the cop. If he hadn't done that, we'd have got away clean."

"You lose the loot?"

Nate shrugged. "An elk antler's not that easy to hide."

"Nope. Sure isn't," Drew agreed.

Sarah saw Drew's unholy grin behind Nate's back before the boy turned in his direction, at which point it disappeared.

"Your days of freedom are over, young man," Sarah said severely, as they reached the Tahoe.

"Aw, Mom," Nate said.

"Not another word, Nate."

As Nate slid into the passenger's seat and closed the door, Drew grinned again over his head and spoke to Sarah across the hood of the Tahoe. "Did the same thing myself when I was his age."

"And?" Sarah prompted, waiting to hear that he'd also been caught.

"Nate's right. Elk antlers are damned hard to hide. I tacked mine up over the barn door."

"Don't you dare tell Nate that story," Sarah hissed. "I'm trying to teach him—"

"The value of honesty and responsibility and other good things," Drew said. "Can we talk after you get him home?"

"It's late. I'm tired. It's been a long day."

"Every minute that passes means clues are getting cold, right? I think I saw that on *Law and Order*."

"Don't be flip," Sarah said sharply.

"Then it's true?" Drew asked.

"I can't—"

"I didn't know the word *can't* was in your vocabulary," Drew said. "How about it, Sarah? Want to help me unravel a mystery and find a murderer?"

Sarah grimaced. "You have five minutes after everyone's in bed. Then you go."

"Fine by me," Drew said. "I'll follow you."

He said the last words as Sarah was opening the door to the Tahoe. Nate heard them, watched Drew open the door to his Porsche and said, "If he's coming home with us, I'll ride with him."

He didn't ask for permission from Drew or wait for

Sarah to deny it. He simply bolted out the door and around the hood of the Porsche and into the passenger's seat of Drew's car.

Sarah waited, expecting Drew to kick Nate out of his car, but Drew just waved at her through his closed window, gunned the Porsche and tore out of the parking lot. She watched until he made a turn in the right direction, then sighed in disgust and followed him.

12

Drew wasn't sure why he hadn't kicked Nate out of his Porsche. Maybe because the boy reminded him of himself at the same age, yearning to be grown up but caught in a boy's body, with a boy's need for adventure. It was harder to prove yourself in the modern world. There were no savage Sioux to battle, no wild mustangs to break, no unexpected blizzards to catch you out on the range and force you to fight your way back home in blinding snow and freezing cold.

So you stole antlers from the town square.

Nate had a teenager's true reverence for fast, sleek cars, and Drew was sorry there wasn't time to stop and let the boy drive. But he could see Sarah's Tahoe in the rearview mirror, and he didn't think she'd appreciate him letting Nate drive his Porsche when she'd just, according to Nate, taken away the keys to the truck for "God knew how long."

Nate launched himself out of the Porsche with the same exuberance with which he'd entered it, talking a mile a minute as he led the way to the front door of Sarah's house. Nate shoved it open, and Drew followed him inside.

Sarah's stepdaughter was sound asleep on the couch, the younger boy tucked against her, dressed in pajamas. The girl woke the moment the door opened and sat up, startled. She instantly checked on the sleeping boy and put her fingertip to her lips and whispered, "Shh. Where have you been? I've been worried sick!"

"I've been riding in Drew's Porsche," Nate whispered back.

"Where's Mom?" the girl asked.

"Right here," Sarah said as she stepped inside behind Drew. "Move, Drew. You're letting all the heat out."

"You should see all the dials in Drew's Porsche, Mom," Nate said excitedly.

His voice was so loud it—or maybe it was the cold air—woke the younger boy.

"Mom?" he said, scrubbing at his eyes. "Where were you? Me and Brooke were worried."

Sarah crossed and sat beside her son and took him in her arms. "You should be in bed."

"Brooke and me waited up for you and Nate. But we fell asleep."

Despite the fact the boy was too big to be carried, Sarah picked him up. Drew instinctively stepped forward and took the burden from her arms. At first she held on, but he said, "Where's his bedroom?" and she turned and headed down the hall.

Drew could hear the two older children following them. Sarah stopped them at the bedroom door and said, "I'll put Ryan to bed. Nate, go take a shower. Brooke, go get ready for bed."

Drew set Ryan down on his bed and stepped back, ready to leave the room. The boy caught his hand and said, "I know you."

"Yeah, we met at breakfast," Drew said.

"What's your name?"

"Drew."

"Hi, Drew," Ryan said. "Did you help Mom spring Nate from jail?"

Drew laughed at the image Ryan's words had conjured. "Your mom did that all by herself."

"Get under the covers, Ryan," Sarah said, pulling the covers down and tucking her son's legs under them. She kissed him on the forehead and said, "Sleep tight. Don't let the bedbugs bite."

Drew backed out of the bedroom quickly, reminded vividly of his own childhood, where such scenes had been few and far between.

He could hear the shower running as he headed down the hall toward the living room. When he got there, Brooke was nowhere in sight. He kept going until he reached a large kitchen that harkened back to the days when families sat around the table and ate every meal together. He stuck his hands in his back pockets and waited for Sarah to find him.

She entered the kitchen a moment later and said, "Coffee?"

"Sure. Thanks."

She scooped some grounds into a coffeemaker, added water and hit the button, then opened the cupboard to retrieve mugs.

"Sugar? Cream?" she asked.

"Neither."

She made a face. "Coffee needs something in it to kill the taste." She retrieved cream from the fridge and a couple of packets of Sweet'N Low. In that short amount of time, the coffee had brewed, and she poured each of them a cup and carried them to the wooden trestle table.

He joined her and they drank their coffee in silence.

The phone rang and Sarah picked it up. She held her hand over the receiver and said, "It's my sergeant. He promised he'd call after he talked to Niles Taylor."

Sarah said "Uh-huh" and frowned and nodded and said "Uh-huh" again before she hung up.

"What did he find out?" Drew asked.

"Taylor said he thought Lourdes was one of the local girls who get invited to the parties he hosts by the woman who plans these events for him. He said Lourdes introduced herself to him as Natalie. He just thought she was pretty and that Clay would enjoy her company."

"That sounds like total bullshit to me," Drew said.

"It might be, but how are you going to prove he's lying?"

"Did your sergeant talk to the woman who planned the party?"

"She said she didn't invite Lourdes. That she'd never laid eyes on her before."

"Back to square one," Drew said in disgust.

"What is it you wanted to say to me that couldn't wait until tomorrow morning?" Sarah asked.

"I don't think Clay was supposed to wake up with that girl in his bed," he said.

"What makes you say that?"

"It doesn't make sense. Clay is worth a lot more to someone as a blackmail victim in his current position than out of politics entirely—which is what'll happen once word of this gets out. As attorney general he can investigate, or choose not to investigate, anything he wants—organized crime, labor unions, political party fundraising, illegal business tactics. As governor—or president—he'd be even more useful as a puppet on a string. Out of politics, he's wasted meat."

"You think someone took pictures of them together and forgot to get rid of the girl?" Sarah asked skeptically.

"I think whoever took blackmail photos thought he had more time to get rid of the girl. Clay said the girl drugged his drink. But Clay never takes more than a sip of any drink. It's how he stays sober over a long night of politicking."

"So he didn't take enough of the drug to put him out for the night," Sarah said.

"Exactly. He woke up eight hours too soon—in time to see someone mucking around on the island with a flashlight."

"Should I call my sergeant?" Sarah asked. "Should we be looking for a murder suspect out there?"

Drew grimaced. "He was gone the next time Clay looked. And if it was the murderer out there, don't you think the arrival of all those cops with flashing lights and sirens would have made him hightail it?"

"There's no way for him to escape the island without going past all those cops," Sarah pointed out. "Each of those Bear Island properties is connected only by a narrow land bridge to the actual island sitting out there in the Snake River."

"So he had a boat tied up on the other side," Drew said. "That way no one sees him coming or going."

"Maybe this guy's still on the river somewhere, or someone saw him on the river tonight." Sarah called the dispatcher and told her to let the field supervisor at the crime scene know about the man who might or might not have been on the island when the murder took place.

"I had one more thought," Drew said after she'd finished her call.

"Drew, I'm exhausted. I—"

"If you accept the premise that the dead girl was supposed to be disposed of and Clay become a cooperative blackmail victim, it would be possible to use the same MO endlessly in the same location."

Drew saw that he had Sarah's full attention.

"You think this has happened on Bear Island in the past? To other political figures?"

"It's a possibility," Drew said. "And raises the intriguing question of what your husband might have seen when he was there doing repairs fifteen months ago."

Sarah's face held an arrested expression. "You think they've buried a body, or bodies, on Bear Island?" Sarah asked. "I can't believe they'd take that kind of risk. It's too close to home."

"But convenient if you're trying to get rid of a large male."

"We looked on the island for Tom," Sarah said. "He wasn't there."

"You didn't find him when you looked the first time," Drew said. "That doesn't mean he isn't there."

Sarah's face paled. "You think Tom saw something? You think they killed him? And buried him on Bear Island?"

"I can't imagine any man leaving you, Sarah. Not of his own free will."

Sarah's eyes glistened suddenly with tears.

"It would be easy to miss a grave in all the undergrowth," Drew continued. "The place is mostly tangled vines and swamp. Just wrap up the body, and when the coast is clear, walk it across to Bear Island on the land bridge, dig a hole in the dark and bury it."

"Who's buried on Bear Island?" Nate said, entering the kitchen with his head bent under a towel he was using to dry his wet hair. He was barefoot and wearing a ratty green terry cloth robe. He pulled the towel free and said, "Mom?"

Sarah stared at him like a deer caught in headlights.

Drew tried to think of something to say that wouldn't provoke the boy into another dangerous adventure. He settled for saying, "No one. At least, no one that we know of."

"Who do you think might be buried there?" Nate persisted.

Drew heard footsteps and Brooke appeared in the kitchen doorway.

"Daddy," she said, her hazel eyes bleak. "Drew thinks Daddy might be buried on Bear Island."

"You're shittin' me, right?" Nate said, his gaze shifting from Brooke to his mother to Drew and back again.

"Watch your language, Nate," Sarah said.

"I heard them talking," Brooke said. "They think Daddy might have seen something bad happen to one of the missing girls, so he was murdered and buried on Bear Island."

"No shit!" Nate exclaimed.

"Nate!" Sarah said as she rose to her feet. "That's enough. You two should be in bed."

"But we're not in bed," Brooke pointed out. "We're here and we heard what you said. There's no taking it back, Mom. We know. So what are you going to do about it?"

"What is it you expect me to do?" Sarah demanded.

"Go to Bear Island," Brooke said. "Find Daddy."

"Brooke," Sarah said, her voice gentle, "it's very unlikely that Daddy—"

"You just don't want to find him!" Brooke said. "You wanted him to go and you're glad he's gone. You don't care that he might be—" Brooke swallowed a sob. "That he might be dead! That he might be buried in some swamp."

Sarah reached for her daughter, but Brooke pulled free and ran for her room. Sarah shot Drew a helpless look and headed after her, leaving him alone with a stunned Nate.

"Do you think it's true?" Nate asked. "Is my father buried on Bear Island?"

"Your mom said they already looked for him there once, and didn't find him," Drew said.

"But it makes sense," Nate said, rubbing harder at his hair with the towel. "Dad did mechanical repairs and handyman stuff whenever the tow business was slow. He was there the day he disappeared. Maybe he did see something."

"You and Brooke stay away from that island," Sarah said, reappearing in the kitchen doorway.

"Are you going to take another look, Mom?" Nate asked.

"I'm an officer of the law. I'd need probable cause and a warrant to go digging around out there. Drew's wild guess about your father being buried there is just that—a crazy idea. So no, I'm not going on a wild-goose chase around Bear Island."

"But, Mom—"

"Neither are you," Sarah said. "Go to bed, Nate. Forget about Bear Island."

Once Nate was gone, Sarah sank into the chair across from Drew and said, "I'm not sure whether I want Tom to be there or not."

"Does that mean you're going to take a second look?" Drew asked.

Sarah sighed. "What I told Nate is true. I'm an officer of the law. And I don't have probable cause."

"A murderer might have been out there tonight. Isn't that probable cause?"

Sarah looked thoughtful. "I might have probable cause, but I'll still need a signed warrant to search."

"I'm not under those constraints," Drew said. "All I need is a good excuse. Which I have."

"You'd be trespassing," Sarah said.

Drew grinned. "I don't plan to get caught. Want to come along?"

"Don't tempt me."

"Didn't know I'd have to. Come on, Sarah. Don't you want to know for sure?"

"What are the chances we could find a body that's been there fifteen months?"

"You have to remove vegetation to dig a grave. It was so dry last summer nothing was growing. All we have to do is search the island for a body-sized barren spot. Are you coming? Or do I go alone?"

"I can't go, Drew. Any evidence that Tom was murdered and buried there that I found without a warrant would be—"

"Fruit of the poisonous tree," Drew recited. "And inadmissible in court. All right, sweetheart. I'll go alone."

"I'm not your sweetheart," Sarah said quietly.

Drew rose and kissed her tenderly on the forehead. "All right. We're just strangers who had sex. Good night, stranger. I'll let you know what I find."

"When are you going?" Sarah asked as she rose to follow him to the front door.

Drew paused and turned to her. "If I go during the day, when it's light enough to look around, I'm liable to get spotted. It'll have to be at night."

"You think a flashlight won't give you away? Or were you planning to search by moonlight."

Drew smiled. "I'm probably not even going to need a flashlight, with the full moon so bright. Don't worry. I'll manage." He turned again to leave, but her voice stopped him.

"Drew."

He turned and saw that Sarah was right behind him. "What is it, Sarah?"

She reached out and gave him a quick hug. "Be careful."

Drew took her face in his hands and kissed her gently on the mouth. "You bet, sweetheart."

He was surprised at how hard it was to let her go. A couple of months ago he'd sworn off women for life. Here he was feeling things he'd promised he'd never let himself feel again.

He reminded himself that Sarah had kids, and that kids were no part of his future. Which meant Sarah could be no part of his future. But that didn't mean that they couldn't enjoy each other right now.

He wondered if the brief connection they'd made would survive the discovery of her husband's body on Bear Island. He didn't know why he was so sure it was there. Maybe he just wanted it to be there. Until Sarah knew what had happened to her husband, she wasn't free to move on. He tried not to think why that mattered to him.

"Get some sleep, Sarah," he said. "This'll all be waiting for you in the morning." He kissed her on the mouth, tasting her warmth one last time, then let her go and stepped out into the cold.

Once outside, Drew realized he wasn't going to be able to sleep until he took a look at that island. The whole area was crawling with police right now, at least where the houses were located. But what if he waited a while and approached from the other side of the river?

Drew drove away wondering how hard it would be to launch his fishing boat at this hour of the night.

Brooke snuck into Nate and Ryan's room without turning on the light. "Nate," she whispered. "You asleep?"

"I was," Nate muttered.

"We have to go to Bear Island," Brooke said. "Right now."

"It's dark out, Brooke, in case you haven't noticed," Nate said.

"We have to go at night so we won't be seen."

"Then how are we supposed to find Dad—if he's even there?" Nate asked.

"There's plenty of moonlight."

From the other side of the room a small voice piped up, "And we can tape red plastic wrap over the front of our flashlights, so they're like, infrared."

"How come you're awake?" Brooke demanded.

"You woke me up talking so loud," Ryan replied.

"You can't come with us," Brooke said.

"Then I'm going to tell Mom what you're doing," Ryan said.

Brooke whirled on Nate and said, "Now see what your loud talking did?"

"I'm not the one who had the brainy idea of going to Bear Island in the middle of the night," Nate said.

"So we're really going?" Ryan said excitedly.

"Shh!" Brooke admonished. "You're going to wake up Mom. If you want to go, get dressed."

Ryan lit the flashlight he kept under his pillow to read after the lights were out, then jumped out of bed and began rummaging through his drawers for clothes.

"Are you really going through with this cockeyed idea?" Nate said.

"With or without you," Brooke assured him.

"Shit," Nate said. "I can't let you go by yourself. You're liable to get lost."

"I've got a better sense of direction than you do," she shot back. "But I need you to paddle the canoe."

"Paddle what canoe?" Nate said as he pulled on jeans over his long johns.

"The one we're going to steal," Brooke said.

Brooke waited for some protest from Nate. He merely continued dressing. Ryan said nothing, but his eyes went so wide they were white all around. "Are you going dressed like that?" she asked her younger brother.

Ryan looked down at his cowboy-patterned pajamas and pulled the top off over his head without unbuttoning the buttons. He pulled the bottoms off, revealing Jockey shorts, then searched through his chest of drawers, pulling out a long john shirt and bottoms and some corduroy trousers, a long-sleeved T-shirt and a wool sweater. Brooke crossed to help, but Ryan said, "I can do it myself."

"How are we going to get the keys to the truck?" Nate asked.

Brooke reached into the pocket of her jeans and pulled out a set of keys which she dangled before him. "Already taken care of that."

Nate grinned. "Guess we're really going to do this."

"Where's the Scotch tape?" Ryan asked, searching around the desk Nate used to do his homework.

"What do you need tape for?" Nate said.

Ryan held up his flashlight and a roll of red plastic kitchen wrap he'd been using to make a school project. "I need to tape some of this stuff—"

"That's stupid," Nate said.

"No, it's not," Brooke countered. "That red plastic wrap will cut the light." She crossed to the desk and searched through the center drawer until she found a roll of Scotch tape. While Nate shoved his feet into Sorel boots, she taped the filmy plastic to Ryan's flashlight.

"You'll drown if you go overboard in those," Brooke said, pointing at Nate's heavy winter boots.

"You know my feet get cold. I'll take my chances."

When she saw her brothers were dressed, Brooke crossed to the door and silently eased it open, looking down the hall toward her mother's room. Light seeped from the crack under the door, and she could hear CNN coverage of the murder on Bear Island on the TV. She turned to face her brothers and put her fingers to her lips, then slipped into the hallway and headed for the kitchen.

Ryan tripped on the rug and the flashlight banged on the wall.

Brooke's heart skipped a beat, and she stared down the hall at her mother's closed door.

"What was that?" her mother called from her room.

Brooke cleared her throat and said, "I was getting a glass of water and I tripped on the rug."

"Are you all right?"

"I'm fine, Mom," Brooke said, shoving the boys past her into the kitchen. She ran the water at the kitchen sink as though filling a glass, then set a glass down on the counter loudly. "Good night, Mom," she said.

"Good night, Brooke."

Brooke followed Nate and Ryan down the street to Nate's friend Clive's house, where they got into the truck and closed the doors with barely a click behind them.

"Where are we going?" Nate asked as he started the truck.

"I have a friend who lives at John Dodge," Brooke said, naming an expensive neighborhood across the river from Bear Island. Every home in John Dodge had a pedestrian walkout to the Snake River. The wide dike that kept the river from overflowing was open to the public. "I saw a canoe beached near their boathouse the last time I visited. We can borrow that."

"How big is this canoe?" Nate asked. "Are we going to be able to get it into the water?"

"Big enough for the three of us," Brooke said. "You and I should be able to carry it."

"Your friend's not going to notice anyone stealing a canoe from their backyard?" Nate said skeptically.

"Their backyard goes back about three acres, so no, they're not going to hear or see a thing," Brooke said.

"Are you sure they're not around?"

"Pretty sure," Brooke said, biting her lip nervously.

"Where do we park Mom's truck?"

"There's a back road that leads to their place. We can park it there."

Nate met Brooke's gaze, glanced down at Ryan, who sat between them, then back at her and said, "What happens if we do find Dad's . . . I mean, what if we do?"

Brooke felt her stomach churn. "We'll cross that bridge when we come to it."

Nate followed Brooke's directions and finally cut the engine on the pickup at the end of a long drive that was bordered by naked birches and tall cypress. "How much snow do you think there is built up on the ground out here?" he asked.

"Not more than two or three inches," Brooke said. "We shouldn't have any problem."

She and Nate each took one of Ryan's hands to help him through the snow. The canoe was where Brooke remembered it being, turned upside down on an open wood frame that was sheltered by a pitched wooden roof. "There it is," she said. It was smaller than she remembered.

"That's barely big enough for two," Nate muttered.

Brooke had remembered the canoe as being bigger than she now realized it was. "It'll be easier for the two of us to maneuver," she said.

"Where do you suppose they keep the paddles?" Nate said as he lifted the canoe by himself.

Brooke looked around and realized the paddles weren't with the canoe. She turned to stare at the house and breathed a sigh of relief when she saw no lights were on. "They probably keep them in the garage," she said. "I'll go get them."

"It's going to be locked," Nate said. "And there's going to be an alarm system."

"I know where they keep a key hidden," Brooke said. Nate raised an eyebrow, but said nothing as Brooke headed for the house. The family vacationed in Jackson a couple of weeks in the summer and sometimes came to ski for a week in the winter. Otherwise, the house was vacant. Brooke had met the girl who lived here when she'd come last year to ski. They'd spent an afternoon talking at the Mangy Moose, after which the girl had invited Brooke back here.

As a policewoman's daughter, Brooke couldn't believe the girl had been so incautious as to retrieve a key from a "rock safe" lying on the ground near the back door when Brooke was watching, especially when they'd only known each other for an afternoon. Brooke had never taken advantage of the girl's naïveté—until now.

She looked for the rock safe where it had been, but it wasn't there. She felt a moment of panic, then saw the rock that held a key inside had been moved to the other side of the back door. She retrieved the rock, and sure enough, the key was inside.

Brooke breathed a sigh of relief and used the key on the kitchen door. She remembered the girl saying they didn't have an alarm system because there was nothing in the house worth stealing. What she meant, of course, was that they had enough money to replace the very expensive furnishings if they were stolen. Brooke had often wondered what it would be like to be rich.

For a moment she allowed herself to imagine what her life might be like if her mother married someone as wealthy as Drew DeWitt. She cut off the fantasy as quickly as it began. What she wanted was her father back . . . alive. She just didn't think that was going to happen.

Brooke would never believe that her father had walked out on them. She was as certain that he loved her as she was that the sun would rise in the morning. He never would have stayed away if he could've come home. Which meant that something bad had happened to him.

She didn't want him to be dead and buried on Bear Island. But she would rather know the truth than live in limbo. If he was there, she planned to find him.

Brooke headed straight for the door that led to the garage from the kitchen. The aluminum paddles were hanging in plain sight on the garage wall a little above her head. She rose on tiptoe to get them but lost her balance, and one of them hit her hard on the head as it came down.

She stood back, stunned, and let them both clatter to the cement floor. She put her hand gently to her head, expecting it to come away bloody, but all she felt was a patch of rough skin where the paddle had skimmed her forehead on its way down.

She breathed an inward sigh of relief. Her head hurt, but so long as there was no blood, she was fine. When she bent to retrieve the paddles, she lost her balance and had to grab onto the workbench along the wall.

She reached up to her head again, wondering if she was hurt worse than she'd thought. She let go of the bench and waited to see if the spurt of dizziness would return. When it didn't, she pulled her wool cap down carefully to hide the spot where she'd been hit, then squatted, rather than bending, and retrieved the paddles.

Her forehead throbbed when the cold air hit her face as she left the house, but she figured her bop on the head was a small price to pay. It could have been a lot worse. Like if there had been blood. "Got 'em," she told Nate, as she met him at the edge of the river.

He had the canoe in the water, attached by a rope tied off on a wooden stake. Ryan was already sitting in it.

"You get in and sit in the front," he said.

Once Brooke was setted, Nate handed her a paddle, then untied the canoe, got in himself and shoved off with the other paddle. If Nate hadn't built so many muscles kayaking on the Snake last summer, they would have been swept downstream.

"The water's moving really fast," Brooke said as she paddled hard upstream.

"What did you expect?" Nate said. "I told you this was a crazy idea."

"Just keep paddling!" Brooke said.

"I want to paddle," Ryan said.

"The current's too fast," Brooke replied.

"I want to help," he persisted.

"If you want to help, turn on your flashlight and aim it at the shore," Brooke said.

With the red plastic wrap on it, the light didn't carry far. "Did you bring another flashlight?" Brooke asked Nate.

"Actually, yeah, I did," Nate said.

He pulled a large flashlight out of the depths of his winter coat and handed it over.

"Give it to Ryan," Brooke said.

"Ryan, shine it toward the shore."

"Aren't you worried about someone seeing us?" Nate asked.

"So far, except for 'borrowing' this canoe, we haven't done anything wrong," Brooke said.

"What about breaking and entering to get the paddles?" Nate said.

"I didn't break in," Brooke countered. "I used a key."

Nate snickered. "I'm sure Mom will see it that way."

"Mom will understand," Brooke said. "If there's any chance at all we can find Dad— "

"Watch out!" Ryan called.

His warning came too late. The small canoe had hit something submerged in the water. It tipped wildly and began filling up fast with water.

"We're sinking!" Ryan cried.

"Push us free!" Brooke yelled at Nate.

"I'm trying! It's not working!"

"Don't lose the flashlights," Brooke said. "We're going to need them when we get to the island."

"How are we going to—" Nate railed.

"We'll have to swim," Brooke interrupted.

"I'll sink with these boots on," Nate said.

"Take them off," Brook said briskly. "Your coat, too. Tie the strings of your shoes together and loop them around your neck."

"There's no time. We're sinking!" Nate protested.

"Do it!" Brooke was yanking her winter hiking boots

off, tying the strings together, then slipping them around her neck and removing her coat, which she dropped on the floor of the canoe. Then she did the same for Ryan. "Nate, you're going to have to help Ryan. Ready, Ryan?"

"I'm scared," Ryan said.

"Don't worry," Brooke said. "Nate's a strong swimmer, and so am I. We won't let anything happen to you."

"The shore looks a long way off," Ryan said.

"It's not as far as it looks," Brooke said.

"Shit, shit, shit! This water's cold as a witch's tit," Nate complained as he eased into the water.

"Suck it up and swim," Brooke shot back as the canoe slid away into the icy depths. Nate was older, but Brooke believed she had a lot more common sense than her brother. She understood how dangerous their situation truly was. She'd seen *Titanic* enough times to know that you could freeze to death pretty quickly in water this cold.

She kicked as hard as she could for shore, urging Ryan to kick, too. Nate swam with Ryan secured in a rescuer's grasp, but the current quickly swept them downstream. Fortunately, they were caught in an eddy that was carrying them toward shore.

"I'm cold, Brooke," her younger brother gasped.

"Keep swimming!" she said. "Don't you dare stop. And hang onto those flashlights!"

They were still twenty feet from shore when Brooke realized she probably wasn't going to make it. She could barely lift her arms.

"Keep going," she told Nate.

"Let's stay together," Nate said.

"I can't keep up with you," she told Nate. She met his gaze in the moonlight and saw the despair there. She could hear his teeth chattering. "Please. Go," she told him. "I'll be right behind you."

"I'll come back for you as soon as I get Ryan to dry land," Nate promised.

"I'll be right behind you," she lied. "Head straight across Bear Island for one of the houses. They can call Mom to come get you."

"To come get *us*," Nate corrected. "Don't give up, Brooke. I'll be right back. I promise."

She could hear him swimming, but with the moonlit shadows on the water, she wasn't sure where he was. She thought about yelling for help, but there was no one to hear. Then she realized she would feel pretty dumb if it turned out there was somebody there to rescue her, and she hadn't opened her mouth to make a sound. She could no longer lift her arms out of the water, and her feet felt like they weighed a hundred pounds.

Brooke took a deep breath and shouted, "Help! Somebody. Anybody! I'm here in the water. Help me, please!" She started sinking and choked on a swallow of icy water.

"I'm drowning!" she cried, terrified. "Heellllp!"

But no one answered. Not even Nate or Ryan.

13

Drew felt his gut churning as he drove away from Sarah's house. He must be pretty desperate to suggest Sarah's missing husband was buried on Bear Island. With the mountains and valleys and forests around Jackson Hole, there were a million better places to hide a body. The girl whose body had been found had been buried a long way from town.

But a grown man's dead weight was a lot heavier to cart around. Maybe whoever was running this black-mail and murder scheme had buried Tom Barndollar's body in the most convenient spot, knowing that if other bodies were discovered far away, no one would ever think to look on Bear Island.

The problem was Tom's missing truck. Men had left home with less. The missing truck gave Tom mobility. The missing truck meant Tom might not be dead, that, despite having a wife and kids he supposedly loved, he'd flown into the wind.

Which made Drew's proposed moonlight venture seem all the more absurd.

Drew snorted in disgust. Talk about a fool for love. Here he was making up scenarios that would free Sarah for a real relationship with him, when he knew damn well he wasn't going to commit himself to someone who had three kids. Hell, one kid would have been too many. He knew better than to think he could be a good parent. He didn't have a role model for the job, and at thirty-five, he was too old to learn.

He found himself turning left instead of right, heading down the road that led home, instead of the road that led to Bear Island. He couldn't help thinking, as he rode down what was normally a pitch-black road, that the moon was certainly right for a nighttime adventure. It was bright enough that he could see the rolled bales of hay in the field beneath a shallow layer of snow.

As he pulled his Porsche into the four-car garage, he noticed the small fishing boat on its trailer at the far end of the garage. Next to it sat his repaired pickup.

Drew lingered in his Porsche long enough for the garage lights to go out automatically. He fought a battle with himself in the dark. It was a wild-goose chase, plain and simple, just as Sarah had said. It was no more than forty degrees out there, although that was warmer than it sounded, since there was little or no humidity in Jackson.

How did he expect to find anything, anyway, when the island was a morass of vegetation? He was going to spend a lot of time and energy tramping around in the cold and the dark and feel like a prize idiot when he was done.

Drew got out of his Porsche and headed into the darkened house. He made straight for the living room without turning on a light in the kitchen. He turned on a lamp with an antler base near a modern wet bar, then proceeded to fix himself a drink. He found some aged scotch, poured it into a crystal tumbler along with some ice, and crossed to the chair by the fireplace.

The housekeeper had removed the ashes and laid a new fire, and Drew struck a match to the kindling before settling into the studded leather chair that was a part of his family history. It sagged in the seat where so many of his powerful forebears had sat their rumps. Drew had known for many years that no descendant of his was going to occupy this chair.

Not that he hadn't imagined what it might be like to have kids of his own. The problem was, a man needed a woman to bear his children. But he'd seen what an angry, unhappy, discontented woman could do to innocent kids. He wasn't going to subject any child of his to that kind of hell.

An image formed in his mind of Ryan reaching out to Sarah, who picked him up, despite the fact he was too heavy for her. Of Sarah rescuing Nate from jail and hugging him to her, before she meted out punishment that was neither cruel nor abusive.

Drew was much more familiar with scenes like the one with Brooke curved protectively around her younger brother on the couch, waiting for a parent who was late coming home. But Sarah's appearance hadn't been the cause of even more fear. Brooke had seemed relieved to see her mother.

Drew realized suddenly that what he'd feared for so many years was not his own ability to love his children, but that the woman he chose to love might not love his children.

Sarah would love any child of hers . . . and yours.

So maybe there were some women who could love their children — any children — wholeheartedly. Maybe there were some women it was safe to love.

The sound of the phone ringing startled him. Who could be calling him? Sarah?

Drew leapt for the phone, aware of the surge in his pulse at the thought that Sarah might be on the other end of the line. He didn't want to care for her, didn't want to find himself falling down that well of vulnerability. But he couldn't seem to stop himself. He picked up the phone, his heart pounding in his chest, but before he could say a word, he heard Jackson Blackthorne on the line.

"I just got a call from a friend of mine," Blackjack said. "Is it true? Was Clay found in bed with a young woman who'd been strangled?"

"Yes, it's true," Drew said. "He called me—"

"Why wasn't I informed immediately?"

"Clay didn't want—"

"I don't give a damn what Clay thinks he wants," Blackjack said. "I'll be there in the morning."

In the background, Drew could hear Blackjack's wife Ren asking for the phone. A moment later he heard her voice.

"Drew? Is Clay all right?"

"He's fine, Mrs. Blackthorne." He was surprised that she sounded so genuinely concerned. Clay was Blackjack's son, not hers.

"What about that poor young woman's family?" Ren asked. "What's being done for them?"

"I don't know," Drew admitted. He hadn't even thought about the girl's family.

"Would you please find out what you can?" Ren said. "I'd like to visit them tomorrow."

"You're coming here?"

"Of course we're coming," Ren said.

A moment later, Blackjack was on the phone again. "You tell that son of mine I'll have him out of there by morning."

"Tomorrow's Sunday," Drew reminded him.

"I don't give a damn what day it is," Blackjack said. "Clay will be out of jail tomorrow morning or I'll know the reason why."

Drew found himself holding a phone that had been disconnected. He set it down quietly.

He'd never known his father. The man had sired him and moved on. He wasn't sure he envied Clay his father. His cousin had been forced to fight all his life to be his own man. Blackjack had stepped right in to solve his son's problems without giving Clay the opportunity to solve them on his own. Drew would have hated that sort of interference in his life.

That was simply another example of how hard it was to be a parent. There were a thousand things you needed to learn. When to step in and when to step away. When help was wanted and appreciated and when it would only be resented. Parenting was a quagmire. Drew couldn't understand why so many people stepped into it. Maybe it was like quicksand. It didn't look as dangerous as it was.

Sarah seemed to have a handle on it. As much as any parent could.

Which brought him full circle to the decision about whether or not to go back out into the cold to look for a body on Bear Island.

"Hell," Drew muttered. Someone had been out on Bear Island the same night a young woman was murdered. He owed it to Clay, and to himself, to at least check it out.

He headed into the kitchen, set his glass on the counter and grabbed his coat from the rack on his way back to the garage. He opened two of the four garage doors, drove his pickup out and backed it up to hitch it to the boat trailer.

Forgotten Valley bordered the confluence of the Gros Ventre River with a tributary of the Snake that was navigable. Drew simply drove to the ramp built on his property and launched the fishing boat. He'd done enough adventuring on the river with Clay when he was younger that he knew where he was going. The small boat engine was surprisingly quiet as he headed upstream in the moonlight.

Few of the homes that bordered the river were lit. Drew knew it was more a case of people not being in residence than of people being asleep. It was a sad truth that most of those who could afford to own homes in Jackson Hole didn't live in them year-round.

Drew was as guilty as the rest, even though he believed that, with its majestic Grand Tetons, its forests of pine and spruce and aspen, and its abundance of wildlife, Jackson Hole was one of the most beautiful places in the world to live.

It was also the kind of place that gave you too much time alone with your thoughts.

Drew still hadn't figured out what to do with the rest of his life. He wasn't sorry to be wealthy, but it gave him almost too many options. He had no interest in doubling or tripling his money. He had no interest in a life of leisure. He wanted to do work that was satisfying and fulfilling and made the world a better place. Being a lawyer had filled that role until now.

But he wasn't sure he wanted to go back to the cut-throat world of large law firm practice. There had to be something else that he would enjoy as much — or more. He just hadn't found it yet.

Drew saw the outlines of Bear Island ahead on his left and wondered where he ought to go ashore. He'd kept an eye out, but so far he hadn't seen anyone else crazy enough to be on the river at this hour of the night, not even the police.

He looked for some sign of life in the houses that were connected to the island, and saw lights on in the one where the murder had occurred earlier in the evening. He guessed the police were still working the scene. The last thing he wanted to do was get caught trespassing.

Drew heard splashing ahead and wondered if he was going to have to deal with a moose that had decided to swim the river. The dopey-looking animals, which could weigh as much as a thousand pounds, were surprisingly aggressive. Or maybe an elk had wandered from the reserve on the north end of town and decided to take a moonlight swim.

Drew was smiling at the image he'd conjured when he heard an honest-to-God shout for help. A female shout for help. He turned up the power on the tiny boat engine as far as it would go and raced toward the sound.

All he could think was that the bad guys needed to dispose of another female. The one female he knew they had was Kate Grayhawk.

"I'm coming, Kate!" he shouted. "Hold on!"

"I'm drowning," he heard in the distance. "Heeel-llp!"

As he rounded a bend in the river, Drew saw some-one splashing in the water not more than twenty feet from shore. As he headed in the girl's direction, he saw her head slip beneath the surface. "Hey!" he shouted. "I'm here!"

He saw the head bob up again and wasn't sure whether she'd heard him or not. He brought the aluminum boat as close to her as he could get, then leaned over and caught hold of her shirt.

Wet hair covered her face, and he couldn't see who it was he'd dragged over the edge of the boat and into his arms. "Kate?" he said anxiously, shoving her hair back. "Is it you?"

Then the moonlight hit the girl's face, and he rec-ognized her. "Brooke? What the hell are you doing out here?"

"Nate," she gasped. "And Ryan. Did you see them?"

"They're in the water, too?" he asked, searching the river in both directions and then the shoreline.

"Our canoe sank," she said, her teeth chattering. "Nate and Ryan were swimming ahead of me."

"I don't see them. We'd better call for help." He reached into his coat and realized he'd been in such a hurry, he hadn't brought his cell phone. He started to swear, remembered she was only fifteen, and bit back the profanity. He grabbed an old wool picnic blanket in the stern and wrapped it around the shivering girl.

"Do you think they made it to shore?" she asked.

"We'll have to find that out after I get you someplace where you can get warm," Drew said, turning the boat toward the opposite shore, where there were homes with a phone.

"No!" she said grabbing his arm. "We have to go look for them. They'll be scared. Nate might go back into the water looking for me. He'll freeze and drown."

Drew hesitated only a moment before he turned the boat back around and grounded it against the shoreline. He jumped out and tied it off. "You stay here," he said. "I'll take a quick look around. If I don't see them, we're outta here."

"I'm coming," Brooke said, clambering over the side of the boat onto the island.

"No, you'll be—"

"I'll be warmer moving around than sitting here in the cold," she said.

She was right, and if he had an eye on her, he could make sure nothing bad happened to her. "Let's go," he said. "Stay with me."

They were already deep in the underbrush before he

realized he hadn't brought a flashlight. "I thought we'd have more light," he muttered.

"That's why we brought flashlights," Brooke said.

"Your brothers have flashlights?"

"If Ryan didn't lose them in the water."

Drew peered ahead through the tangled undergrowth, hoping to see a beam of light. "We'll never find them in this stuff."

"I told them to head for the houses on the other side of the island," Brooke said.

"I thought you said Nate would head back into the water."

"If he didn't come back looking for me," Brooke said somberly, "it's because he couldn't."

Drew remembered the man with the flashlight Clay had seen earlier that night on the island. He didn't want to think about what might have happened to the two boys, assuming they'd actually made it to shore. "Can you walk any faster?"

"Walk as fast as you want," Brooke said. "I'll keep up."

Drew abruptly put a hand out to stop her, and said, "Shh." He pointed in the direction of a bobbing red light. "Someone's coming."

He heard Brooke draw breath to shout and clamped a hand over her mouth. In her ear he whispered, "Wait until we see who it is."

She looked up at him with frightened eyes, the whites reflecting in the moonlight. She nodded, and he let her go.

Drew stood, holding his breath, and watched as a

man with a red-beamed flashlight marched two persons, one tall, one short, ahead of him back toward the water.

"It's—" Brooke began.

Drew clamped a hand across Brooke's mouth again as he recognized her two brothers in the faint red glow. He strained to see who was holding the light, but to no avail. What he did see was the outline of a handgun.

". . . right back into the water," a male voice said.

Drew realized that whoever had caught the two boys was marching them right back to the river—to drown them. He tried to think of a way he could save them without putting Brooke at risk. The underbrush would make a lot of noise if he tried to intercept them. But what other choice did he have?

"Lie down," he told Brooke. "I want you out of the line of fire if he starts shooting."

"But—"

"Do it!"

As soon as she was down, he shouted, "Police! Drop your gun! We have you surrounded."

As soon as he said it, he realized how much it sounded like a bad TV script, but to his amazement, it had the exact effect he'd hoped it would. The man with the flashlight turned toward the sound of his voice, and with the light off of them, he heard the two boys take off running.

Unfortunately, the light found him, and the instant the man realized Drew wasn't the police, and that the kids had taken off running, he made a growling sound and shot at Drew.

Drew had anticipated the shot, and the bullet that would have hit him in the heart only tugged at his sleeve as he dove to the ground. Drew wondered if the noise of the shot had carried to the police still in the house, or whether the wind had carried it away or the noise of the river had drowned it out.

An instant later the flashlight went out and Drew heard the sound of someone running back toward the houses on shore.

Drew wanted very badly to go after him, but Brooke grabbed at his ankle and cried, "Don't leave me!"

As he turned to help her up, he heard Nate calling, "Is that you, Brooke?"

"Yes, it's me!" she called back. "Are you and Ryan okay?"

Drew watched as the siblings fell into each other's arms, Ryan and Brooke crying, Nate trying very hard not to cry.

"We need to get the hell out of here," Drew said. "Before that guy comes back with help."

"We can't leave," Nate said. "They'll move Dad if we do."

"What?" Drew said.

"When Ryan and I came ashore, we saw a light in the brush ahead of us. We walked in that direction and that's when we saw them. They were digging up a body."

"*They* were digging?" Drew said. "That guy *is* going for help. Let's—"

"How do you know it's Daddy they were digging up?" Brooke interrupted.

"I saw his shirt in the light. That blue-and-white-and-green plaid one he was wearing the day he disappeared," Nate said.

Brooke turned to Drew and said, "We can't leave, Drew. If that is our dad, we have to—"

"I'm sorry if that was your dad they were digging up, Brooke, but those guys mean business. We need to get out of here now, while we still can. They're not going to want witnesses."

"We're not going," she said, her teeth chattering from fear as much as the cold, Drew believed. She turned to Nate and said, "Do you think you could find your way back to . . . there?"

"Sure. Let's go."

Drew watched as Sarah's children took off in the same direction the man with the gun had taken. They were holding hands to stay together in the dark, single-minded in the pursuit of their father's corpse.

"Sonofabitch," Drew muttered as he hurried after them. He understood why Sarah's children were determined to go on. He just hoped like hell he could protect them from whatever danger lay ahead.

Sarah didn't know what woke her. Some premonition? Mother's intuition? She sat up with a start, knowing something was wrong. She eased open the drawer in the chest beside her bed where she kept her Glock and slowly chambered a round. Then she rose soundlessly from the bed and headed on tiptoe down the hall.

She had kept night-lights in plugs around the house since Ryan was a baby, so she could see without turning on an overhead light. There was also a surprising amount of moonlight.

She reached the boys' room first, eased the open door wide—and gasped when she saw the two empty beds.

She whirled and hurried down the hall to Brooke's room. She shoved open her stepdaughter's door to discover her bed not only empty, but unslept-in.

It didn't take Sherlock Holmes to figure out where her children had gone. Both Nate and Brooke had overheard her discussion with Drew about the possibility of their father being buried on Bear Island. What she couldn't understand was why they would have taken Ryan with them. He was just a baby!

Sarah's heart leapt to her throat when she realized her children would probably attempt to reach the island from the river. Ryan had only learned to swim late last summer. Surely Nate and Brooke wouldn't put him in a boat without a life jacket!

And where were they going to find a boat to get them to the island? Sarah tried to think of anyone her children knew who might have a canoe or a fishing boat or a raft, but couldn't think of anyone who wasn't a seasonal resident.

Maybe they hadn't been daring enough to borrow—or steal—a boat. Then she thought of Nate's recent theft of antlers from the town square. He was certainly bold enough to do something as stupid as this.

Sarah felt her cheeks grow hot, as the blood rushed to her face. She was furiously angry with her children.

And terrified by the possibility of what might happen to them alone on the river at night.

She'd slept in her long johns, and she hurried back to her bedroom to pull on jeans, a wool sweater and hiking boots. She debated whether to call on one or more of her fellow officers to help her find her children and then realized Nate would certainly end up in trouble with the juvenile authorities if he had indeed "borrowed" someone's boat without asking.

Nate had spent enough time with friends rafting down the Snake during the summer to be good on the water, and Brooke swam like a fish. But the water would be frigid. If they had an accident . . .

As Sarah gunned the engine on her Chevy Tahoe, she remembered that Drew had said he would be going to the island tonight. She pulled out her cell phone and called his home number. And got his answering machine.

"This is Sarah. If you're there, Drew, please pick up. My kids are missing. I think they've gone to Bear Island. If you get this message, call me."

She didn't have Drew's cell phone number and she wasn't sure how she could get it. She hoped that the reason he hadn't answered his phone was that he had, in fact, gone to the island, and that if her kids showed up there, he would take good care of them and make sure they got home all right.

Which presumed her kids would run into Drew, and not someone bent on doing bad things.

Sarah glanced down the street to where the pickup had been parked earlier that night. It was gone. She swore under her breath as she headed straight to the house where the murder had occurred.

Police had "frozen" the scene, preserving it until the arrival of special agents from the Wyoming DCI in Cheyenne. Sarah drove up to the house and parked but didn't join the cluster of deputies outside. She took her heavy-duty lantern from the Tahoe, made sure her Glock was loaded and walked around the house toward the footbridge that led onto Bear Island.

The area of the island closest to the houses had been cleared as a picnic site, but Sarah walked past it and onto the part of the island that had been left as natural habitat. There were no paths here, and the footing was uneven and treacherous.

She cursed when she caught her foot on a root and fell onto her hands and knees. The lantern tumbled out of her hand and the light went out. She hadn't realized how the trees overhead would block out the moonlight. She groped around with her gloved hands in the area where she thought the lantern had gone when it flew out of her grasp, but all she felt was frozen marsh.

"Damn, damn, damn!" she muttered. She stood up and kicked the underbrush with her boot, but no luck. Sarah was debating whether to go back to her Tahoe for a flashlight when she heard an echo of sound running downwind. A gunshot?

Sarah froze. She looked around, wondering if the police at the house had heard the shot, but realized the wind had carried most of the sound in the opposite direction.

She pulled her portable radio from the pocket of her

coat and said to the dispatcher, "Shots fired. Officer needs assistance. Bear Island—the actual island. Bring lights. It's dark as hell out here. And hurry!"

She wanted to run, but she didn't have enough light to see where to put her feet. She retrieved her Glock, made sure a round was chambered and began moving through the tangled growth as quickly as she could. Her eyes were intent, the eyes of a predator.

"I'm coming, my darlings. Just hang on until I get there."

14

Drew caught up to Brooke and said, "Don't you think it would be better not to subject Ryan to the sight of his father's rotting body? Come to think of it, you and Nate ought not to be looking at it either."

His intent was to shock her into a realization of what it was they were doing, but Brooke never broke stride.

"I've known Daddy was dead for a long time," she replied. "He would have come home to us if he were alive."

Drew was surprised by the certainty in her voice. "I still think—"

"I'd rather see him, and know that he's dead, than wonder forever what happened to him," she said.

"Brooke's right," Nate said. "This is something we have to do."

"Why not let the police take care of this?" Drew suggested. "Your mother—"

"Mom doesn't care," Brooke said. "She wouldn't even come here looking for Daddy."

"She explained that," Drew said, rising to Sarah's defense. "She needs probable cause to—"

"How about someone shooting at us?" Nate interrupted angrily. "You think that's probable cause something hinky is going on around here?"

"If these guys were digging up a body, it was only because they want to move it somewhere else," Drew said. "They're going to be highly pissed off if you get in the way."

"We already have," Brooke pointed out. "We're still alive and they're gone."

"That doesn't mean they won't come back," Drew argued. "We should be running as fast as we can in the other direction."

"We're not turning around," Brooke said.

"Then at least be careful," Drew warned.

"We're going to look before we leap," Nate assured him.

"But we *are* going to look," Brooke said.

"I'm cold," Ryan said through chattering teeth.

Drew realized he was still wearing his dry overcoat, while all three kids were wet. So much for protective paternal instincts. He unzipped his parka and pulled it off.

"Hold up a minute," he said. He stuffed Ryan's small arms into his coat and zipped it up.

"Thanks," Ryan said. "This is warm."

Drew quickly realized that the boy's hands were caught mid-elbow in the sleeves of the parka and that the hem nearly dragged the ground. Afraid the boy might trip, he scooped him up into his arms.

"Hey!" Ryan said. "I'm not a baby."

"No, you're not," Drew replied. "But your legs aren't as long as ours, and with danger lurking, we may need to move fast."

"Danger?" Ryan said, his eyes wide.

Drew cursed inwardly. He hadn't meant to scare the boy, but obviously Ryan hadn't been paying attention to the conversation he'd been having with Brooke and Nate. "There's at least one man out there somewhere with a gun. If we have to run, I don't want you to get left behind."

"Me, neither," Ryan agreed. "Okay," he said. "You can carry me."

Drew tried to think of the last time he'd carried a child like this. He'd carted one of his female cousins across Bitter Creek at a Christmas get-together at the Blackthorne ranch when he was twelve. But that was a long time ago.

The boy's arms circled his neck and after another minute of slogging their way through the thick underbrush, Ryan laid his head on Drew's shoulder. Drew gradually became aware that he was holding dead weight and realized the little boy must have fallen asleep. He shifted Ryan's weight and tightened his hold to make sure the child would be safe in his arms.

"There it is," Nate whispered at last, pointing toward a shallow grave that had been partially excavated. Moonlight shone in a clearing on the newly dug soil. "Dad's grave."

"You can't know that without taking a closer look," Drew said.

"I . . . I don't think I want to do that," Nate admitted.

"I will," Brooke said.

Drew handed Nate the sleeping boy and stepped in front of Brooke. "I'll do it."

"How will you recognize Daddy?" Brooke said. "You've never met him."

"I saw a picture of him and your mom on the piano in your living room," Drew said. He'd been looking at a more youthful, happier Sarah, but he hadn't missed seeing Tom. "You've told me he was wearing a blue-and-white-and-green plaid shirt." Which he needed to know, because there likely wasn't much of Tom Barndollar's face left to identify. "You guys wait here where you can't be seen. And be quiet."

Drew moved toward the grave site as quietly as he could. He'd done enough hunting to know how to stalk prey, but he'd never been the object of the hunt. He felt his neck hairs hackle and stopped dead.

Someone was out there.

Drew was well aware that if anything happened to him, Sarah's kids would be sitting ducks. Imagining Sarah's devastation if anything happened to one of her children made his stomach churn. There was no room here for error. Precious lives were at stake. He remained motionless, straining to see movement in the dark.

The grave site appeared to be abandoned.

Drew didn't want to look at a decomposed body, but he'd promised Sarah's kids he would determine whether or not their father was buried in the disturbed dirt. He moved forward cautiously, his eyes and ears alert for any sign that the man who'd shot at him had returned.

He heard nothing.

Drew let his gaze roam the area for a long time before he moved out of the concealing underbrush toward the mound of dirt and debris and the shovel that lay beside it. He knelt and saw the bones of a human hand. It was a grave all right. He released a soughing breath he hadn't realized he'd been holding.

"Stay where you are," a voice commanded.

Drew felt every muscle in his body tense.

"Stand up, but don't turn around," the voice ordered. "I have a gun aimed at your back, so don't try to run."

Drew knew he was a dead man if he didn't run, so running made a whole lot more sense than staying where he was. What he needed was something to distract the man with the gun, to give him a fighting chance to escape.

Then he spied the shovel.

The shovel was pointed, but more importantly, it had a long wooden handle. If he could reach it, he could swing it to some effect. He might injure or disarm, and would certainly distract the man with the gun, so he could make a run for it.

"Hey, mister!" he heard Nate shout from the bushes.

Drew cursed the kid for exposing himself and at the same time rose and whirled with the shovel in his hands, swinging it in a death-dealing arc.

Unfortunately, the man with the gun was too far away for the shovel to make contact. When Drew let go and the shovel took off, the gunman merely jerked aside, and the shovel flew by without even scratching him.

He stood there, gun in hand, moonlight reflecting

off teeth that were bared in a horrific grin. "Game's up," he said.

"You're right about that," a female voice said from behind him. "Don't move. You're—"

Drew dove for the bushes as the gunman pivoted and fired at the voice behind him. Drew heard the explosion of a second shot in almost the same instant. When he looked back, the gunman lay crumpled on the ground.

And Sarah stepped into the moonlight.

"What the hell are you doing here?" she demanded. "And where the hell are my kids?"

"Mom!" Nate shouted as he crashed through the undergrowth toward her, Ryan awake and wailing against his shoulder.

"Are you hurt?" Brooke cried, rushing toward her mother.

Drew saw the shock and relief on Sarah's face as she enfolded her children in her arms, like a mother hen gathering chicks.

Only this hen was still holding a smoking Glock.

He rose and checked the pulse of the man Sarah had shot.

"How is he?" she asked as Nate transferred Ryan into her arms.

"Dead," Drew replied. He was amazed at how calm she seemed, how unperturbed that she'd just killed a man. Then she tipped her head up and he got a better look at her eyes in the moonlight. Stark. Agonized. And he saw how her jaw was clamped. She wasn't as unaffected as she wanted him to believe.

He rose and slid an arm around her and felt her slump against him. He hadn't been wrong then. She needed a strong shoulder to lean on. His shoulder.

For a few moments, they all simply huddled together, gathering warmth and comfort. Then Sarah lifted her head and asked, "Why was he pointing a gun at you?"

He met Sarah's gaze over her children's heads. "He was digging up a body." He glanced down significantly at the half-covered plaid shirt revealed in the moonlight. "And we caught him at it."

In the distance Drew heard shouts and saw bobbing lights in the crackling underbrush. "Sounds like the cavalry has arrived."

"I called for help. I'll need to stay here to answer questions. Can you take the kids— "

"Mom, we found Daddy," Brooke said in a choked voice.

Drew watched as tears welled in Sarah's eyes. She threaded the fingers of her free hand through Brooke's tangled hair and pulled her stepdaughter close enough to kiss her brow. "I know, baby. I know."

"That sonofabitch killed him." Nate turned and kicked the dead body and then burst into unmanly tears. Drew pulled the boy to him and Nate clutched him tight, muffling his sobs against Drew's shoulder.

Sarah met Drew's gaze and said, "Can you get the kids checked out at the hospital?"

"Mom, we're fine," Brooke protested. "Just cold."

"I know," Sarah said. "Freezing cold! That's what I'm worried about."

"Cripes, it's gotta be forty-five degrees out here," Nate said. "That's not freezing."

"All we need is a warm bath," Brooke argued.

"I can see you're both shivering," Sarah said.

"I'll be fine when I get out of these wet clothes," Nate said. "I'm not going to the hospital. And that's final."

Drew's throat was tight as he watched Sarah draw her children close and kiss each one. He swallowed hard and said, "I'll take them home, if you want."

Then he remembered how he'd arrived on Bear Island. "As long as someone can give us a ride."

He saw the moment Sarah realized she was still holding her gun. She stuffed it into her holster, dug into her coat pocket and handed him a set of keys. "Take my Tahoe."

"But, Mom, no one's allowed—"

"This is an emergency, Nate," Sarah said, cutting him off. "I'll be home as soon as I can get there. I need to stay here a while and explain . . ." Sarah's voice trailed off and Drew heard her swallow hard.

He stepped closer and said for her ears only, "Are you all right?"

"I'm a little shaken," she admitted. "I've never shot anyone before."

He could feel her hands trembling as she transferred Ryan into his arms. He slid an arm around her shoulder and pulled her close enough to give her the comforting kiss on the forehead she'd conferred on each of her children. "Don't worry about the kids. I'll make sure they get warmed up and into bed."

Sarah looked up at him, her eyes shining in the moonlight, and said, "Thank you, Drew."

He felt his heart swell. "You're welcome, Sarah."

Then, as though he'd done it all his life, Drew turned to the two older children and said, "Let's go, kids. We've got a little hike ahead of us. When we get home, I want you all to take a hot shower and get right into bed."

He looked down when Brooke grabbed his crooked arm, but she was staring straight ahead, ignoring him. Nate strode along beside him, excited, now that it was all over, and rhapsodizing about how his mother had gotten the draw on the bad guy. Ryan wrapped his arms around Drew's neck, laid his head on Drew's shoulder and fell soundly asleep.

Unable to sleep, Libby had turned on the TV a little after two in the morning, staring transfixed as she heard the news of Clay's arrest on CNN. She made a phone call to the captain of the Teton County Jail, who was a friend, asking him if she could talk to Clay Blackthorne, since the girl he'd supposedly murdered had also been a missing person, like her daughter Kate. When he said yes, she threw on some clothes and raced into town.

Libby didn't need the heater in her Outback. Her body felt hot, flushed with anger. The man she'd considered making love to had ended up in bed with another woman the same evening. And the woman—only a girl, really—had ended up dead.

Libby couldn't believe Clay was guilty, but what was

he doing in bed with some woman when he was supposed to be focused on helping her hunt for their
daughter? And why hadn't he called to let her know
what had happened?

She gnawed her cheek. Reporters, print and television alike, were surely swarming the Teton County Jail
by now, hoping for some juicy tidbit to feed the ravenous public. Once they started looking into Clay's background, asking the locals questions, digging for dirt,
they might connect Clay to Kate, might even find pictures of the two of them together.

Libby shuddered to think of what kind of media
frenzy it would create if they discovered a young
woman who'd visited Clay whenever he was in Jackson
Hole had disappeared within the past forty-eight hours.
That much attention focused on Kate could get her
killed.

On the way into town, she heard Kate's name
being spoken on the radio. She turned up the volume
and heard the female reporter say that Kate was the
third local girl to be reported missing over the past fifteen months. She explained how a Nevada runaway
was found dead several months ago in the nearby
mountains. How the first local working girl reported
missing was still missing. And how a second missing
local girl, Lourdes Ramirez, had now turned up murdered. And finally, speculated about what Kate's fate
might be.

"Oh, God." The words slipped out. A prayer. A plea.
Libby had tried very hard to believe Kate would come
home safe and sound. Every hour her daughter was

gone with no word, Libby had sunk deeper into a well of terror.

Libby was grateful that Hank Studdard, the captain of the jail, was a hunter, and that she'd taken him on a couple of guided trips without charging him any fee. An enormous, trophy-sized stuffed turkey he'd bagged on one of their trips occupied the corner of Hank's office. Hank's noble, if homely bird, of which he was infinitely proud, stood as tall as a four-year-old boy and had saggy red wattles and a stringy black beard.

When she'd called and asked Hank if she could come to the jail to talk to Clay, he'd said, "Don't know why you'd want to march through that circus of reporters outside, but I owe you one, so come on. By the way, your daddy's here."

Her breath had caught in her chest. "What?"

"King Grayhawk himself," Hank said. "Said he has a word or two to say to the judge about bail for this prisoner."

"I'll be there in a few minutes, Hank," she'd said.

"Come to the back door," he said, "and I'll let you in."

The Teton County Jail was in a separate building across the parking lot from the sheriff's office, and as she'd feared, both buildings were surrounded by camera crews and reporters who'd flown in from television stations around the country. She parked three blocks away and forced herself to walk slow enough that she didn't end up slipping and breaking her neck on the melting ice and snow.

She rang the buzzer at the back door and Hank let

her in. "Come on in, sweetie," he said. "Your daddy's been keeping us all in stitches."

Libby stared at her father in disbelief. Her daughter was missing. A girl was dead. And all her father could do was make jokes, no doubt at Clay's expense. That was King Grayhawk, vindictive to the end.

"Where's Clay Blackthorne?" Libby asked the captain. "I'd like to talk to him."

"Sorry, sweetie," Hank said. "No one gets in to see him."

"On the phone you promised—"

Hank shrugged. "Can't help it, sweetie. Didn't know there were going to be so many folks around."

"Why did you let me in, if you weren't going to let me see him?" Libby asked with asperity.

A deputy approached Hank and whispered in his ear.

"Now the shit will hit the fan," Hank muttered.

"What's wrong?" Libby asked.

"Seems that boy's daddy has shown up here on my doorstep."

"Jackson Blackthorne is here?" Libby glanced at her father, who was regaling a circle of deputy sheriffs with another story.

Hank followed her gaze and said, "Don't see how I can get King to leave or the other to stay away. Bound to be some fireworks here in a minute."

"Let me talk to Mr. Blackthorne," she said. "Maybe I can convince him that this isn't the best time—"

She was too late. Jackson Blackthorne had evidently talked his way inside.

Libby was amazed at how much alike her father and

Blackjack looked. Both were tall, both broad-shouldered, both still lean.

Blackjack's hair was silver, his brows black, his gray eyes as implacable as stone. He was wearing a dark blue Western suit, with a crisply starched white Western shirt held at the throat by a silver bolo tie. He stood with his feet widespread in expensive alligator boots. The clothes might have been civilized, but there was no mistaking the craggy, sharp-featured face for anything but a man who'd spent his life fighting the elements.

Her own father's hair was still thick and dark brown, though it was never seen, always hidden beneath a Stetson, as it was now. His wide-set eyes were a clear, bright blue, like the arctic sea. He used his cane like a king's scepter to give him majesty as he limped—long step, short step, long step, short step—toward his enemy.

Blackjack focused cold gray eyes on King Grayhawk and said, "You've got no business here. This doesn't concern you."

"The hell I don't!" her father shot back. "You know as well as I do I have an interest in the charges against your boy. 'Specially in light of recent events."

Libby saw the threat in King's words: that he would reveal the secret Clay had kept for so long—his relationship to Kate, and at a time when it was liable to do the most damage to Clay's career.

Libby had seen two massive bull elk face off and lock antlers with a clamor that echoed through the forest. The clash of wills between these two men was no less violent.

"I intend to have my son out of here by morning," Blackjack said.

"He stays where he is," King replied.

"He's innocent."

"Guilty as sin," King shot back. "Of more than just this girl's death."

"What's that you're saying?" Hank interjected. "You've got evidence of more than just this girl's death? You think Blackhorne knows something about Kate's disappearance?"

"Stay out of this, Hank," King said.

Hank eyed both men and backed off.

"I called Judge Wilkerson from Washington," Blackjack said. "He's willing to have a bail hearing first thing tomorrow morning."

"Bail hearing doesn't mean your son is getting out on bail," King said. "Here in Jackson, we don't allow murderers to roam the streets."

"My son is innocent."

"Ain't till it's proven so," King said.

"You've got that backward," Blackjack countered. "A man is innocent until—"

"We'll prove him guilty," King said. "Don't you worry about that."

Blackjack turned from King to the captain and said, "I want to speak with my son."

"No," King said.

Blackjack never took his eyes off the captain, and Libby watched with a sick feeling in her stomach as Hank shot a look at King and visibly wilted.

"Sorry, sir," Hank said. "Can't let you do that. Only

his attorney can speak with him before the bail hearing."

Libby knew that rules like that were broken all the time. At the moment, it appeared Hank was more frightened of whatever repercussions her father might have promised than what this stranger might do to him.

Blackjack didn't argue. He simply turned on his booted heel and left the jail.

Hank spit the dark liquid residue of his chewing tobacco into a Styrofoam coffee cup he was carrying and said, "Whew! That is one angry motherf—"

"There are ladies present, Hank," King said, glancing at Libby. "I'll see you tomorrow morning at the hearing. I trust no one will be visiting the prisoner before then."

Hank gave a jerky nod. "No, sir. No one."

"Except for me, Daddy," Libby said. "Hank promised I could speak with his prisoner."

King crossed to her and said, "I can't imagine what you have to say to that . . . man."

"His name is Clay Blackthorne, Daddy. And what I have to say to him is none of your business."

"That pack of coyotes should have stayed in Texas where they belong," King said, glancing at the door Blackjack had exited.

Libby knew better than to argue with her father. "Good night, Daddy."

King Grayhawk harrumphed a dismissal and limped away without another word.

Libby made sure her father was gone before she

turned back to Hank. "I'm ready when you are," she said.

"This is a dangerous prisoner," Hank said. "I'm not sure—"

"Daddy isn't going to make any more fuss," she assured the nervous captain. "And for Kate's sake, I'm willing to take the risk."

Hank took her to an isolation cell where Clay was being held. Above her, on the second floor, she saw a deputy in a glass-walled box who had a view of the entire jail. Hank stopped in front of a door in which the only openings were a food port and a small window and punched in the combination to a Cypher lock on the wall.

When the cell door opened, she flinched at the sight of Clay wearing a bright yellow jumpsuit. She struggled not to wrinkle her nose at the smell in the spartan cell, with its stainless steel toilet attached to the wall. Then her gaze locked with Clay's.

Libby wasn't sure what she'd expected, maybe regret, maybe anxiety, even apprehension. What she saw was cold, hard anger. Defiance. Hostility. Scorn. And the arrogance of a man who had no intention of tolerating the treatment he was receiving, a man certain that it would be rectified immediately, if not sooner.

"Why am I still in here?" Clay asked.

"Bail hearing is scheduled at ten in the morning," Hank replied.

"I think he'll talk more freely if I speak with him alone," Libby said.

Hank shook his head. "I don't think—"

"If my father has no objection, I don't see why you should," Libby said.

"Your father was here?" Clay asked, his body suddenly taut.

"Please, Hank," Libby said. "I need a few minutes alone—"

"Three minutes," Hank said abruptly. "Then you're out of here. This is supposed to be a goddamn isolation cell. 'Scuse the French."

"Thank you, Hank." She put a hand on the captain's chest, and he backed out of the cell and closed the door partway.

"I'll be right here, Blackthorne," Hank said from the other side of the door. "Don't try anything."

Libby followed Clay as he moved to the rear of the tiny cell to give them more privacy.

The first words out of his mouth were, "The girl who was murdered was with Kate yesterday."

"What?" That fact had not been on the news. "How do you know?"

"She told me so."

Libby felt a chill at her core. "You didn't hurt that girl to make her tell you—"

"I didn't lay a hand on her. She was afraid to talk to me in the crowd and led me to an upstairs bedroom. My drink was drugged, and when I woke up, I was in bed with her and she was dead."

"Why would anyone do such a thing? Who hates you enough—"

"North," Clay said. "Your brother North was there last night."

Libby stared at him aghast. "Are you suggesting North—"

"He's killed before."

"That death was ruled an *accident*!" Libby's breathing was harsh, and she felt her hackles rise in response to the threat against her brother. Slowly and succinctly she said, "It wasn't North."

"What's his connection to Niles Taylor?" Clay asked.

Libby shoved a curl behind her ear in agitation. "They're members of the same oil consortium."

"That's all? Nothing else?"

"How should I know?" she said angrily. "I don't keep track of everything North does. But if you're suggesting my brother is involved in anything illegal—"

"I don't know if that oil consortium is dirty or not," Clay said. "If it is, North would certainly have a reason to want me in a compromising position, since my office is investigating it."

"How would killing that girl help North?" Libby demanded.

"I don't think I was supposed to wake up before the girl's body had been removed," Clay said.

Libby shook her head in confusion. "I don't understand."

"Drew thinks someone took pictures of me with the dead girl, that her murder was part of a blackmail scheme to make me dance like a puppet on a string."

"Drew was there, too?" Libby asked.

"Not at the party. I called him after I woke up and found myself in bed with a dead girl."

Libby felt her heart squeeze. "You called him, but not me? You trust him, but not me?"

"It has nothing to do with trust," Clay said brusquely. "Drew's an attorney. I needed legal advice."

"You could have called me later," Libby said.

"I didn't want to get you involved."

Libby's mouth twisted cynically. "You mean you didn't want anyone making a connection between the two of us, especially with Kate missing. You wanted to protect your career."

Clay opened his mouth to say something, then shut it. For the first time she saw something like remorse in his eyes.

"It crossed my mind," he admitted. He shoved a hand through his black hair, leaving it askew as he paced the narrow width of the cell. "But that wasn't my only reason for wanting to keep you out of this."

"What other reason is there?"

"I didn't want reporters squatting on your doorstep, getting in the way of finding Kate."

"Have you told the police what you just told me — about the girl who was murdered being with Kate earlier in the day?" Libby said.

"Yes."

"Then why aren't they out looking for our daughter?"

"They're trying to find the person who brought Natalie — Lourdes — to that party. Maybe he can lead them back to wherever Kate is being kept. They'll find him . . . unless he's already dead."

"What do you mean?" Libby asked.

"The man Sarah Barndollar shot on Bear Island last

night was there digging up the body of Sarah's husband Tom, who's been missing for the past fifteen months."

"You think the man who was shot brought Lourdes to that party?" Libby said.

"He was on Bear Island in the dark, carrying a gun on the night of the murder," Clay said. "So, yes, I think he could be one of the bad guys."

Libby clasped her hands so tightly together the knuckles turned white, to keep from wringing them in despair. "What if it was him, Clay? What if the only person who could have led us to Kate is dead? How are we going to find our daughter before something like what happened to that poor girl happens to her?"

"Come here," he said.

Libby stepped into his embrace and welcomed the feel of his arms closing around her in comfort. "I'm so scared, Clay."

"I should be out of here later this morning," he said. "We'll find out everything we can about the man who was killed. He had to know someone at that party. And we'll start looking at every isolated cabin around here— by air, by snowmobile, on skis. If this was an ongoing blackmail scheme, it won't work anymore because it's been exposed."

Libby suddenly had an idea. "Maybe there are other blackmail victims," she said. "You could request that anyone who's been blackmailed in a similar manner step forward, anonymously if they must, and tell you who's benefited. Surely that would lead us to the bad guys. And if we know who they are—"

Clay hugged her quickly and let her go. "A lot of

cameras will be on me when I'm released on bail. I'll make my plea then."

"Do you think someone will come forward?" Libby asked.

"Maybe. If anyone else has been blackmailed. And if they believe they can do it without the bad guys coming after them. These guys play for keeps."

Libby stepped back when she heard Hank's stern voice outside the door saying, "No one's allowed to speak with Mr. Blackthorne except his attorney."

"I am his attorney," a confident voice replied.

Libby looked at Clay, a brow cocked in question, and he said, "That sounds like Morgan."

Clay stepped to the door and pulled it open. "I'm so glad you're here, Morgan." He reached out and shook the hand of a man who was blond like Drew, but without Drew's height or good looks.

Morgan DeWitt's smile was friendly and confident. Libby could easily imagine him as Clay's chief of staff, making sure Clay's orders got carried out. His tie was pulled up tight, his alligator belt and wingtip shoes looked new, and his tailored gray suit looked expensive but not ostentatious. He was just tall enough not to be labeled short, and he made no attempt to hide the fact his hairline was receding.

"If this guy's your attorney," Hank said, "who's that behind him?"

Morgan stepped aside to reveal an absolutely stunning auburn-haired woman wearing a classic black Chanel suit and Manolo Blahnik high heels.

"Jocelyn!" Clay exclaimed.

Libby stood back as the statuesque young woman threw herself into Clay's arms.

"Clay! I've been so worried about you."

Clay met Libby's eyes over the beautiful young woman's head and said, "This is Jocelyn Montrose. Giselle's younger sister."

Jocelyn turned toward Libby, dabbing with a lace handkerchief at the tears in the corners of her beautiful violet eyes. Libby hadn't believed eyes could be that color purple, but Jocelyn's were. The woman's accent, a combination of crisp New England and seductive Paris, France, made her sound sophisticated and exotic, and the raspy texture of her voice raised the hairs on Libby's nape.

"I'm so glad to meet you, Libby," Jocelyn said. "Clay and Giselle have told me so much about you and Kate."

Of course Clay's late wife had known about Kate's relationship to her husband. It appeared that Jocelyn did, too. Libby glanced at Morgan DeWitt and realized he must know, as well. Clay couldn't have traveled to Jackson so often without explaining to his chief of staff why he was going there.

Libby worked hard to keep the frown from her face. How many people were aware of Clay's relationship with Kate? Was that how the kidnappers had known to take her? Had someone revealed Clay's secret to some enemy of his?

Jocelyn turned back to Clay and said, "Your father and mother were nice enough to give Morgan and me a ride here in their private jet. Now all I need is a place to stay. With all the reporters in town, there isn't a free room any closer than Pinedale."

"There's room at Forgotten Valley, but Drew and I are both staying there, so you'd be stuck with a couple of bachelors."

"I have an extra room," Libby heard herself offer.

"Oh," Jocelyn said.

Libby found herself the focus of the young woman's disconcerting violet eyes. "You're welcome to use my guest room until you can find another place."

"You're so kind," Jocelyn said in her cultured voice. "Thank you."

Libby didn't want to like Jocelyn Montrose. The young woman was far too beautiful and sophisticated and charming—all the qualities Clay Blackthorne needed in a wife. She already seemed to have Clay's attention, and his affection, if that greeting was anything to judge by.

"Did Wilkerson agree to call a bail hearing?" Morgan asked Clay.

"At ten this morning," Clay replied. "Drew's acting as my attorney."

Libby saw one of Morgan's eyelids flicker before he said, "Don't you think you ought to get a criminal attorney in here to represent you?"

"I can do that once I'm out of jail," Clay said.

"I can see we've interrupted you," Jocelyn said to Clay. "Morgan and I can wait outside while you finish your conversation with Libby."

"There are a lot of reporters in front of the building," Libby said. "You might want to go out the back way."

"I can give Jocelyn a ride to your house and wait for you there," Morgan offered. "If you give me directions."

While Libby gave Morgan directions, she was aware of Jocelyn leaning up to whisper in Clay's ear. She felt the green-eyed monster awaken in her breast and did her best to beat it back down.

"I'll see you later, Jocelyn," Clay said.

"*Au revoir*," the statuesque woman said.

Hank stuck his head in the door after Jocelyn and Morgan had left and said, "You two about done?"

"One more minute please, Hank," Libby said. When Hank was gone, Libby turned to Clay and said, "She's very beautiful. Are you going to marry her?"

Clay laughed a little too heartily. "She's my late wife's little sister. We're just friends."

"Friends don't fly halfway across the country in the middle of the night to see someone accused of murder," Libby said. "She's in love with you."

"Maybe she is," Clay conceded. "That doesn't mean I have the same feelings for her."

"Don't you?" Libby asked.

Clay put his hands on her shoulders but Libby stiffened when he tried to pull her close. "We can talk about this when I get out of here."

"What if you don't get out of here?"

"There's no chance of that," Clay said. "I'm a public figure. I have no reason to run. I have property in this community and—"

"You were found in bed with a dead woman. That's rather difficult to explain away. What makes you think this judge will let a suspected murderer out on bail?"

Clay's lips curved in a sardonic smile. "My father's a good friend of the judge."

Libby met his gaze and said, "So is mine."

"They've faced off before and my dad has come up the winner," Clay pointed out.

"My father's been waiting for a chance like this for a long time. He won't let the opportunity to punish you slip through his fingers."

"Then I guess we'll have to wait and see how things turn out."

"That's enough," Hank said, pushing the door open. "Come on out of there, Libby."

"Good luck at the hearing," Libby said as she backed out of the cell.

"Don't worry about me," Clay replied. "I'll be out of here by—"

The cell door slammed before he finished speaking.

15

A fierce argument outside the canvas walls woke Kate. There was enough morning light to see her hand in front of her face, which meant she'd survived her second cold, terrifying night of captivity. She scooted across the rough wooden floor on her hands and knees toward the drafty, boarded-up window, where the raucous sound was loudest, and listened hard.

"How the hell have you managed to get everything so fucked up?" a harsh male voice demanded. "Why wasn't that girl's body removed immediately? You've ruined everything!"

Body? Kate thought. *Lourdes's body? Is Lourdes dead?* Her heart began to pound.

"He was drugged," a gruff male voice replied. "How could I know he'd wake up so soon? None of the others did."

"That's your job," the harsh voice said. "You kill the girl, take pictures of the man and the dead girl in bed, and get rid of the girl. It's that simple."

"If it's so simple," the gruff voice replied, "why don't you do it yourself next time?"

Next time? Kate felt her heart leap to her throat, threatening to choke her. *Am I next?*

"There isn't going to be any next time," the harsh voice said. "We're done. I'm going to have to come up with another plan to get what I want. This one isn't going to work anymore."

"Just because this girl has a family looking for her—"

"You fool!" the harsh voice interrupted. "She not only isn't a runaway, that idiot from Midland picked up King Grayhawk's granddaughter!"

"Lester said he was ordered to pick her up."

"Not by me! You two don't know what you've done. Every policeman in the country is looking for that girl. Christ! She also happens to be Clay Blackthorne's daughter."

"How the hell was I supposed to know that? Who even knew he had a daughter?"

Kate felt a chill run down her spine. Only a very few people knew the truth about her father. She could count them on two hands. Whoever was out there, whoever had been killing girls and taking pictures of them with drugged men, was someone who knew her mother or her father well enough to know that she was Clay Blackthorne's daughter.

Which made her situation all the more sinister. Whichever acquaintance it was couldn't take the chance of letting her go. Which meant sooner or later—probably sooner—she was going to be killed and dumped somewhere no one would ever find her.

Or left here to die of hunger and thirst.

When Lourdes had been taken last night, no food or

water had been left for Kate. Her throat was raw and her tongue thick. What made it worse was knowing there was so much snow right outside the door. If she could reach it, if she could melt it, she could drink, and ease her thirst.

But it might as well be snow in Timbuktu, as much chance as she had of reaching it. She was going to die with her tongue swollen up and purple in her mouth, her eyes bugged out and her body shrunken like an old prune.

Kate cursed her vivid imagination. Her mother and father, and her stepgrandmother and grandfathers, were probably searching for her at this very moment. She knew from past experience that whenever someone in her family wanted something done, they made it happen. Neither Blackthornes nor Grayhawks let anything, or anyone, get in their way.

But what if someone in her extended family really was responsible for this murder and blackmail scheme? That person would be in a position to thwart the attempts to find her. That person could make sure all efforts to locate her failed. That person could make sure she died.

Kate ran through the short list of people who knew she was Clay Blackthorne's daughter: her mother, her father, Ren and Blackjack, King, her eldest uncles North and Matt Grayhawk, her father's wife Giselle — but she was dead — and Giselle's sister Jocelyn, her father's personal secretary and his chief of staff, and her father's cousin and partner at the ranch, Drew DeWitt, whom she thought of as another uncle.

Her father's relatives in Texas knew, as well, including her father's twin brother Owen and Owen's wife, and her father's younger sister Summer and her husband Billy. But they all lived in Texas, which made their involvement in a Wyoming blackmail scheme unlikely. But not impossible, she realized.

She had two more uncles and two more aunts on her mother's side, and it was possible they knew the truth, but they lived in Texas, and she'd never even heard any of them mention Clay Blackthorne.

Her father might have told a few people how she was related to him, but it had been made clear to her from the time she was old enough to understand words, that the truth might be devastating to his political career. She doubted he'd shared such potentially destructive information with many—if any—others.

Which of her relatives was capable of blackmail and murder? Kate's heart was pounding as she admitted the truth. Any or all of them, under the right circumstances.

Grandpa King had told her the story of her grandmother, Clay's mother Eve, who'd planned her own death by suicide and tried to make it look like Clay's father Blackjack had murdered her. Her uncle Owen was a Texas Ranger and had killed men. Her uncle North had accidentally killed a man—against whom he'd co-incidentally held a grudge.

Her family were no strangers to violence.

Kate had learned to shoot when she was big enough to carry a rifle. She'd killed a buck once but had never gone hunting again. She hadn't liked the way she'd felt when she looked into the glazed brown eyes of the dying animal.

"So how do we get rid of her?" the gruff voice asked.

Kate was jerked from her musings by the gruff man's question and listened with bated breath to hear her fate.

"It's dangerous to move her right now," the harsh-voiced man said. "There are too many cops out there looking for her."

Silence. More silence. Kate wanted to scream at them to let her go. That she wouldn't talk. That she didn't know who they were. At least, she didn't recognize either of the two voices. Shouldn't she, if it was someone she knew?

Of course, the two men could have been hired by one of her relatives. Almost all of them were filthy rich, starting with both her grandfathers, who not only seemed to have all the money they could ever need, but seemed hell-bent on earning even more.

In the end, Kate couldn't remain silent. She had to beg for her life.

"Let me go!" she screamed. "I won't talk. I don't even know who you are!"

"Have you been in there listening all this time?" the harsh voice asked.

Kate hesitated a beat too long before she replied, "No."

She heard the harsh voice swearing, using words so foul she'd never heard them before, though she had no doubt what they meant.

"You're a little too smart for your britches, young lady," the harsh voice said.

"Please let me go," Kate begged. "I promise—"

"Shut up!" the harsh voice said. "I need to think."

Kate rose and pressed her ear against the planking that covered the plastic window, her eyes closed, her fingers crossed, praying for a miracle.

"We don't have to do anything right now," she heard the harsh-voiced man say. "Nobody's going to find this place. It's too well hidden. Let's just let things cool down."

"When do you want to meet again?" the gruff voice asked.

"In a couple of days," the harsh voice replied.

In a couple of days she would be dead of thirst. "I need water and food!" she cried. "Please. I'm thirsty and hungry."

"You want me to do anything about that?" the gruff voice asked.

"Might as well keep her alive," the harsh voice replied. "If things go belly-up, we might need her as a bargaining tool."

"I didn't bring anything with me," the gruff voice said. "I'll have to go back to town and get something."

"Wait till dark to come back here. I don't want you being seen," the harsh voice said.

"I'm thirsty now!" Kate protested.

A flat hand slapped against the wood on the outside of the window and Kate jumped back.

"Get the hell away from that window," the harsh voice said.

Kate stared at the light filtering through the boarded-up window, her whole body trembling with fear and fatigue. Then she realized she could see the two men standing outside.

She squinted as a ray of sunlight hit her eyes. At first the two men were merely black outlines. As her eyes adjusted, she began to make out the shapes of their faces. She didn't recognize the younger of the two and turned her attention to the other man.

Kate gasped in shock and horror when she realized who it was.

16

Sarah was exhausted, both physically and emotionally. It had been the longest day of her life. Or rather, the second longest. The longest had been the day Tom hadn't come home. At least this day had come to an end. Finally.

"You sure you're okay by yourself?" her boss said as he stopped in front of her house in the wee hours of the morning.

"I'm fine, Jim." Sarah didn't want to remind him that Drew had taken her kids home, so she wouldn't be alone. She reached up to shove an errant strand of hair behind her ear and realized her hand was trembling. She quickly pulled it down, but it was too late.

"Yeah, sure. You're fine," her boss muttered as he eyed her shaking hands. "Stay home tomorrow. Get some rest."

"I'm fine," Sarah protested. "Really."

"You're on administrative leave until you talk to a psychologist and he says you're all right—up here," Jim said, tapping his temple. "Those are the rules."

"Really, I—"

"Shut up and get out of the car," he said.

Sarah knew there was no use arguing. Her sergeant was a stickler for the rules. As she headed for the front door, she realized she might very well need the day off, depending on what shape her kids were in physically and emotionally.

Sarah had been anxious about what she might find at home. She certainly hadn't expected all the lights to be off and for everyone, including Drew, who lay prone on the living room couch, to be sound asleep. She closed the front door quietly, relieved that she could put off talking about what had happened. She wasn't sure she could relive the past night without falling apart.

She'd killed a man.

And she'd found Tom. Or rather, her kids had found Tom.

Sarah tiptoed down the hallway in the dim yellow glow of the night-light and checked in the boys' room to make sure they were all right.

She pulled the covers up over Ryan's shoulder and brushed a damp mop of hair from his brow before pressing her cheek against his forehead to see if he had a fever. He felt warm, but not hot. Then she crossed to Nate's bed, laid a hand gently against his warm— again, not hot—cheek and slid the covers over the one bare foot that always hung out at the bottom of the bed. Before she'd finished, the foot had found its way back out from under the covers.

She closed their door quietly and moved farther down the hall to Brooke's room, where she could see a light on under the door. She knocked softly and whispered, "Brooke?" as she opened the door.

Brooke was sitting cross-legged at the head of her bed wrapped in a blanket, the volume in her earphones so loud that Sarah could hear the raucous rap music across the room. Tears had dried on her stepdaughter's cheeks.

Sarah settled near enough to Brooke to lay a hand on her knee. "Do you want to talk?"

Brooke shook her head.

That wasn't unusual. Brooke never wanted to share her troubles. Sarah was reluctant to leave without offering what comfort she could. She didn't ask Brooke to remove her earphones, or even to turn down the volume. She simply talked, sharing her feelings about the discovery of Tom's body.

"As horrible as it was to find your dad that way, I feel relieved to know what happened to him," she began. "I never really believed he left us. But his truck was gone, and he'd threatened . . ." Sarah stopped and swallowed past the painful lump in her throat.

She looked into Brooke's dark, wounded eyes and said, "Now we know for sure that he loved us all too much ever to leave us, if he'd had a choice." She looked down, unable to meet Brooke's gaze, and continued speaking.

The thumping, rhythmic cant in the background suddenly stopped.

Sarah looked up to see more tears sliding down Brooke's cheeks. She opened her arms and Brooke threw herself against Sarah's body.

Sarah held tight as the girl sobbed, "Poor Daddy. Oh, poor, poor Daddy."

The mournful cries were muffled against Sarah's shoulder. She patted Brooke's back, her own throat aching with unshed tears. She hadn't cried yet for Tom, afraid to let go for fear that she wouldn't be able to stop.

Sarah wasn't sure how long they remained locked in each other's arms, but at last she felt the tension ease in Brooke's body and realized the exhausted girl had fallen asleep.

She laid Brooke down and covered her with the blanket that had been wrapped around her, kissing her on the cheek before she turned and left the room. She stepped into her own room, then realized she should cover Drew with a blanket. He was liable to get cold before morning. She grabbed a crocheted quilt from the foot of her bed and headed back to the living room.

To her surprise, Drew was no longer on the couch. She looked around and saw him standing in the doorway to the darkened kitchen.

"You're up," she said.

"I should go," he said. "It's late."

She smiled wanly and said, "No, it's early."

"How are you?" he asked.

She felt her chin quiver and gritted her teeth. She tried smiling again, but it didn't work. Her lips wobbled, and then crumpled. She wasn't sure which one of them moved first, but a moment later Drew's arms were wrapped tightly around her. She felt herself sagging as she gave in to grief. She felt him pick her up in his arms as she pressed her mouth against his chest and wailed out her sorrow.

"It's all right," Drew crooned in her ear, as he settled both of them on the couch with her in his lap. "Cry all you want. I'm here, Sarah. I'll take care of you."

Which made her wail all the harder and press her face even harder against his shoulder to muffle the sound. She didn't want to wake up the kids, or frighten them with the depth of her despair. She clung to Drew, her arms around his neck, her body as close as she could get it to his. She would have climbed inside him, if she could.

She was shuddering and shivering and couldn't seem to stop.

"Sarah?" Drew said.

She heard the concern in his voice and leaned back to look up into his face. "Did you see Tom?" she choked out. "Nobody seemed to think anything of digging him up right in front of me. He was . . . he was . . ."

"Oh, baby," Drew said, tucking her head under his chin and holding her close. "I wondered why you seemed so calm. You didn't react and I thought . . . We're all stupid idiots. Me, most of all. I should have known you'd be torn apart inside. You don't have to be so strong, Sarah. I'm here."

They were powerful, moving words to hear. A man to support her. A man to lean on. A man to trust. Sarah had been self-reliant for so very long. She'd been on her own for over a year, managing fine. But so lonely. And so scared all the time that she would make a wrong choice and the kids would suffer for it.

Drew was talking again, and she had to concentrate

to understand what he was saying. "I suppose you're a basket case over that guy you shot, too," he said. "I'm so sorry, Sarah. I wish I'd realized sooner how you felt. I would have sent the kids home with someone else and stayed with you."

"No," she said, shaking her head. "I would have worried about them if they hadn't been with someone I trust."

He slid a finger under her chin and lifted her face so he could look into her eyes. "You trust me, Sarah? With your kids? I'm the last person—"

"You're not like that miserable grandmother of yours," she said softly, but fiercely. "You're a good man, Drew. I'd trust you with my kids any day of the week."

She heard him swallow noisily.

"Thanks, Sarah." He cleared his throat and said, "I'd better get out of here so you can get some sleep."

"I can sleep in tomorrow. I'm on administrative leave for a couple of days."

"Why's that?" he asked. "They're not giving you a hassle about shooting that guy, are they? Because if they are, I—"

"It's nothing like that. I had to answer a lot of questions, and I had to turn in my Glock as evidence, but they gave me a replacement weapon. I just have to get checked out by a psychologist to make sure I'm okay about the shooting before I can go back to work."

His hand cupped her head and stroked her hair as he asked, "How are you feeling about it?"

"Sick to my stomach," Sarah admitted. "Sick at heart. I would do it again, if I had to. But I hope I never have to. What I really want is to be a part of the investigation. I want to find out whether the guy I shot is connected to any of the politicians at that party."

"Who says you can't?" Drew asked.

"I'm on administrative leave," she reminded him.

"So what? Haven't you ever done any investigating when you weren't on duty?"

Sarah snickered. "Are you kidding? I've worked more hours off the clock over the past year than on, trying to find those missing girls. It's important to me, but I'm not the only deputy out there following up on leads and looking for Kate. My kids need me here."

"I think they're fine, as far as their dousing in the river goes. I made sure they got hot baths or showers and were dressed warmly for bed."

"Thank you," Sarah said. "They seemed okay when I checked on them."

"I suppose only time will tell whether they need some counseling."

"It's available, if it comes to that," Sarah said.

"I should leave now," Drew said. "And let you get some sleep."

"Don't go."

Sarah saw the surprise on Drew's face. She couldn't quite believe she'd asked him to stay, but she didn't want to be alone for what remained of the night. She looked into his eyes, to make sure he understood that she wasn't offering sex, that all she wanted was comfort, a strong shoulder to lean on and a warm body next to hers to fend off the cold creeping through her.

"I'm here for you, Sarah, as long as you need me," Drew said.

Sarah sagged against him, allowing the rigidity of control to seep from her body. "Thank you," she whispered.

She was still on his lap, and she laid her head against his shoulder and slid her fingers into the soft hair at his nape. His heart thumped steadily against her ear.

"Sleep now," he murmured, his hand threading through her hair to massage her scalp. "I've got you. You're safe with me."

They were words she hadn't realized how much she needed to hear. Forty-eight hours ago she'd never even heard of Drew DeWitt. Now she would have trusted him with her life. She didn't want to think how she was going to feel when he left.

It was only a matter of time. The rich folks never stayed long. Jackson was too isolated. They came to enjoy the majesty of the Grand Tetons, to hunt or to take a whitewater raft trip down the Snake, or to ski the double diamond slopes. And then they were gone.

Drew was here to recuperate from a broken heart. When it was healed, he would go back to some big law firm in some big city to work. In the meantime, she was glad he was here.

"Drew," she murmured.

"Yes, sweetheart," he murmured back.

"Thank you for being here."

"I can't think of anywhere else I'd rather be," he said. "Sleep now, Sarah. Rest."

Sarah closed her eyes and listened for the thump of

Drew's heart. She heard the house creak. And the heater come on. And felt an ache in her throat.

The tears slid silently down her cheeks. She felt Drew brush at one with his thumb, then lean down to kiss away another. She turned her face up to his, and their lips caught and held. Then she laid her head once more on his shoulder and gave in to the powerful lethargy that claimed her.

Drew woke up on Sarah's lumpy living room couch. Dawn had finally arrived. He smelled coffee. And bacon. He sat up, straightening his crooked neck carefully, and realized Sarah must have thrown the crocheted blanket over him when she got up to fix breakfast.

He lifted the blanket and smelled it, inhaling her scent. He was astounded at how short a time he'd known Sarah Barndollar, and how profoundly she'd affected his life. No one he knew would have believed he'd spent the night baby-sitting. Children hadn't been a part of his world—or his plans for the future.

While he'd experienced a great deal of passion with his former lover, Grayson Choate, he'd rarely felt the sort of connection he'd experienced with Sarah last night. He'd held her in his arms till she was asleep, and then, as gently as he could, had put her into her own bed, kissed her brow and left the room.

That sort of tenderness with a woman was much more frightening—and threatening—to the walls he'd built around himself than a tempestuous night of sex would have been.

He'd returned to the living room with the urge to bolt, to get out, to get away, to escape from the ties he could feel beginning to bind him to this family. The sense of panic was overwhelming.

Which was when he'd realized he didn't have a car to leave in. He'd considered calling a cab, but wasn't sure how likely a cabbie was to gossip about Sarah. He'd sat down on the couch and stared at the moonlight coming through the front window, wondering how he'd gotten himself so involved with this family. He remembered thinking how tired he was and how he wished he were home in his own bed.

He must have fallen asleep.

Drew still had the urge to flee, but even stronger was the urge to see Sarah. To know that she was all right. To comfort her. To protect her.

Shit. He sounded like some romance novel hero. But dammit, that was how he felt.

He scrubbed the sand out of his eyes and brushed his fingers through his lanky blond hair to flatten what was standing straight up and lift what had flattened against his scalp. He ran a hand across the dark stubble on his face and scratched his chin. And grinned. He must look like something the cat had dragged in.

He rose, stretched his arms high over his head and leaned back until his ribs almost cracked, then hitched up his jeans and headed for the kitchen.

Sarah stood at the stove with her back to him, humming a Faith Hill tune and wagging her jean-clad fanny in time to the music.

"Good morning," he said.

She turned abruptly and a half-cooked piece of bacon went flying and landed on the counter next to the sink. She stared at it, looked wide-eyed at him, and laughed. "You startled me."

He retrieved the hot piece of bacon with two fingers, crossed to her, and dropped it back in the pan. "Sorry about that. Thanks for loaning me your couch."

"Thanks for taking care of me."

"You're very welcome," he said. And meant it.

"I never asked if the kids gave you any problems last night," she said.

He saw her anxiety and decided not to tell her how Brooke had been a real pain in the ass. The teenager had challenged him on everything from which pajamas he put on Ryan to whether Nate could have a snack before going to bed.

After the boys were down, she'd refused to go to bed herself, saying she preferred to stay up until her mother got home. He'd finally threatened to pick her up bodily and cart her to her room, if she didn't travel there in a hurry on her own two feet.

"The kids were great," he said, smiling so Sarah would believe him.

She narrowed her eyes and said, "Brooke didn't give you any trouble?"

He shrugged. "She was okay. How are you feeling this morning?"

She shook her head and turned back to the stove. "As well as can be expected. I promised Ryan I'd make blueberry pancakes for breakfast this morning." She grimaced. "But I didn't get to the grocery store, so he's going to have to settle for French toast and bacon."

Drew took a step forward, aligning his body with hers. When she leaned back into him, he slid his arms around her waist and hooked his hands together over her belly. He set his chin on her shoulder and said, "Tough night all around."

She moved the bacon around in the pan, found a slice that looked done, and lifted it out onto a paper towel she'd laid on the counter. "I'm handling it." She gave him a sad smile over her shoulder and said, "I always do."

"I know it wasn't easy finding your husband like that."

"To have my kids see Tom—" She dropped the fork on the counter and turned, sliding her arms up around his neck and laying her cheek against his chest. "I'm afraid to think what kind of nightmares they'll have. Especially Ryan."

"He made it through last night. That's a good start."

"Part of the reason I was so late getting home was that I waited around to see if the coroner could make a guess about how Tom died. He found a bullet hole in the back of Tom's skull. He said it looked like he'd been shot at close range, just like that girl who was found dead in the mountains."

"So both deaths might be linked to whatever scheme they tried to run on Clay last night," Drew said.

She nodded.

Drew picked up the fork she'd dropped, turned a

piece of sizzling bacon and set the fork back down. "Who did the guy you shot turn out to be?"

"His name was Lester Wallace," she replied. "He had a Texas driver's license and an address in Midland. A lot of priors. No permit for the gun. We've asked the Midland/Odessa PD to find out who he worked for and whatever else they can about him."

"Texas, huh? He's a long way from home. Wonder how he knew where that body was."

"I imagine because he buried Tom there fifteen months ago," Sarah said. "Forensics in Cheyenne will see if they can match the bullet that killed Tom with Lester's gun."

"Why would a guy from Texas shoot Tom?" Drew asked.

"Probably because Tom saw something he wasn't supposed to see."

"Like what?" Drew asked.

"It'll be easier to hazard a guess once we know more about Lester Wallace," Sarah said. "Like what he was doing here in Wyoming in the first place."

Drew put his hands on either side of Sarah's face, looked into her eyes and said, "How are you this morning, really?"

"Sad. Angry. Guilty." She shot him a defiant glance. "How should I feel? I shot and killed a man last night—who probably shot and killed my husband—who's been lying buried all this time not ten miles from here, while I've been . . ."

Tears welled in her eyes as she met his gaze and spilled over as she choked back a sob. "While I've been—"

"Shh. Shh," Drew said, tightening his arms around her. "You've done nothing wrong, Sarah. Tom was gone for more than a year without a word. You've suspected for a long time what must have happened to him. Now you know for sure. He didn't leave you. He didn't leave his kids. He was taken from all of you against his will."

One by one, he kissed the salty tears from her cheeks, then lifted her chin with his forefinger so he could reach her lips, which were pliant and giving. He deepened the kiss, offering comfort and . . . something more. "It's over, Sarah," he murmured. "You can all go on with your lives."

"What are you doing to my mother? Get away from her!"

Drew had been totally absorbed with comforting Sarah, so he was stunned by the rake of fingernails on his arm as Brooke clawed at him. He backed off, holding his hands up to keep her pummeling fists from doing any more harm.

Sarah wrapped her arms around Brooke from behind and said, "That's enough, Brooke. Stop it!"

Brooke sagged in her mother's hold, huge tears sending clumps of black mascara rolling down her cheeks, her mouth crumpling in a wail of pain and anger. "You stay away from my mom!"

"Behave yourself, Brooke," Sarah admonished.

Brooke jerked herself free and said, "How can you kiss another man, when we just found out Daddy's dead?"

Drew met Sarah's stricken glance. He'd only meant to give her a kiss of comfort. He had no idea how or why it had become so much more. Maybe because they'd both needed each other so much. He got no further than that thought before both boys arrived at the kitchen door in their pajamas.

"What's going on?" Nate demanded. "Why is Brooke screeching like a wildcat?"

"I caught him kissing Mom!" Brooke said, pointing a chipped, scarlet-painted fingernail at Drew.

"So?" Nate said. "What's the big deal?"

"Mom is married!" Brooke spat.

"Dad is dead," Nate shot back brutally. "He has been for more than a year."

"I know that," Brooke retorted. "But *he* didn't know that until last night."

Drew had to admit she was right. "I'm sorry, Brooke, for any pain I caused you. Your mother and I—" Drew realized he had no idea where to go from there. His brief relationship with Sarah had been based on sexual attraction. He wasn't sure how it had become so much more complicated.

He met Sarah's agonized gaze, hoping she would know how to explain what he could not.

"I think you should leave," she said softly, her eyes stark.

Drew looked around the room and realized he didn't belong here. They didn't want or need him. He was the outsider, the one who would never fit in. Not that he wanted to. "Yeah. Sure," he said.

He didn't look at Sarah or her kids on his way to the living room to get his coat. He was at the front door when he remembered—again—that he'd driven

Sarah's Tahoe from Bear Island. He didn't have his cell phone with him, either. It was in his pickup, which he'd left at the landing where he'd launched his fishing boat.

"Screw it," he said as he opened Sarah's front door and stepped into the frigid cold. It wasn't that long a walk down the mountain to town. He could call a cab when he found a pay phone.

He didn't bother saying good-bye to anyone. Good-byes didn't matter, because he wasn't coming back.

17

In the end, Drew didn't have to walk very far, because an older man in a pickup stopped to see if he wanted a ride into town. Drew couldn't help thinking that sort of thing never would have happened to him in Houston. In a big city, every stranger was a potential robber, rapist or murderer. In a small town, strangers were soon identified as neighbors.

Except, that hadn't been the case lately in Jackson Hole. Far too many innocent young women had become victims.

Drew had his new friend drop him off at the jail. He'd talked with Clay on the phone in the wee hours of the morning and knew that, despite the fact it was Sunday morning, a bail hearing had been scheduled in the circuit court at ten o'clock—for which Drew was supposed to act as Clay's counsel.

Since Drew had previously only represented white-collar criminals, he'd urged Clay to contact an attorney who specialized in representing clients accused of murder.

"No need for that," Clay had said. "All you have to do is show up. Bail will be set and I'll be out of here."

Drew wanted to make one last plea to Clay in person to postpone the bail hearing and get a good criminal attorney to represent him.

It was after six, but the area outside the jail was deserted. Apparently, all the television folks were still tucked into their warm, cozy beds. Drew told the deputy on duty he was there as Clay's attorney, and Clay was brought—in manacles—to a room where they could talk.

"You look like hell," Drew said, leaning against the wall as Clay paced the room in his yellow jumpsuit.

"You don't look much better," his cousin replied. "What are you doing here at this godforsaken hour of the morning?"

"You need someone who specializes in criminal law, Clay," Drew said. "If the judge starts asking questions and expecting me to spout case law, I'm not going to know diddly-squat. To be honest, if it were me, and someone told me the facts of this case, I wouldn't let you out on bail. The evidence is too damning."

"Then I'm glad you're not the judge," Clay said, twisting his body from side to side to stretch out the kinks. "Anyway, I took your advice. I talked to some hotshot criminal attorney in New York last night who's agreed to represent me. Unfortunately, he can't make it to Jackson in time for the bail hearing this morning."

"Get it postponed," Drew said. "That shouldn't be a problem."

Clay shook his head. "I don't want to spend one more minute in that cell than I have to."

"It's your neck," Drew said, resigned to representing

Clay, at least for the bail hearing. "Any idea who set you up?"

"The person I want to talk to is Niles Taylor. It's a little coincidental, don't you think, that Lester Wallace is from Midland, too?" Clay said. "Once I'm released, I plan to make a plea on TV to anyone who might have been blackmailed in a similar way to come forward—anonymously, if necessary."

"You think some politician or businessman or judge who's been—maybe still is being—blackmailed is actually going to admit he paid off a blackmailer in return for not being exposed as a murderer?"

Clay shrugged. "Stranger things have happened."

"I think you're barking up the wrong tree."

"I'll be glad to bark up a different tree, if you can show me one."

But Drew didn't have any better ideas to offer. "Do you think Kate's disappearance is part of this blackmail scheme?"

Clay frowned. "I think it has to be. I just don't understand why no one's contacted me. There's been no ransom demand, no threats on Kate's life, nothing."

"The fact that she was picked up almost immediately after she arrived in town suggests someone knew she was coming and was waiting for her," Drew said. "Has Morgan been able to determine the origin of that e-mail?"

"I got distracted and forgot to ask him about it when he was here last night—or rather, very early this morning."

"Morgan was here at the jail?"

Clay smiled. "Morgan and Jocelyn flew in with my parents on their Citation."

"Why would Jocelyn come all the way out here?" Drew asked. "Is there something going on between the two of you that you haven't told me about?"

"She was around a lot when Giselle was in the hospital, and we got to be friends," Clay said. "Lately, she's been my hostess at a couple of parties and my date when I've needed one at social functions. My parents offered her the ride and she took it. It's as simple as that."

"Right," Drew said skeptically. "In my experience, a woman who flies halfway across the country to see a man accused of murder considers herself more than 'just a friend.' "

"Do me a favor. Forget about Jocelyn. Find Morgan and ask him about that e-mail to Kate."

"Where is he staying?"

Clay raked an agitated hand through his hair. "He didn't stop by and see you at the ranch?"

Drew hesitated, then admitted, "I didn't sleep there last night." He gave Clay a look that didn't invite questions.

"Jocelyn should know where he is," Clay said.

"Where is she staying?"

Clay looked bemused as he said, "With Libby."

Drew whistled. "How the hell did that happen?"

"Jocelyn couldn't find a hotel room, so Libby offered her a bed at her house."

"Don't you think that's a little strange?"

"Why should it be?" Clay said. "Jocelyn is just a friend."

"Uh huh," Drew said. "And what does that make Libby? Just another friend?"

"Yes. Now go," Clay said. "Find Morgan."

"I'm gone," Drew said. "I'll bring you something to wear to the hearing."

Drew called Libby's house from the jail and Jocelyn told him that Morgan was staying at the Antler Motel on Pearl Street. Drew left the jail and walked the short distance to the motel, which appealed to tourists because it was constructed of logs and featured rooms with fireplaces and the inevitable Western decor.

He knocked on the outside door to Morgan's room, but there was no answer. Either Morgan wasn't in, or Jocelyn had given him the wrong room number.

When Drew checked at the registration desk, the clerk said, "Mr. DeWitt picked up a rental car last night. Haven't seen him since."

Drew figured Morgan must have gone out for an early breakfast. He checked at the Wagon Wheel restaurant across the street, but there was no sign of his stepbrother. Drew realized he'd rather be having coffee and bacon and French toast with Sarah, but since that wasn't a choice, he decided to treat himself to sausage and biscuits at Bubba's.

It was a long walk down Broadway to Bubba's, but there was no wind, and it was so dry in Jackson it didn't feel as cold as he knew it was. Drew realized why the sun hadn't made an appearance when feathery snowflakes began to fall. He grinned and stuck out his tongue to catch a few.

Bubba's was cheerfully noisy and warm and, to his

surprise, Drew saw Morgan sitting at a booth, deep in conversation with two men he didn't recognize. Since there was an empty seat, he told the hostess he was with friends and crossed the room to join them.

"Hey, Morgan," he said, smiling at his stepbrother.

"Drew! Son of a gun! I didn't realize you were in town."

Morgan was sitting by himself on one side of the booth, and he slid out and threw an arm around Drew, turning him toward the other two men. "This is my little brother Drew," Morgan said. "Drew, this is Niles Taylor and Jimmy Joe Stovall."

Each man rose up and reached across the table to greet Drew and shake his hand.

"Are you with someone? Can you join us?" Morgan asked.

"I'm all yours." Drew gestured toward the booth and said to Morgan, "After you."

Drew crowded in after his stepbrother and ordered his breakfast from the waitress who magically appeared. Without asking, she poured him a cup of coffee. Drew reached for the hot cup and only then noticed that no one had said another word since he'd sat down.

"What's got all of you up so early?" he asked.

"Clay, of course," Morgan said.

"I feel like this is all my fault," Niles said. "I was the one who invited him to that party last night and introduced him to that girl. Who knew he would drink so much?"

"I believe he was drugged," Drew said.

"Well, yes, that's what he says," Niles said.

Drew knew that if any of the more sophisticated drugs had been used, there would be no evidence of any drug left in Clay's body to prove his point. "I believe Clay," he said.

"I feel bad because I was working at the house," Jimmy Joe said. "I just didn't see any suspicious characters or hear anything out of the ordinary."

"Working? But not on duty?" Drew said, staring at the Teton County patrolman's uniform Jimmy Joe was wearing. "Aren't you a deputy sheriff?"

Jimmy Joe swallowed the coffee in his mouth and said, "I was off-duty, working as a rent-a-cop to earn a little cash, keeping an eye on things for the homeowner."

Drew wasn't going to say what he was thinking. That Jimmy Joe hadn't done his job very well, and a girl had ended up dead. "Who owns that home on Bear Island?" Drew asked.

"A friend of mine, a congressman," Niles said. "He offered it to me for the party. I hired Jimmy Joe here at his recommendation."

"Has this friend of yours loaned you his home before?" Drew said. *For other parties where other women got killed and other men got blackmailed?*

"Once or twice." Niles smiled and said, "Don't imagine he'll be loaning it to anyone again anytime soon."

"What's his name?"

"Whose name?" Niles asked.

"This congressman friend of yours."

"I don't think—"

"I can look it up in the county records," Drew said. Only it was more of a threat.

Niles narrowed his eyes, turned to Morgan and said, "Your brother doesn't play nice."

Morgan grinned and said, "You don't want to get him mad. Drew's hell on wheels when—"

"The name?" Drew interrupted.

"Harvey Donnelly," Niles said.

"He's not a congressman," Drew said sharply. "He's the governor of Texas!"

"I suppose I never think of him as Governor Donnelly," Niles said. "He was Congressman Harvey Donnelly when I met him."

Drew could see all the puzzle pieces fitting nicely into place. He'd often been guilty of making a leap in logic: A therefore D, skipping steps B and C. It had gotten him into trouble before, and it likely would again. But if he laid everything out, he got the same result.

A. Clay's office in Washington was investigating an oil consortium doing business with the Japanese.

B. Niles Taylor was the Midland oilman who'd organized the consortium.

C. With incriminating pictures of Clay in bed with a dead woman, Niles could force Clay to end his investigation, or at least make sure it never turned up anything negative.

Jimmy Joe Stovall was on hand to ensure that the local police and county deputies stayed away while the girl was murdered and the body removed. Except, Sarah's kids had interfered, and Sarah had shot the gunman from Midland, the possible—make that probable—murderer of Lourdes Ramirez.

Dupes like Congressman—now Governor—Donnelly, who might himself have been a blackmail victim once upon a time, provided the site of the intrigue, while being able to offer the alibi of being far, far from the scene of the crime.

D. Crime solved. Villains exposed.

Drew had heard it said that the most obvious solution to a puzzle was often the right one. It had only taken one mistake—not removing Lourdes's body before Clay woke up and called the police—to bring the whole scheme tumbling down.

The problem now, of course, was how to prove his theory and clear Clay's name.

The biggest question remaining was how Kate's abduction fit into the picture. He could see no purpose for her kidnapping if Niles had intended to blackmail Clay all along. Or maybe he'd worried that the blackmail scheme would fail and wanted insurance that Clay would cooperate. That was still a possibility.

"If you gentlemen will excuse me," Drew said, "There's something I need to discuss privately with my brother." He stood and said, "Can you step outside with me a minute, Morgan?"

"We're done with our breakfast," Niles said, swiping his mouth with his napkin. "Why don't we excuse ourselves?"

Jimmy Joe picked up his coffee cup and slurped the rest of it down, then scooted across the booth after Niles and said, "Nice seeing you, Morgan. Drew."

When they were gone, Drew sat down on the other side of the booth.

The waitress cleared the table and said, "Your breakfast will be right up."

"What is it, little brother?" Morgan asked.

"Clay wants to know if you've discovered who sent that e-mail to Kate."

Morgan shook his head. "Somebody clever, is all I know."

"How is it you ended up having breakfast with Niles and his friend?" Drew asked.

Morgan's eyes narrowed. "Why do you ask?"

"Why don't you want to tell me?"

Morgan grinned. "Why so suspicious?"

"You're avoiding my question."

Morgan shook his head and said, "I knew Niles had hosted the party last night—"

"How did you know that?" Drew interrupted.

"Clay told me. Hey," Morgan said. "What's going on here? I'm one of the good guys."

"Then how do you know Niles Taylor?"

"Only in the context of the ongoing investigation of his oil consortium," Morgan said. "I sat down here to see if I could find out any more about what happened last night on Bear Island."

"Who else is involved in that oil consortium?" Drew asked.

"A bunch of Texas oilmen, including Niles Taylor. And the Grayhawks—King and North."

Drew hissed in a breath. "Why are a couple of Wyoming oilmen involved in a Texas oil deal?"

"King bought up a lot of mineral leases in Texas when the bottom fell out of the oil industry. He owns just about as much oil—and land—in Texas as he does in Wyoming."

Drew suddenly realized why Kate Grayhawk might have been taken. Not as a threat against Clay, but as a threat to be used against King. There was no question that Kate was King Grayhawk's grand-daughter. If what Clay had told him was true, the old man might have wanted Kate aborted before she was born, but once she'd shown up, he'd claimed her as his progeny.

So what was it Niles Taylor wanted King Grayhawk to do? Get out of the deal? Be quiet about whatever was wrong with it? Give up more of the profits to the con-sortium—or to Niles himself? The best way to find out was to ask the old man. And the sooner the better.

"I've got someone to see," Drew said abruptly.

"If I'm not mistaken, that's the waitress with your breakfast," Morgan said, as the waitress set a plate in front of Drew.

Drew took one long, regretful look at the steaming white gravy with sausage that had been ladled over fluffy homemade biscuits. He knew if he took one bite he'd want to eat it all, and he had a lot to do before the hear-ing. He shoved the plate aside and said, "How would you like to give me a ride out to Forgotten Valley?"

"Sure. No problem."

Morgan's rental car turned out to be a four-wheel drive Jeep. It looked like his stepbrother had already done a great deal of back-country driving.

"Where have you been to sling up this much mud?" Drew asked as he eyed the Jeep.

"I took a drive out to the elk refuge at dawn."

Drew had made the drive north out of town himself a couple of times to watch the elk in the early morning. It wasn't a muddy trip. As he buckled himself into the passenger's seat, Drew eyed his stepbrother, wondering if Morgan himself might be a victim of blackmail.

As Clay's chief of staff in Washington, Morgan wielded a great deal of power. As Clay moved on and became governor of Texas, and eventually president, Morgan would almost certainly go with him as a trusted advisor.

That made Drew's stepbrother a very powerful man, and a potential target for the kind of blackmail scheme that had been tried on Clay.

"Are you in trouble?" Drew asked, as his brother made the turn onto Spring Gulch Road.

Morgan shot Drew a startled glance. "What?"

"Has someone tried to blackmail you? Are you being blackmailed right now?"

Morgan spluttered and laughed. "Are you crazy? What gave you an idea like that?"

"Clay's current predicament," Drew replied. "It was a set-up, Morgan. Someone wants a hold on Clay and planned to get it by blackmailing him with pictures of him in bed with a dead girl."

"Is that what Clay told you?"

"I figured it out for myself."

"That sounds like a pretty elaborate set-up when

Clay was only invited to the party yesterday morning," Morgan said.

"How do you know he was only invited yesterday morning?"

"Niles mentioned it at breakfast," Morgan said. "Which means that if what Clay says is true, someone set up this intricate blackmail scheme in less than twelve hours. That doesn't make sense to me."

Drew understood now why Clay prized Morgan's advice. Drew had never looked at it that way. But he knew for a fact that Clay hadn't intended to go to the party on Bear Island before yesterday at breakfast.

"They snatched the girl three months ago," Drew mused aloud. "She was available on the spur of the moment. They could easily have had the drug handy. All they needed was Clay."

"And someone to commit the murder," Morgan pointed out. "Jimmy Joe told me that he didn't see anyone suspicious coming or going from the house. He had a guest list and was checking people off as they came in, which means the murderer was someone who was invited to the party."

"Or that Jimmy Joe left the door sometime during the night and the murderer walked in without being noticed," Drew suggested.

"Which sounds more likely," Morgan agreed. "Although it probably wouldn't hurt to talk to everyone on the guest list."

"The cops are already on it," Drew said. But he wondered how cooperative the influential guests had been, considering their high profiles and the fact this was a homicide.

"Here we are," Morgan said as he pulled up to the back door of the main house at Forgotten Valley.

"You're welcome to stay here," Drew said.

"Thanks, but I've got a room in town."

Drew didn't question Morgan further. All the De-Witt kids had their quirks. Needing his own space was one of Morgan's.

"Are you going to be at the bail hearing?" Drew asked.

"Clay will get in touch when he needs me." Morgan grinned and said, "I hear you're his attorney."

Drew made a face. "Against all good sense. He keeps telling me it's a done deal, that all I have to do is show up, and he'll be out of jail on bail."

"I'm betting that's exactly what will happen."

"I hope you're right," Drew said as he let himself out of the Jeep. "See you . . . when?"

"Later," Morgan said.

Drew watched his stepbrother back up and drive away. He wished they were closer. He wished they saw each other more often, or at least talked on the phone. Drew wasn't in touch with his other step-siblings, either. It was as though they'd all made a pact to disavow the past and live their lives forward, never looking back.

Drew glanced into the garage on his way into the house and saw his foreman had retrieved his fishing boat and pickup. He crossed to the pickup and retrieved his cell phone. And found three messages—all of them from Sarah. He remembered he'd written the number on a pad and left it by the phone in her kitchen last night, with a note to call if she needed him.

He debated whether to call her back. Until he realized all three calls had been made after he'd left her house this morning. After she'd sent him away.

Had something happened? Was she all right? Were the kids all right? Had some new information come in about Tom's murder? Or the charges against Clay?

Drew felt his heart racing as he reached for the button to call Sarah back.

Before he could punch in her number, the phone rang.

18

Drew had never before been nervous in a courtroom, except perhaps for his first appearance before a judge. He'd also never before represented a client accused of murder. He'd spent time on the phone with Clay's criminal attorney in New York, confirming what he ought to say on Clay's behalf and what Clay ought to say. Drew didn't know why he felt so anxious. He only knew he was.

The hickory benches in the Teton County circuit courtroom were packed with interested spectators, including media and townspeople. More troubling to Drew was the presence of both Jackson Blackthorne and King Grayhawk. He knew from stories Clay had told him just how much the two men hated each other. He knew King wanted to keep Clay in jail. Drew only hoped Blackjack had as much sway with the circuit court judge as Clay had said his father did.

Clay sat beside Drew at the defendant's table dressed in a dark gray wool-blend suit Drew had brought to him, with a crisply starched white shirt and a subdued tie. He looked like the influential and respectable political figure he was. What amazed Drew was the total lack of concern in his cousin's demeanor.

"You look like you're here as a spectator, rather than the defendant," he said to Clay.

Clay smiled, an easy, confident smile, and said, "That's because I know I'm innocent."

"Lots of innocent men have gone to jail," Drew retorted.

"Once I'm out of here," Clay said, "you and I are going to get together with Detective Barndollar and figure out who the real murderer is."

Drew groaned.

"What's wrong?" Clay asked.

"Nothing that can't be fixed." Clay's mention of Sarah had reminded Drew that he'd never returned her three calls. Clay's high-priced New York attorney had called immediately after Drew had seen the notice of Sarah's calls and kept him on the phone so long that he'd neither called Sarah back nor sought out King Grayhawk. He'd raced just to get showered and dressed for court.

Whatever Sarah wanted to talk about must have been important, or she wouldn't have called three times. Now that he had time to think about it, that niggling worry was back. Was she all right? Were the kids all right? He needed to know why she'd called.

As he reached for his cell phone, the excited hum in the background was replaced by scraping feet and rustling clothes as the bailiff said, "All rise."

"That's not Judge Wilkerson," Clay said under his breath.

One of the part-time magistrates entered the courtroom and took a seat at the bench, which was on a raised dais angled in the corner of the courtroom. Drew heard the ripple of excitement run through the crowd as everyone realized a substitution had been made.

"Be seated," the judge said. "I'm Judge Warner. Judge Wilkerson has recused himself because of a close relationship to the defendant through his father."

Drew heard a buzzing in his ears. He'd known things would go to hell. He just hadn't been sure how it would happen. He glanced at Clay, whose head was turned and whose eyes were locked with his father's.

Drew turned his own gaze across the courtroom and saw the smug look on King Grayhawk's face. Apparently King had done a little wheeling and dealing of his own overnight.

The district attorney rose and began his presentation, in very short order coming to precisely the conclusion Drew had expected. "The state believes there is a significant risk of flight if the defendant is released on bail, and therefore asks that bail be denied."

Drew wiped his sweaty hands on his suit trousers under the table as he listened to the DA list the reasons why he believed flight to be a possibility, ending with, "The defendant has a personal jet waiting at the airport as we speak."

The judge called on Drew to speak next.

Drew made all the arguments he'd discussed with Clay's high-priced New York criminal attorney, wishing with his heart and soul that Clay had been wise enough to wait, or that he'd been a big enough bastard to refuse to help his cousin. Because he knew, as sure as hogs made bacon, what was going to happen the instant he sat down.

"Bail is denied," the magistrate said.

The courtroom erupted, with the media running for the doors to file their stories, while a deputy put hand-cuffs on Clay and led him away. Drew had to hand it to his cousin. Clay's face never showed one bit of the fury Drew was sure he felt.

Drew heard low, angry voices and turned to find King and Blackjack faced off behind him in the nearly empty courtroom.

"Told you I'd get him one day," King said viciously. "You can kiss good-bye any hopes you ever had of that bastard son of yours becoming president."

"My son only took what your daughter freely of-fered," Blackjack shot back. "If a bitch wags her tail hard enough, she'll get what she's asking for."

Drew heard a gasp and realized it had come from behind Blackjack.

"Dammit all to hell!" Blackjack said, as he took a step aside and revealed Libby Grayhawk. "Didn't real-ize you were standing back there, girl."

Libby's face was ashen.

Drew wondered how Libby Grayhawk had ended up on the Blackthorne side of the courtroom. Then he saw Jocelyn Montrose and realized Libby must have brought her house guest here this morning and stayed by her side out of courtesy.

"I need to be getting home," Libby said. Drew saw her hands were shaking as she pulled on her coat.

Before she could leave, Blackjack's wife Ren slid an arm through Libby's and said, "My husband wants to apologize first."

Drew watched the ice melt in Blackjack's cold gray eyes as his wife looked up at him.

"I'm sorry, Ms. Grayhawk," Blackjack said. "That was discourteous of me."

King Grayhawk laughed. It wasn't a nice sound. "Easy to see who wears the pants in your family."

"Shut up, Daddy," Libby said matter-of-factly. She turned to Blackjack and said, "Thank you, Mr. Blackthorne. I do need to get home. There are chores to do." She turned to the elegant woman at her side and said, "Do you want to come with me, Jocelyn?"

"But of course," Jocelyn said.

When Libby and Jocelyn were gone, Blackjack turned back to King and said, "I know other judges."

"So do I," King said. "That boy of yours is going to stay behind bars till hell freezes over."

"Clay can take care of himself," Blackjack said. "I want to know what you've done with Kate. Where's my granddaughter?"

For the first time King looked rattled. His shoulders lost their stiffness and his complexion turned ashy. "I don't have her. I wish to God I did."

"You mean to say you have no idea—"

"I told you I don't!" King interrupted. "I've got every hand on my spread out looking for her. No one knows where she is. She's just plain disappeared. When I get my hands on the sonofabitch who took her—"

"Vengeance is going to be cold comfort if Kate turns up dead," Blackjack said brutally.

King looked stricken. "I'm doing everything in my power—"

"Maybe this is going to take both of us . . . working together," Blackjack said.

Drew expected King to come back with another malicious retort, but the old man said, "I'm willing to call a truce if you are. We can pick up our guns again when Kate is safe."

Drew felt like gasping himself, as Blackjack extended his hand and King Grayhawk clasped it.

"Till Kate is found," King said.

"Till Kate is found," Blackjack repeated.

Drew hadn't realized either man was aware of him until Blackjack turned to him and said, "What information can you give us about who might have taken Kate?"

Drew found himself the focus of all eyes. He glanced at King Grayhawk, then at Blackjack and said, "I do have a theory about why she might have been taken."

"Speak up, man," King said.

"Are you involved in an oil consortium doing a deal with the Japanese?" Drew asked King.

"I backed out of that." King turned to Blackjack and said, "Heard that boy of yours was investigating the deal, so I took a closer look at it myself. Didn't like what I found."

"When did you back out?" Drew said.

King lifted his Stetson, scratched his head,

smoothed his hair and tugged his Stetson back down low on his forehead. "Two weeks ago, maybe."

"Have you been getting any pressure from anyone to get back in?"

"Are you suggesting Niles Taylor and that gang are responsible for Kate's disappearance?" King said. "Because if you are—"

"Have you been getting pressure from anyone to get back in the Japanese deal?" Drew said impatiently.

"I got a call from . . ." King turned to Blackjack and said, "You and I need to talk."

"The police—" Drew began.

"No need to involve a bunch of Barney Fifes," King said, cutting him off. "I can handle this."

King glanced at Blackjack, who turned to Drew and said, "The two of us certainly can."

"What about Clay?" Drew asked Blackjack.

"Clay isn't going anywhere," Blackjack said with a sardonic twist of his mouth. "I'm sure he'd appreciate anything you can do to help him find out who killed that young woman."

"I want to be there when you talk to Taylor," Drew said.

Blackjack glanced at King, who nodded, then said, "All right. I'll give you a call." He slipped an arm around Ren's shoulder, gestured King down the courtroom aisle and said, "Shall we go?"

Drew's jaw was agape as he watched the two powerful enemies stride away like old friends. Men who'd grown up on the Western frontier were definitely a different breed. In order to survive, they'd learned to set aside their personal animosity to fight mutual enemies—the Sioux or the Blackfoot or natural disasters—knowing they could fight each other at a more convenient time.

He'd never expected to see two lifelong rivals join hands to work together. But to save their granddaughter, they had.

He only hoped King and Blackjack would succeed. An image formed in his mind of Jackson Blackthorne throttling Niles Taylor and he smiled grimly. The man would talk, all right.

Drew was closing his briefcase when he saw movement from the corner of his eye. He looked up and caught his breath at the sight of Sarah Barndollar. She looked even more beautiful than he remembered. Probably because he saw her now as forbidden fruit. He'd walked away. He meant to stay away. Better not to be nice. Better to put a fence up before she closed the distance between them.

"Don't you ever take a day off?" he said, letting his irritation that she was off-limits come out in his voice.

He watched her chin come up pugnaciously before she said, "I left three messages for you this morning. You never called me back."

"Oh, shit." He'd forgotten. Again. "I'm sorry. I was going to call you but—"

"I got an anonymous call from a man who said he'd been blackmailed the same way someone attempted to blackmail Clay."

Drew froze in the act of shutting his briefcase. "Does he know who's at the bottom of this?"

"He suggested a place where he thought the kidnapped girls might be held. I thought you might want to come along."

"You're not calling in the cavalry?" Drew asked.

"I'm on administrative leave," Sarah said. "If I call it in, my sergeant will assign someone else to check it out. Besides, I'm not sure it's a legitimate lead. I'd rather take a look myself first. I can always call in help later, if I need it."

"I'm glad you came to me," Drew said as he snapped his briefcase closed. "How are we getting there?"

"We'll need to ski up Game Creek Canyon," she said.

Drew hesitated. "This place is near the top, I suppose."

"Where else?" Sarah said with a smile.

Game Creek Canyon was another place he hadn't skied much since he'd been buried under five feet of snow at 25 Short—because it was one of those places where avalanche was always a danger.

But Kate might be up there somewhere. And Sarah had asked for his help.

"I'll need to stop by my place to change clothes and get some gear," he said.

"Thanks, Drew," Sarah said. "I'd like to take my Tahoe, in case I need to use the radio to call for help later." She followed him outside and said, "I can give you a ride to your place, if you like, and we can go from there."

The few flakes of snow Drew had seen first thing in the morning had become a full-fledged snowstorm. "Not the best weather to be heading up into Game Creek Canyon," he said.

"I don't want to wait."

Drew could understand Sarah's urgency, but he couldn't help wondering how they were going to see to get where they were going. He didn't want to think about the very real possibility of an avalanche, if it kept snowing this hard and the wind kept blowing.

"Who's taking care of the kids while you ride to Kate's rescue?" Drew asked as Sarah turned onto Spring Gulch Road.

"Nate and Brooke can take care of themselves," Sarah replied. "They both look after Ryan." She glanced at him and said, "I didn't want to leave them alone so soon after last night. But Brooke overheard me talking on the phone with that anonymous caller and mentioned it to Nate. The kids want me to do whatever I can to find the man responsible for their father's murder."

"They're amazing kids," Drew said.

"They're normal kids," Sarah countered. "They have their good days and their bad days. They'll always miss their father."

"Will you miss him?" Drew could have bitten out his tongue for asking such a revealing question, for which the answer was obvious.

"I'm glad to know he didn't run away from us," Sarah said soberly. "From me. We'd argued that last morning. Tom didn't want me to work such long hours. He wanted me to spend more time with him and the kids."

Drew wasn't sure what to say. He settled for, "That sounds reasonable."

"I tried explaining to him why I needed so badly to

find those missing girls." She glanced at him and said, "My sister disappeared when I was fourteen. She was never found."

"I'm sorry," Drew said. "I had no idea."

"Tom said the past didn't matter, that I should put my family first."

"It sounds like you both had a point."

Her lips twisted ruefully. "You're not taking sides?"

"I can see both sides," Drew said. "Is one necessarily right and one wrong?"

"The problem was that Tom and I could never find a middle ground." Sarah looked at Drew, then back at the road and said, "After Tom disappeared, I think I spent even more time at work, to the detriment of my kids."

"They're doing fine," Drew said.

She grimaced and said, "Would Nate have been out stealing antlers from the town square if he had a mother at home keeping an eye on him? Would Brooke be starving herself every chance she gets and dressing like a Brooklyn hooker if I was there every morning and evening? Would Ryan—"

"Whoa, whoa," Drew said. "You're being way too hard on yourself. If you're looking for ugly stepmothers, I can tell you stories about my grandfather's second wife that'll singe your eyebrows. I know what a cruel, uncaring woman does when she wants to hurt the ones she's supposed to love.

"You're nothing like that, Sarah. You love your kids. You care about them. They're happy and well-adjusted and—"

Sarah abruptly braked and the Tahoe skidded into a snowbank at the side of the narrow dirt road.

Drew saw her eyes had welled with tears and realized she could no longer see to drive. She stared straight ahead, her jaw clenched, her chin quivering.

Drew pulled her fingers free of the wheel, pulled her close and settled his arms around her. "Sarah, Sarah," he crooned. "Everything's going to be all right."

She shoved her cold nose hard against his neck and said in a low, grating voice, "I don't know if I can raise three kids all by myself. I'm a terrible mother. I—"

"Stop right there," he said, grasping her face with both hands and forcing her to look into his eyes. "I've seen abused kids. I was one," he admitted, feeling his heartbeat rachet up at the admission he'd never made to anyone.

She stared at him wide-eyed. "But you're rich!"

"Rich folks can brutalize their kids with the best of them," he said. "In my case it was a stepgrandmother who did all the damage. I'm only telling you this because I've spent enough time with your kids to know there's nothing abusive, emotionally or physically, about your relationship with them. Nate and Brooke and Ryan all love you. They all look to you for help when they need it. They trust you to be there for them."

"Thank you, Drew," she said, leaning forward to press her forehead against his.

They were nose to nose, their mouths a breath apart. It would have taken very little to close the distance. But he drew back. "You're getting tears on my suit," he said with a gentle smile. He wasn't going to let himself kiss her. It was too damned dangerous. She was too damned attractive. And he wanted her too damned much.

He had no intention of hanging around Jackson Hole, Wyoming, the rest of his life. He had places to go. Things to do—that is, once he figured out what they were.

He let go of her and she eased back into the driver's seat, brushing at the tears on her cheeks with the back of her hand.

"I hate crying," she said, swiping at her nose with her sleeve.

"You're beautiful when you cry."

She half-laughed, half-sobbed and said, "Now you're lying."

He'd never meant anything more in his life. But it was better that she didn't know that. "You okay to drive now?" he asked.

She sniffed once and said, "Yeah," then started up the Tahoe.

They didn't say another word the rest of the way to the main house at Forgotten Valley.

"Come on in," he said as he headed for the kitchen door. "I won't be long. You can make us some coffee to take along. Coffee's in the cupboard over the sink and the coffeemaker's by the stove. I've got a thermos in the cupboard over the stove."

He hurried down the hall, afraid that if he stayed another minute in the kitchen he'd take her in his arms and never let her go.

*   *   *

"If you don't mind, I need to stop by and see my brother North before we go back to my place," Libby said.

"I'm sorry I've put you to so much trouble," Jocelyn said.

Libby snorted inelegantly. "You haven't been any trouble at all. It's that father of mine—and Clay's father—who need an attitude readjustment."

Jocelyn smiled. "I must say that was an impressively terrifying battle of wills."

"You get used to it," Libby said. "As far back as I can remember, my father's always gotten his own way. If he wants something, he goes after it. Nine-and-a-half times out of ten, he gets it. Trouble is, he's raised seven children, including me, who expect the same results when we want something. And cry bloody murder when we don't get it."

Jocelyn laughed and eyed her askance.

Libby figured the demure young woman was probably trying to decide whether she'd been using hyperbole. She might have exaggerated a little, but not much. Libby had grown up in a cutthroat, dog-eat-dog family where it was a way of life to fight for what you wanted and never to settle for less.

Which was why Libby had defied her father and left home with her illegitimate daughter when she was eighteen. And why she hadn't been satisfied with any other man, once she'd given her heart to Clay Blackthorne.

Now it looked like she was going to lose Clay to yet another woman.

Libby had watched Jocelyn Montrose when the

graceful young woman greeted Clay in the courtroom and noticed Jocelyn's whole demeanor had become soft and adoring. It was plain as the exquisite nose on the young woman's face and the doting look in her amazing violet eyes, that Jocelyn was in love with her late sister's husband.

Libby had wanted to yank the other woman's hair out.

Which told her more than she wanted to know about her own highly irrational, emotionally immature—all right, ferociously jealous—feelings for the father of her child.

The problem was, and always had been, that Blackthornes were as used to getting their own way as Grayhawks. Once Clay had realized the depth of her betrayal all those years ago, he'd walked away from her and never looked back.

Libby had tried hard to believe that there was more than one man in the world with whom she could be happy. She'd finally admitted, after breaking her engagement rather than marrying a second time, that she'd never committed her whole heart to either man she'd tried to love, because she hadn't possessed a whole heart to give.

Was she now supposed to step back and give Jocelyn Montrose the freedom to pursue the man Libby loved, had always loved, and would continue to love until the day she died?

No. Hell, no. Absolutely, positively not. No self-respecting Grayhawk would concede the battle without a fight.

But Libby had far too much on her plate as it was. Her first priority was finding her daughter. She was also determined to find out who'd framed Clay, and why. She didn't have time right now to worry about the threat Jocelyn Montrose posed to her future happiness.

But she couldn't ignore the other woman, either.

Libby had to believe that Kate would be found safe and sound, and that Clay would be cleared of the spurious charges against him. When that day finally came, she didn't want Jocelyn Montrose waiting in the wings to entice Clay away. And she knew just the man to distract her rival.

Her brother North.

Since desperate situations required desperate measures, Libby had decided to kill two birds with one stone. She would simply take Jocelyn along when she went to see North to ask him what he knew about Niles Taylor. And introduce him to the violet-eyed woman.

Libby had no illusions that North would settle down happily ever after with a woman like Jocelyn. She was far too delicate a hothouse flower to share the rugged life North lived on his Wyoming ranch. She would quickly wilt and die.

But Jocelyn was exactly the sort of woman North took to his bed. Beautiful, big-bosomed and long-legged.

North's previous partners had also been overtly sexy. At first glance, Jocelyn didn't seem to fit that description. Especially not with the way she kept her clothes buttoned up to the throat and her hair bound up in a

French twist. But her loveliness would surely catch North's eye.

Libby would simply have to put the two of them together and keep her fingers crossed. With any luck, North would distract Jocelyn long enough that, when things settled down, Libby would have the chance, at long last, to make amends with Clay.

Libby knew North would be at home this morning. In fact, Sundays were virtually the only time he did stay at home. As she drove up, he was outside picking up a load of firewood from the side of the house. He hesitated as she pulled up, then headed toward her.

She got out as he approached and said, "The judge didn't grant Clay bail."

"Never figured he would." North bent and glanced through her open car door to the other side of the front seat and said, "Who's that with you?"

Jocelyn leaned toward the driver's side, smiled at North and said in her melodious, French-accented voice, "Good morning. I'm Jocelyn Montrose."

Libby was watching North closely but saw not the slightest flicker of interest in his eyes. She pressed her lips flat. Maybe he needed to see how tall Jocelyn was. Or get a better look at her arresting violet eyes.

"Can we come in for a minute?" she said to her brother.

This time she saw a flicker of annoyance cross his face. Sundays were his day to sit back, put his feet up and relax by himself. But she wasn't about to let him send her away. "I really need to talk to you."

He'd never turned her away. And he didn't now.

"Come on in." He didn't wait for them, just turned his back and headed for the door with the load of firewood in his arms.

"Maybe I should wait here," Jocelyn said, eyeing North's broad, dismissive back.

Libby smiled. She was determined to get the two of them together in the same room. "Please come inside. I'd worry about you sitting out here in the cold. I shouldn't be long."

North was setting another log on the crackling fire in the living room by the time Libby and Jocelyn joined him. Libby had always loved North's house. It was totally masculine and smelled of leather and the mesquite he put on the fire.

The inside walls were composed of chinked logs. Above the stone mantel hung a massive oil painting of longhorns being herded across a deep ravine by cowboys on horseback wearing yellow slickers. The furniture was brown leather, and colorful Navajo rugs lay on the hickory wood floor. The immense wall of windows on the opposite side of the room revealed a stunning view of the snowcapped Grand Tetons in the distance.

When at last North turned to face Jocelyn, Libby kept her fingers crossed that she'd see some sparks. She gritted her teeth when North evidenced absolutely no reaction to the beautiful woman.

Instead he turned to Libby and said, "Do you want to talk in here, or do we need to go to my office?"

"Here is fine," Libby replied. "Jocelyn is Clay's late wife's younger sister. She knows about Kate."

North grunted, and Libby felt like kicking him. A

woman as sophisticated as Jocelyn Montrose wasn't going to be attracted to a grunting man.

"I wanted to ask you what you know about Niles Taylor," she said bluntly.

"He's a Texas oilman."

"I knew that much," Libby said with asperity. "Why were you at his party on Saturday?"

"He invited me."

Libby made a frustrated sound in her throat. "Do you know any reason why Niles would want to cause trouble for Clay?"

"You worry too much about that man," North replied.

"Answer the question."

"I think Niles wants to talk Clay out of investigating an oil consortium he set up."

"Would he resort to blackmail and murder to stop him?" Libby asked.

North's eyes narrowed, but he said nothing.

"Would he have an innocent girl drug Clay's drink and then murder her and put them in bed together?" Libby persisted.

"I don't know," North said.

"Can't you make a guess?"

"I'll ask him the next time I see him," North said sardonically.

Libby stared at her older brother, knowing that he couldn't be pushed. She exhaled. She hadn't gotten much information from him, but that didn't mean he wouldn't find out the answers to the questions she'd asked.

She glanced from North to Jocelyn and realized the other woman's cheeks were flushed. Maybe there was some attraction, and all she needed to do was leave them alone for it to spark to life.

"I could use a cup of coffee," she said.

"Help yourself," North said. "It's in the kitchen."

Libby couldn't believe her brother was acting so boorishly in front of company. She'd fix him. She'd leave him alone with Jocelyn while she went for coffee.

"Why don't you keep Jocelyn entertained while I get the two of us some coffee? Would you like a cup, North?" Libby asked.

This time her brother's pained expression was all too apparent. "No coffee for me."

Jocelyn was still standing in the middle of the living room as Libby headed for the kitchen. She almost turned to suggest that Jocelyn make herself comfortable but realized it would probably be better if she let the two of them work things out on their own. "I'll just be a minute," she said as she exited the room.

A long hallway and a swinging door separated the living room from the kitchen. Libby held the door open for a moment before letting it swing closed, hoping to hear some conversation in the living room, but it was too far away for voices to carry.

Her brother had nothing resembling a china cup and saucer in the kitchen, only man-sized mugs. Libby picked two of the smaller ones without chips and poured coffee for herself and Jocelyn. She knew Jocelyn liked hers black with sweetener because she'd served her coffee earlier that morning.

Libby was trying to think of some way to postpone her return to the living room, when the swinging door slammed open and Jocelyn strode into the kitchen, her fists clenched, her face flaming and her stormy violet eyes bright with unshed tears.

"I want to leave," she said, her voice breaking.

"What's wrong?" Libby asked, alarmed. "Did North—"

"I want to leave," she repeated, her voice pitifully high-pitched.

An instant later, North shoved his way through the kitchen doorway. Libby was astonished to see that his reddened right cheek bore the clear white imprint of a hand.

She turned on her brother and demanded, "What did you do to her?"

She watched a muscle in North's jaw flex. He stared at Jocelyn, his eyes narrowed, and said nothing.

Libby turned to Jocelyn and asked, "Are you all right? What did he do to you?"

"I'm fine," Jocelyn said, her eyes focused on the floor, her chin wobbling. "But I wish to leave."

Still no explanation from either one of what North had said or done to provoke a woman as self-possessed and dignified as Jocelyn Montrose into slapping his face.

"I'll talk to you later," Libby said to her brother. It was clear Jocelyn Montrose wouldn't care if she never saw North Grayhawk again. Libby tried telling herself it was only a short distance between love and hate. But it was clear that she was going to have to come up with someone else to distract Jocelyn's attention from Clay.

She put an arm around Jocelyn's shoulder to lead her away and realized the young woman was still wearing her coat. What on earth had North said or done to raise such a ruckus when Jocelyn hadn't even taken off her coat?

In the short time they'd been inside, nearly an inch of snow had collected on the ground. Libby's stomach clenched when she realized the snow was going to obliterate any signs of Kate's trail in the wilderness.

Libby didn't ask questions once they were back in the car. She couldn't believe how wrong things had gone between North and Jocelyn. She'd wanted to make the situation better, not worse.

Jocelyn didn't speak until Libby stopped the car at her cabin on the edge of North's spread. "I shouldn't have slapped him," she said.

"What happened?" Libby asked.

Jocelyn bit her lip and shook her head. Her eyes brimmed with tears. "I can't . . . I don't . . ."

"Never mind," Libby said. "Forget I asked. In fact, forget I have a brother named North."

Jocelyn choked on a laugh. "You've been so good to me. I feel so bad about slapping your brother." She turned to Libby and said, "But he deserved it."

Libby felt a spurt of guilt. She hadn't been at all *good* to Jocelyn. She'd been plotting and planning to get rid of her. "I'm sorry," Libby said. Maybe she ought to tell the other woman the truth about her own feelings for Clay. Maybe Jocelyn was no more interested in Clay Blackthorne than the man in the moon.

But Jocelyn spoke first.

"I don't know if I should be telling you this," Jocelyn said. She hesitated, sighed, then said, "I have feelings for Clay."

Libby barely managed to hide her despair.

"I've loved Clay ever since I first laid eyes on him," Jocelyn said. "I met him first, before my sister. Did you know that?"

"No, I didn't," Libby said.

Jocelyn nodded and dabbed gracefully at the tears on her cheeks with a lace handkerchief. "But he took one look at Giselle and forgot all about me. They were inseparable. I rarely visited my sister during the years she was married. It was too painful to see him with her. I was jealous, you see."

Libby nodded, but said nothing. Her throat had swollen so thick it hurt to swallow.

"Then Giselle got cancer. When it was too late, I realized how much precious time I'd lost by being jealous of my sister's happiness. I spent as much time as I could with her those last months. I never once looked at Clay . . . or coveted my sister's husband."

Jocelyn turned toward Libby and said, "Toward the end, when Giselle knew she didn't have much time left, she looked at me and whispered, 'Promise you'll take care of him for me, Jocelyn. He's going to be lost. He'll need you. Stay with him. Love him for me.'"

The last words were barely audible.

Libby gripped the steering wheel, afraid to let go, hearing in Giselle's confession the death knell to her dreams of a life with Clay. "So you've been doing what your sister asked," she said quietly.

Jocelyn nodded. "I'm torn in two. I never told her that I've always loved him."

"She must have known," Libby murmured.

"Do you think so? I've wondered sometimes. I've tried to do what she asked. Sometimes I think Clay cares for me. Sometimes I'm not sure. What am I going to do?"

Libby felt like wailing. Here she was acting as a confidante to the woman who was the greatest threat to her own hope of living happily ever after.

Libby was grateful that at least Jocelyn didn't know the truth about her matchmaking attempt. No wonder Jocelyn had repelled whatever advance North had made.

"I only wish there was something I could do to help Clay," Jocelyn said, her hands threaded together and clutched tightly in her lap. "I feel so useless. I don't even have the right clothes for a place like this."

"You might fit into some of Kate's things," Libby said. "She's tall like you."

An ache rose unexpectedly in Libby's chest as she spoke Kate's name. Where was her daughter? What was happening to her? How was she ever going to find her?

Libby's cell phone rang and she grabbed for it without looking at the caller ID. "Kate? Is that you?"

She glanced at Jocelyn, her eyes wide, and exclaimed, "Clay? Where are you? . . . You're out? How on earth did that happen? . . . That's wonderful!"

"Clay's out of jail?" Jocelyn whispered.

Libby nodded distractedly, then gripped the phone

harder as she said, "No, I haven't heard anything from Kate . . . What? Where did the caller say she might be? . . . Of course I'd be willing to bring the dogs. Where is it we're going?" She glanced at Jocelyn and said, "I'll be waiting for you at my cabin."

Libby stuck her cell phone in her pocket, shoved open the car door and headed for the kitchen door.

"What's going on?" Jocelyn asked, following Libby into the house.

"Clay got an anonymous tip where we might find Kate."

"Has he called the police?" Jocelyn asked.

"He's afraid of what the police might do. He wants to look on his own before he contacts them."

"With you?" Jocelyn said, frowning.

"Tracking is what I do." Libby stared out the kitchen window at the blowing snow and wondered how much scent would be left for the dogs to follow.

"You're leaving me behind?"

"You couldn't keep up," Libby said bluntly.

Jocelyn turned and leaned forward, her voice excited and earnest. "I'm stronger than you think, Libby. I want to go along. I want to help Clay find his daughter."

"You'll slow us down," Libby insisted.

"Then you can leave me behind on the trail."

"You might get lost trying to find your way back. You could freeze to death. I'm sorry, but you can't go."

"All right," she said with a disappointed sigh. "I'll stay behind. At least I'll be by the phone if someone calls with information about Kate."

"Thank you. That would be a big help."

Libby spent a moment feeling sorry for the other woman, who was so out of her element here. But a moment was all she had. She needed to figure out the best way to reach the area Clay had mentioned, and which of her hunting rifles, with their long-distance scopes, she was going to take along.

19

Sarah snapped her cell phone closed and tucked it into her trouser pocket, then held her hands out to the roaring fire in Drew's fireplace. "The weather service says the wind is near gale force, the temperature is dropping and to expect six to eight inches of snow in the mountains."

"So are we going, or not?"

Sarah looked at the blizzard raging outside, then met Drew's gaze and said, "Not right now. It's too dangerous. We have to wait out the storm."

"But Kate—"

"We'd have trouble even finding the trail in a whiteout like this," Sarah said. "Let alone taking off into the wilderness on some wild-goose chase."

"Did the guy who called you sound like he was sending you off on a wild-goose chase?" Drew asked.

"He sounded rational. That doesn't mean he was telling the truth. Or that his directions will lead us to Kate. It's not going to help if we end up having to be rescued ourselves."

Drew threw a log onto the fire, sending up a hail of sparks. "This sucks."

"Big-time," Sarah agreed. "Kate was alive yesterday. We have to presume she's being kept somewhere safe. I promise you, as soon as the weather breaks even a little, we'll go."

"It's hard not to want to go anyway, blizzard or no blizzard," Drew said.

"If we can't see our hands in front of our faces right now, the bad guys can't, either," Sarah pointed out.

"Do you need to get home?" Drew asked.

"The kids have orders not to step foot over the threshold today. They're to do nothing but rest and recuperate."

Drew smiled wryly. "And you expect them to obey you, after what they did last night?"

"Those were extraordinary circumstances," Sarah said. "And yes, I do expect my children to obey me. There are consequences when they don't."

"Such as?" Drew asked.

"Getting grounded. Losing privileges. Believe me, a week without Metroid for Nate, or without Harry Potter for Ryan, or without the phone for Brooke, is a terrible punishment."

Drew grinned. "With a mother as mean as you, I'd be good."

Sarah looked at him earnestly and said, "Discipline is important. It helps a child grow into a responsible person."

"I agree," he said, sobering. "I'm just not used to—" He stopped himself and said, "You're good at parenting, Sarah. It shows."

Sarah let herself imagine for a moment that he was

Nate and Brooke and Ryan's father. It was too bad he didn't like kids, because she thought he'd be good at it. But she'd learned not to indulge in fantasy, so she turned the subject away from her kids. She walked to the window being pelted with crystals of wind-driven snow and said, "I'm glad I'm in here and not out there."

Drew joined her and said, "I've always known the weather was unpredictable in Wyoming, but I'm still always amazed to see it change from gentle snow to blizzard conditions in twenty minutes."

"I wish the storm had held off long enough for us to get up Game Creek Canyon and back," Sarah said. "I imagine every minute Kate Grayhawk spends out there in the wilderness feels like a lifetime. With any luck, this'll blow through in a couple of hours."

"Until then, I guess we're stuck here together," Drew said.

Their eyes caught and held.

Sarah felt a tingling in her breasts and a tightness in her belly that signaled a desire so strong it frightened her. She could feel her pulse racing, feel the heat in her throat as her body flushed with sexual awareness.

Her eyes remained riveted on Drew's, so she was aware of how his pupils grew large and dark as he drank in the sight of her. She watched his nostrils flare for the scent of her, saw his sensual appetite awaken and grow.

Sarah knew she ought to flee, but she felt frozen in place by the force of Drew's intense gaze.

He stretched out a hand almost lazily, like a sleek cat that knows its quarry is trapped and cannot escape. He circled her waist and pulled her toward him until her hips cradled his thighs. His body was hard against hers, his arousal unmistakable.

His eyes never left hers as his hands slid up to cup her derriere and settle her snugly against him. His nose nuzzled her throat, and his mouth followed. He nipped gently, then laved with his tongue, his hot breath sending shivers down her spine.

Until that moment, Sarah had been passive in his arms.

When his hot gaze met hers again, she slid her hands into his hair and pressed the full length of her body against his, so her breasts were crushed against the hardness of his chest. She lifted her mouth and found his, her tongue urgent in its quest to be inside tasting him, joining his in a search for mutual pleasure.

Drew surprised her when he picked her up in his arms. She stared at him, her heart beating frantically, her breath coming in short bursts, her body flushed and pulsing with desire.

He headed for his bedroom without a word. He set her on her feet beside the bed and said, "I want to undress you."

"Fine. As long as I'm allowed to return the favor."

She was wearing layers for the trip up the canyon, so when Drew tugged her sweater off over her head, he found a wool shirt. She was surprised how slowly he unbuttoned her shirt and tugged the tails out of her jeans, especially considering that all he could see beneath it was her long johns. He smiled as he tossed her shirt onto a nearby chair.

She could feel his callused fingertips against her skin

as he freed the long john shirt from her trousers and eased it up over her head, leaving her wearing only a bra. And not a very fancy bra, at that. Women who'd been married a long time wore functional, rather than sexy, underwear. And Sarah, who hadn't had a man in the house for a year, had allowed her underwear to get woefully shabby.

She put her hands over her worn-out bra and said, "This should have gone into the trash a long time ago."

Drew smiled and said, "Fine by me." He reached up to unhook her bra, forcing her hands away from her chest, then pulled the straps off her shoulders before tossing the frayed lingerie into the trash can across the room.

Sarah laughed. "I'm going to need that later."

"You can pick up another one at home." Drew unbuckled her belt and pulled it through the loops slowly and sensuously, then dropped it onto the floor.

He unsnapped her jeans and was reaching for the zipper when she caught his wrist and said, "My turn."

She kept her eyes on his as she unbuttoned his plaid wool shirt and pulled it down his arms. When it wouldn't come off, she realized his hands were too big for the shirt to come off unless she undid the buttons at the wrist. And then realized that with the shirt binding his hands, he was essentially her prisoner, to do with as she wished.

She left his hands bound as she shoved his long john shirt up high enough to expose most of his chest. She kissed his navel, and he hissed and sucked in his stomach. She chuckled and kissed her way up to his nipples, first teasing them with her tongue and then nipping, until Drew hissed and jerked back a step and began struggling to get his hands free.

"Uh uh," Sarah said. "It's still my turn."

She unbuckled his belt and didn't bother pulling it from his jeans before she unzipped them and slid her hand inside his underwear to cup his warm, hard and silky flesh.

Drew froze and stared down at her. A moment later, his mouth was latched to hers, his tongue thrusting deep, mimicking the sex act. She heard a button pop, and one of his hands was free, and then cloth ripping as he tore his shirt off and pitched it across the room.

Then his hands were on her breasts, his thumbs brushing the nipples, causing them to harden and peak, his mouth hot on hers, demanding equal passion, his body pressed hard against her hand, seeking the pleasure she offered.

"I want to be inside you," he said in a throaty growl, shoving at her jeans, long johns and underwear, trying to get her naked.

She let go of him to help him pull at her clothes, then stopped and said, "Boots! Boots!" when she realized her clothes wouldn't come off over her winter boots.

He tipped her onto her fanny on the bed and went to work on her laces, as she shimmied out of her clothes, so that by the time he was done and had her boots and socks off, he could pull the rest of her clothes off over her pointed toes.

"Sit," she said, standing up and pushing him down

onto the bed. She knelt at his feet naked and went to work on his shoelaces while his hands played with her breasts.

"God, I can't get enough of you," he said. "I'm dying out here. Hurry up. I want to be inside you."

She moaned as her body began to ache with need.

She yanked his boots off and tossed them, pulling on his socks as he shoved the rest of his clothes off. Then he lifted her up and impaled her as she dropped down onto his lap, her knees on either side of his hips.

Her arms went round his neck and she latched onto his shoulder with her mouth, as they moved together desperately, seeking release.

"Sarah," he breathed, his mouth seeking hers. "Sarah, I want you. I need you."

Sarah realized she was waiting for more, for Drew to say *I love you.*

But the words never came. At least, not before the two of them did.

Sarah's climax was shattering, more so because the lack of special words being spoken by Drew should have made the sex act less intense, should have kept her from giving everything she had to give.

Drew clutched her tightly as he spilled himself inside her, his face pressed against her breast, his body rigid in exultation.

They were both breathing hard, and the smell of sweat and sex was strong in the warm room.

Sarah waited for the moment when Drew would separate them, and she would have to look into his eyes and see that what they had done was not as special for him as it had been for her. That he did not feel for her what she was coming to realize she felt for him.

She brushed aside the sweaty curls from his brow and kissed him gently there, tasting the salt, before she laid her cheek on his shoulder.

His hands were roaming her back, soothing, loving.

Sarah realized she shouldn't have used that word, *loving*. Drew didn't love her. He'd said he *wanted* and *needed* her. Both were important, but they weren't *love*.

"I told myself I wasn't going to do this," Sarah said, as she tried to disengage herself from Drew.

He caught her at the waist with both hands and kept her from moving. She could feel him stirring inside her and her eyes widened.

"Did you think we were done?" he said with a twinkle in his eye.

"Well, yes," she admitted with a shy smile.

He leaned her backward and lowered his mouth and put his lips to her breast and suckled.

Sarah gasped as an aching need built inside her. "How do you do that to me?" she asked breathlessly. "I want you again."

He lifted his head, grinned at her and said, "Good. Because you've got me."

He lay back on the bed, and she lowered her body over his. He reached up and freed her hair from its French braid and slid his hands into it. "Your hair's so silky," he said.

She lowered her head, letting her hair flow across his body, as she found his mouth with hers.

The lovemaking was slower this time, each searching out places on the other's body to kiss, moving as one, rolling so she was beneath him. He slid his hands beneath her buttocks and lifted her as he began once more to thrust.

"You're beautiful, Sarah," he said.

Sarah barely managed to keep from blurting, "Haven't you seen all those silver stretch marks?" Instead, she grinned, arched her body into his, and replied, "I love it when you say things like that."

His hands played with her hair, and his mouth tantalized her body, as he moved first with grace and then with urgency.

Sarah cried out as her body began to spasm with almost unbearable pleasure, and she heard Drew's guttural response as he spilled himself inside her.

He kept most of his weight on his arms, but she'd wrapped her legs around him and they lay that way until their breathing slowed. Drew slid to his side and pulled her close, his chin resting against her brow.

"I don't want to get up," Sarah said.

"Then don't," Drew murmured.

"I should call and check on my kids."

"They're supposed to be tucked in safe at home."

"Yes, but knowing my kids, it never hurts to check."

Sarah pressed her nose against Drew's flesh and inhaled the man-scent of him. Her eyes felt heavy and she let them slide closed as she snuggled against him.

"Don't let me fall asleep," she mumbled.

Drew didn't answer, and Sarah realized from his deep, even breathing, it was because he was already asleep. She relaxed against him, liking the way the coarse hair on his chest tickled her nose. She laid her hand on his chest, then laid her cheek against her hand. She was warm and comfortable and happy.

She decided it wouldn't hurt just to rest a little while until the storm passed them by. She could check on her kids before she and Drew headed up the canyon.

Drew never slept long after sex because he was used to having to get up and leave whatever bed he was in. He froze when he realized Sarah was still snuggled up next to him. It was her hair tickling his nose that had woken him.

He wondered if he should wake her, but one glance toward the window confirmed that the storm was still blowing. He took advantage of the opportunity to look his fill.

Sarah's body was long and sleek, and her golden brown hair teasingly hid breasts he'd discovered were just the right size to fit his hands. Tiny lines of worry had etched their way onto her brow. She was lucky they weren't much deeper, he thought wryly, considering the bucketful of responsibility—and the occasional wild escapade—her kids must provide.

What dawned on Drew, as he lay beside her waiting for the storm to abate, was how anxious he felt himself about Nate and Brooke and Ryan being home alone right now. They were probably just fine. But his stomach was knotted with worry.

Over kids he hadn't even known forty-eight hours ago. Over kids that had mostly been a pain in the ass. Over kids that he realized he cared about in a way he'd sworn to himself that he'd never allow himself to care.

The same way he cared for Sarah.

Her anguish made his heart hurt. Her terror made him want to protect her. His arm tightened convulsively around her, and Sarah protested with a grunt before her eyes blinked open.

"Sorry," he said, easing his hold on her.

When she lifted her head to look out the window he said, "Still blizzarding out there."

She laid her head back on his shoulder trustingly, eased one leg over his hip to put them body to body and murmured, "Hmmm. You feel good."

"So do you," he said.

Drew couldn't remember ever making love to a woman when the act hadn't been preceded by recognizable physical desire. But making love to Sarah this time was motivated by something entirely different. He was afraid to name it even to himself. Offering comfort was a safer word than the truth.

Yet, in the beginning, comfort was all there was.

He held Sarah snug in his arms, feeling the warmth of her, wishing he could lift some of the heavy burdens she carried from her slender shoulders. He hadn't expected her to press her hips against his and whisper, "Make love to me, Drew." He hadn't expected his own response.

He'd taken her face in both hands, looked into her eyes and seen the desperate need to be connected intimately, completely, to another human being. He'd answered her plea by giving everything he had to her. His heart. His body. And his soul. Oh, yes, his soul.

Drew hadn't known it was possible to love someone

so deeply, so completely, in such a short time. He had no idea how it had happened. He only knew it had.

Loving Sarah was terrifying because of the promises he'd made to himself that he would need to break in order to keep her in his life.

I will never have children.

I will never love a woman who can break my heart.

Loving Sarah meant taking the risk of being a parent to her children. Present tense. It wasn't even a question of having children of his own someday in the future. There was nothing future about it, because Nate and Brooke and Ryan already existed.

At which point, a startling thought lodged like a painful fishhook in his gut. If he was going to break his vow by parenting Sarah's children, why not go all the way? Why not have a child—or two or three—with Sarah?

Which brought him to the second vow he'd made.

For a woman to break his heart, he would have to love her. And she would have to betray him.

He'd never doubted his ability to love. Just as he'd never doubted that eventual betrayal. It had happened with every woman he'd ever known and loved, especially those closest to him, most notably, his stepgrandmother, and most recently, the woman he'd left behind in Houston, Grayson Choate.

Drew had guarded his heart as much as he could. But whenever he'd given it, as he inevitably had, he'd been disappointed. How could he expect things to be any different with Sarah Barndollar?

Drew was jolted by another thought. He knew he

loved Sarah, but he had no idea how she felt about him. She'd only recently found out she was a widow. It was wishful thinking to believe she could have been as smitten with him over the past forty-eight hours as he had been by her.

He found himself fantasizing about what it would be like to live here with her. To wake up with her soft, warm body next to his, to get dressed together and make breakfast together.

He stopped himself right there.

He needed to add three loud, quarrelsome and intrusive kids to the picture.

As much as Drew tried to make the image unpleasant, it wasn't. Maybe he was being naive. Probably he was being naive. But he'd liked having siblings. He'd liked the noise and the laughter—for as long as it had lasted. But it never lasted long.

Drew had learned not to believe in happily-ever-after. He'd learned not to trust. It was hard to hope, when his hopes had been dashed so ruthlessly in the past. It would be far safer to walk away and never look back. Now. While he still could.

Sarah drifted in and out of sleep, aware of something niggling at her, something that wouldn't let her completely relax. When Drew's phone rang, she sat bolt upright.

"What time is it?" Drew said, rolling over onto his back and rubbing the sleep from his eyes.

Sarah's glance jumped to the window, and she was forced to squint against the bright sunshine. "The storm is over." She looked at the digital clock beside Drew's bed and said, "It's a little after one o'clock." And then, staring at the ringing phone, "Are you going to get that?"

Drew reached across the bed and picked up the receiver. "Who's calling?" he asked irritably.

Sarah snatched her trousers from the floor and searched the pockets for her cell phone, looking to see if the kids had called. They hadn't. She hit the button to call home and waited while the phone rang and rang until the answering machine picked up.

"If you're there, pick up," she said. She waited, but the phone remained unanswered. Then she called the cell phone Brooke carried when the kids left the house. All she got was voice mail. "Where are you guys?" she said. "I'm on my way home. If you get this message, meet me there. I'm going to want a damned good explanation why you disobeyed me and left the house."

Drew appeared before her wearing unsnapped jeans and scratching his belly. "You'll never guess who that was," he said.

"I hope it was my kids. They haven't called me and they aren't at home," Sarah said. "If they went out in this storm—"

"Hey, calm down," Drew said, trying to pull her into his arms.

Sarah batted his hands away. "My kids are gone. I'm not in the mood for sex."

A flicker of hurt darted in Drew's blue eyes and Sarah realized she'd mistaken his offer of comfort for something else. "I'm sorry." She rose and slid her arms around Drew's waist to hug him, then leaned back and looked up into his eyes. "I know I'm acting like an idiot, but after the stunt they pulled last night, I'm a little skittish."

"Maybe they went to a friend's house," Drew said.

"I'll feel better when I know they're all right," Sarah said. "I'm sorry I snapped at you."

"Forget it," Drew said, returning her hug.

"Who was that on the phone?" she asked.

"Clay."

"Do you need to go down to the jail?"

Drew grinned. "It seems the judge had a change of heart. Clay's out on bail."

"That's amazing!" Sarah said.

"Yeah, amazing what two powerful old men can accomplish when they join forces," Drew said cynically. "What's even more interesting is that Clay got the same anonymous call you did—about where to find Kate. He said he had to threaten to tie Libby to a chair to keep her from going after Kate in the storm."

"I suppose we can all go together now," Sarah said.

"I've got a meeting to go to first."

Sarah raised a questioning brow. "What's up?"

"King and Blackjack are planning to confront Niles Taylor," Drew explained. "Clay invited me to be there when they ask him some pointed questions."

"What about rescuing Kate? Shouldn't that take precedence?"

"Clay seems to think he'll get more precise information about where Kate is from Niles."

"In that case, I'd like to be there, too," Sarah said.

"Don't you have to check on your kids?"

"We can do that on the way."

"You weren't invited to this party, Sarah."

"So I'll show up uninvited." When Drew's face remained implacable, Sarah said, "Niles Taylor may have arranged my husband's murder, Drew. I want to be there. I just need to check on my kids first and make sure they're all right."

"Fine. I'll come with you."

Sarah opened her mouth to tell Drew she could meet him later and closed it again. She might very well need his help if it turned out the kids had run her pickup into a snowy ditch somewhere. "Thanks," she said.

Sarah felt a strange lethargy, an unwillingness to let go of Drew and finish dressing. It felt wonderful to be held in a man's arms, to acknowledge his strength and know he was there to support and comfort her. She'd learned enough about Drew DeWitt in the short time they'd been acquainted to understand why he might want to keep their relationship strictly casual, which is to say, sexual.

She couldn't help wanting more. She knew the chemistry between them was something special. She liked him and admired him. And she trusted him. Which was a lot to say based on such short acquaintance. Could you fall in love with a man over a weekend? Sarah was afraid she had.

She lifted her face to his for one last kiss and said, "We'd better get moving."

They walked hand in hand to the bedroom and dressed in companionable silence. As though they were already a married couple, Sarah thought. She flushed, then glanced at Drew and realized he had no way of discerning her thoughts.

He smiled when he saw her eyes on him and said, "I'll bring my pickup, in case we need to drive around looking for them."

"Good. I'll meet you at my house," Sarah said.

Drew helped her put on her coat, wrapped her scarf around her neck and placed one more kiss on her mouth before he shoved her out his kitchen door ahead of him.

Sarah basked in the warm afterglow of feeling loved—even though she knew it wasn't the real thing— all the way home.

Alarm bells went off when she pulled up to the house and found the pickup gone. She'd left the keys for the truck in a kitchen drawer in case of emergency, but she'd warned Nate, "It better be a real emergency, or you aren't going to be driving again until summer!"

Drew was right behind her as she hurried into the house and called out, "Anybody home?"

No answer.

She hurried to the phone to check the answering machine, to see if the kids had left her a message.

And found a handwritten note from Brooke on the counter. Her heart nearly stopped when she read it.

"Oh, no," she whispered.

"What is it?" Drew asked.

She handed him the note without speaking. Her heart squeezed in terror as she read it again along with Drew.

Dear Mom,

Nate and Ryan and I are following the directions you got over the phone this morning to that hideout in Game Creek Canyon. I did that pencil thing over the outline of your writing on the notepad so I could read what you wrote. We plan to meet up with you there, but if we don't, you'll know where we are. Love,

Brooke

Sarah's throat had swollen closed by the time she got to the "Love" Brooke had squeezed in as an after-thought above her signature.

"My kids," she choked out as she turned to Drew, tears springing to her eyes. "My kids were out in that storm. I've got to find them."

Sarah headed for the door, but Drew hooked her arm and turned her around.

"Let go of me!" she snarled.

Drew had both her arms now, and was holding tight, so Sarah couldn't pull free.

"I'm scared shitless, too," he said. "But think, Sarah! Niles Taylor may be able to tell us exactly where Kate is being held. We'd have a better chance of finding your kids if we know where they might end up."

"I can't wait," Sarah wailed. "They might be—" Sarah couldn't say what she feared. If Nate and Brooke and Ryan hadn't found shelter, they might have frozen to death in the storm. Her best hope was that they'd found the place where Kate was being held captive and were holed up with her.

Then she envisioned what the men who'd brutally murdered Lourdes Ramirez would do to her children if they found them. She stared into Drew's agonized eyes and moaned.

He pulled her into his embrace, and Sarah held on tight.

"Just hang on," he muttered in her ear. "We'll find them, Sarah. I promise you, we'll find them."

Sarah swallowed over the painful knot in her throat and said, "They're alive, holed up somewhere. I just know it. My kids are resourceful. And smart. And—"

Her voice hitched and quavered, and Drew folded her more tightly into his arms. His own voice wasn't too steady as he said, "And when we do find them, I intend to give those disobedient whelps a good piece of my mind!"

Sarah realized he sounded exactly like . . . a parent.

20

Drew was surprised, when he and Sarah drove up to King Grayhawk's ranch house at Kingdom Come, to find Niles Taylor just arriving. The ten-thousand-square-foot log house, with its immense stone chimney, was set on a beautiful hillside surrounded by aspens and evergreens and had a breathtaking view of the Grand Tetons.

Niles stepped out of a chauffeur-driven limo and smiled broadly. "Why, hello, Drew. What brings you here?"

"Same thing that brings you here, I expect," Drew replied. He didn't reach out to take the hand Niles extended, and the other man withdrew it with a frown.

"I see you've got a deputy with you," Niles said, eyeing Sarah.

"That's Detective Barndollar to you," Sarah said in a cold voice.

Drew watched as Niles surveyed the other cars parked along the circular drive. "Looks like quite a few folks were invited to this shindig." He stared up at the imposing house, then back at Drew and Sarah, then at the open limo door.

"Don't even think about it," Drew said.

Niles smiled and gave the door a little push. It closed with an expensive-sounding *thunk*. "Wouldn't dream of leaving before I see who's come to the party."

Drew felt Sarah bristle beside him as they followed Niles up a stone walk to the front door. Niles didn't get a chance to ring the brass bell announcing his arrival before one of the double front doors opened and North Grayhawk said, "Come in, Niles."

Drew saw the older man stiffen when he realized that Blackjack and Clay were standing beside the stone fireplace, while King sat in a leather chair near the fire.

Drew heard Sarah draw a sharp breath when they entered the great room, which had a thirty-foot ceiling framed by log beams and featured a second-story walkway leading from one side of the house to the other. Oak floors shone beneath an impressive central chandelier made of elk and deer and moose antlers. Floor-to-ceiling stone covered the wall that held the fireplace, where a cheery fire crackled.

It was as good a place as any for a showdown, Drew supposed.

"Come in and take a seat, Niles," King said.

"I'd rather stand," Niles said, eyeing the two Blackthorne men at the fireplace and watching as Sarah and Drew crossed to join them.

"We weren't expecting you, Detective Barndollar," King said. "But you're welcome."

Sarah gave King a jerky nod, then focused her gaze once more on Niles.

"You might wonder why I've asked you here," King began.

"I have a pretty good idea," Niles said sardonically.

"Shut up," King said, stamping his cane on the floor with a sharp crack of wood against wood and then rising to his full imposing height. "I'll make this simple. Tell me where my granddaughter is."

"What are you offering me if I do?" Niles said.

Drew heard Sarah suck in a gasp of air at this blatant admission that Niles knew where Kate Grayhawk was.

"I'll let you live," King said.

"I'm making no promises," Blackjack said.

Niles blanched. "I'm not going to tell anyone who Kate Grayhawk is." He glanced at Clay and said, "I mean, that she's your daughter."

"What makes you think Kate Grayhawk is my daughter?" Clay said.

"You're here, aren't you," Niles said snidely. "I know the truth about you and your bastard brat. That should have been enough to keep you dancing like a puppet on a string for years. But no," he snarled, "that wasn't good enough. He said we had to set you up with the girl and take pictures."

"Who are you working for?" North demanded. "Who's in charge of this filthy racket?"

Niles's eyes narrowed. "Wouldn't you like to know. Maybe I do have some negotiating room here." He turned to Clay and said, "I'll tell you his name for a pass on investigating the consortium."

"No deal," Clay said. "You're going to jail. With any luck, you won't have a pot to piss in when you do."

"You sure as hell aren't going to be the one prosecuting me," Niles shot back. "You're going to be resigning in disgrace!"

"Where's my granddaughter?" King repeated, reminding them why they were all there.

"Are my three children with her?" Sarah asked.

Drew saw surprise on Niles's face before he answered, "Why would anyone want to kidnap your kids?"

Drew watched Sarah clamp her teeth to keep her jaw from quivering and said, "The detective's children are missing. We think they headed up Game Creek Canyon before the storm."

"I don't know anything about them," Niles said.

"Sarah and Clay each got an anonymous call giving directions to where Kate is supposedly being kept," Drew said.

"Then why do you need my help finding her?" Niles snapped.

"We need to know how accurate the directions we got are," Drew said.

"They're good," Clay interjected.

Drew frowned and said, "How do you know?"

"Because the 'anonymous' man who called was Governor Harvey Donnelly. Harvey and I roomed together in college. When he heard what happened to me, Harvey called to say the same thing had happened to him. One of the guys who removed the body when he was blackmailed bragged about how they'd kept the girl captive in Game Creek Canyon.

"Harvey went up there afterward and found the spot where the tent they'd used had been set up. He said there was no guarantee it would be in the same place this time, but because these guys lacked imagination, he'd be willing to bet it wouldn't be far off."

"Where is Kate being held, exactly?" Blackjack said, taking a menacing step toward Niles.

Niles took a half step back, then stopped and squared his shoulders. "I want a guarantee—"

Without warning, King swung his oak cane, which landed with a bone-crunching *thwack* across Niles's solar plexus, doubling him in half.

Niles grabbed his belly and retched.

Drew looked at Sarah to see whether she would protest this brutal assault, but her jaw was clamped and her hands were knotted into fists.

"Where is Kate?" King said in a steely voice. "You've got thirty seconds to tell me before I brain you with this thing."

Niles put his hands up to cover his head, but was still unable to stand up straight. "You're the law," he said to Sarah. "Do something! Help me."

"I won't let him kill you," Sarah said.

But it was clear to Drew, if not to Niles, that she wouldn't stop King much short of it.

Niles coughed and gagged and said, "She's up Game Creek Canyon."

"How far?" Sarah demanded. "How do we get there?"

"I don't know," Niles admitted. "I never went there myself."

"How do we know you're telling the truth?" Sarah demanded.

"Because a worm like him wouldn't soil his hands doing his own dirty work," North said in disgust.

"Get out of my sight, you slimy bastard," King said.

Niles turned and stumbled toward the door, fumbling to get it open and slamming it closed behind him as he left.

"Are you just going to let him go?" Sarah asked incredulously.

"He's not going far," Clay said. "The FBI is waiting for him at the airport."

"How do we find Kate?" Sarah asked. "And my kids?"

"We follow the directions Harvey gave us," Clay said.

"What are we waiting for?" Drew said. "Let's go."

21

Drew couldn't help feeling that any second the mountain of snow above him was going to slide down. His heart rate had skyrocketed as the walls of Game Creek Canyon began to rise on either side of them. He caught himself holding his breath until his chest ached and realized he was anticipating an avalanche that never came. He forced himself to breathe evenly, or as evenly as he could.

He glanced at Clay and saw his cousin was having an even worse time of it than he was. He knew Clay had never really recovered from the experience of digging him out of the snow on 25 Short. Clay was sweating profusely, and his jaw was set in a grimace of determination. But he'd never once suggested slowing down or turning back.

Which any sane person would have done.

By the time he and Sarah and Clay and Libby had met at Game Creek Road, just south of Jackson on Highway 191, conditions were *perfect* for an avalanche. Tons of snow had been dumped in the storm, and a warm, gusty chinook wind had blown in right behind it, windloading the powdery snow on angled slopes and sending the clouds scattering, making way for a surprisingly hot morning sun.

Considering the danger involved in snowshoeing up the trail, Drew had asked Sarah why they couldn't make a quick trip over the canyon in a helicopter looking for the four missing kids.

"I've already had someone up in a Bell 407 taking a look," she admitted. "But he didn't see anything from the air, which isn't really surprising. Otherwise, that hideout would have been discovered long ago. He also didn't see any sign of Nate or Brooke or Ryan."

Drew mentally acknowledged how impossible it would have been to discern three small, snow-covered bodies from the air.

"It's dangerous to fly too low with the avalanche conditions what they are," Sarah said. "Vibrations from above could start an avalanche as easily as one misstep on the ground.

"Which is also why we're snowshoeing rather than taking snowmobiles," she said.

Because of the deep, powdery snow, Sarah had suggested they use snowshoes instead of skis. Motorized vehicles weren't allowed in the wilderness areas of Game Creek, but Sarah had apparently considered using them anyway.

"I've got a GPS to mark our location if and when we need to call for help," she said.

Drew and Sarah, and Clay and Libby, and Libby's two redbone coonhounds had traveled about three miles along the bottom of the canyon when they reached a fork in the trail. Drew was surprised to see snowmobile tracks. Someone had been there before them earlier that same day after the snow had stopped falling.

"What do you think?" Clay asked Drew. "The kidnapper?"

He turned to Sarah and said, "Guess someone isn't as worried as you are about their motorized vehicle starting an avalanche."

"Someone is taking his life in his hands," Sarah snapped.

That was the most she'd said in the thirty minutes it had taken them to get to the fork in the trail.

"I've been thinking about who might be anxious enough to risk coming up this trail in these avalanche conditions," Drew said. "I keep coming up with the same answer."

"It's some kid who wants to ride his snowmobile in all this powder," Sarah said.

"Or someone who knows about that hideout up there and what's in it and wants to check on it after the storm," Drew said. "Maybe even the person who kidnapped Kate."

"I hope the hell that is who it is," Clay said. "When I get my hands on—"

"There isn't going to be any vigilante justice," Sarah said. "If we catch someone with Kate, I'll arrest him."

"You're on administrative leave," Drew reminded her. But he knew for a fact she was carrying the replacement Glock, and he didn't think a little technicality like not being on duty was going to keep her from arresting anyone she thought needed arresting.

"As long as Kate is found safe and sound," Clay said, "I don't give a damn what you do with anyone else you find."

Drew noticed nobody suggested the possibility that Kate might not be found safe and sound.

"It's amazing to me that someone would hide a kidnap victim so close to town," Libby said.

"The less traveling a kidnapper has to do with a body in the trunk, the better," Sarah said. "Besides, this terrain is rugged enough to discourage anyone skiing off the trail. And that hideout has to be well hidden to go undetected by the forest service, since they're up here all the time."

"If that snowmobile is being ridden by the kidnapper, why didn't he bother hiding his tracks?" Libby asked.

"Good point," Drew said.

"There's no reason to hide his tracks—until he leaves the trail," Sarah pointed out.

"So we should be watching for a place to the side of the trail where the snow is disturbed, where this guy might have brushed out his tracks?" Drew asked.

"Exactly," Sarah said. "With any luck, he'll only try to hide them for a while, and we can pick up his trail again in the rough."

"The dogs can help us with that," Libby said. She put Doc and Snoopy on the trail of the snowmobile, and not far up the canyon they bounded off into the undergrowth.

"He did a pretty good job of hiding the fact that he left the main trail," Libby said when they reached the spot.

"Which makes it unlikely that this was a kid enjoying the powder," Drew said.

"It doesn't look like there's much room to take a snowmobile between all that foliage," Clay said, his eyes narrowed as he gauged the dense undergrowth through which they would have to travel.

"There's got to be a trail," Sarah said. "All we have to do is follow where the snowmobile leads us."

"Are we sure this is the way to go?" Drew asked. "Does this jibe with what Donnelly said?"

"He said we should turn off the main trail into the wilderness at a blazed tree about twenty minutes after the fork," Sarah said. "We haven't gone that far yet, but I suppose whoever is on that snowmobile knows a quicker, easier way to get where we're hopefully going."

"If we're going, let's go," Clay said. "Day's wasting."

Drew had heard Blackjack use the same expression to his cowhands when they began a roundup. He watched as Clay pushed out ahead of everyone, with Libby on his heels, both of them following the two coonhounds, whose noses were leading them ever higher up the canyon.

Drew was last in line. Which might be the safest place to be if the dogs or Clay triggered an avalanche. Although, sometimes the first person crossing a fracture in the snow only loosened it, and it didn't come free until two or three more skiers had passed by.

There is no safe place on this goddamn mountain, Drew thought.

"Avalaaannnche!"

Even though Drew had been expecting the worst, his heart took a quick leap into his throat as Clay's warning echoed back to him. What astonished Drew was that he found himself skiing hell-bent *toward* the sound of Clay's voice, rather than away from it.

As Drew looked up in horror, he saw that the snow had fractured along a hundred-foot line above them and was barreling down the mountain, pulverizing trees and burying brush. He saw Clay grab Libby's hand and yank her after him as he sped away from the closest edge of the onrushing snow.

As he watched, Clay pulled Libby tight against his chest and braced his back against a thick aspen, waiting for the snow to race past them. Drew heard one of the dogs yelp and realized they'd been too far ahead of Libby and Clay to make it back to safety.

Drew caught up to Sarah, who'd stopped in her tracks, and slid a reassuring arm around her. "Are you all right?" he said.

She nodded, then pointed, her eyes stark.

Drew saw the silky red head of one of the dogs appear above the tumbling snow and disappear again as the thundering avalanche continued down the mountain. The second redbone hound appeared briefly, disappeared and then reappeared paddling along the top of the snow as though he were swimming.

The slide stopped sooner than Drew would have expected, only a couple of hundred feet down. The instant it did, the hound that was still on top of the snow freed itself, raced twenty feet up the mountain and began digging.

"That's Snoopy," Drew heard Libby cry. "He must be digging for Doc."

Drew saw Libby take off across the tumbled snow, Clay on her heels, grabbing for the shovel in his pack.

Drew's gaze shot to the top of the mountain, wondering if more of it was going to come down. But when Sarah took off to join Libby and Clay, he followed.

A moment later, the four of them were digging— with Snoopy, make that five. They were racing time, knowing that the buried hound would suffocate in a matter of minutes.

"I found a paw!" Clay said.

"I've found another," Sarah said.

Libby carefully cleared the area where they believed the dog's head to be and found a cold black nose. Soon, Doc's whole head was visible. When Clay finally pulled the redbone hound free of the snow, he let out a baying howl.

Libby hugged the dog, laughing and crying, then rose to fling herself into Clay's arms. "Thank you!" she cried. "Thank you!"

Drew watched as Clay rocked Libby in his arms, while both dogs bounded around them, apparently fine after their avalanche adventure. Libby was smiling up at Clay when he said something Drew couldn't hear. Her smile suddenly disappeared. Abruptly, they stepped apart. Libby bent down to fondle Doc's ears, while Clay folded up his shovel and put it back in his pack.

Drew shook his head. Those two were meant for each other, but he doubted Clay would ever allow the past to be forgotten—or forgiven.

He turned to Sarah and said, "That could have been a helluva lot worse. And there's more snow where that came from."

"Are you suggesting we turn back?" she asked.

Drew realized there was no turning back, no matter how great the danger. There were four precious lives at risk. Even so, the cost of saving them might be too high. He met Sarah's gaze and said, "I don't want to lose you."

Sarah seemed surprised by the admission. She avoided acknowledging its import by saying, "We'd better get moving if we want to catch up to that snowmobile."

"If we move across this slide to the other side, the dogs should be able to pick up the scent," Libby said.

They were soon across the slide area and headed back up into the high timber. Sooner than any of them expected, the dogs found the snowmobile's tracks.

Which was when Drew realized that the passing snowmobile had probably precipitated the avalanche.

"I wouldn't have thought he'd keep on concealing his tracks once he got off the main trail," Libby said.

"He probably has something tied on the back of the snowmobile to brush them out, and it's easier just to leave it there than to stop and remove it," Clay said.

"If the kidnapper wants the location of his hideout to remain a secret, he has to be this careful," Sarah said.

"I wonder how close we are," Libby said.

"We're not going up anymore," Drew said. Which was important to him, because it was often along the ridges that the snow fractured and an avalanche began.

Clay halted and pointed ahead. "There's something up there. Do you see it?"

Libby called the dogs to her and put them on a lead. "I don't want them smelling Kate and making a beeline for her," she said. "Assuming she's there," she added softly.

Drew had to squint to see the strange-looking structure through the thick underbrush that surrounded it. He turned to Sarah and said, "What is that?"

"It's a yurt!" she said. "No wonder it was never found! They probably put it up when they need it and take it down when they're done."

"What's a yurt?" Drew said.

"It's what's being used these days as a portable ski cabin," Sarah said. "Mongolian nomads who roamed China and central Asia thousands of years ago invented them. They're made of locking wood poles and have a conical roof with a hole in the top for smoke to escape."

"So it's the Mongolian version of a tepee," Drew said.

"Rounder and flatter," Sarah said, "but every bit as fast and easy to dismantle and transport. In the old days they were covered by animal skins. The modern ones have a wood framework covered in canvas or some fabric."

"How do we do this?" Drew asked. "Do we ski up there and announce ourselves? Do we sneak up? What?"

"I go. You all wait here," Sarah said.

"No way," Clay said. "There could have been two people on that snowmobile. There might be others at that yurt. If they see a lone woman—"

"I'm a deputy sheriff." Sarah smiled and added, "And I have a gun to even the odds."

Drew wondered how often men underestimated Sarah because of her sex. Her voice had been patient, but firm, as she insisted on being treated like what she was—the law in these parts.

"I wouldn't mind having you all handy as backup," she said. "I want to know where you are, so I'm not shooting in your direction if bullets start flying."

Drew was right behind Sarah as they moved quietly toward the yurt, trying to stay hidden as they watched for any movement.

"The door's on the other side," he said to Sarah. "How are we going to get there without being seen?"

"Very carefully," Sarah said.

Sarah had put up a brave front, but she moved toward the yurt with a heavy heart. Was it possible her children had found this remote destination and were safe inside? Even if they'd escaped the storm, how safe could they be if this place was truly the den of a murderous kidnapper?

She wanted to believe she would find all four children safe inside, but as she turned the corner and saw there were *two* snowmobiles parked out front, and no one to be seen, she realized that rescuing the four children—if they were all there—might not be that easy.

Should she wait for whoever was riding the snowmobiles to come back outside? Should she organize everyone to charge through the door and subdue whomever they found there? Or should they all wait while she called in the cavalry?

Sarah realized that all three options had risks. The kidnappers—there must be at least two—might even now be planning Kate Grayhawk's death. Or how to rid themselves of three meddlesome kids who'd shown up on their doorstep.

She eased toward the boarded-up window, cupping her hands over her eyes against a crack in the wood planking, trying to see inside. She saw figures on the floor, but before she could determine how many and what sex, two men walked out of the entrance to the yurt, their backs to her, arguing.

"I've pre-armed the explosive to start the avalanche," the first voice said. "I'm using a two-kilo charge. All we have to do is get ourselves to a safe place and light the fuse."

"And all our troubles will be buried and gone," the second voice said with satisfaction.

Sarah leaned back against the thick canvas wall of the yurt, making a smaller target of herself as she listened. She thought she recognized the first voice, but she couldn't place it. Then the man turned at an angle and she nearly gasped aloud.

Jimmy Joe Stovall was a Teton County Deputy Sheriff! And he'd just announced how he planned to commit a multiple murder and make it look like an accident.

"Wonder when they'll find the bodies," Jimmy Joe said.

"Maybe in the spring. Maybe never," the second man said.

Suddenly, Clay Blackthorne burst from his hiding place and crossed the trampled snow near the yurt to confront the two men, Libby beside him, her rifle aimed at the second man's heart.

The instant they appeared, Jimmy Joe pulled his Glock and aimed it at Libby. "Keep your finger off that trigger," he warned.

"*You* did this, Morgan?" Clay cried in an angry, anguished voice. "*You* took Kate? Why?"

"It was a stupid mistake," the man Clay had called Morgan said. "But as long as I had her, it made things a lot easier."

"What things?" Clay demanded.

"That Japanese oil deal, for one. The old man was about to step out of it. Needed him in. Mentioned the girl and bingo! He's back in again."

"Which old man?" Libby said. "My father?"

"Bingo," Morgan said again.

"He knew you had Kate?" Libby said.

"Didn't know it was me, exactly," Morgan replied. "Just that she was being held and that he'd better do as he was told."

Drew realized King Grayhawk had been playing his cards very close to the vest, indeed. He'd never let on that he'd previously been in contact with Kate's kidnapper.

"What happens now?" Clay said.

"First, Libby puts the rifle down," Morgan said.

"No," Libby said.

While Sarah watched, Morgan reached over his shoulder into his backpack and pulled out a bulky object, which turned out to be two round cylindrical objects—each as wide as a quart water bottle, but shorter—taped together. Then he reached into his pocket for a lighter.

"In case you're wondering," Morgan said, "this is two kilos—4.4 pounds—of PETN and TNT. It's already armed. All I have to do is light the fuse. So I'm going to ask you one more time, Libby, to put down that rifle."

Libby exchanged a despairing glance with Clay, then carefully laid the rifle in the snow at her feet.

"Back away from it," Jimmy Joe ordered.

Libby and Clay backed away.

"Let the children go," Libby pleaded.

"Sorry," Morgan said "No can do."

"Kate!" Libby cried. "Are you in there? Answer me!"

But there was no sound from the yurt.

"Are you going to shoot us?" Clay asked.

"No need to do that," Morgan said. "We can bury you alive, along with your kid. Too bad she's out cold. She's going to miss the happy reunion."

Sarah had already drawn her Glock and aimed it at the two men, watching to see what they would do. She stayed hidden, unwilling to expose herself in case someone else remained inside.

Drew caught her eye from the trees, and she motioned for him to join her. He took advantage of the distraction Clay and Libby had provided to join her.

"Did you see if they both have guns?" Sarah whispered.

"The deputy's got one," Drew said. "My brother Morgan is the one holding the explosives."

"Your *brother*?" Sarah said.

"Stepbrother," Drew said bitterly.

Sarah's heart went out to him. Yet another betrayal by someone he loved.

"Kate, are you in there?" Clay shouted.

No response.

"Is anyone in there?" Clay shouted.

No response.

"What have you done to my daughter?" Clay said through tight jaws.

"She's fine," Morgan replied. "We just gave them something to put them out—until the snow buries them."

"Them?" Clay said.

"Some kids took refuge here during the snowstorm. The bunch of them were getting ready to light out of here when we showed up. Bad timing for them," Morgan said.

Sarah fought back a joyous sob of relief, even as her heart pounded with terror. Her kids were alive, and she'd found at least one of the missing girls alive and well.

But her work wasn't nearly done. They might all still become victims of an avalanche, unless she could find a way to stop Morgan DeWitt. She was tempted to shoot first and ask questions later. But that wasn't how she was made. She had to do this right. She also had to act fast. These men were cold-bloodedly planning the murder of six people.

"I'll give you anything," Clay said. "I'll do anything. Just let the kids go."

As Sarah watched, Morgan slowly shook his head.

"No can do, boss," Morgan said. "I think you're all going to be lost in a terrible avalanche."

"People will know this was no accident," Clay said.

Morgan shrugged. "By the time the snow melts in the spring and uncovers you, I'll be back in Washington and the Japanese deal will be done. Get inside," he said, gesturing with the gun.

Clay and Libby had started for the door to the yurt, when Morgan said, "Wait." His eyes narrowed and he did a slow, visual check of the vicinity, the barrel of his gun leading the way.

Sarah put a warning hand over Drew's chest. She made herself as small as she could against the canvas structure, and in fact, even ceased to breathe.

"How did you know to come here?" Morgan said suspiciously. "How did you find this place?"

"I got an anonymous call," Clay said. "Someone told me there was a place up here where I might find Kate. Libby's dogs helped us find the way."

That seemed to satisfy Morgan, who said, "Go ahead. Get inside."

"She's dead!" Libby cried as she entered the yurt.

Her agonized wail nearly sent Sarah running for the door herself, but Drew grabbed her arm to keep her in place. When she turned angrily in his direction, he put his fingertip to his lips, met her gaze, and shook his head.

Sarah felt her breath catch as she looked into eyes that had become two shards of ice. The carefree playboy was gone. Every muscle in Drew's body looked tense, and she had the sense of a savage animal, feral and merciless, ready to pounce. She felt her body quiver in response to the deadly aura of the man beside her.

Sarah was distracted by sounds of a scuffle and realized Clay must have gone for Morgan's throat. Then she heard the sickening sound of metal against bone, Libby's shriek of rage and fear, and the sound of a body collapsing.

Morgan's breathless voice said, "You didn't have to hit him so hard."

Jimmy Joe replied angrily, "What was I supposed to do? What does it matter, anyway? In twenty minutes, they'll all be dead. Do you want me to knock her out, too?"

Sarah realized Jimmy Joe was referring to Libby.

"She's not going anywhere without him," Morgan said derisively, "or her kid. And neither of them are going anywhere anytime soon. Brace that door closed with a log, and let's get out of here."

Sarah watched as Morgan took off his backpack, carefully returned the explosives to it, then put it back on, before retrieving Libby's rifle and setting it against the wall of the yurt. Meanwhile, Jimmy Joe made grunting noises as he hefted Clay's inert body.

She turned to Drew and whispered, "Go around the yurt to the opposite side to distract them. I'll come up behind them."

She was asking him to risk his life. He might be shot when Morgan and Jimmy Joe realized that Clay and Libby weren't alone. Sarah waited to see what he would do.

Drew's eyes were cold and menacing as he glanced over her shoulder at the two men. He caught her in a painfully tight grasp, kissed her hard, and said in a harsh, guttural voice, "In case I don't get a chance to say it later, I love you."

Then he was gone, stalking the two men as stealthily and ruthlessly as a panther.

She heard Morgan and Jimmy Joe close the door of the yurt behind them before Drew said, "Hey there, Morgan. What's up?"

"Goddamn sonofabitch!" Morgan said. "How the hell did you get here?"

"Same way half the sheriff's office is going to get here in a few minutes."

Sarah realized the hesitation for what it was. Morgan DeWitt deciding whether to shoot his brother and make a run for it, or just to make a run for it.

It was now or never.

Sarah wished she could be sure the two men were far enough from the yurt that they wouldn't be tempted to jump back inside. But there was no more time to think.

She stepped out from her hiding place and said, "Police. Drop your weapons and put your hands up."

Jimmy Joe yelled "Holy shit!" and dropped Clay like a sack of potatoes, then raced for his snowmobile.

Drew launched himself at Jimmy Joe with an animal cry, but their struggle for Jimmy Joe's gun blocked Sarah from shooting at Morgan, who reached one of the snowmobiles, revved the machine, and disappeared into the forest.

Furious at having her quarry escape, Sarah pointed her Glock at Jimmy Joe and said, "Let go of that gun, Jimmy Joe Stovall, or so help me I'll blow your head off!"

Jimmy Joe, who'd seen her expert shooting in more than one competition at the police range, let go.

Drew backed off from his bloodied quarry, his teeth bared in a savage grimace.

"Hands behind your back, Jimmy Joe," Sarah ordered.

"Do it!" Drew snapped in a voice that demanded obedience.

Jimmy Joe shrank from Drew's wild countenance. "All right. Just don't hit me again."

As Sarah cuffed him, Drew grabbed a handful of Jimmy Joe's shirt, pointed the Glock he'd retrieved at Jimmy Joe's heart and snapped, "Where is Morgan going?"

When Jimmy Joe didn't answer quickly enough, Drew shifted his grip to Jimmy Joe's throat to cut off the deputy's air and said, "Spill it!"

"Top of the mountain," Jimmy Joe croaked. "You'd better catch him, or we're all going to be buried alive!"

Drew's face contorted as though he'd swallowed a piece of bad meat. "I have half a mind to smother you before I go."

"Drew," Sarah warned. He looked dangerous enough—and powerful enough—to do it.

Drew released Jimmy Joe's throat with a sound of disgust, turned his back and stalked away from her, singleminded in his pursuit of the man who'd betrayed them all. He was already revving the second snowmobile by the time Sarah caught up to him and climbed on behind.

"What are you doing?" he said.

"I'm coming with you."

He bent one savage glance on her, then turned forward. She felt the steel in his back, the hard cord of muscle in his body, as she grabbed hold to avoid being tumbled off when the snowmobile suddenly accelerated.

"What did you do with Jimmy Joe?" Drew yelled back at her as the snowmobile's engine protested the speed he was demanding.

"He's taking a nap."

"Good," Drew said with guttural satisfaction.

Sarah hadn't known she was capable of knocking someone out with the butt of her Glock. But she couldn't afford to leave Jimmy Joe awake and able to wreak havoc.

Morgan's trail was easy to follow in the fresh snow, but there was no sign of him ahead of them, only the distant whine of machinery.

The transformation in Drew was surprising, but Sarah realized she'd known deep down, all along, that there was a darkness inside him that he kept hidden. His stepbrother's betrayal had ripped off the mask of civility Drew normally wore and exposed the jumble of fierce emotions inside. Ruthlessness. Cruelty. Menace.

And yet, with Sarah, he'd held that violence in check. She could only imagine the self-control it had taken to appear so carefree, when he was anything but.

22

As soon as the door to the yurt closed, Libby was on the ground beside Clay, whose head was bleeding badly where he'd been struck. She put two fingers to his throat and found his pulse strong, if a little erratic. She heard voices outside and realized Sarah and Drew were making their move.

Everything happened fast. A moment later, they were gone.

Libby understood why Drew and Sarah had jumped on the second snowmobile and raced after Morgan. It was their best hope of saving everyone. But what if they didn't succeed?

Libby's heart was pounding as she turned to look for something to stanch Clay's bleeding head. She was shocked to find the four children sitting up and staring wide-eyed back at her.

"Mom?"

"Oh, my God. Kate!"

Kate launched herself toward Libby, who hugged her daughter tight and rocked her back and forth. Libby's throat swelled with emotion and tears stung her nose as she forced her daughter back far enough that

Sarah focused on what Drew had said to her before they'd started their attack. *I love you.*

She wished she'd said the words back. She opened her mouth to speak them now but realized the wind would whip them away. When she told Drew she loved him, she wanted to be looking into his eyes. She wanted him to hear what she was saying and understand that she would be his solace in the dark times— and his joy in the light.

Sarah wanted desperately to tell Drew how she felt. To live happily ever after with the man she loved. And her children. And their children.

"Do you think we can catch Morgan in time?" she yelled into Drew's ear.

Drew didn't answer in words. He simply revved the engine until it screamed.

she could look into her eyes. "Are you all right?" she asked, searching Kate's face for any signs of trauma. "Morgan said he'd drugged you."

"We didn't drink the water he gave us," Kate said. "Lourdes had warned me what they would do. We dumped the water and pretended to fall asleep."

"Lourdes?" Libby said.

"The girl who was here before me. They took her away." Kate's eyes darkened as she said, "I didn't know what had happened to her—until these guys showed up and told me she was murdered."

Libby turned her attention to Sarah Barndollar's children. The younger boy was sitting in the girl's lap, while the older boy sat beside her protectively. "You must be Nate and Brooke and Ryan," she said.

"We are," the girl answered. "When can we get out of here?"

Libby saw that none of the children had shoes or coats. And Clay was still unconscious. "I think we should wait here for your mother to get back."

"What if she doesn't come back?" Brooke said. "What if that guy Morgan manages to start an avalanche? I think we need to get as far from here as we can as fast as we can."

"I can't leave Clay," Libby said. "You go. I'll wait here until he—"

"We can carry him, Mom," Kate said. "We'll rig something, some kind of travois and—"

"You're right," Libby said. She hadn't wanted to face the truth, but there was no denying how desperate their situation was. "We can't count on being saved. We're going to have to save ourselves." She eyed the children's stocking feet and said, "What are we going to do to keep your feet from freezing?"

"We've got it all figured out," Kate said. "We'd already planned how to escape when that Jimmy Joe guy and Morgan showed up."

"That deputy went through our backpacks and frisked us," Brooke said. "But he missed a couple of things." She grinned broadly, revealing shiny metal braces, and held up a small penknife. "We don't have to get through the door. We can cut our way through the canvas wall."

As the kids began to move around, Libby realized they'd already used the pen knife to cut through their trousers below the knee. They pulled off the sheaths of cloth and pulled them onto their feet to use as makeshift shoes, tying them with strips of cloth they'd torn from their long john undershirts.

"I'm impressed," Libby said. She looked around for something to make a travois, but there was nothing to be found. The yurt had been stripped of anything useful.

Then she realized they could use parts of the yurt itself. The interior wooden poles could be pulled down, and the canvas would make a bed for the travois. The only question was, could they do everything that had to be done in time?

Libby listened hard for the sound of the snowmobiles in the distance. She heard nothing but the wind in the pines. "We'd better get moving," she said. "I don't imagine we have much time."

She tied on Ryan's makeshift shoes while Kate and Brooke and Nate pulled down two of the poles. The problem arose when they tried to cut the thick canvas with Brooke's small penknife. It was hard, slow going.

And they were running out of time.

"Maybe we can carry Clay," Kate suggested.

"I might be able to manage a fireman's carry," Nate said.

Libby eyed Clay's powerful, over-six-foot frame and imagined it draped over Nate's lanky teenage body. She didn't think it was going to work, but she said, "We might as well give it a try."

Libby got on one side of Clay, Kate and Brooke on the other, and they lifted him upright. It took all of them to heave Clay up over Nate's shoulder.

Nate staggered a step or two, then sank to his knees. "I'm sorry," he said, his throat working as he swallowed back despair. "He's too heavy for me."

"Unh."

Libby wasn't sure she'd heard the sound at first. When it came again, she realized Clay was awake. "Clay?"

As she helped ease Clay off Nate's shoulder and onto his back on the ground, his eyes fluttered open.

She watched him survey the faces above him and saw his relief when he spied Kate.

"Hey, Kitten," he said in a hoarse voice. He reached out a wobbly hand and touched her cheek.

"Hey, Daddy," Kate said, moving his hand to her mouth and kissing his fingertips. Then she froze, looked guiltily up at her mother, and around to the three strangers before whom she'd revealed something that was supposed to remain a secret. "I mean Clay," she said.

"I like 'Daddy' better," Clay said.

"Oh, Daddy," Kate said, laying her head across his chest and holding him tight.

His hand came up to caress her hair, and Libby saw something she'd never seen before.

There were tears in Clay Blackthorne's eyes.

He eased his head in Libby's direction, winced and said, "What's going on?"

"Morgan took off on one of the snowmobiles, and Drew and Sarah are chasing after him on the other one. Sarah handcuffed the other man and knocked him out. Morgan seems determined to start an avalanche," she said. "We need to get out of here, if we can."

"What's stopping us?" Clay asked.

Libby smiled and said, "We couldn't move your carcass."

"Help me up," he said.

Libby and Kate each slid an arm under Clay's shoulders and helped him lurch to his feet. He secured an arm around Libby's waist and leaned heavily against her.

He closed his eyes and muttered, "Damned yurt keeps moving."

Libby realized he ought to be lying down, but that was a luxury they couldn't afford. "Do you think you can walk?"

"I'll walk," he said through gritted teeth.

When he tried, he stumbled, and if Kate hadn't

helped Libby hold him up, he would have fallen flat on his face.

"We'll help you, Daddy," Kate said, easing an arm around his waist. "Lean on me."

The look of love on Clay's face as he said, "Thanks, Kate," made Libby's throat ache.

"If you guys are ready, we need to get moving," Brooke said. She'd taken Ryan's hand and was standing by the broken lattice framing the slit they'd made in the canvas wall.

Libby was awed by the teenager's composure. "We'll follow you," she said.

Brooke shoved her way through the tear in the canvas, followed by Ryan and Nate. Libby went next, pulling Clay through while Kate pushed. Once they were outside, they found Jimmy Joe sitting on the ground moaning.

"What do we do with him?" Nate asked.

"Leave him there," Brooke said coldly.

"You can't leave me here to die!" Jimmy Joe protested.

"Why not?" Kate said. "You're a murderer. You bragged about killing Lourdes. I bet you killed the girls that were here before her."

Jimmy Joe's face flushed a livid red. "Leave me here, and you'll all be murderers, too," he said heatedly.

"If you can walk, you can follow us out," Libby said.

"I can walk," Jimmy Joe said, struggling to his feet.

As Jimmy Joe rose, Libby felt Clay once more become dead weight in her arms. "Clay!" she cried.

He was too heavy for her and Kate to hold upright,

and Libby sank to her knees as they lowered him onto the snow.

"What are we going to do now?" Kate cried. "We can't leave him here!"

"Jimmy Joe can carry him," Brooke suggested.

"I'm cuffed," Jimmy Joe protested. "Besides, I'm hurt."

"I can get you out of those cuffs," Brooke said.

"You got a key, kid?" Jimmy Joe said with a sneer.

"No, but I've got a hair pin." Brooke pulled a jeweled bobby pin from her hair, stretched it wide and inserted one end into one of the cuffs behind Jimmy Joe's back. Ten seconds later, it sprang open.

Jimmy Joe pulled his hands around in front of him, rubbing his wrists. "How the hell did you do that?"

"I practiced on my mom's cuffs," Brooke said. "Now pick him up, and let's go."

"Not sure I'm going to do that," Jimmy Joe said, his eyes narrowing maliciously. "Figure I can run a lot faster without all that extra weight."

"We let you go," Kate said angrily. "Now help us."

"Sorry, little girl. Ain't gonna happen."

Before any of them could stop him, Jimmy Joe Stovall took off running into the woods. Nate headed after him and had almost disappeared in the trees when Brooke shouted, "Nate, stop! Come back! He's going the wrong direction."

"The wrong direction?" Libby said.

"He's heading farther into the canyon, not back toward the main trail," Brooke said.

Libby stared at the mountain above them, wondering how much more time they could possibly have. Would Drew and Sarah stop Morgan? Or were they all destined to suffocate beneath tons of snow?

She looked down at Clay, who was out cold. "I want you kids to leave," she said. "I'll stay here with Clay."

"No," Kate said, putting her arms around Libby's waist and hugging her tightly. "I'm not leaving you, Mom. Or Daddy."

Libby met Brooke's gaze and said, "You should go. While you still have time."

Brooke stared into the treeline, waiting for Nate to come huffing back to her.

"I could have caught him, if you hadn't called me back," Nate said.

"I know," Brooke said. "But what would you have done with him when you did?"

"I could have—" Nate began.

Brooke cut him off with, "Kate and her mom have decided to stay here with Mr. Blackthorne. I need to know whether you want to leave them behind and try to make it out, or whether you want to stay here with them . . . and trust Mom and Drew to save us."

"That's easy," Nate said.

Brooke lifted a brow and said, "It is?"

"Sure," Nate said, picking Ryan up in one arm and circling Brooke with the other. "We wait here for Mom and Drew to save us."

Drew had never been in a race where the stakes were so high. He took terrible chances, cutting corners around trees that would have sent him and Sarah flying, if they'd clipped them. At one point, he lost sight of Morgan, and his heart pounded its way up into his throat until he saw movement ahead of him again.

Too late, Drew realized it had been a mistake for both of them to come. One of them should have stayed behind to try and move the children out of harm's way. He'd been too consumed by hurt and blinded by anger at Morgan to stop and think.

Drew had honestly never seen this coming. The more Drew thought of the devastation Morgan had wreaked and the lives he'd ruined, the faster he drove.

"I see where he's heading," Sarah shouted in his ear. "I know a shortcut."

"You'd only be guessing where he's going to end up," Drew said.

"We're never going to catch him in time if we don't do something," Sarah replied. "We have to take the risk."

That was the last thing Drew wanted to do. Cold calculation was safer than taking chances. He was hanging on to control of his anger by a bare thread. But Morgan had moved beyond his sight again, and he knew that he had no choice.

"All right," he said. "Point me in the right direction."

"He's heading for the Divide. If we cut across, we can get there ahead of him."

Drew followed Sarah's pointing finger and headed off at an angle to the route they'd been following. He increased his speed as much as he dared, bouncing and skidding and sliding as fast as the snowmobile would travel. If they could get ahead of Morgan, they could intercept him before he reached the top of the mountain, where it was likely he'd set the charge.

The terrain was so steep, Drew had to zigzag to move upward. Then he had a paralyzing thought.

"What are the chances we're going to start an avalanche ourselves?" he shouted back at Sarah.

"Less than the absolute certainty that Morgan is going to start one," she replied.

Suddenly, they were at the top of the mountain. Drew stopped abruptly and let the engine idle as he searched the horizon for signs of Morgan. "Dammit! He's not here!"

"Turn this thing off," Sarah said. "Listen."

Drew did, and heard the faint sound of an engine. "Do we wait here?" he asked Sarah. "Or head in his direction?"

Then the other engine stopped.

"We go to him," she said.

"He's going to hear us coming," Drew said as he revved the engine and took off.

"Just move this thing!" Sarah said.

In a matter of minutes, Drew could see Morgan standing beside his snowmobile, his eyes focused on something he was doing with his hands. Checking the fuse and cap, most likely, Drew thought, to make sure they were securely taped to the charge.

Morgan looked up at him. And smiled.

"How can you smile, you sonofabitch," Drew said through tight jaws. "Knowing what you're about to do?"

"Lean to the left," Sarah said.

Drew veered to the left.

"Put this godforsaken machine back on course and *lean* as far left as you can," Sarah said.

Then Drew spotted the Glock in her right hand.

It was an impossible shot. The ride was too bumpy. The distance was too far. The target was too small.

"Don't do it, Morgan!" Drew shouted.

Morgan turned to face them, yelled "Fire in the hole!" and lobbed the explosive charge right at them. Then he mounted his snowmobile like it was a horse, waved cheerily at Drew and took off in the opposite direction.

"We've got ninety seconds before that detonates," Sarah yelled. "Drop me off and—"

"Take the shot first," he said viciously. "Take it!"

Drew's right eardrum reverberated with the blast, as Sarah pulled the trigger.

To Drew's surprise, Morgan toppled off his snowmobile.

"I got him!" Sarah cried.

But an instant later, he was up again, stumbling toward his snowmobile, getting back on and racing away.

It took twenty seconds to reach the deadly package of PETN and TNT. Sarah grabbed it up and began tearing at the tape that held the fuse and sensitive cap, which was the detonating device, in place.

"How can I help?" Drew said, his stomach churning as he watched her unwind mounds of black tape.

"Go!" she yelled. "Don't let him get away."

"I love you, Sarah," he said fiercely.

"I love you, too," she said, sparing him a single glance. "Now get the hell out of here!"

Drew drove after Morgan like a bat out of hell, his heart in his throat. He counted the seconds, knowing Sarah didn't have much time. He willed her to succeed, and prayed to God, promising to love Sarah and her kids and take care of them as long as he lived, if they could all just be safe.

The ninety seconds was up.

Drew held his breath and finally heard a sharp crack, like a firecracker going off. The much smaller explosion meant Sarah had managed to pull the fuse and cap free. The only question was whether she'd managed to throw them away before the cap exploded and the shrapnel from it took off her hand.

Desperate to know if Sarah was all right, Drew dared a look over his shoulder.

And saw Sarah with her hands—both hands—widespread above her head in triumph, a broad smile across her face.

Seconds later, Drew was alongside Morgan. He had Jimmy Joe's Glock in his hand and death in his heart as he aimed the gun at his stepbrother. "Stop that thing, Morgan. It's over."

Morgan had one hand on his stomach, where bright red blood stained his blue ski jacket. "You're going to have to kill me, Drew."

Drew felt a strange coldness inside. A willingness to kill. And fought it down. He accelerated and drove his shrieking machine into the path of the other, causing both to flip.

He rolled onto his feet and looked around for Morgan. He found him lying face down beside his whining snowmobile. Drew reached for the key and turned it off. Then he turned Morgan over and wiped the snow from his eyes and nostrils.

"Why, Morgan?" Drew asked in an agonized voice. "You had everything. Clay would have taken you with him to the Oval Office."

Morgan spit blood and shoved Drew away. "It was taking too long. You've always had money. I never did. My mother didn't get anything in the divorce, and your grandfather didn't leave anything to me. It was going to take another ten years for Clay to make it to Pennsylvania Avenue. I got sick and tired of waiting for the cash to start rolling in."

"You could have asked me for money anytime," Drew said. "You would have been welcome to anything I have."

"I didn't want your charity," Morgan snarled.

Drew left him lying there—dying, he believed—and went to retrieve his snowmobile. He had it upright, when he heard the other machine roar to life. He was barely able to leap aside before Morgan roared past him on his snowmobile, heading downward across the slope, back into the forest from which they'd come.

Drew had just hopped onto his machine when he heard an ominous rumble. His heart skipped a beat. He knew that sound. It was snow, breaking off from the crest of the mountain. It was the avalanche he and Sarah had been trying so desperately to prevent.

"Sarah!" he cried, as he gunned the engine and raced back toward where he'd left her. "Sarah!"

But he was too late. The avalanche had swept her up. Drew saw everything in a single tortured glance.

Morgan's snowmobile tumbling over and over like a ball caught in a powerful wave. Morgan's arms flying out from his body, his legs splayed, his face a mask of horror.

And Sarah's frightened face as she dog-paddled her way toward the edge of the thundering snow.

He drove like a maniac downhill along the edge of the tumbling snow. As he neared Sarah, he reached out and yelled, "Give me your hand!"

"I can't reach!" she cried.

"Take my hand, Sarah!" he said, willing her hand into his own.

He caught her hand and yanked with all his might. He fell backward off the snowmobile with Sarah in his arms. The machine veered off from the avalanche with a whine and kept on going. Drew held Sarah tight as tons of snow and debris roared past them.

"Thank God you're safe," he said fervently.

"My kids!" she said, shoving herself away and rising to watch the snow pummel its way down the mountain, leveling everything in its path. "My kids are down there. We have to go!"

Drew stood at her side for another moment, watching the devastation wrought by the powerful white wave. Morgan was buried down there somewhere under tons of snow. There was no chance of finding him before the snow snuffed out his life. But there were others they still might be able to save.

"Let's go." Drew looked around for the snowmobile and found it nestled under the lowest branches of a spruce.

"Please hurry!" Sarah said as she climbed on behind him.

Drew drove even faster down the mountain than he had coming up. It could take as little as two minutes to suffocate in an avalanche. It had taken them more than five just to get down the mountain. He knew what Sarah expected to find. He refused to believe the worst. He was going to stay hopeful until there was no hope.

"How far down do you think the avalanche traveled?" Sarah asked.

"They're going to be safe, Sarah," he said. "Believe it."

The yurt came into sight. The lower part of the door was covered by two feet of snow, but the structure was still upright.

"Where are Nate and Brooke and Ryan?" Sarah said, her voice frantic. "I don't see them."

Then a girl with flyaway hair came around the corner of the house. Mother and daughter cried out to each other simultaneously.

"Brooke!"

"Mom!"

Drew stopped the snowmobile as Sarah leaped off and pulled her stepdaughter into her arms. He could see both of them were crying and felt his throat swell with emotion. A moment later, Nate and Ryan joined Brooke. Drew was surprised when Nate left his mother's embrace and gave Drew a hard hug.

"Boy, are we glad to see you," Nate said, grinning broadly. "We were afraid you got caught in the avalanche."

Then Brooke turned to him and said, "Thank you, Drew. We knew you and Mom would save us."

"It was sheer luck that that avalanche stopped before it ran you over," Drew said.

Sarah was shaking her head. "The avalanche Morgan started wasn't as big as the one he'd planned to detonate. Stopping him saved everyone."

"You dismantled the charge," Drew said. "Not me."

"You caught up to Morgan so I could do it," Sarah said.

"You're *both* heroes!" Ryan said with a grin.

"Thanks for settling that for us," Drew said with a laugh, sweeping Ryan up into his arms for a hug. He walked to the front of the yurt with Ryan sitting on his arm, Sarah and Brooke on one side and Nate on the other.

When Kate saw Drew, she ran toward him and hugged him and said, "I'm so glad to see you!"

Libby embraced Sarah and said, "Thank you for saving all our lives."

"How is Mr. Blackthorne?" Sarah asked.

"He's coming around," Libby replied. "Do you think it would be safe to have a helicopter come get us?"

"The snow above us has already come down," Sarah said. "So I don't see why not." She made the call for a helicopter, then asked, "Where's Jimmy Joe?"

"He ran off into the woods," Kate replied. "Right into the avalanche. I hope that murdering bas—"

"Kate," Libby said. "That language—"

"But he *is* a murderer," Kate said, tears springing to her eyes. She turned to Sarah and Drew and said, "He admitted that he killed Lourdes."

"He probably killed Daddy, too," Brooke said.

"We've got his gun," Drew said, pulling the Glock from where he'd stuck it in his belt and handing it to Sarah. "You can do ballistics tests to see if this gun was used to kill Tom."

Ryan tugged on Sarah's coat and said, "Can we go home now?"

Drew met Sarah's gaze. *Home* sounded pretty damn good to him.

The helicopter Sarah had called made a *flucketa, flucketa* sound as it landed in a nearby meadow.

"Kate and I are going with Clay to the hospital," Libby said to Drew. She hugged Sarah as Kate hugged Nate and Brooke.

"See you 'round," Kate said.

"Sure," Nate replied, his voice cracking.

Brooke grinned, "I think she likes you."

Nate turned beet red as Kate smiled and trotted off with her mother toward the helicopter.

"How would you like to ride in a helicopter?" Drew said to Ryan.

"Can we, Mom?" Ryan asked, jumping up and down. "Can we?"

"I don't know—" Sarah said.

"Can I borrow your cell phone?" Drew said to Sarah. When she handed it to him, he made a call and said, "Everything's arranged."

"What's arranged?" Sarah asked.

"A Bell 407 will be here for us in a little while."

"I can't afford—"

"I can," Drew said.

"Are you really rich?" Brooke asked, her eyes narrowed.

"Really, really rich," Drew replied with a smile.

"This is not a topic any of us should be discussing," Sarah said firmly.

"Unless I'm going to be a part of this family," Drew said.

He watched Sarah's eyes widen in surprise. "I hardly know you," she said.

"I love you," he said. "And I'm not going anywhere."

"I think you should marry him, Mom," Nate said.

"Nate!" Sarah said, shocked.

"He's got a Porsche," Nate explained.

"We can take a vacation in Paris," Brooke said with a faraway look in her eyes.

"I can get a pony," Ryan said.

"Wait just one minute," Sarah said, her hands on her hips. "You don't marry a man because he has money, Brooke."

"No. You marry him because you love him," Brooke said. "You love Drew, don't you, Mom?"

Sarah turned to Drew, her heart in her eyes.

"I've seen how you look at Drew, Mom," Nate said. "You love him. Admit it."

"Drew is nice," Ryan said. "You can marry him, Mom. It's okay with me."

Sarah laughed. A broad smile spread across her face as she turned to Drew and shrugged. "I guess I have to marry you. Ryan wants a pony. Brooke wants a trip to Paris. And Nate wants a Porsche."

"How about you, Sarah?" Drew said, his gaze focused on hers. "What do you want?"

"I just want you."

Drew wasn't sure who moved first, but a moment later they were holding each other tight. He kissed her long and deep. He was looking forward to coming home each day from now on to the woman he loved. And her three adventuresome children.

"Euuwww, they're kissing," Ryan said, as Nate and Brooke each took one of his hands to lead him away.

"Leave the poor things alone," Brooke said. "Can't you see they're in love?"

"Forget about them," Nate said, sliding an arm around Brooke's shoulder. "Do you think Kate really wants to see me again?"

Drew broke the kiss and smiled into Sarah's eyes. "I can't wait till we have one of our own."

Sarah laughed. "I wouldn't mind getting married first."

"Will you?" Drew asked.

"Will I what?" Sarah asked.

"Marry me?"

"I'm only saying yes so that when we're old and gray you can tell our grandkids that their Pap-Pap proposed to their Nana forty-eight hours after he met her. I'm expecting a long engagement."

Drew smiled and pulled her into his arms. "How about until the aspens turn gold?"

He felt Sarah's cold nose against his throat as she said, "October sounds like a lovely month for a wedding."

EPILOGUE

Drew's life was about to change forever. Today he was getting married. His surviving family had all come from Texas for the wedding. All except Morgan, whose body had never been found.

The snowmobile Morgan had been riding had been discovered in the spring halfway down the mountain. What was left of Jimmy Joe Stovall's body, which had been ravaged by some wild animal, had been found by hikers. No sign had been seen of Morgan's remains. He was presumed dead, his body perhaps buried by some animal who would dig it up later to eat.

Drew wondered. Until Morgan's body turned up, he wasn't going to believe his stepbrother was dead.

"What has you looking so thoughtful?" Sarah said.

Drew turned and opened his arms and his almost-wife walked into them. He kissed Sarah tenderly, then turned her so her back aligned with his front and laid his hands across the precious burden she carried. "I was wondering what kind of trouble Morgan is going to bring with him when he shows up," Drew admitted.

"He's dead," Sarah said. "He isn't going to come back to haunt any of us."

"I hope you're right." Drew nuzzled her neck and

said, "I thought the groom wasn't supposed to see the bride before the wedding."

"I'm not wearing my wedding dress," Sarah said. "So this doesn't count."

"I never thought this wedding would turn out to be such a big affair," he said. "I wish we'd just gone to the courthouse and stood in front of a judge."

"It's good to celebrate a wedding with family and friends." Sarah grinned and added, "I just never thought so many of your friends and relatives from Texas would show up."

Luke Blackthorne, Drew's best friend when he'd worked in Houston, had come to town to be Drew's best man and brought his wife Amy and their three kids. His cousin Clay had flown in to be one of Drew's groomsmen, and had brought his fiancée, Jocelyn Montrose.

That had been a surprise.

Clay had been offered a federal judgeship, and though he'd have to be confirmed by Congress, it seemed he was going to get the job, which would take him back to South Texas. Apparently, Jocelyn had her heart set on a June wedding.

"I was sure Clay would end up with Libby," Drew said.

Sarah looked up at him and said, "He's not married yet."

"What does that mean?"

"North is heading to his ranch in Texas, and he's asked Libby to go with him. She's considering it seriously, since Kate's a freshman at UT."

"The plot thickens," Drew said with a smile. "When does this wedding of ours start?" he asked.

"In about two hours," Sarah said. "Are you ready?"

Was he ready to be a husband? Was he ready to be a father?

It was a sign of how much Drew had changed in the year since he'd come to Jackson Hole, that he could answer yes to both questions. He was not only *in love* with Sarah, he *loved* her.

He was staying in Jackson to practice environmental law, work that would give his life meaning and purpose. But the greatest metamorphosis had occurred in Drew's attitude toward being a father. He no longer feared he would mess up Nate or Brooke or Ryan's lives. He believed he could help Sarah's half-grown kids become better people. He was still daunted by the thought of raising a baby from scratch. Or would have been, if he hadn't had Sarah's promise to help.

He laid his hand on Sarah's belly and said, "I'm ready, Sarah. For whatever life brings. As long as I can spend all those days and nights ahead with you."

Tears glistened in Sarah's eyes as her smile widened. "I love you, Drew. You're going to be a wonderful husband and an amazing father."

Drew swallowed over the sudden lump in his throat. He leaned down and kissed Sarah, feeling the supple give of her lips and the equal fervor with which she returned his kiss. For the first time in his life he believed . . . in happily ever after.

Dear Readers,

For those of you who would like to see more of North Grayhawk, and have been patiently waiting for Clay Blackthorne's story, they're on the way! I'm continuing the saga of the Grayhawks and Blackthornes in Texas in my next novel, *The Next Mrs. Blackthorne*.

The Bitter Creek Saga also includes *The Cowboy, The Texan, The Loner,* and *The Price*. You should be able to order them on the Internet or find them in your local bookstore.

If you're looking for something to read in the meantime, watch for *Honey and The Hired Hand, The Men of Bitter Creek* and *Sweetwater Seduction,* all coming soon!

If you'd like to read more about the Blackthorne family, look for my Captive Hearts series set in Regency England, including *Captive, After the Kiss, The Bodyguard,* and *The Bridegroom*. For those of you intrigued by the Creeds and the Coburns, check out the Sisters of the Lone Star trilogy, *Frontier Woman, Comanche Woman,* and *Texas Woman*.

I love hearing from you! You can contact me directly through my Web site, www.joanjohnston.com. I answer e-mail as I receive it. Or you can write to me by snail mail at P.O. Box 7834, St. Petersburg, FL 33734–7834. If you'd like a reply, please enclose a self-addressed stamped envelope.

Happy reading,

Joan Johnston

Visit
❖ **Pocket Books** ❖
online at

....

www.SimonSays.com

....

Keep up on the latest new
releases from your favorite
authors, as well as author
appearances, news, chats,
special offers and more.

SIMON & SCHUSTER
A VIACOM COMPANY
www.SimonSays.com

Pocket
Books

2381-01